Michelle Paver was born in Malawi; her father was South African and her mother is Belgian. They moved to England when she was small and she was brought up in Wimbledon, where she still lives. After gaining a first in biochemistry at Oxford she became a lawyer and was until recently a partner of a large City law firm, specialising in patent litigation. She has now given up the law to write full-time. *A Place in the Hills* is her second novel; her first, *Without Charity*, is also published by Corgi.

To find out more about Michelle Paver and her novels visit her website at www.michellepaver.com.

D1051521

www.**booksattransworld**.co.uk

Also by Michelle Paver

WITHOUT CHARITY

and published by Corgi Books

A Place in the Hills

Michelle Paver

CORGI BOOKS

A PLACE IN THE HILLS
A CORGI BOOK : 0 552 14753 2

First publication in Great Britain

PRINTING HISTORY
Corgi edition published 2001

1 3 5 7 9 10 8 6 4 2

Copyright © Michelle Paver 2001

The right of Michelle Paver to be identified as the author of this
work has been asserted in accordance with sections 77 and 78 of
the Copyright Designs and Patents Act 1988.

In this work of fiction, the characters, places and events are either
the product of the author's imagination or they are used entirely
fictitiously, and any resemblance to actual persons, living or dead,
is purely coincidental.

Condition of Sale
This book is sold subject to the condition that it shall not, by way of
trade or otherwise, be lent, re-sold, hired out or otherwise circulated
in any form of binding or cover other than that in which it is
published and without a similar condition including this condition
being imposed on the subsequent purchaser.

Set in 10/12pt Sabon by
Phoenix Typesetting, Ilkley, West Yorkshire.

Corgi Books are published by Transworld Publishers,
61–63 Uxbridge Road, London W5 5SA,
a division of The Random House Group Ltd,
in Australia by Random House Australia (Pty) Ltd,
20 Alfred Street, Milsons Point, Sydney, NSW 2061, Australia,
in New Zealand by Random House New Zealand Ltd,
18 Poland Road, Glenfield, Auckland 10, New Zealand
and in South Africa by Random House (Pty) Ltd,
Endulini, 5a Jubilee Road, Parktown 2193, South Africa.

Printed and bound in Great Britain by
Cox & Wyman Ltd, Reading, Berkshire.

A PLACE IN THE HILLS

PART ONE

CHAPTER ONE

Rome, 24 March 53 BC

It was noon on the Day of Blood when he first saw her.

The procession was nearing the doorway where he and Plautius were standing, and above the heads of the other onlookers Cassius had just glimpsed the Great Mother's effigy, lurching crazily towards them on the shoulders of her priests.

Rome wore a chaotically festive air that day. People thronged the narrow streets, and hung out of windows and balconies. It was the sort of spectacle which made educated men debate the nature of faith, and congratulate themselves on being above such foolishness. Besides, when else could you watch a barbarian mob howling through the streets of Rome, delirious on drugs and devotion and self-inflicted agony?

Afterwards, Cassius thought how incredible it was that in the crush he had managed to catch sight of her at all. He was to think of that a lot in the years to come. And of how different his life would have been if he hadn't glanced her way.

He had just picked a potsherd from the pavement and was turning it idly in his palm, for it was a fragment of a prayer-lamp, of the kind which the peasants back in Gaul sold to pilgrims in their hundreds. At this time of year, the Goddess' sanctuary contained so many lamps that he could see it at night from his garden: a faint glow far up the gorge; an eye in the mountain.

Thinking of that, he felt a wave of homesickness so strong that it took his breath away. That was when he saw her.

She was standing in the doorway across the street. Like him, she held a fragment of pottery in her palm. She was frowning a little as she examined the reliefs.

'Pretty,' said Plautius, following his gaze.

'No,' Cassius replied. 'Beautiful.' He shrugged. 'Like – what, about one in three of the women in this crowd? Must be something to do with being idle all day, and having plenty to eat.'

She was of medium height, and young, with straight dark hair and brows, and a chiselled mouth. He could tell from the way she wore her hair – in a simple horse-tail at the nape of the neck – that she was not yet married.

His first thought was that she must be some patrician miss who had come down from the Palatine for a little excitement. At her side stood a large coarse-featured slave-girl in a brown wool tunic, whose job was obviously to shade her with a sun umbrella. And no doubt when the young mistress had tired of barbarian processions, a litter would emerge from a side-street and carry her home.

Everything about the girl spoke of impeccable good breeding. Her dress was of some subtle blue-green stuff, belted at the waist and again beneath the breasts with a fine gilded cord; and she wore a dazzling white mantle with one fold draped decorously over the back of her head. Her clothes were spotless, and as fine as gossamer. Probably linen rather than silk, which no doubt would be thought indelicate for so correct a young girl.

Although come to think of it, he might be completely wrong about her. For all he knew she was a high-class courtesan, simply *pretending* to be an *ingénue*. Or perhaps a rich divorcée, indulging in a spot of amateur whoring for kicks. In Rome such distinctions weren't easy to spot. And he had been on campaign for so long that he'd forgotten the signs.

So maybe the dress *was* Egyptian linen, the genuine article – or maybe just a street-market imitation. And maybe those beads trembling at her ears *were* Persian emeralds and Indian pearls, or maybe just bits of coloured glass and paste.

But the heavy twisted chain about her neck had the sheen of real gold, no doubt about that, and on it she wore an amulet which intrigued him. A small crescent moon. Did that make her a believer in the Goddess?

Surely not. She didn't look ecstatic as she studied that shard in her hand. Merely puzzled.

Softly, the crescent moon rode the pulse at the base of her throat.

His gaze moved to her face, and he found with a start that she was watching him. Her eyes were fine and dark, and distinctly annoyed at being the object of his scrutiny.

He returned her stare for just long enough to prove that he wasn't disconcerted, then turned back to the procession and put her firmly from his mind. The day belonged to Plautius, his best and oldest friend. He would not allow some haughty little miss to interfere with that.

Suddenly the procession was upon them, and the girl disappeared behind a baying frenzy of eunuch priests. Flutes shrilled, cymbals clashed, and trumpets blared.

Sunlight blazed off the towering silver form of the Mother on her saffron-painted litter. Her sightless face of jagged black stone communed with a horizon which mere mortals would never see.

'Make way for the Mother!' howled the believers in Latin and Phrygian and Phoenician and Greek, and many other tongues which Cassius didn't know. Stinking to Heaven, they whirled about their Deity. Blood-spattered robes floated. Long hair streamed. Scrawny limbs ran crimson as scrouges crackled through the bright air.

The street seemed as hot as Hades. The sunlight was a knife in the brain, the din enough to split eardrums. The air was thick with the smell of balsam and trampled roses, and the salty, metallic undertow of blood.

Next to him, Cassius felt Plautius sag. 'Are you all right?' he said in the old man's ear. 'If you like we can go—'

Plautius shook his head with an impatient frown, though when Cassius offered him his good arm, he leaned on it gratefully.

'Are you sure you wouldn't rather leave?' Cassius insisted.

'Quite sure,' Plautius told him. He was enjoying himself *immensely*, he said, hadn't observed the Syrian cult at such close quarters for years. Although the sun was perhaps excessively strong for this time of year, and they must take care to drink plenty of peppermint tea the instant they were safely back in the house. Come to think of it, would Cassius care for one of his lozenges in the meantime? Wild cucumber and ground dog's gall, just the thing for inflammation of the eyes, which was sure to ensue with all this dust.

Cassius quickly assured him that he'd taken one before they left the house.

'A wise precaution,' nodded Plautius, favouring his companion with a blast of the anise he chewed every morning to ward off toothache.

The Goddess' litter moved on, and the high priest, swaying dreamily in Her wake, drew level with them. A silver image of the Mother bumped against the eunuch's ribs, and at each step he lashed himself with a knotted scourge, shuddering in wide-eyed ecstasy as the whip hit his back.

Cassius wondered what pose the priest had struck as he stood beneath the altar, waiting for the bull's lifeblood to pour down upon him. Had he kept his eyes open throughout the sacrifice? Had his mouth been agape to catch the purifying flood?

Although of course, it wasn't a *pose* at all. None of this was. You only had to look at the faces of these believers to see that they were oblivious to the laughing, fascinated, horrified, disbelieving crowd around them.

How Cassius envied them such blind conviction.

The high priest flicked back his long hair, spattering the ladies in the crowd with blood, so that they shrieked in delighted horror. Perhaps it had been a while since they'd been this close to shredded male flesh.

The Day of Blood never failed to draw the upper classes. And who could blame them? Compared to Jupiter Best and Greatest in all His infinite dullness, this was *religion*. Painful, steaming, and intense. And of course, there was always a strong military presence in case of trouble – and soldiers never failed to pull in the women. Long-necked patrician socialites were always on the look-out for a bit of rough. Cassius should know about that.

When he'd first come to Rome as an eighteen-year-old, he thought he'd stumbled into Elysium. It had taken a while to work out that with Roman women, what you saw was, disappointingly, what you got. A brief exchange of flirtatious nothings along more or less predictable lines; a few steamy couplings between rank sheets while a compliant maid kept a lookout for trouble; a string of tantrums over increasingly costly presents; and finally, the inevitable door slammed in the face.

You could get all that from whores with less risk and fewer histrionics. Which was why none of his poems had ever dealt with love.

'You know,' Plautius exclaimed, dragging him back to the present, 'after all these years I think I finally grasp the attraction of the Syrian cult. Some sort of – *connection*, isn't it? The sacrificial blood washes away the believer's sins, thereby bringing him into closer communion with the Deity. And presumably the self-castration helps as well. Hm. An interesting idea. Enlightenment through suffering.'

Cassius bit back a smile. It was good to see his old friend so much in his element: observing, questioning, modestly enjoying the exercise of his powerful intellect.

But he, Cassius, why had *he* come? Why did he always come on this particular day, when he was not – or he didn't think he was – a believer? Was it to find out if maybe this time, *this* time, he would feel the presence of something higher and deeper than what he could only see and touch?

But how was that possible, when it was all nonsense, mere peasant superstition which he'd put away when he became a man? He had been to university, for Heaven's sake. He had studied Greek. So why did he feel as if he had lost something along the way?

Just then the procession thinned to a straggle, and the girl across the street reappeared.

Still here? thought Cassius in irritation. Haven't you seen enough?

'She's someone's daughter, as I recall,' remarked Plautius.

'They usually are,' said Cassius drily.

'No, I mean to say – a *personage*.'

'Mm. She looks it. Out with the maid for a bit of excitement. Though I bet she'd run a mile if she found any.' He shook himself as if to get rid of an unwelcome impression. 'Come along, old friend. Shall we go?'

'So soon?' said Plautius, trying not to look relieved.

'Well, I don't know about you, but I could do with a drink.'

Plautius' thin lips compressed into his version of a smile. 'My boy, you have read my mind.'

Cassius laughed. 'I haven't been a boy for decades, I'm thirty-three years old!'

'Ah, but to me you'll always be a boy, you know that! The same boy to whom I taught rhetoric in Massilia – that is, when *you* weren't catching *me* out.'

'Only because you let me.'

'But you had the wit to perceive that. And the grace to let it pass.'

They turned to go.

Obscurely, Cassius felt angry with himself.

For what? he wondered. For being caught staring by a prim little miss who's half your age?

Plautius is right, you've been out in the sun too long. Or perhaps you simply need that drink.

'Proposition One,' Tacita's philosophy tutor had dictated to her that morning: 'the gods are indifferent to the world and have no effect upon it; *therefore* there is no point in worshipping them. Proposition Two: the gods determine all things down to the smallest detail; *therefore* man has no freedom of choice, *therefore* good and evil are meaningless abstractions. Compare and contrast. With special reference – *if* you must – to this barbaric procession you're so intent upon witnessing.'

A randomly configured world, or the complete absence of free will. Watching the rapt faces of the believers, Tacita wondered if there wasn't anything in between.

After all, what kind of compulsion makes a man like that priest take a knife and cut off his own manhood, then walk through the streets carving up his back with a knotted scourge? He must believe in something, to do that.

Mustn't he?

And she, Tacita – why was *she* here? To make notes for her next philosophy lesson? Or because she envied that priest his conviction, and wanted in some small way to experience it, or at least to understand?

'Not bad, for a soldier,' said Albia her slave, nudging her arm.

Without seeming to, Tacita took in the tall bearded officer across the street. She needn't have worried about being caught staring, for he was far too absorbed in watching the procession's approach.

His face was thoughtful, but she couldn't tell if he was amused, intrigued, or genuinely moved by what he saw. Perhaps he was a believer. Lots of soldiers were. Although it would be more unusual in an officer like him. With a practised eye Tacita had already taken in the fact that he wore the gold ring of the equestrian class, and armour of tinned bronze and gilded hide beneath a cloak of fine white wool.

He was tall, with thick dark-blond hair, and a short, straight beard clipped close to the strong line of the jaw. Beards were unusual in Rome, but perhaps he kept his out of convenience, as some career officers did. Which would tally with the fact that, unlike some of the other officers in the crowd, he hadn't bothered to bring his helmet along. Clearly he wasn't one for show.

But Albia was right, it was a handsome face: high-browed and intelligent, though perhaps a little too grave. Maybe he was in pain, for his right arm was bandaged from elbow to wrist.

Then she noticed with surprise that the old man leaning on his good arm was – of all people – Lucius Faenius Plautius, the advocate. A friend of her father's. Or rather, a frequent and much-respected opponent in the courts.

'Quick!' hissed Albia. 'He's turning this way!' Wildly the slave looked round, then stooped and pressed a potsherd into her mistress' hand.

'What am I supposed to do with this?' said Tacita crossly.

'Just keep your eyes on it and look modest and intriguing. Trust me. I know what I'm doing.'

'No you don't.'

'Listen, mistress, you were the one who wanted to experience life. Well, there it is, all six-foot-something of it. Strongly built, nicely battle-scarred – though not too much – and with that pensive expression you say you find so attractive.'

'I never said that.'

'And it's not as if he's a ranker, so that's all right.'

17

'He's a plebeian, though. No getting round that.'

'Yes, but compared to you, *everyone's* a pleb.'

'And he has a tan.' Tacita frowned. 'So vulgar. Like a farmer or a slave.'

'With shoulders like that, who cares? Ooh, I only wish he was looking at me the way he's looking at you. It's been two weeks since I last—'

'That'll do, Albia,' said Tacita severely. With a sigh she studied the shard in her hand. Sometimes it was better to play along with her slave's little games. It tended to get them over sooner.

Besides, now that she came to examine it, the shard was interesting. A fragment of some largish vessel, perhaps a *kántharos* or some other type of drinking-cup, which bore a section of a finely moulded relief. Tacita recognized Hercules in his lion's skin – she could see a paw dangling off one over-muscled shoulder – but she couldn't work out which of the Labours he was supposed to be performing. Although self-evidently it wasn't that of the Nemean lion, since he was already wearing it.

A deafening clash of cymbals made her jump. Across the street, the officer was still watching her. To her annoyance she felt herself blushing. Pointedly she returned his stare. Didn't he know not to gawp at his betters? Then she turned her head slowly and renewed her study of the procession.

When she glanced back again, the officer had gone. She felt let down – and angry with herself for feeling anything at all. So much for the stoical detachment she had been cultivating over the past few weeks.

On the way home, Albia kept running off to look for the officer, then dashing back to check on her mistress, like a puppy let loose on its first walk. Then, as they approached the turning for Victory Hill and the long climb home, Albia gave a triumphant yelp and disappeared down a side-street.

Moments later, Plautius and the officer emerged from the *opposite* side-street. The old man saw Tacita stamping her foot and calling in vain, recognized her, comprehensively misunderstood her, and despite her protests, set off in chivalrous pursuit of the errant slave. Which of course was exactly what Albia had intended. And as no officer would leave a young girl of good breeding unattended in a crowded street, Tacita was forced to wait beside him until Albia should deign to reappear. Her decision to leave the litter at home – in the teeth of her mother's objections – began to look like a serious mistake.

I will tan that girl's hide when I get my hands on her, she thought, gritting her teeth and trying to appear at ease. Which was difficult, for they were on the corner of Etruscan Street and Victory Hill, and had continually to step back to let people through. Tacita felt uncomfortably hemmed in. At her back was a cobbler's stall whose sharp-eyed proprietor she had always disliked; to her right stood the officer, and to her left, a large and worryingly unsteady jar of sesame oil.

To her irritation, the officer seemed disinclined to speak. Had he no manners whatsoever?

'So,' she said briskly, to break the silence, 'how long are you in Rome?'

'That depends on my orders,' he replied. 'But it'll be a couple of months at least.' Surprisingly, he had an educated voice, without a hint of a provincial accent. Although with that fair hair he must surely be from Gaul, equestrian class or not.

'So you're up for a spot of big city sophistication,' she

remarked, letting a hint of scorn leach into her voice. 'Must be quite a change, after fighting Germans.'

As she said it she heard her mother's voice inside her head: *Tacita, Tacita, do at least try to curb your tongue! Just because these things occur to you doesn't mean you have to say them!*

'In fact,' said the officer, 'Germany isn't a bad guess. Perhaps I should return the favour and guess what you're doing down here.' He threw her a measuring glance. 'I'd say you were born and bred on the Palatine, and thought you'd amuse yourself with a look at the Syrian orgies. At a safe distance, of course. And no doubt on a pretty short leash.'

'What's that supposed to mean?'

He shrugged. 'Presumably you have the usual strict papa. Although I'm surprised you're not married at your age. You must be – what? Seventeen?'

'Sixteen.' That stung, for most of her friends had been married for years. But it was hardly her fault if her father couldn't find a man with blood pure enough to ally with his only daughter. 'So what about you?' she retorted sweetly. 'You must be – what, about twice my age? Presumably you have a wife and several brats in some cosy little house down by the Meat Market?'

He looked amused. 'I'm not married. I'm a soldier.'

'I'd noticed.'

'And you are . . .'

'Not a soldier.'

One corner of his mouth went up. It was a good mouth, but it wasn't much of a smile. He didn't look as if he smiled very often.

The procession was far away by now, wending its way south towards the Porta Capena, and the banks of the Almo. At this distance all that reached them was a discordant rumour of cymbals and harsh singing.

Etruscan Street was returning to normal, its vendors once more intent on their everyday business of charging the highest prices in Rome – 'but for the kind of goods, young mistress, which you just can't *get* anywhere else'.

The air stank with the mingled smells of urine, roses and sour wine, and underfoot the ground was crunchy with broken offerings: shattered beakers of wild pear blossom, and tiny glass jars of cinnamon, bought to be dashed against walls in small powdery explosions of perfumed dust.

Tacita stirred the debris with the toe of her sandal. Albia must be leading poor old Plautius a merry dance. Where *was* the wretched girl?

'So,' said the officer at last, 'was I right? Did you come down to see how the Syrians handle these things?'

'Something like that, I suppose.'

'And what did you think of it? Did you find what you were looking for?'

She frowned. Abruptly, her talent for riposte deserted her. 'I don't know,' she said at last. 'I don't know why I came, or what I was looking for. I – don't know.'

Absurdly, she felt close to tears. He shouldn't go around accosting girls with bizarre questions, it wasn't fair. She cast about for a change of subject. 'You're left-handed,' she said at random. He had ink stains on the fingers of his good hand.

'Then it was lucky for me that I sprained my right wrist, wasn't it?'

'I'm surprised you have ink stains at all. I didn't think soldiers had much time for writing.'

'I'm a poet.'

'You said you were a soldier.'

'Can't I be both?'

At last she felt on firmer ground. The doors had been flung open for ridicule, and that was something she could never resist. 'But of *course* you can,' she said with mock solemnity. 'At least, you can try. And you won't be alone, will you? Why, every officers' mess has its gaggle of hopeful scribblers. I've met your kind at my father's parties. You have – what shall we call them? *Literary aspirations?*' She said the phrase slowly, extracting every drop of sarcasm. 'Now let me see. I believe I can guess your background without being told. You're one of our New Men, aren't you? Your father was a citizen – although perhaps only just – who made good out in the provinces. Probably somewhere in Narbonese Gaul?'

He nodded, his face expressionless.

'That's what I thought. And clearly the fond papa bought his son the best education he could afford – although at a keen price, of course. Good local school. Decent – albeit local – university. Perhaps even a bit of Greek on the cheap.'

'Quite right. Though we couldn't afford the grand tour to Athens.'

'Oh couldn't you? *What* a pity. You don't know what you missed.'

'On the contrary. I think I do.'

That made her feel ashamed. But she'd started, so she soldiered on. She hadn't forgotten that crack about the leash. 'So. You thought that as you were in Rome, you'd take in a bit of the local colour. Perhaps to get some ideas for your next masterpiece.'

'That wasn't originally the reason.'

'But now it is?'

For the first time he looked her full in the face. He took his time, and she felt the heat rise to her cheeks.

'Well,' he said softly, 'right now I'm certainly getting ideas.'

'That's coarse and impertinent,' she snapped, 'and hardly poetic.'

'What can I do? I'm a soldier.'

'I thought you were a poet.'

'And I thought you were a lady. It seems we're both wrong.'

At that moment, Plautius hurried up with an unrepentant Albia, and swamped them in a flurry of wheezy introductions. But as the old man was embarking upon a lengthy message of greetings to Tacita's father, she abruptly ceased to hear a word of what he was saying.

She ceased to hear a word immediately after Plautius told her the officer's name. From then on, she was too appalled to hear anything except the thunder of her own blood in her ears.

'*I'm a poet,*' the officer had said in his offhand way. But if Tacita had known to whom she was speaking, she would have replied: No, you're not *a* poet – you're *The* Poet. You're Gaius Cassius Vitalis. We've all read you, we know you by heart. You're the man who broke all the rules of poetry, who isn't afraid to peel back his own skin and write what he feels, in words that fly up and sing like neat wine in the blood.

No. She wouldn't have said any of that. She wouldn't have said a word. She would have been far too intimidated to open her mouth.

And *this* was the man she had been happily insulting to his face.

'I don't know what to say,' she said simply.

'Well, that's a first,' he remarked.

'I – didn't recognize you. I mean, I've never seen you before. I never managed to get to one of your readings.'

'I don't give many. I'm not often in Rome.' He paused, then added. 'Too busy fighting Germans, I suppose.'

She nodded slowly, accepting that as just punishment.

'But you've read my work?' he asked.

Again she nodded, pressing her lips together to prevent more ineptitudes escaping.

'Well?' he said. 'Any comments? Are the – um, literary aspirations justified?'

He spoke without irony, but she wasn't going to let him catch her out again. Whatever words of praise she uttered now would damn her for ever. She would be easy fodder for one of his clean-slicing little epigrams, preserved for all eternity as the pretentious patrician socialite in love with her own non-existent wit.

Her chin went up. 'If you don't mind, I'd rather not tell you what I think. I see no point in trying to summarize a man's whole experience, when you've been doing that in your poems for years. How could I possibly better them?' She thought she sounded both pompous and illogical, but to her surprise he only smiled.

'That's a novel approach to criticism. But I wasn't trying to catch you out. I wanted to know what you think.'

He sounded as if he meant it. And for an instant, he looked as surprised about that as she.

For the first time she met his glance.

His eyes were a startling light-filled grey, with an edge of smoky blue about the iris. Looking into them was like looking into his soul.

The breath caught in her throat. The sounds of the bustling street receded.

Dimly she became aware that beside her Albia was waxing impatient. That old Plautius was tapping his friend's shoulder. She could not move.

She had no idea how long they stood there. Again Plautius tapped the poet's shoulder, and murmured something about getting out of the sun.

Gaius Cassius Vitalis didn't seem to hear. His smile had vanished. She knew – she *knew* – that it was the same for him.

'Gaius,' the old man said uneasily. 'We really ought to be going.'

Tacita watched the poet slowly return to himself. He opened his mouth to speak. Then cleared his throat and started again. 'Will you –' he said to her. 'Will you – be at the Games next week?'

It was so unexpected that it caught her off guard, and her reply came out more tartly than she'd intended. 'That depends on how short they keep my leash.'

He took that gravely, in silence. But it had not been an idle question – it had cost him to ask – and she bitterly regretted her sharpness.

But by the time she had regained her wits, he had already turned and was walking away with the old man. 'I don't know,' she called after him. 'Maybe I will. I'll try.'

But by then he was already halfway down the street, and she didn't think he heard.

'Cassius,' said Plautius at his side. 'No.'

'Why?'

'You know why. She's a patrician and you're not.'

'I don't see wh—'

'Do you *know* who her father is? He's Publius Tacitus Silanus, for Heaven's sake! You've seen him in the law courts, you know what he's like – what that whole *family's* like! One of the oldest clans in Rome, and not about to let anyone forget it. Strike first, think later, and

25

pay for the funeral. That's their motto where the honour of the family is concerned.'

Cassius heard the words but he didn't understand them. He felt the paving-stones beneath his feet, and the wind in his hair, and the sun on his face, and smelt the trampled roses and the blood – all of it more intensely real than ever before in his life, and yet at the same time more bizarre and unintelligible. As if he were a stranger to the world, seeing it for the first time.

'Cassius. No. No. I won't see you hurt.'

Glancing over his shoulder, Cassius watched her walk away up Victory Hill. Her back was very straight, and she did not turn round.

But she had said that she would try to get to the Games. That was what she had said.

'I'll see you there,' he called after her. But he didn't think she heard.

CHAPTER TWO

Gorges de Sarac, south-eastern French Pyrenees,
July 1972

How *like* Toni to run away from a riding lesson, thought her father furiously as he scrambled up the sweltering mountain track.

All little girls love horses, but not Toni. Oh, no. Toni was different. Toni was at war with them.

'It *bit* me!' she'd yelled, her small goblin's face purple with outrage. '*Bad* pony!'

Then she'd punched it on the nose. Not a warning smack, but an all-out, clobbering punch.

Her mother and sister had been mortified, the villagers thought it a huge joke, and the sturdy mountain pony scarcely blinked. No doubt it had received worse beatings in its time.

So now here was Charles Hunt: choked with dust, lathered in sweat, and deafened by cicadas, skinning his knees on a track of blinding white rubble which led to God alone knew where. All because his eight-year-old hated riding.

Ahead of him the path forked. To the right it carried on up the gorge, clinging to the mountainside two hundred feet above the river. To the left it wound past a minuscule terrace of vines before disappearing into the jagged, sun-baked scrubland of the *garrigue*.

Among the vines, an old man in villainously dirty overalls was burning brambles.

Charles Hunt detested the French, but this attempt at viticulture impressed even him. Give these people a patch of rubble the size of a postage stamp and they'd shove in a vine.

'Excusez-moi,' he called out, wincing at his own strangulated English accent. 'Avez-vouz vu une petite fille par ici?'

The old man took his time about acknowledging him, but at last he ambled over to the front of the terrace.

Charles saw that the man was younger than he had first appeared, perhaps in his early fifties, with startling blue eyes in a seamed mahogany face.

The farmer hawked, spat, and barked a brusque question in impenetrable French. At least, Charles guessed it was French. For all he knew it could have been Spanish or Catalan or Chinese.

Had his wife been there, she would have remarked that he ought to have anticipated that. 'I mean, anywhere west of Nice is practically Spain, isn't it, darling? So what do you expect in the foothills of the Pyrenees?'

At last Charles grasped that the man wished to know, bizarrely, whether he was a German. Startled, Charles replied that he was not. The farmer gave a satisfied nod, then jerked his head towards the right-hand fork. 'La Sourça,' he muttered, already turning back to his vines.

It took Charles a moment to work out that 'La Sourça' meant the underground spring which, according to his Michelin map, was located in a limestone cave about a mile and half up the gorge. Its official name was

'La Fontaine del bon Cristia'. The Fountain of the Good Christ.

'Good Christ is about bloody right,' muttered Charles, setting his teeth and starting up the right-hand track. A mile and a half? Oh, *Toni*!

He kneaded his temples. The relentless rasp of the cicadas was giving him a headache.

Half an hour later he finally reached the cave, a startling semicircle of darkness overshadowed by a massive overhang of black-streaked rock.

There was no sign of his daughter. If she had wandered in and got lost, he would throttle her.

He flung himself down in the shade of the stunted oak which guarded the cave mouth. He was drenched in sweat and his heart was pounding unevenly. Any minute now and he'd have a coronary.

Now what do I do? he wondered. Say a prayer to whatever benighted spirit haunts this place, and hope for the best?

Sunspots darted before his eyes, and from deep within the cave came the bubbling song of water. His archaeologist's mind noted automatically that this was a perfect site for a shrine to the Mother Goddess. And no doubt the spring inside welled up from some kind of cleft, which the Romans who had colonized the area would have regarded as a *mundus*, a doorway between the worlds of the living and the dead.

A deeper, less rational part of his mind assured him that all this was true. The cave was indeed a shrine to the Lady of the Wild Things, and it did indeed contain a door to the land of the dead.

Which of course was perfectly ridiculous. But he shivered, just the same.

'*Daddy!*' cried a familiar voice from the darkness,

startling him into the present. 'You came *after* me, all this way!'

And there she was, her plain little face filthy with dust and tears, but lit up like a Christmas tree at the sight of him. Both her podgy knees were black with dirt, and her T-shirt looked as if it had been dragged through a thorn-bush. Evelyn would not be amused. The T-shirt was a Lacoste.

'Toni!' he exploded. 'This is the bloody *limit*!'

She stood awkwardly before him, digging her bare toes into the dirt. She had tied the laces of her tennis shoes together and hung them round her neck, which he thought ineffably vulgar.

He snatched them off and began unpicking the knot.

'Sorry, Daddy,' she muttered. 'But I *really* don't want to go riding.'

'Well, you've got to, that's all there is to it.'

'Oh *please*. I hate it. Ponies are horrible.'

'No they're not. Besides, your mother insists.' Belatedly, he added, 'And so do I.'

Privately, he wondered if the riding lessons weren't a mistake, like the tennis coaching and the ballet classes. 'It'll draw her out,' Evelyn always said, failing to recognize that her efforts only sapped the child's confidence the more.

Still, none of that was really his concern, thank God. The girls were Evelyn's responsibility, they had agreed so from the start. Which made it all the more outrageous that he should be dragged into this now, on his holiday.

'But, Daddy, I don't *want* to learn to ride.'

'Why not? All little girls love horses. What's wrong with you?'

Her face closed, and her lower lip thrust out.

He had a shrewd idea that if she had been older and

better able to articulate her feelings, she would have replied: what's wrong with me is this. I'm fat and shy and the school swot, and Mummy prefers Caroline, who isn't.

And what would he have said to that? What *could* he have said, when it was all true? Besides, he preferred Caroline himself. His elder daughter was a sweet, pretty, undemanding eleven-year-old. She was easy to love.

Evelyn always said that Toni should have been a boy. Studying her now, Charles thought how cruelly accurate that was. She was too tall and solid for a girl, and her bottle-top glasses made her eyes appear piggy. Everything about her was inappropriate. Inappropriate to be the offspring of a woman as lovely as Evelyn, and a man as lean and graceful as himself.

There was no getting away from it: Antonia was a changeling. And the worst of it was, she knew.

Sometimes he felt sorry for her. Usually, merely guilty and a little embarrassed. Today he was simply annoyed.

Without a word he got to his feet and started swiftly down the track. He heard her struggling with her tennis shoes, then scrambling after him. Moments later she appeared at his side.

She put out her hand to take his, but he jammed them both into the pockets of his shorts. Damned if he was going to reward her after what she'd put him through.

Silently she dropped her hand, her face carefully blank.

Her legs had to work twice as hard as his to keep up, and after a while he eased up on the pace.

'Are we going to buy that house by the river?' she asked shyly. 'The one that used to be a mill?'

He suppressed a snort. That 'we' was rich. She knew as well as he did that all the money was Evelyn's. Or rather, poor darling Uncle Gerald's wonderful fortune, now safely tucked away in Lloyd's, where it could grow even more enormous by the minute.

'Perhaps,' he muttered. 'It'd be a good place for me to work during the long vacation. And it's in the right valley.'

'Do you mean the right valley for Cassius?'

'Mm-hm.' It irritated him that she spoke of his pet project with such familiarity. Today everything about her irritated him.

'Are you sure he lived here, Daddy? In this actual valley?'

'Of course I'm sure.'

'Why?'

'*Because!*' he snapped. Why couldn't she simply believe what he said? Christ, it was bad enough fielding that sort of inquisition at the faculty, without getting it from his own daughter.

He knew he was being unfair. If Caroline had asked the same question he would have been overjoyed at her showing an interest in his work. So why not Toni? It wasn't her fault if she had the kind of mind which couldn't take things on trust. He ought to encourage that. He ought to be proud of her independent thinking, of her precocious, prickly intelligence.

So why did he only feel this irrational resentment? Jealous of an eight-year-old? Absurd. And wrong to take out his frustrations on a child. It just showed how low he had sunk.

Charles Hunt the gentleman amateur, the faculty joke – whom they only kept on for his connections ('so handy for funding') and for his beautiful wife, who lent any gathering a touch of class.

'Daddy?'

'*What*.'

'Why do you think Cas—'

'Toni, I'm not going into all that now! It's stinking hot and I'm exhausted, and desperately in need of a drink. Let's just get this over with as soon as we can, shall we?'

Her father had asked why she didn't want to go riding, but Antonia knew that he didn't really want to know. And if she told him, it would only make him crosser.

That morning her big sister had remarked in her kindly way, not meaning to hurt, that Antonia's Dinosaur Club badge was a bit young, wasn't it, and it did clash horribly with her T-shirt, so presumably she wasn't going to wear it for riding?

Antonia didn't know what 'clashing' meant, except that it had something to do with colours, but Caroline must be right about it, because Caroline knew those sorts of things. The trouble was, Antonia had been counting on the Dinosaur Club badge to protect her from the ponies.

So the stark choice was either to confront the ponies *with* the badge, but 'clash' (whatever that meant) – or to leave the badge behind, and face the ponies un-protected. In the end she went for the second option, and her fears were justified. She was bitten, painfully, on her upper arm. Not hard enough to bleed, but hard enough to cause a big purple bruise, and to prove that she had been right. Ponies hated her as much as she feared them.

But if she tried to explain all that to her father he would never understand. He would tell her not to be ridiculous. Surely she had grown out of dinosaurs years ago?

Cassius had understood. Cassius always understood.

He might be a grown-up and a Roman, but that didn't stop him writing poems about sea monsters, and horses that flew. And no-one ever told *him* to grow out of Pegasus.

And somehow when Cassius was with her, she wasn't a bit scared of Pegasus – even though Pegasus was, technically, a horse. Up in the cave when she had explained about the Dinosaur Club, Cassius had promised to write her a poem about a triceratops. She wished she was back there now, with him. Cassius was the only person she could tell things to, and he never laughed at her or told her she was wrong.

She *adored* the cave. As soon as she found it she had felt safe and accepted as never before. Even her hiccups had stopped. And she knew immediately that it was a magic place. That was why she had taken off her sneakers before she went inside.

The darkness had felt wonderfully cool, the dust as soft as talcum powder between her toes, and when she put her hand in the cleft in the rock, the water she drew out in her cupped palm was icily sweet.

Then, as she padded back to the cave mouth, a small green lizard had scuttled past her foot, and turned, and *looked* at her. He was so close that she could see his sides panting in and out, his skin all shiny and bumpy like a fruit pastille.

That was when she knew that Cassius had been here too.

'*I know a place in the hills,*' he had written in one of her favourite bits in the book in her father's study, '*where the gods walk the earth. A place where each life you encounter – the emerald lizard, the drop-eared goat, the wheeling hawk – regards you silently, without fear.*

34

For here you are scarcely more than they, in the face of a greater power.'

'What's that in your hand?' her father said, making her jump.

She swallowed. 'I found it in the cave.' Shyly she held out the scrap of pottery. 'I think it's Roman. Red and shiny, like in your book? Maybe it's a clue that Cassius used to go there.'

But to her horror, the sight of her treasure made her father explode. 'Oh, *Toni*! This is so typical of you!'

Her mouth fell open.

'Where did you find this? Mm?'

'In the ca—'

'Don't you know by now that if you ever find anything old, you're *not to move it*?'

Her face felt hot. Any moment now she'd get hiccups all over again.

'You never listen, do you? You say you want to learn, then you do something like this. Acting like some asinine tourist who doesn't know any better.'

'I – I could put it back.'

'No you can't. Not in exactly the same place where you found it. The damage is done. Whatever we *might* have learned from this particular shard is gone for ever. Because of you.'

She felt sick.

They walked on in silence. When they were almost at the mill, her father told her to cheer up, in the voice he used when he knew he had gone too far.

She took a deep breath which turned into a gulp. 'I'm sorry about the find, Daddy.'

'It doesn't matter,' he muttered. 'It's only a piece of Samian ware. Common as muck. Doesn't tell us a thing.'

'So you don't think it means he—'

'Cassius wouldn't have gone up there, Toni! It's just a local shrine for peasants – if it's anything at all, which I doubt.'

She bit her lip. She knew he was wrong, but she wasn't about to provoke another outburst – or worse still, make him stop talking about his work altogether. He hardly ever spoke to her about Cassius, and now that he'd started, she wanted their walk to last for ever.

But he didn't say anything else, and the silence lengthened.

It was all her fault. She had made him cross, and now he would never talk to her again.

Antonia had always known that Caroline was her mother's favourite, and she used to think that to even things out, she must be her father's. Now she realized that things don't work like that.

'How about this,' said her father at last. 'When you grow up, you can be an archaeologist like me, and help me solve the riddle Cassius left behind. Then we'll be famous. We'll go to conferences together, and tell everyone how we did it.'

And then you'll love me as much as you love Caroline, thought Antonia.

She looked up at him and asked, 'What do I have to do to be an archaeologist?'

CHAPTER THREE

Saturday, 3 September 1988

'*Fuck* archaeology,' said Myles when he called Patrick the night before.

He was on speed again. Patrick could tell. He was talking too fast, with long breathy pauses in between. And as always, he was oblivious of the phone bill. Why worry? It was only money. His mother took care of all that.

'So I guess the dig's not going too well, huh?' Patrick had replied.

'Fuck knows,' said Myles, 'I haven't been down there for a week. Why should I? I'm a volunteer. And we haven't found a thing in eight fucking weeks.'

'What, nothing at all?'

'A few bits of old flowerpot.'

'Did Romans have flowerpots?'

'How should I know? You can ask that prick of a supervisor when you get here, if you're so interested.'

'Right.'

'God, I hate it when you do that.'

'Do what?'

'Go all self-righteous on me. It's so *American*.'

'I'm not self-righteous.'

'Yes you are.'

'I was only wondering why, if this dig is such a fiasco, you still want me to come out, is all.'

'*Because*. I don't need a reason.'

And because Myles was Myles, Patrick was now on a plane to Toulouse, wondering what the hell he was getting himself into.

Because Myles, for all his crazy mood swings and bizarre public-school snobberies, was Patrick's best friend. The only person who had thrown him a lifeline in that first horrible week at Oxford, when the scholarship money hadn't come through in time, and the other 'freshers' – Jesus, these British had a nickname for everything – had congealed into terrified cliques and repelled all comers.

That was when Myles, in his filthy Volkswagen Golf, had nearly flattened Patrick at an intersection, and after berating him for cycling on the wrong side of the road, had suggested they go for a curry. There he had got roaring drunk, and said, 'Listen, Paddy, or whatever the fuck your name is. You can't stay in Hall, it'll be ghastly, you'll never meet anyone worth meeting. Why don't you take the spare room in my house?'

So Patrick did.

His friend's *house*, for Christ's sake. Myles' mother was some kind of high-flying attorney, who'd bought it as a reward when he scraped into Oxford at the third attempt. And it was to her 'weekend retreat' in the South of France that Patrick was now flying, having spent the past two months schooling horses at a riding stable, to save up the fare.

He'd never even met Mrs Passmore, and he wanted to keep it that way, as she sounded pretty overwhelming. He was glad that neither she nor her husband, Myles' stepfather, would be at La Bastide during his stay.

In the three years that Patrick had lived in the house in Norham Gardens, Mrs Passmore had never once visited her son. Nor had Myles' father, who was a surgeon. Nor had his stepfather, who was a judge. Myles said he didn't mind, but Patrick knew better. And that made him feel bad, for he would be delighted if he never met *any* of them. It embarrassed him to be taking Myles' charity, for at his friend's insistence and over his own objections, he didn't pay rent. In the end, to assuage his conscience, he had taken to putting what he thought was an OK amount in a bank account from time to time. Myles would get around to spending it in the end. On drugs, if Patrick knew his friend.

His friend.

It still struck Patrick as odd that he should have a friend. After his mom walked out he had never seen the point. Why get attached to people? They only left. But somehow, Myles had slipped through the net.

Maybe it was because they were both a couple of years older than the others on the course – Patrick because he had worked his way through college and the scholarship exams, and Myles because of re-takes, though he told everyone he'd been in Hong Kong, getting work experience.

Whatever the reason, somehow they muddled along just fine. They went to parties together, where Myles got hammered, and teased Patrick because he didn't drink. They picked up women. They studied. They passed. Or, in Myles' case, flunked. Myles preferred educating Patrick in what he called 'the essentials'. Like wearing the right kind of collar stiffeners, and how it was OK if your kitchen stank in hot weather, but you mustn't ever *roll up* the sleeves of your sweater or you'd look like a grammar-school boy, which for some reason was right out.

'And I'll tell you another thing,' Myles had said. 'Dr Hunt is a prick. No getting round it. A twenty-four-carat prick of the first water.'

That had made Patrick laugh. To Myles, everyone was a prick. Including Myles. 'Myles, who cares? You don't want to be an archaeologist, you're going to be Director-General of the BBC.'

'And you, Paddy my boy, will be my own personal therapist, when I crack up from the strain of subverting the Great Unwashed.'

'So,' Patrick had said, 'you're not on this dig for the thrill of the find. So who is she?'

'I thought you'd never ask, me old chum. Ah, the Vestal Virgin! Yum yum *yum*!'

With a *ping* the sign for fastening seat-belts lit up.

Patrick turned to gaze at the flawless sky. He bit his lip. From what Myles had told him, Antonia Hunt sounded like someone he could do without. Classy English girls put him on edge. They invariably patronized him when they learned that he was from Wyoming. 'Isn't that where cowboys come from?' they would say. 'And *My Friend Flicka*? *Where* did you say you're from? Dew-boys? What's that, a town?' He knew he was being over-sensitive, but within five minutes he would feel himself reverting to an awkward, check-shirted hick from the boondocks.

And Antonia Hunt was clever, too, so bang went his last line of defence.

'So I guess Miranda is a thing of the past, huh?' he had said to Myles.

'You mean Nerissa.'

'Nerissa, right.'

A chuckle. 'God, you Yanks are so old-fashioned! It's really rather endearing.'

40

'I guess that means it's not goodbye to Nerissa.'

'What's wrong with keeping them both on their toes? Poor darling Toni hasn't a clue what's going on, so it can't possibly hurt her, and Nissa doesn't care one way or the other.'

From what Myles had told him about Nerissa, Patrick didn't like the sound of her either. According to Myles she was a dead ringer for the young Brigitte Bardot, and *serious* class. And on top of it all, she also happened to be Myles' stepsister. Which made her the daughter of the judge, from a previous marriage.

Shit.

His stomach clenched. He had the same feeling of blinding white fear as when he'd emerged from the subway on his first day in London, and come face to face with more ancient and beautiful buildings than he'd ever seen in his life. Buildings which the Londoners used with Olympian unconcern as diners and 'building societies', whatever the hell those were.

And now here he was on his way to the South of France – the *South of France*, for Christ's sake. Grace Kelly and Cary Grant; cravats and croupiers and private yachts, and classy English girls with cool disparaging stares.

Shit.

Get a grip, he told himself. You can do this. Set yourself more than you can do, and you'll do it. Right?

He had read that in a *Reader's Digest* when he was nine, the day after his mother walked out. He had been playing truant in the drugstore, numbly rifling the magazines, and wondering what he had done to make her leave. *Set yourself more than you can do.*

But what, the nine-year-old Patrick had asked, do I want to do? And all of a sudden, he knew. He wanted to end up the opposite of his father. He wanted to end up *not* humiliated, and *not* in a trailer home, and *not* a drunk.

As always when he thought of his father, he felt the familiar pain.

The only thing the poor guy ever wanted was to be proud of you. So what did you do? You killed him. Doesn't matter what the doctors said. You know it's true. You broke his heart. And now you've got to live with that. Too late to make it better now.

The pretty stewardess came down the aisle. 'Bar's closing, sir. Last chance for another drink.' She looked him straight in the eyes and gave him a brilliant smile. 'Would you like something a little stronger than a Coke?'

Politely, he declined.

Still smiling, she leaned over to clear his tray-table.

She had very pretty teeth. Hell, she was pretty all over. Mid-twenties, about his own age. And she'd been back twice already to check on him. If he made a move, they could have a coffee somewhere in the airport, and she would probably be available for a bout of what he and Myles called 'Teflon sex'. Fun for a couple of hours, no strings, *adios*, and let's move right along. Which was exactly the way Patrick preferred it.

Though of course there would be no time for anything like that today, for Myles would be waiting at the airport.

Myles wasn't.

Patrick stood around for an hour on the concourse, which was as hot and humid as a steamed-up bathroom. Then he spent another twenty minutes trying to call the house at La Bastide. Eventually he got a ringing tone, but no-one picked up.

Then he became seriously hungry. Tried to buy the smallest, plainest roll he could find at the airport café. Succeeded after a struggle, and wished he hadn't, for it was mind-blowingly expensive. Jesus, what would a round of drinks cost out here? Or maybe they didn't *have* rounds of drinks in the South of France. Maybe you just sold off an organ or two, and drank champagne through a straw.

Another hour went by. He thought about getting a bus into Toulouse and finding a train. Gave up on the idea – and not just because it would probably swallow his entire month's spending money, all seventy-five pounds and fifty pence. He was beginning to realize that not speaking French was going to be a problem, for his high-school Spanish cut no ice with the French.

Why hadn't he learned French in high school? He could have, but he'd chosen Latin instead. 'With Latin you're halfway there in most European languages,' his mother had airily assured him once, and he'd swallowed it whole, as he'd swallowed everything else she told him.

Looking back, that seemed like just another of her British tricks for tightening the cultural thumbscrews on her only son and her poor dumb hick of a husband – who'd never been further than Lander in his whole life, not even for his own funeral.

Thanks, Mom. Wherever you are.

Myles Cantellow awoke with a start and stared at the ceiling, wondering, as he always did, where he was and who was beside him.

Ah, yes. You're at the mill with Toni. Yes. So everything's all right.

Like the rest of the mill, her room was shabby and scantily furnished, but he found that endearing. Her mother – the Ageing Débutante, as he liked to call her – had stopped coming to La Bastide years ago, and neither Toni nor her father bothered much with their surroundings.

Which was fine by Myles. He liked her bedroom just the way it was. The walls were discoloured, the linoleum curled, and the mirror had silvery patches – but the bed creaked satisfyingly when put to good use, much to the disgust of Toni's father, whose study was directly beneath. Even at midday it was dim and cool, in the perpetual shadow of the Roc. And the thunder of the river was a soothing antidote to the rasp of the cicadas.

Toni lay on her side with her back to him, but he could tell from her breathing that she wasn't asleep.

She hadn't enjoyed the sex. She hadn't said anything about it – she rarely did – but he could tell. He, on the other hand, was still coming down from somewhere among the chimney-stacks. Though there was no point in telling her that.

'I don't know about you,' he said quietly, 'but for me it wasn't that great.' He watched her turn and raise herself on her elbow to look at him. 'Maybe,' he added, 'I can only have good sex with women I don't like.'

She regarded him impassively, as she always did when he had hurt her. 'Maybe so,' she said at last.

'The trouble with you,' he said, 'is you lack the confidence to say what you feel.'

'The trouble with you,' she replied evenly, 'is that you'd use it against me if I did.'

He grinned. 'Paranoid.'

Her lip curled. 'Machiavelli.'

He wasn't sure what she meant, but it sounded like a compliment, so he let it pass.

He was constantly amazed at how a girl like her, who

could fearlessly contradict professors, and manage a team of volunteers like a four-star general, was going out with him. Myles Cantellow, fuckwit *extraordinaire*, and this summer's lucky recipient of a Gentleman's Third in PPP – while she had a First in Classics *and* a fucking PhD, and was waiting to hear about a Cambridge lectureship which she was bound to get.

What the hell was she doing with him? If the roles had been reversed he wouldn't have given her the time of day. But they had been together now for just over two months, which was twice as long as any other relationship he'd ever had.

Sometimes he wondered if it was all the fault of her family. The Ageing Débutante must be pretty hard to take at the best of times, and so was Dr Hunt the Prick, still bumping along the bottom of the academic world at his disgusting redbrick university. Then there was the gorgeous dumb-blonde sister, who had clearly perfected the art of making Toni feel the ugly duckling, but who – as Myles could personally confirm – was a surprisingly lousy lay.

With a family like that, no wonder escaping to Oxford had seemed like such a miracle to poor Toni.

Once, in a fit of openness, she had told him how she had taken herself in hand in her first term there. Contact lenses, new clothes, a bit of makeup. And as she had been too excited to eat, the puppy fat had just tumbled off.

It didn't sound like much to Myles, but obviously it meant a lot to her. Women were so ridiculously vulnerable about their appearance. Even the clever ones. Especially the clever ones. Oh well, who was he to complain, when it meant that she'd never found the time or the courage to get a boyfriend? Lucky, lucky Myles.

Although sometimes he felt sorry for her, stumbling across *him*, of all people, at her very first attempt.

He could have told her from the start that she was wasting her time with him. No-one stayed with Myles Cantellow for long. They ended up hating him, and left.

When he thought about Toni leaving him, his chest hollowed out and he felt sick. To shake it off, he jumped out of bed and went naked to the chest of drawers.

In the mirror he saw her reflection watching him. He really liked the way she looked. The long, crinkly black hair. The pale skin that refused to tan.

His gaze shifted to his own face. He wasn't handsome, but women didn't seem to mind, so he didn't either. What he minded was that he was just *under* six feet tall, with a small girlish mouth, and hair that was too thin and too blond, when everyone knew that only dark men, like Patrick, got taken seriously.

But at least his eyebrows were good. Brown and thick, and aggressively curved. Fuck-you eyebrows.

A cold sore was developing at the corner of her mouth. Fuck. He'd caught herpes from a Dutch girl when he was thirteen, and it had put him off kissing for life. With Toni he'd turned that into a virtue, telling her they mustn't kiss, as he didn't want to pass it on. She believed him, as she always did. He didn't know if he despised or pitied her for that.

God, he hated women. There were times when he wanted to fuck every single woman in the world.

'I don't know,' he said to Toni's reflection. 'Maybe you're frigid.'

She blinked. Absorbing the hurt without showing it. Her own peculiar response to pain.

'Maybe,' he went on, 'we should stop sleeping together.'

'If you like.'

Mission accomplished. Now she had something to think about while he was in Toulouse, and he'd got rid of the hollowness in his chest. 'I've got to go,' he said.

'You had to go an hour ago, when you came in. You should be at the airport by now.'

'Patrick can wait. He'll have to. He hasn't got anywhere else to go.' He paused. 'Maybe I'll take Nerissa along for the ride.'

'If you do that,' she countered evenly, 'you'll have to take Simon along too, and there's not enough room in the jeep.'

'Oh yes there is. Simon's a shrimp, and Nerissa's such a tiny little thing.' Maybe that was laying it on a bit thick, but he couldn't resist it. It was reassuring to know that he could really screw her up if he ever told her about Nerissa. Maybe that was what Patrick had meant when he'd said that Myles only slept with Nerissa to assert his independence from Toni. Fuck off, Myles had replied, to hide his pleasure, for he loved it when Patrick analysed him.

But what Toni didn't understand was that it was crucial to be several hours late to pick up his friend. Can't have Myles Cantellow hanging around looking keen, like some fucking Boy Scout, now can we? Not when he's the one with the house and the public-school background and the villa in France, while Patrick's just some poor-white Yank from the middle of nowhere.

'So what do you think,' he said, pulling on cut-offs and his favourite Gieves & Hawkes shirt with the rip in the back. 'Should I take Nerissa, or just Modge?'

'Take whom you like.'

'D'you want to come?'

She shook her head. 'I've got work to do.'

'You're so conscientious, Toni. It's a real turn-off.'

She shrugged. 'That's one thing I'm not about to change, not even for you.'

He knew she meant it. That was what he found so exciting about her. No matter how hopelessly inexperienced she was with men, there was always that strong, deep-rooted passion for something he couldn't begin to understand.

He gathered his spare change from the chest of drawers, along with his Amex card and the Roman coin his mother had given him when he got into university. He jammed the whole lot in his back pocket and said, 'I almost forgot. I won't be helping out at the Source any more. None of us will.'

That made her sit up. 'Why not?'

'Your father's pulling us off it. Didn't he tell you?'

'Wha – t?'

'He says there's no point in carrying on up there when we've only got three weeks left, and he needs everyone down on the main site, and anyway, the Source is obviously nothing to do with your fave Roman, and – oh, yes – he can't devote any more manpower to your childhood fantasy. Yup. I think that about covers it.'

He watched her take it all in. As he had known she would, she flicked a glance at the bedside cabinet, where her precious little secret was securely locked up: her own attempt at translating the Cassius *Poems*, along with a note of her screwball theories on the poet. It was all desperately heretical and personal, and secret – or so she thought. Poor Toni. He could screw her up about that too, any time he liked.

'Sometimes,' she said quietly, 'it feels as if he doesn't want me to succeed in anything I do.'

48

'Well, two cheers for you, Toni! You got there at last! Parents fuck you up. Didn't you know?'

Doubtfully, she met his eyes. It was amazing. She just didn't get it.

He paused in the doorway. 'I thought I'd take the jeep instead of the Panda.' The jeep was her father's, and looked so much cooler than the Panda, which belonged to his mother.

'OK by me,' she said.

'Oh, and by the way,' he added. 'About the sex. – Maybe we should keep trying a bit longer.'

If Myles was right about her father, thought Antonia as she pulled on shorts and a Peruvian cotton top and padded downstairs, she was going to be a good deal busier from now on. She would have to get up at least two hours earlier every day in order to put in time at the Source before joining the main dig.

It hadn't occurred to her to give up the Source. The Source was her personal project. She had funded it from her savings, negotiated with the landowner for permission to dig, and designed the excavation strategy herself. After years of waiting and hoping, she had finally won the chance to prove what she had always known, and what her father had long since dismissed as make-believe: that two thousand years ago, Cassius had lived in the valley of the Sarac, and had worshipped at the Source.

Contrary to what her father clearly believed, she wasn't doing it to prove him wrong. Quite the opposite. She wanted to get closer to Cassius because by doing that she got closer to solving the riddle, and fulfilling the pact she had made with her father sixteen years before. Together they would solve the riddle and become famous. Together. Once they did that, everything else would fall into place.

The kitchen was a cool, dim cavern, and it was empty. Everyone was up at the main dig, or across the courtyard in the pot-shed. Not that there were very many of them. By any standards, the dig was woefully undermanned. Apart from herself and her father, there was only Myles and Nerissa (when they felt like it), Simon (because he needed the credits for his degree), and the ever-faithful Modge. It was hardly much of a team.

Maybe Daddy was right about the Source. Maybe they *should* just concentrate on what the university expected them to do. Keep on doggedly excavating the patch above the river, which had looked so promising as the site of a Roman villa. At least, it had looked promising from the aerial photos.

Judging by the mess on the kitchen table, her father had recently had lunch. On it were two dirty plates, a dish of oily butter studded with dead flies, a wedge of liquefying Brie, and half a *pain de campagne* which was rapidly turning to stone.

Antonia snapped off the end of the loaf. If she hurried, she could reach the main site in under five minutes. Maybe her father wouldn't notice that she'd been gone for over two hours.

She reminded herself that it didn't matter if he *did* notice. She was twenty-four years old, for heaven's sake, she could do what she liked. So why did he still have this knack of making her feel in the wrong?

Hurrying out into the scullery, she almost fell over Modge.

The little girl started guiltily. She had been studying her reflection in the mirror over the sink. To judge from her expression, she hated what she saw.

'Myles said I could go with him to the airport to meet Patrick,' she blurted out. 'He's gone to fetch the jeep.' Then, as if to reassure herself that her half-brother hadn't already left without her, she added, 'He promised last night that I could go.'

Last night, thought Antonia. So all that talk about taking Nerissa instead of Modge had been a lot of rubbish. What careful games Myles played. Merely thinking about them made her tired. So don't think about them, she told herself. And don't even *begin* to think about what he said about your being frigid. That's just another of his little games.

Isn't it?

To start with, being with Myles had been amazing. She had known of him vaguely at university, but never to speak to. Myles Cantellow belonged to the fast set, which took hard drugs, was far too cool to do any work, and stared straight through people like her.

She had been amazed and exhilarated when she realized that he wanted to go to bed with her. And he had been surprisingly nice when he learned that, freakishly, she was still a virgin.

But that had been back at the end of June, when he was still reeling from getting a Third. It seemed like years ago, now. Well, she told herself briskly, if he's nothing but trouble, why put up with him? No-one's forcing you. You've only yourself to blame.

But when she thought about dumping him, her skin prickled as if she was going to throw up. Which was odd, because she wasn't in love with him, and he definitely wasn't in love with her. But he needed her, so maybe that was it. Maybe she needed to be needed.

Modge was on the verge of tears as she fought a losing battle to secure her ponytail with a plastic clip of fluorescent green. Her brown hair was too thin and greasy to take the clip, which kept sliding off and clattering onto the tiles.

She wore an eye-popping lime-green T-shirt tucked into tight purple shorts which bit into her high, round midriff. The final *coup de grâce* was a *Star Trek* knapsack bulging awkwardly between her shoulder-blades.

When she saw Antonia eyeing the knapsack, she shrugged it off and chucked it on the floor. 'Myles says only toddlers wear knapsacks,' she mumbled, 'but I *need* it! It's got my sunglasses and comic and some tissues and a bottle of water in case I get thirsty.'

Antonia hated to see the anxiety on the small sallow face. It wasn't fair. Why should it matter how an eight-year-old looked?

Without having met Patrick McMullan, she was angry with him for inspiring such passionate devotion. He would probably turn out to be just another Great Manipulator, like Myles: coldly exploring the limits of his own permafrosted nature by inflicting pain on others.

'Sometimes,' she said, 'I could clobber Myles.'

Modge's jaw dropped.

'Sometimes,' Antonia went on, 'I think he isn't a human being at all. I think he's a robot from outer space. Or maybe an android.'

Modge blinked. Then she giggled. No-one made fun of her half-brother.

'Come here, you,' said Antonia, pulling Modge towards her. The little girl's shoulders felt hot and frail, like a kitten. 'You know,' she said, 'you'd feel better if you wore the T-shirt outside the shorts. Like this. And the way to wear a knapsack and not look like a toddler is to wear it over just one shoulder. There. Now you look radical.'

Modge threw her an uncertain look. 'Is that good?'

'Oh, yes. It's the ultimate in cool. Now how about losing that clip, and just using your usual one? Where is it, inside the knapsack? There. We know this one'll stay in place. But let's pep it up a bit, shall we?' She undid the ribbons from her own ponytail and tied them round Modge's. '*Et voilà*. A garnish of sapphire and silver – which, if I remember rightly, are the colours of the United Federation of Planets.'

Modge turned pink. '*Radical*,' she said.

CHAPTER FOUR

Modge sat stiffly in the front of the jeep and tried not to flinch at her half-brother's driving.

When they nearly bumped into a lorry on the motorway, or lurched scarily as they rounded a bend, she sucked in her lips and struggled not to wince.

Earlier, as they were manoeuvring out of the courtyard at the mill, Myles had done something wrong to the gears, and the jeep had continued going backwards when they should have gone forwards, and nearly backed into the wall. Antonia, watching from the porch, had laughed, and Modge had giggled, and Myles had nearly chucked her out.

He was quite capable of chucking her out at a petrol station, and leaving her there. Myles was capable of anything. He was *so* wicked. Modge longed to do something he'd admire.

If only he wouldn't tease her so much. Grown-ups always said 'it's only a joke' when they wanted to be nasty without actually having a fight. Simon Toynbee said it all the time. Once in the pot-shed she'd seen him accidentally knock over the ink they used for labelling shards, and it went all over the context sheets, and when Dr Hunt came in and was furious, Simon blamed Alfonse, the mill cat. Modge was *outraged*. She would have sprung to Alfonse's defence, but Dr Hunt only fumed but didn't actually take it out on Alfonse, so she kept quiet. She had learned that if you try to blame a grown-up, you're the one who gets into trouble. 'It was only a joke,' Simon said, when he caught her glaring at him.

Simon Toynbee was exactly the way his name sounded: thin and whiny and a sneak. Names were important to Modge, because she *hated* hers, especially her nickname. Antonia had lent her a Book of Names, and she'd looked everyone's up. She wasn't a bit surprised to learn that her sister Nerissa – who looked so perfect it was scary – was named after a sea nymph.

Or that her own name didn't mean anything at all, but was simply someone else's name, which had been wrongly spelt in a play. That stood to reason, because Modge had once overheard her mother telling a friend that Modge had been 'a mistake'. *Modge-Podge.* Like a biscuit cobbled together from leftover scraps of dough.

Patrick had told her that if she really wanted to, she could change her name when she was older, but he hoped she wouldn't, as he liked it. She couldn't work out if he really meant that, or was only trying to make her feel better.

'Cat got your tongue, Modge-Podge?' said Myles.

She gripped her seat, and wondered what he meant. It didn't sound very nice. Alfonse would never do a thing like that. 'No,' she said carefully.

'Nervous about meeting your boyfriend again?'

'He's not my boyfriend.'

He laughed. 'No need to get in a strop!'

Modge dug her thumbnail into the seat. 'I'm not,' she muttered. 'It's just that he's not my boyfriend.'

'Then why are you all togged up? Bells on your toes and ribbons in your hair.'

Her stomach turned over. Now that Myles had noticed the ribbons, she was desperate to take them off, for if he mentioned them to Patrick she would die. But if she *did* take them off, Antonia would be hurt, so it looked like she was stuck with them. Next to Patrick – and Myles when he wasn't being nasty – Antonia was her favourite person in the whole galaxy. Apart from Mummy, of course.

'Don't worry, Modge,' Myles said. 'I won't tell Patrick.'

She shot him a look. She'd heard *that* before.

Android, she told him silently in her head. It made her feel immensely better.

She settled back and concentrated on thinking about Patrick. She had only met him once before, on one never-to-be-forgotten Sunday, when he and Myles had descended on her school without warning, and taken her out for tea. The other girls had been *so* jealous. Two incredibly dashing young men, one of them a real American.

Afterwards, she had told all the girls how clever Patrick was, and how he was studying something with a long name which he said was about finding trapdoors inside people's heads, and very gently cleaning out the cobwebs. Or something like that. She hadn't understood exactly, but it was lovely having a grown-up talk to her as if she was a grown-up too. And she thought Patrick would be the right person to do the cleaning-up thing with the cobwebs.

They reached the airport. She was scared of airports, but knew better than to show it in front of Myles. The tarmac in the car park was hot and squidgy beneath her sandals, and the electric doors made a horrible hissing noise. She wanted to hold Myles' hand when they went through them, but he was walking too fast, so she clutched her *Star Trek* pack and hurried after him.

'What's the time?' he said when they were inside, weaving through the crowds. He never wore a watch.

Modge consulted the Vulcan Time-Scanner on her wrist. 'Six minutes to three.'

Myles hooted. 'Oh, *man*! This time I've really done it, even for me! The poor bastard's plane got in at twelve.'

Modge's jaw dropped. Did he mean to say that they'd kept Patrick waiting for *three hours*?

Black despair opened up before her. Patrick would be furious. In fact, maybe he was *so* furious that he hadn't bothered to wait for them, and had just turned round and gone back to England.

Then suddenly there he was, and he was even handsomer than she remembered. He was Lancelot and Cassius and Luke Skywalker all rolled into one. And he didn't look in the slightest bit cross. He was laughing, and he gave Myles the sort of punch in the tummy which boys do when they're pleased to see each other, although this must have been quite a hard one, as it made Myles gasp and bend over double. But when Myles straightened up, he was laughing too, and Modge could tell that he was trying not to show how incredibly pleased he was to see his friend.

Shyly, she waited with her knapsack at her feet. She was so happy she wanted to cry.

Then Patrick reached down and hoisted his rucksack over one shoulder, *exactly* as Antonia had taught *her* to do. Casually, Modge did the same with hers. She moved to Patrick's side, hoping Myles wouldn't notice her. Myles hadn't said anything about the ribbons, or about Patrick being her boyfriend, but she didn't want to jog his memory.

Patrick looked down at her and grinned. A proper grin, as if he really was pleased to see her. 'Hi, Imogen,' he said.

By the time they were nearing the village of La Bastide, Patrick was fed up with France, Myles, and the British. But mostly with Myles.

'Well, it was your own fucking fault for flying to Toulouse instead of Perpignan,' Myles had said at the airport, as he chucked Patrick's rucksack in the jeep. 'Perpignan's so much *nearer*, it's just down the road.'

'Yeah,' said Patrick drily, 'and British Airways is about twice as expensive as Air Express.'

Myles rolled his eyes. 'Oh, *money*! Is that all you think about?'

Patrick – hot, tired, hungry and apprehensive – decided to ignore him. It was either that or deck him in the parking lot.

Knowing he was in the wrong made Myles drive even more appallingly than usual. Modge sat in the back gripping the edge of her seat, and Patrick concentrated on the scenery.

The South of France wasn't what he'd expected at all. He'd expected something like Beverly Hills. Palm trees and country clubs, and turquoise swimming pools. Instead he found himself in a harsh, lonely country of blinding silver rock and dusty thorn-scrub; a crazy geometry of dizzying gorges, towering pinnacles, and sun-baked uplands.

'*The Fenouillèdes*', said the guidebook he had found in Oxford Central Library, '*are the last major hills before the Pyrenees. In many ways they are more isolated and less explored than their larger cousins.*'

He could understand why. Even for Europe, the roads

were ridiculously narrow and tortuous, and in the few villages they passed through, the pedestrians had to step into doorways to avoid the jeep. Not that there were many people about. The villages were practically deserted.

Every other hilltop bore the traceried ruin of a castle. He'd read about that, too. Hundreds of years ago, this had been the border between France and Spain, a place of bloody feuds and bitter last stands. But the book hadn't prepared him for the sheer number of the damn things.

Still, at least there was one small reminder of home. Most of the roadsigns were pitted with buckshot. It seemed that the French used them for target practice, just like they did in Wyoming.

After about an hour and a half they reached a bridge across a fast-running river which foamed from the mouth of a narrow, steep-sided gorge. The entrance to the gorge was guarded by two massive, crazily leaning rock buttresses, several hundred feet high.

Halfway across the bridge, Myles cut the engine. 'We're here. That's La Bastide up ahead.'

Beyond the bridge, the road veered sharply away from the mouth of the gorge and wound up to a jumble of Spanish-looking houses clinging to a steep hill. Patrick saw terracotta roofs, thick whitewashed walls, and tiny shuttered windows. Terraces of vines and olive trees occupied every spare inch in between. A small church squatted beside a capacious cemetery dotted with cypresses, and at the top of the hill, the obligatory ruined castle towered over the village. From there a stony ridge ran in a long swooping curve to join the eastern buttress of the gorge.

'Our house,' said Myles, 'is Les Limoniers – the one just below the castle.' He pointed to a large whitewashed villa with sky-blue awnings, several terraces, and a garden of bougainvillea and lemon trees. 'The views are amazing. Best in the village.'

That figures, thought Patrick sourly, determined not to be overwhelmed.

Without the noise of the engine, the sounds of the countryside surged in on him. The thunder of the river, the rasp of the cicadas. A distant creak as someone in the village opened a shutter. The air was sharp with the tang of woodsmoke, and a dusty undertone of sage.

He pointed to the slope beyond the bridge, where, just below the first house in the village, an area the size of three tennis courts had been cleared and staked out in squares. 'I guess that's the main site, huh?'

'Got it in one,' said Myles. 'The skinny shit shaking his head is our esteemed leader, Dr Hunt. The gawky redhead with the ponytail is Simon the Dork. And the blonde doing nothing in the shade is of course the luscious Nissa.'

The young Brigitte Bardot, thought Patrick with a sinking feeling. Right down to the shades.

'Tell you what,' said Myles, drumming his fingers on the steering wheel. 'You get out here with Modge-Podge and go and meet everyone, and I'll take your pack up to the house.'

Patrick opened his mouth to protest, but Myles cut him short. 'No time like the present, Patroclus. Go on – please.'

Patrick shot him a glance. His friend's eyes were bloodshot and jittery, and there was a thin sheen of sweat on his upper lip. He needed a hit.

Patrick wondered if speed was still the flavour of the month, or whether coke had taken over. With Myles it could be anything. Just so long as his little sister wasn't around to see him take it. Myles had no compunction about swearing in front of Modge, or getting dead drunk, or keeping her up till all hours, but about drugs he had an absolute rule.

Patrick gave a brisk nod, and opened the door. 'We'll catch you later. Come on, Imogen.'

The elder Dr Hunt turned out to have querulous grey eyes and a nicotine-stained beard which drew attention to a bitter mouth. He neither welcomed Patrick nor introduced him to the others, but merely gave him the briefest of handshakes, and told him to go and find his daughter, who would give him a site plan and a list of Do's and Don'ts.

'That would be Dr Hunt the younger?' Patrick said.

The thin lips became perceptibly thinner. Clearly, on this dig there was only *one* Dr Hunt.

Well, screw you, thought Patrick, watching him go, and feeling the remains of his goodwill evaporating fast. Out loud, he said to the blonde who had wandered over to inspect him: 'I guess I've just offended the Professor, huh?'

'Oh, don't mind him,' she said, 'he's just in a strop because he had a row with Toni. And by the way,' she took off her shades and favoured him with a cool smile, 'he isn't a professor. I know you Americans call everyone a professor, but over here they're not as common as they are in the States.'

Patrick nodded gravely.

She was extremely pretty in a feline sort of way, with large greenish-grey eyes and a flawless complexion tanned a beautiful honey-gold. She wore a wide straw hat and a short, floaty flowered dress which seemed wildly out of place on a dig, but suited her smallness and femininity.

Judging from the way in which she was calmly sizing him up, she would probably be available if he wanted her. He did not. If they slept together she would never let him forget who was doing whom the almighty favour. Besides, she was sleeping with Myles, so it was out of the question.

The tall redheaded guy had also wandered over. Hadn't Myles said this was Nerissa's boyfriend? Or maybe he just *wanted* to be her boyfriend. Whatever, he was welcome to her, so he could stop looking as if he'd just swallowed a lemon.

'So,' said Simon Toynbee, 'you're an American. Does that mean you don't speak French?'

'Well, I'm not sure about that as a definition,' Patrick said evenly, 'but yeah, it does.'

Simon tried not to look pleased. 'That'll set you back a bit.'

'Don't worry,' said Nerissa. 'We'll look after you.'

'Thanks,' said Patrick. 'In fact, your sister's been doing a pretty good job of that already.'

'Half-sister,' Nerissa put in sharply, with a glance at Modge. 'Same father, different mothers.'

At Patrick's side, the little girl flushed.

Patrick bit back his irritation. 'You know, it's getting kind of late. Why don't we let you finish up here and—'

'Yes, why don't you?' said Simon. 'Toni's probably down at the mill, you can check in with her.'

Shyly, Modge took his hand. 'Come along. I'll show you the way.'

They left Simon and Nerissa, and started back towards the bridge. Behind them, Patrick overheard Nerissa remark to Simon, 'So that's Myles' friend from the sticks. Not what I'd expected. Not at all. A bit grammar school for Myles, don't you think?'

'Absolutely,' said Simon.

'Good shoulders, though,' Nerissa said.

They were too far away to catch Simon's reply.

'Patrick,' said Modge. 'What's grammar school?'

'The opposite of Myles,' said Patrick grimly.

'Oh,' said Modge. 'Well, that *must* be good.'

Patrick laughed, and flicked her ribbons.

Just before they reached the bridge, Modge took a side-road on the left which Patrick hadn't noticed before, for it dropped steeply below the level of the parapet. They climbed down through pines, cypresses and oaks, and finally reached a dark ivy-choked ruin at the water's edge.

The Moulin de Sarac must once have housed a pretty wealthy miller, for it was built around a spacious court-yard, and reached through an impressive stone archway. It would have been magnificent about four hundred years ago, but since then it had slipped a bit. The roof was a patchwork of moss and broken terracotta, half the outer wall had disappeared beneath a mountain of ivy, and the other half had subsided into the river. The tiny shuttered windows and the general air of decay made Patrick think of the Brothers Grimm.

The location didn't help, either. It was jammed beneath the towering eastern buttress of the gorge, which Modge told him was called the Roc de St Pastou – as if that made up for the fact that it looked about to flatten the mill.

With growing reluctance he followed her towards the archway. He had no desire to meet Antonia Hunt. He'd had enough of patronizing English girls for one day.

The Gorges de Sarac, he decided, was a truly horrible place. Above his head the black-streaked Roc shut out the sun. The riverbanks were choked with tumbled boulders and fallen trees, from which rose the sour tang of rottenness. If there were birds, Patrick couldn't see any. He couldn't hear any, either. He couldn't hear anything above the thunder of the river, which reverberated through the gorge. You could be murdered down here, and no-one would hear you scream.

'Hey, Modge,' he said suddenly, 'I'll bet Antonia wants to be by herself right now, after that row with her dad. What say we skip the mill and you show me this Source you're so keen on?'

To hell with Dr Hunt the younger. She wasn't the only one who wanted to be on her own.

They took a dirt road which branched off from the mill track and snaked steeply up the Roc, hugging a stony slope of sun-bleached thistles on which an occasional twisted olive tree struggled to survive.

It was a steep climb, but after ten minutes they rounded the buttress and left La Bastide behind.

Suddenly Patrick found himself in a different world: harsher, wilder, and astonishingly remote.

He had always thought of Europe as a crowded place, but looking around, he couldn't see a single rooftop, or other sign of human occupation. There was nothing to show that this country was inhabited at all, or had *ever* been inhabited. All he could see were the splintered hills marching grimly towards the horizon, and the stark white brilliance of the Pyrenees.

After about a mile they came to an aluminium farm gate wedged open with a rock, and immediately after that, the track split. Modge told him that the left-hand fork, which was deeply rutted with tyre tracks, continued over the Roc to a farm called Le Figarol, where old Monsieur Panabière, who owned the Source, lived with his invalid wife. He was also the owner of the tiny terrace of vines ten yards down.

'You don't speak German, do you?' Modge asked anxiously.

Patrick assured her that he did not.

'Whew,' said Modge. She told him that Monsieur Panabière had had a horrible time in the war, and didn't tolerate Germans on his land. He had been known to fire warning shots at hikers he suspected of Teutonic origins, and if he was having a *really* bad day, being fair-haired could be enough to set him off.

They continued up the right-hand track. The air grew hotter, dizzy with the scent of wild thyme. The cicadas were deafening.

After another few hundred yards, the track became a footpath. The rocks threw back the heat like a furnace, and Patrick wished he had kept his pack with him, and could have changed into a pair of shorts. When he left Oxford that morning it had been 'unseasonably cool' – as the British endearingly termed their lousy summers – so he was wearing jeans and a heavy cotton polo shirt. His clothes felt like sodden wool against his skin.

They reached a rusty footbridge spanning a deep tributary gorge, and on the other side the track forked again.

'That's the Ravin de Verdura,' said Modge, with enviably good pronunciation. 'You *don't* want to go down there. Myles did once, and ended up on the *garrigue*, which you can't see from here as it's over the hill, but it's just rocks and there's no water at all, so he's jolly lucky to be alive.'

'Yikes,' said Patrick.

He was starting to feel bad about dragging her along. Even after he had relieved her of the *Star Trek* pack, her funny little face remained the colour of a ripe plum. But when he suggested that maybe she should wait under an olive tree while he carried on for a bit, she looked so crestfallen that he dropped it. The Source, she said, was a magic place, she absolutely *loved* it, and he would too.

He forbore from telling her that he didn't care what the hell the wretched Source was like, just so long as he could be alone for a while and get his head together before returning to the fray.

They climbed further up the gorge, going more slowly, for Modge's sake. Pebbles loosed by their footsteps trickled over the edge. It was a long way down, and Patrick put Modge on the side furthest from the drop.

As he got into his stride, the irritations of the day fell away. This was the same track – the *same track*, for Christ's sake – which the pilgrims had taken thousands of years before, when they had believed that the Source possessed healing powers. He had read about that on the plane. And the 'Fontaine del Bon Cristia' was, by European standards, a pretty recent name, cobbled together by medieval Christians in an attempt to stamp out the last traces of paganism. The old name, which Modge said the locals still used, was 'La Source du Cheval'. The Spring of the Horse. Patrick wondered why they called it that. Up here you would need a mountain goat, not a horse.

As he walked, an odd feeling came over him that they were not alone. He was no stranger to lonely places, but never before had he been so sharply aware of all the small, secret lives thronging round him.

The ravens cawing from the pine tops. The swallows wheeling about the cliff face. The midges and cicadas and bees. They were all part of it, an endless current of life down the years.

A lizard froze on a tree root to watch him pass. A bird fled into the sage with a soft, strong thrumming of wings. He heard goat bells, discordant and mythical. Then a goat appeared silently by an olive tree on the slope above him. It was coal-black, with split yellow eyes and soft, drooping ears. For a moment it regarded him silently, and he felt a shiver of superstitious fear. Then it rose on tiny delicate hind hooves, and began to nibble leaves.

They reached the end of the track. Ahead, a massive overhang framed a semicircle of pure darkness.

'See how it's a horseshoe shape?' panted Modge. 'There's a reason for that. Antonia told me. On Easter Day the Devil fought a terrible battle with St Pastou, and the Devil lost, and *leapt* on his horse and galloped up the gorge, and St Pastou chased after him. And just here, the Devil's horse gave a huge jump and left his hoof-print in the mountain. So St Pastou made a spring in the cave, to wash it clean again. Which means,' she added, in case Patrick hadn't yet got it, 'that the cave is *actually* a giant hoof-print.'

The cave was a good forty feet below the cliff top. 'What was the Devil doing all the way down here?' murmured Patrick. 'Scrabbling for a foothold?'

'A hoof-hold,' said Modge with a grin.

Patrick went to the mouth of the cave, then stopped. Cold breath seemed to emanate from within. He felt strangely reluctant to enter. An interloper. Peering into the gloom, he saw that the cave was perhaps fifty feet deep, and roofed by stalactites which gave it a frozen, chaotic feel.

Narrowing his eyes to adjust to the dimness, he saw a thin black stream of water trickling from a narrow cleft in the back wall. It pooled in a small natural basin of rock, then seeped over the rim and disappeared down a crack in the floor.

Patrick thought of the poem he had read on the plane. '*I know a place in the hills where the gods walk the earth.*'

Standing before the darkness of the cave, he could believe it. At his back he heard the death rattle of the wind in the dry sage pods. He heard its velvet sighs in the oak at the cave mouth, and its deep marine soughing in the pine further down the track. And he could believe, as the pagans had believed, that a different spirit inhabited each plant.

The ravens above his head *were* the messengers of the gods. The cypresses *were* reaching towards heaven. And that black goat by the olive tree was the oldest god of all.

From deep within the cave he heard the sybilline voice of the spring talking to itself.

'Would you mind awfully,' said a voice from the darkness of the cave, 'if you didn't come inside?'

Patrick's heart jerked.

'Sorry if I startled you,' said the voice, which was a girl's. 'But there's a grid in here, and if you don't know where to walk you might damage something.'

Patrick licked dry lips. For an instant, as her voice issued from the darkness, he had thought an oracle had spoken.

He cleared his throat. Then he said hoarsely, 'I guess you'd be the second Dr Hunt?'

'Sorry, yes,' said the voice. 'I was in the side-chamber, that's why you didn't see me, and I was just finishing up,

68

so I'd turned off the lamp to save gas. Modge, take this lot for me, will you?'

A girl emerged from the cave and handed Modge a trowel and a clipboard and some plastic bags with bits of rubble in them, while she rummaged in an elderly blue vinyl knapsack hanging from one shoulder. Awkwardly she offered Patrick her other hand, but he was too startled to take it, and by the time he had regained his wits and extended his, she had already dropped hers.

To his astonishment, he realized that she was nervous. He watched her brush the dust off her hands, drop her rucksack, stoop to retrieve it and brush the dust off it, then notice that she'd just dirtied her palms again and brush them off on the seat of her shorts, before once more extending her hand to him. This time he took it.

She flicked back her ponytail and cast him a shy glance which did not reach his eyes.

What the hell does a girl like this have to be nervous about? he thought in bemusement.

Myles had nicknamed her the Vestal Virgin, but that was all wrong. She didn't look Roman, she looked Minoan. He could picture her turning ceremonial cartwheels across a bull's back. Although before she did so, she would probably apologize to the bull.

She was tall, only a few inches shorter than he, with wide, straight shoulders, a narrow waist, and generous hips and bosom. Her colouring was clear and dramatic: pale skin, dark eyes, long dark hair with a kink to it. A wide mouth, and a fine straight nose with a high Grecian bridge.

The high priestess, he thought numbly.

And like a priestess, she was ablaze with colour in the late afternoon sun. She wore wine-red shorts and a sleeveless top throbbing with zigzags of pure colour: emerald, sapphire, topaz and ruby. Her hair was tied back with a twist of satin ribbons – one the colour of ripe grapes, the other a deep, burning saffron – and from her ears hung tiny papier-mâché parrots. After the sun-bleached hues of the climb, so much richness hurt his eyes.

Belatedly, it occurred to him that he still had Modge's pink *Star Trek* bag dangling from one hand. He must look like an idiot. But Antonia Hunt didn't seem to notice. She was retrieving her specimens from Modge and packing them in her rucksack. Over her shoulder she said, 'Myles said you're from Wyoming?'

Patrick braced himself. But she surprised him by asking if that meant he'd learned Spanish in school.

'Uh-huh,' he replied warily.

'Lucky you,' she said with feeling. 'You'll probably get on far better with the locals than we do with our Parisian French. I still have to make them repeat everything three times. The Catalan accent's impenetrable.'

'You speak *Spanish*?' said Modge, looking up at him. 'Wow.'

Embarrassed, he took Antonia Hunt's now bulging rucksack from her – in the teeth of her protestations that she could manage, honestly – and they started down the track.

'I'm sorry you had to hike all this way to find me,' she said, still without looking at him.

'Well in fact I wasn't—'

'– and I do hope you won't be bored out here. People often do get bored on a dig, you know, it's so much less exciting – I mean, less *immediately* exciting – than they expect. And I'm afraid we haven't had much luck on this one. In fact, none at all. We were hoping for traces of Roman occupancy, but it's been a huge disappointment.'

'That's OK with me,' he put in, when she paused for breath. 'I mean, I don't know much archaeology, but I've been on a couple of digs, so I know what to expect.'

'Oh, *have* you? But that's marvellous! I wish Myles had told me. We're crying out for experienced help.'

'I wouldn't say I was exactly—'

'You've no idea how hard it is to get *anyone* to help out here.'

Modge looked round at them and beamed, and skipped ahead with Antonia's clipboard in her arms.

Patrick still couldn't think of anything to say. He felt as if he'd been kicked in the chest. Luckily, Antonia Hunt was keeping up an edgy torrent of conversation enough for two.

She told him about the dig – about both digs – and he noticed that she was curiously self-deprecating about herself, and over-generous when it came to her father. She even defended his decision to pull all the volunteers off the dig at the Source, when clearly it meant the world to her.

But strangely, when she started telling him about the Roman poet, Cassius, who she thought might be linked with the Source, she became a different girl. Focused, incisive, and not flustered at all. And she made no concessions whatsoever to Patrick as a non-classicist: he could either follow what she told him, or ask if he didn't, but until then, she would simply assume that he could keep up.

He liked her for that. It made a change from being patronized. But he didn't ask many questions. In fact, he didn't ask any. She was nothing like what he had expected.

What on earth was Myles playing at with a girl like

this? Why didn't he stick with someone of his own kind, like Nerissa?

'So what do you think of the Source?' asked Antonia Hunt, cutting across his thoughts.

'The Source,' he echoed stupidly.

'Sorry, that's what we call it. I mean the cave back there.'

He wondered what to say. With anyone else he would have made some quip and left it at that. But with this girl he couldn't do that. For the first time since they had met, she was actually looking at him. Her face was open and exposed and slightly anxious, as if it really mattered what he thought.

He thought of the way her father's lips had thinned at the mention of her name, and what Myles had said about her. '*Ah, the Vestal Virgin, yum yum yum . . . Don't worry about me and Nerissa. What poor darling Toni doesn't know can't possibly hurt her!*'

That made Patrick feel curiously protective, and obliged to tell her the truth. 'I guess . . .' he began at last, searching for words, '"haunted" isn't the right expression for a place like that. It feels as if – as if something lives there. Or lived there once.' He shook his head, colouring. 'No, that's not right. I guess what I mean is, it's a place where the past feels very close.'

Her lips parted. 'That's so well put. That's exactly how it feels.'

Then she smiled at him. Not the quick edgy smile she had given him at the Source, but a wide, genuine smile which took his breath away.

'Come along, you two!' shouted Modge from further down the track.

'Coming!' Antonia Hunt called back, and started after the little girl.

Dimly, Patrick sensed the sun on his back and the smell of the wild thyme, and the breeze softly whipping the dust around his ankles.

Slowly he followed Antonia Hunt down the track.

To Patrick's relief, Myles noticed nothing when he and Modge finally reached Les Limoniers, having left Antonia Hunt at the mill.

Myles was in too good a mood to notice anything: restored, refreshed, and almost puppyish in his desire to show Patrick the room he had prepared for him. It was large and airy, and painted brilliant white, with a cool, blue-tiled floor, and a breathtaking view across the ridge towards the Roc de St Pastou.

Myles had gone to some care (for Myles) to make his friend comfortable, finding a pair of clean sheets and a pillow, and even putting a sprig of bougainvillea in a jam jar in the window, where it had wilted in the sun and dropped its petals all over the sill.

He left Patrick to unpack, and went off to fetch the champagne he'd put on ice, and the *tarte tatin* he'd bought in the village bakery, and the *pâté de sanglier*, which they would have to eat without bread, as he'd forgotten to buy any.

Patrick, emerging newly showered onto the terrace in shorts and a T-shirt, found the omission of the bread obscurely touching. It made him feel worse.

He sat in one of the wrought-iron chairs facing the mountains, and listened to Myles swapping jokes with Modge in the kitchen. After a while he leaned forward and put his elbows on the rail.

An overwhelming sense of danger swept over him.

He had never felt like this. Not once. Not even close. It was terrifying. It felt as if someone had pulled away a scab and exposed his raw flesh to the burning sun.

He sucked in a deep draught of the lemon-scented air. A passage from Cassius came back to him.

> *Doesn't that wretched Boy ever get tired*
> *of plugging away at us with his wretched arrows?*
> *Hunting mortals must be a pretty poor sport for a*
>   *god.*
> *We can't get away, we can't fight back;*
> *all we can do is bleed.*
> *Doesn't He ever get tired of it?*

You've got to get out of here, Patrick thought suddenly. Make some excuse, fall sick, it doesn't matter what. Just get out of here and go back to England.

Myles will be furious, but what can he do?

For what's the alternative? Stay here, and try to steal your best friend's girl? Or sit back and watch him screw her up?

Great choice. Oh, yeah.

You've got to get out of here fast.

CHAPTER FIVE

Rome, 31 March 53 BC

Cassius had been in a terrible mood all week.

He tried not to let it show when he was with Plautius, but the old man was too perceptive to be fooled for long.

Determined to distract his 'young friend' as best he could, he had arranged two elegant little dinners, a musical recital, and several brisk discussions on philosophy, astronomy and ethics. Cassius strove to pretend that he was enjoying it all.

But finally the evening came when Plautius took a little too much raisin wine, and made the mistake of congratulating Cassius on the 'honourable' course he had taken in avoiding another encounter with the daughter of Publius Tacitus Silanus.

'Rome's *full* of pretty girls!' he cried, with the blithe unconcern of a sixty-eight-year-old who has put such foolishness behind him. 'You did the right thing, my boy! The honourable thing. I'm proud of you.'

Cassius set his teeth, and barked at the freedman to refill his wine cup.

He didn't need Plautius to tell him he was doing the right thing. What choice did he have? One glance at her father's house had been enough to tell him that anything else would be madness.

Three days after the Day of Blood, he had wandered up onto the Palatine and sought out the house.

It was dusk – he had just got off duty – and compared to the din of the barracks, the Palatine Hill was like a tomb. Her father's house was in one of the quietest and most exclusive streets, far removed from the stink which wafted up from the Tiber. Every brick, every tile, murmured discreetly of old money. *We don't need to put on a show*, breathed the house. *Ostentation is for plebeians and parvenus.*

It had a windowless frontage which was unadorned by casements or balconies, and painted a plain Etruscan red. A modest doorstep of yellow Numidian marble, a simple door of studded beech.

No show, whispered the house. *We keep our luxury in the back. The fountains and the frescoes, the flower gardens and the inlaid marble floors.*

So of course he had been right to stay away. To bury himself in his duties and forget all about her. He only wished that Plautius didn't feel the need to applaud him so fulsomely, to his face.

But unfortunately the old man did, so Cassius snapped at him, and then felt bad. Which prompted him to make amends by offering to take his friend's place at a poetry evening, when Plautius sprained his ankle getting out of the bath.

Ah, how the gods enjoy their little jokes! Who would have thought that Plautius, of all people, would be his undoing?

The gathering was on the other side of the city, and as Cassius had feared, it turned out to be excruciatingly dull. The host was an elderly crony of Plautius' from the law courts, who had chosen to delight his friends by reading the unabridged version of his 'poetic discourse' on 'The Legends of the Deeps'. Plautius, who had been favoured with an advance copy, had generously pronounced it 'a fine, scholarly work on a sorely neglected theme'.

Not neglected enough, thought Cassius sourly, swallowing a yawn.

He wished he was back with the old man. At least then he wouldn't have to wear this wretched toga, which after his uniform felt unfamiliar and cumbersome. And at least then he could get properly drunk. He had left Plautius reclining comfortably on a couch on the terrace with a flask of wine, from where he could supervise his slaves in one of his favourite pastimes: a moonlit snail hunt in the vegetable patch. 'Over *there*, Solon! Don't let the little rascals get into the broccoli!'

Kind, clever, modest old Plautius, thought Cassius with a twinge of guilt. What did he do to deserve an ungrateful friend like me?

Stifling another yawn, he started counting the heads of the audience, for something to do.

She was two rows ahead of him, and across the aisle on his left. Sitting very straight and still, and staring in front of her with a rigid intensity which told him instantly that she knew he was behind her.

She wore a sleeveless gown of deep sapphire, the colour of a clear night sky just before the last light fades. Pearls in her ears, and the same gold half-moon at her breast. No rings, except for a signet on the little finger of her right hand, which he glimpsed when she brushed a strand of dark hair from her cheek.

So she was not betrothed. He had wondered about that, and cursed himself for not having noticed when they met.

She wore no rouge or eyeblack, and no white lead upon her face. She didn't need it. Her skin glowed against the midnight darkness of her gown.

Abruptly the reading came to an end, and there was a smattering of exhausted applause. People stood up, stretched, chatted, and began drifting towards the dining room.

Cassius watched her turn and make some appeal to the thickset, youngish man – her brother? – sitting beside her. *It's hot*, she seemed to be saying, fanning herself. *May I go outside for some air?*

The brother considered, then bestowed a gracious nod. Presumably he was eager to attain the dining room. Besides, what harm could she come to at a gathering like this?

Still fanning herself, she rose and glided out onto the terrace.

What in Hades do I do now? wondered Cassius, his heart racing.

The sensible – indeed, the only – choice would be to say a swift goodbye to his host, and leave as rapidly as he could. That would also be the cowardly choice, and the cruel one. And discourteous, too. At the very least he ought to apologize for leading her on the other day at the procession.

Fool, said a waspish little voice inside his head. *You don't honestly believe that this has anything to do with courtesy?*

The lawyer's garden was a pleasant place of smooth, sandy walks hedged with rosemary and box, and dimly illuminated by torches and moonlight. Which still left plenty of shadowy patches beneath the fruit trees.

He found her at the end of an arcade of mulberries.

She made no pretence at being surprised that he

should have followed her outside, but merely drew back so that anyone passing the other end of the arcade would believe that he was alone.

'You weren't at the Games,' she said in a low voice.

No preamble. No dissemination. He thought that brave. 'I had duties,' he lied.

'You said you'd be there.'

'Yes.'

'Yet you never came.'

'– No.'

'You were playing games with me.'

'No. No.'

Her face was grave, and he could see that she was trembling. Her hands were taut at her sides, clutching the stuff of her dress. 'I offended you,' she said abruptly, startling him – for that was the last thing he thought.

'Wh – at?'

'That day when we met. I was rude. I sneered at you.' Her chin went up. 'I'm sorry.'

'No,' he put in quickly. 'It's I who should apologize to you. I should have introduced myself, not led you on like that, it wasn't fair. That's why I came out here. To apologize.' Another lie. His cheeks darkened with shame. He hoped the moonlight was too dim for her to see. 'I had no idea,' he said, 'that you'd be here tonight. If I'd known, I wouldn't have come.' He realized how that must sound, and flushed anew.

Her lip curled. 'My father does sometimes let me out, you know. Provided my brother can come with me, and the gathering is sufficiently dull and worthy. I think the family tolerates my interest in poetry because it keeps me out of trouble.'

There was a silence, while they both thought about how that sounded.

She bowed her head. 'You've been avoiding me, haven't you?'

'– Yes,' he said gently.

'Why?'

'You know why.'

Her head came up and she met his eyes. He felt himself sway.

'This is too dangerous,' he said. 'For both of us. You know that. You must go inside, now. Find your brother and make him take you home. At once. I'll wait here until you've gone.'

He stood back to let her pass, but she did not move. He watched her face turn pale. It tore his heart to see with what prickly dignity she strove to master her hurt. But at length a tear welled from her eye and spilled down her cheek.

'No,' he said. 'No. You mustn't cry.'

Without knowing what he did, he put out his hand and stopped the tear with his finger.

She stood perfectly still while he touched her cheek. Then with a fine, proud gesture that was to stay with him for years, she twisted round with her back to him so that he wouldn't see more tears.

In the moonlight her hair was a ribbon of darkness down her back. Her neck was pale and exposed.

He stood with his fists at his sides, watching the silent rise and fall of her shoulders as she cried.

At last he reached out and turned her gently round, and drew her into his arms.

CHAPTER SIX

Sunday, 18 September 1988

Before Patrick had come to La Bastide, Antonia used to spend Saturday nights with Myles at Les Limoniers. Then on Sundays she would get up early, pull on her kimono, and wander out onto the terrace to watch the sun rise.

But for the past fortnight she had been too self-conscious to wander around in her kimono. It embarrassed her to bump into Patrick after she had slept with Myles.

She told herself she was being ridiculous, she could sleep with whoever she pleased. It didn't work. At night she would lie awake wondering if Patrick could hear when she and Myles had sex. That was hardly likely, as his room was at the other end of the house. But these days Myles made *such* a noise. As if he wanted his friend to hear.

This particular Sunday morning, she lay in bed for longer than usual. Her face felt stiff with fatigue. Working at the Source as well as the main site was taking its toll. And last night had been late for everyone. Myles and Nerissa had insisted on driving twenty-five miles to Sainte Eulalie-les-Thermes for dinner at a three-star Michelin, and as Antonia's father refused to look after Modge, they had to take her with them. Modge spent the evening curled up asleep in the Panda, and Antonia spent the evening getting up to check on her.

It was after two when they returned to La Bastide. They dropped Simon and Nerissa at the mill, then drove up to Les Limoniers. Myles decided to watch the opening ceremony of the Olympics on TV. Patrick deposited the sleeping Modge in her room, then joined Myles in the sitting room. Antonia went to bed.

Now she lay watching the play of sunlight on the ceiling, while Myles whiffled into the pillow beside her.

Last night's redeeming feature, she thought, was that she had been asleep when he came in, so they didn't have sex. Then it occurred to her that this was not how one ought to feel about one's boyfriend. Maybe Myles was right, and she really was frigid. Or maybe they were just wrong for each other.

She felt too tired and too confused to deal with that now. And badly in need of a cup of coffee. She slid out of bed and pulled on shorts, a bra and a T-shirt. Then she twisted her hair into a plait, and padded downstairs.

Through the french windows she saw Modge and Patrick having breakfast on the terrace. Modge was shakily pouring Patrick a mug of coffee. His face was impassive as he watched the eight-year-old man-handle the coffee-pot in one unsteady hand. She had already slopped a generous amount onto the table, but he pretended not to notice, though he swiftly took charge of his mug before she could spill that too. He thanked her gravely, and she sucked in her cheeks so as not to look too pleased.

Watching the little charade, Antonia wished Patrick liked her as much as he seemed to like Modge. Or even at all. But since his arrival he had avoided her whenever he could. On the dig he would listen politely to her instructions, then move away at the first opportunity. He never chatted or cracked jokes with her. And he never called her Toni. She didn't *like* her nickname, but she minded that he did not use it. 'Antonia' sounded so imperious; impossible to say without a drawl.

You botched things from the start, she told herself. That first day up at the Source, when you had to go rabbiting on like a demented schoolmarm. '*Oh, that's so well put!*' Who wouldn't feel patronized by that?

Since then, it had only got worse. When Patrick was around she became self-conscious, which made her all the more likely to say the wrong thing. Like the other day at lunch, when he had asked one of his rare questions about Cassius, and she had tried to show what she meant by marking a passage in his copy of the *Poems*. Quietly he had asked her not to, explaining that it was a library book. 'Oh I'm sorry,' she had said quickly, 'of course.' Then she realized how that must sound. *Of course* it's from a library. Of course you can't afford to buy new books. Of course, of course, of course.

So you could hardly blame him for disliking her.

Why, then, did she sometimes get the feeling that he was protecting her? Like yesterday evening, when she had been digging for ten hours straight, and Myles was being particularly Myles-ish, and her father had decided to pick a fight with her about how to handle the next section. Patrick had wandered over and casually distracted them both, giving her a much-needed breathing space.

It didn't make sense. *He* didn't make sense.

Myles said Patrick was self-confident: 'You'd have to be, to grow up in Wyoming and believe you could get into Oxford.' But there were times when Antonia wondered about that.

Like the night before, in the kitchen at Les Limoniers.

Myles had gone to the mill to collect the jeep, so they could take two cars to the restaurant. As always when they went anywhere 'good', he had been on edge, and his parting shot about her dress had rattled her. 'You're too tall to wear an emerald green cheongsan. You look like a fucking parakeet.'

Pondering this, she had gone downstairs and found Patrick alone in the kitchen, gazing out of the window. He hadn't heard her come in.

He wore a plain white cotton shirt, stone-coloured flannels, and boat shoes. Myles had lent him a pair of gold cufflinks, but he must have become impatient with them, for he had simply rolled up his shirt-sleeves, and the cufflinks lay discarded on the table.

After two weeks in the sun he was tanned, and his dark hair had glints of chestnut. Antonia thought him unnervingly handsome, and felt more of a parakeet than ever.

At that moment, a car had hooted in the street, and Patrick had leaned out and shouted to Myles that they were coming. Then to her surprise he had paused, squared his shoulders and lifted his chin, and taken a couple of deep, slow breaths, like an actor steeling himself to go out on stage.

But he can't be *nervous*, she had thought in astonishment. What could someone like that be nervous about?

For the first time she tried to see Les Limoniers through Patrick's eyes. The eyes of a twenty-four-year-old American whose father had spent his life in a factory making football boots. A young man so anxious to avoid spongeing off his rich friend that Myles went through hoops to stop him bankrupting himself to pay his way.

She had taken in the state-of-the-art kitchen with its marble tiles and granite worktops. She had pictured the restaurant in Sainte Eulalie, which Myles had booked without thinking of the cost. He'd had to explain to Patrick about Michelin stars, as they didn't have them in Wyoming.

At that moment Patrick had turned and found her watching him. He had very clear, light-filled blue eyes which she always found startling. She had tried to smile, but he hadn't smiled back. Perhaps he thought she'd been spying on him.

And now, this morning, if he chanced to turn his head, he would find her watching him again, as she had watched him last night. Quickly, she stepped out into the sunshine.

'Morning,' she said brightly, taking a chair opposite him.

'Hi, Antonia,' he said evenly.

This time, she resolved, it'll be different. I'll really try.

She watched him spread thick mountain honey on a brioche. He wore dusty jeans and a washed-out navy T-shirt. Bluish shadows beneath his eyes gave him a slightly bruised look.

She took a brioche from the basket. 'Myles is still asleep,' she said.

He gave a slow nod.

Well, full marks, Antonia. Ten out of ten for stating the obvious. And for making him feel like a gooseberry.

She tried again. Asked him what he thought of the restaurant last night.

'OK. I guess . . . It went on a bit.'

'You're telling me. I was ready to go home an hour before we left.'

Again he nodded.

'*I* slept through the whole thing,' said Modge, pouring Antonia a mug of coffee and carrying it over to her.

'I know,' said Patrick with a smile. He had a nice smile. Antonia wished she got to see it more often.

The sun was becoming stronger. Patrick got up from the table and pulled out the awning.

'Patrick,' said Modge through a mouthful of brioche. 'Myles says you don't drink, but he's wrong. You *do* drink. I've seen you.'

He grinned at her. 'He means I don't drink alcohol.'

'Oh,' said Modge.

Antonia had wondered about that. Now she plucked up her courage and asked, 'Is that because you don't like it?'

He shook his head. Then he said simply, 'My dad was an alcoholic. It kind of put me off.'

She blinked.

'What's an alcoholic?' asked Modge.

'Someone who drinks too much and can't stop,' Patrick replied.

Modge looked at him with round eyes.

'That must have been rough,' Antonia ventured.

He thought for a moment. Then he said quietly, 'My dad was all right.'

'I'm sorry,' she said quickly, 'I didn't mean—'

'I know you didn't,' he said with a slight smile.

They continued eating in awkward silence.

'Patrick,' Modge said again.

'Mm?'

'Who was your best friend when you were eight?'

'Lots of kids,' he said, without looking up.

'But didn't you have a *best* friend?'

'Nope.'

Modge considered that. Then she turned to Antonia. 'Who was yours?'

That caught her off guard. 'I – sort of had an imaginary one,' she said.

She caught a surprised glance from Patrick.

'Who?' said Modge.

'What?' said Antonia.

'Who was your imaginary friend.'

'Um.' She hesitated. 'I can't remember.'

'I bet you can,' muttered Modge, 'but you're just not telling.'

Antonia poured herself more coffee. She wondered if Patrick guessed who the imaginary friend had been. Probably. Myles was always teasing her about Cassius.

Terrific, she thought. Now he thinks you're crazy as well as patronizing.

Suddenly she wanted to be anywhere but here on the terrace with him. She wanted to be alone somewhere, far from Myles and Patrick and the whole damn thing.

From the sitting room came the sound of someone knocking over a lamp and swearing savagely. Myles wandered out, yawning and rubbing his elbow. He threw himself onto a sun-lounger, stretched, and gave another tremendous yawn. 'Modge-Podge, save my life. Coffee, no milk, *tons* of sugar . . . Ah, you're an angel!'

Modge blushed.

'D'you know,' said Myles, 'I'm still so drunk I can't see straight? It'll be one hell of a hangover when it finally arrives.' He hooked his arm around Antonia's waist and pulled her down beside him.

She told him to let her go, as she had things to do.

'What can you possibly have to do at half-past ten on a Sunday morning?'

She improvised, and said she had to go to the Source.

He rolled his eyes. 'You know, Paddy, sometimes it's a bloody bore going out with a Vestal Virgin.'

'My name,' she said, 'is Antonia. Or Toni. You might try using one or the other now and again.'

'And mine's Imogen,' said Modge, plucking up her courage.

Myles chuckled. 'Who-ho! What's got into these two?'

Antonia tried to remove his arm from her waist.

'I've got a brilliant idea,' he said, tightening his grip. 'Let's go to Antibes and have drinks on the beach, then observe that hallowed Gallic tradition of a Sunday blow-out somewhere good.'

'Yuk,' said Modge bravely. 'Last time we went to the beach I got stung by a jellyfish. I'm staying here.'

'Me too,' said Antonia.

'Oh give me a bloody break,' said Myles.

'I've got the magnetometer for the day,' she said. 'I'm taking it up to the Source.'

'Stop sulking! Just because I called you a Vestal Virgin—'

'I'm not sulking, I just—'

'Yes you are.'

'I've never been to Antibes,' Patrick put in evenly. 'It sounds kind of fun.'

'Now you've blown it,' Myles told him. 'Don't you know that fun and Vestal Virgins don't mix? This one runs a mile from anything that smacks of fun! Can't dance, can't get drunk. Never even swears. In fact, she has trouble letting go at all, don't you, my sweet? And you must have noticed how she's absolutely *terrified* of horses? Last time I took Modge for a pony ride, Toni wouldn't even go near the poor little brute. And when I—'

'Shut up, Myles,' snapped Antonia.

Patrick got to his feet. 'I think I'll take Imogen down to that bakery, or whatever you call it—'

'The *depôt de pain*,' put in Modge.

'Right. We can pick up some stuff for this trip to the beach, in case we can't find a "good" enough restaurant, and some lunch for the two of you.'

Modge leapt to her feet. 'Can I have *pain au chocolat* as well as *tarte tatin*?'

'Sure you can,' said Patrick.

Myles laughed. 'Paddy, you're amazing! In one fell swoop you've restored family values *and* apple pie to us decadent Europeans.'

Patrick told him mildly to get lost.

'Where to, Patroclus?' Myles said with a smile. 'It's my terrace, isn't it?'

'It sure is,' said Patrick. His cheeks darkened.

'Patroclus?' Antonia snorted. 'No prizes for guessing who Achilles is supposed to be. Even if he is getting a bit thin on top.'

Myles' grin hardened at the edges.

She would pay for that, but she didn't care. He had it coming.

Myles crossed his arms behind his head and lay back. 'Achilles the golden boy,' he murmured, 'that's me. A short life but a glorious one.'

'As if,' said Patrick drily. 'But you might not want to push that Achilles–Patroclus thing too far, buddy-boy. Those guys slept together, didn't they?'

'Wanker,' said Myles, chucking a brioche at him.

Patrick laughed and threw it back.

Myles dodged it like a cat. Then he got up and stretched, and wandered back into the house. 'Toni darling,' he called over his shoulder, 'when you've finished, come back to bed for a bit, there's a love.'

'I told you, I'm going up to the Source.'

'Oh, suit yourself!'

Antonia drew her feet up under her.

Modge ran off to find her sandals. Patrick hung back in the doorway. 'Listen,' he said suddenly. 'If you want help taking that magnetic thing up to the Source, I can do it before we go.'

She stared at him. He had never offered to help at the Source before. 'That's OK,' she said automatically, 'I'll take the jeep.'

'But the road doesn't go all the way up. You'll have to carry it.'

'It's not heavy.'

He gave her a long look which she couldn't read.

It occurred to her that maybe he *wanted* to come to the Source. 'Sorry,' she said quickly, 'I didn't mean to stop you, if you wanted—'

'That's OK. Anyhow, I'd better go to Antibes with Myles.'

She nodded.

He turned to go.

'Patrick,' she said suddenly. She felt herself blushing, for she didn't often call him by name. 'About your father . . .'

He waited, his face impassive.

'What I said about its being rough for you, I mean, about him being an alcoholic. I didn't mean to pry, or anything.'

'I know,' he said.

'Well. Anyway, I'm sorry.'

'You're always saying sorry,' he said. 'But you don't have anything to be sorry about.'

Before she could reply, he had turned and left the terrace. A few minutes later he appeared in the street below. She watched him walking down the hill, with Modge skipping round him like a puppy.

Myles sometimes teased him about the slight limp he'd acquired from a high-school football injury. According to Myles, it was something to do with a ligament in the knee, and surgery would fix it, but Patrick hadn't got around to having it done.

Watching him now, Antonia could detect no sign of a limp. She thought he moved well, with a kind of contained energy – as if he might be capable of erupting into violence, but kept it well in check. She liked the way he moved. She liked him.

And she wanted him to like her.

Myles had promised Modge that they would be back from Antibes by seven at the latest, and could have supper together on the terrace, with champagne for the grownups, and a *diabolo menthe* – her favourite – which he would make especially for her.

When there was still no sign of them by nine o'clock, Antonia gave Modge a boiled egg and soldiers, and put her to bed in the spare room at the mill. Modge was subdued but not especially downcast. She was accustomed to being overlooked.

Antonia and her father ate a largely silent meal in the kitchen, then went their separate ways – he to work in his study, she to unlock her bedside cabinet and put in a few hours on her notes. At midnight she went to bed.

She was woken at two by her father's angry voice

down in the courtyard. A door slammed. A girl laughed. A car-horn hooted. Then came an outraged yowl from Alfonse. The cat was always sleeping in doorways, and her father was always treading on him.

Sick with fatigue, Antonia pulled on her kimono and stumbled downstairs.

She found her father standing in his pyjamas on the kitchen doorstep, blinking in the harsh porch light. Myles, Simon and Nerissa were slumped in the Panda, while Patrick sat behind the wheel, looking tired. Myles was yelling for Modge at the top of his voice. He was either very drunk or very high, or both.

'Over to you,' Dr Hunt muttered to her between clenched teeth before disappearing inside. Moments later his door slammed with a force that shook the house.

Antonia rubbed her face and stifled a yawn. 'Myles, go home. It's two in the morning.'

'Where's *Modge*?' he cried. 'I've come to c'llect my sister!'

'Myles,' muttered Patrick. 'Come on. This was a mistake. We're going home.'

'Fuck *off*, Paddy! I've come to c'llect *Modge*!'

'You'll do nothing of the sort,' snapped Antonia, 'so clear off! And that goes for Simon and Nerissa too. If you two can't come home at a decent hour you can jolly well stay at Myles' for a change. Now get lost.'

All four of them stared back at her.

She had a sudden image of herself – not in a short green kimono, but as a nagging housewife in a kitchen-sink melodrama. The killjoy, the shrew: with her hair in curlers and cold cream on her face, clutching a dirty bathrobe to her chest. Nag, nag, nag, that's all you ever do.

Well, if you feel left out, she told herself angrily, it's your own bloody fault. You could have gone with them to Antibes, there was nothing to stop you. But Myles is right, you're just too much of a coward to have any fun.

Patrick started the engine, and Myles turned ostentatiously away. There would be trouble tomorrow.

Simon had slumped against the window and passed out. Nerissa sat beside Patrick, giggling helplessly, with one arm around his neck. Her thumb was gently rubbing the base of his throat.

As Patrick put the Panda into gear, he turned and looked at Antonia. 'I'm sorry,' he said. 'I didn't want this to happen.'

She made no reply.

The Panda roared out of the courtyard in a spray of dust and gravel, and she stood watching the headlights make their way up the hill.

'I'm sorry too,' she said.

CHAPTER SEVEN

'I wonder,' said Myles as he rolled off Nerissa, 'what I'll
have to do to make up with Toni. She was in a bit of a
strop just now, wasn't she?'

Nerissa yawned and looked at her watch. Three
o'clock in the morning. Damn. If she didn't get some
sleep soon, she'd look appalling.

'How would I know?' she murmured. 'People like her
are a closed book to me.'

Myles snorted. 'Why bother with the qualification?'

She didn't understand what he meant, but felt disinclined to ask.

She was peeved. In fact, now that she thought about
it, she was *extremely* peeved. She had enjoyed the day
in Antibes, but it hadn't ended the way she had hoped.
She had been looking forward to a long, clean, blissful,
sex-free sleep down at the mill, in the big, cool double
bed she shared with Simon. Simon would not have
bothered her for sex. He would have been out cold, just
as he was now, in one of Les Limoniers' spare rooms.
But the row with Toni had spoilt all that. So here she
was with a sweaty man in a bed which hadn't been
changed for ages.

'A bonus,' Myles had called it.

Speak for yourself, thought Nerissa.

Not that she disliked sex. Sometimes she quite

enjoyed it, especially the undressing and stroking beforehand. But not every night.

That was why she stayed with Simon down at the mill. He was so easily managed, and so incredibly grateful when she said yes. And the really brilliant thing was that he believed everything she said, including her useful little fiction about being small 'down there', so that he must be extremely careful and not do it too often, or he'd make her sore. That never failed with men like Si. It made them feel big and manly and protective. With others she had to be more careful. She had learned that a surprising number – Myles included – found it a turn-on to hurt a girl.

She swung her legs over the side of the bed and stood up. 'I'm going for a Coke.'

'Mm,' mumbled Myles into the pillow. With any luck he would be asleep before she got back. Or slumped in front of the Olympics.

She wandered naked into her own room, which she rarely used, now that she was seeing Simon. In a drawer she found a short slip of heavy oyster satin and slid it over her head, enjoying the slithery coolness against her skin. She couldn't understand girls who slept in an old T-shirt. Nerissa did not *own* a T-shirt. Or a man's shirt. Or a pair of jeans.

Before leaving, she checked her appearance in the mirror. '*Nerissa Passmore has heavy strawberry blond hair, a small firm body of supple porcelain, and eyes like agates in a sunlit river.*' That was how the review of her first film would begin.

The comparison with agates and porcelain was not imaginary. Her art teacher had whispered it in the storeroom when she was fourteen, just before she lost her virginity. Poor bastard. A shuddering bundle of middle-aged lust wrapped up in a lot of rubbish about a joining of souls. Maybe that had fooled him, but it certainly hadn't fooled her.

'*Needless to say*,' the review would continue, '*the camera adores her*.' And the camera would. Men and women all over the world would gaze at her luminous image and cry, because she was so much more beautiful than they.

The kitchen was a cool expanse of marble, bathed in the luminous blue glow of an insect lamp. Honestly, Myles ought to get a maid. The sink was overflowing. Yuk. Men.

She got a Diet Coke from the fridge, which contained nothing much, except for rows of white wine and Charles Heidsieck. Then she curled up on the bench by the open window.

She was halfway through the second paragraph of her review, when Patrick entered the kitchen. He wore a pair of cut-offs and nothing else, and he didn't see her until he had taken a Coke from the fridge and snapped the ring.

'Oh. Hi,' he said, his face expressionless.

She thought that was taking it a bit far, as she must look gorgeous: butterscotch-smooth legs curled beneath her, and one strap sliding obligingly off her shoulder.

She raised her Coke in a silent toast. 'So you couldn't sleep either.'

He shook his head. He leaned against the fridge with his legs crossed at the ankles, holding the Coke can against his chest. He did not seem at all turned on by her, but she didn't mind. In fact she found it curiously restful. He was keeping his distance because she was sleeping with his best friend, which was fine for now. For now she was happy to lean back and admire the view.

'You've got a good body,' she remarked.

'Thanks,' he said carefully.

He had long legs – a surprisingly rare feature in a man – and a fine, beautifully muscled torso. He would probably photograph well.

In fact, they would look fantastic together. The fragile porcelain blonde and the tall, dark, angry-looking young man. Black and white film would be preferable to colour. It would bring out his cheekbones and his chiselled mouth, and make her appear even more delicate and vulnerable: a latter-day Titania to his slightly rough-diamond Oberon.

'Nerissa?' he said after a while.

'Mm?'

'Why did you come on this dig?'

Her eyes widened. It was the last thing she'd expected him to say. 'Why?' she echoed.

'Yeah. Why. Was it because of Myles?'

'Myles? What do you mean?'

He shrugged.

She smiled. 'Oh, I'm not hung up on him, if that's what you think! I just thought it'd be fun to come along.'

'And is it?'

'What?'

'Are you having fun?'

To be honest, lately she had been getting a bit fed up. The dig itself was a terrible bore, and recently Myles wanted sex *all* the time. Even Simon was becoming too hung up on her for comfort. There would be fireworks if he found out about her and Myles. And she loathed fireworks.

So now that she thought about it, no, she wasn't having fun. 'It got a lot better when you arrived,' she said with perfect truth.

He gave her a disbelieving look.

Myles wandered into the kitchen. He wore an orange T-shirt with a rip across the stomach, and no boxer shorts. Nerissa thought he looked absolutely disgusting.

He opened a bottle of Côtes de Roussillon, and rummaged in the drawer for a spliff. 'Are you chatting up my stepsister, Patroclus?'

'No,' said Patrick, 'I think she was chatting me up.'

Myles grinned. 'Don't hold it against her. The little baggage can't help herself.'

Nerissa uncurled her legs and got to her feet. 'Actually, you're both wrong.' She stretched, knowing that the hem of her slip was riding high, and they were both watching. Let them watch. It was all they would get at this time of night.

Myles reached over and slapped her hard on the rump. 'Be off, you little strumpet. I'll be through in a minute. First I want a word with Patroclus.'

Take as long as you like, she thought, rubbing her bottom. She would be asleep, or giving a damned good imitation of it, by the time he came back to bed.

'OK, golden boy,' said Patrick, following Myles out onto the terrace. 'What's on your mind?'

Myles hitched himself up on the table and sat jiggling one foot, with the Côtes de Roussillon resting on his thigh. He inhaled deeply, then handed the spliff to Patrick. 'I was going to ask you the same thing. I've been getting waves of disapproval from you all evening. So I thought, if I'm in for a bollocking, I might as well get it over with.'

Patrick tilted back his head and blew a smoke-ring at the stars, and handed back the spliff. 'Sorry. You're not going to get a bollocking.'

It was a beautiful night, with a huge, nearly full moon glowing in an indigo sky seamed with stars. Patrick noted it mechanically, and without pleasure. He felt exhausted, his limbs heavy with fatigue. But sleep had been impossible. He kept seeing the way Antonia had looked at him as she stood on the mill steps, caught – literally – in the headlights.

Ah, Jesus, you should have stuck to your guns and left this bloody place! Why didn't you?

Because, when he had told Myles two weeks ago that he was returning to England, his friend had not been angry, but resigned. 'So you're leaving,' he said quietly. Then he took the coin from his pocket – the Roman one his mother had given him – and turned it in his fingers. 'I knew this would happen,' he said at last.

'Don't be like this,' Patrick had told him. 'It's just that things seem pretty complicated for you right now, what with Antonia and Nerissa and all, and I figure you don't need me around making it worse.'

To his surprise, Myles had looked enormously relieved. 'Well, why didn't you *say* so? If it's Nerissa you want, be my guest! I'll chuck her today, no problem at all! You're far more important than her.'

The way he had said it. The openness, the hope.

That was when Patrick knew that he couldn't leave.

In the moonlight, Myles had stopped jiggling his foot. 'It's about Toni, isn't it?' he said suddenly.

Patrick's heart lurched. Thank Christ the light was too poor for Myles to see his face.

'Look,' said Myles. 'It isn't my fault. Toni's always working, and Nissa's so fucking available! Jesus, you saw her just now, it's more than flesh and blood can stand!'

Patrick could find nothing to say to that.

'If you want to know,' Myles added, 'I've been thinking about straightening things out.'

'How?'

'Chucking Nissa, and making a go of it with Toni. That's what you think I should do, isn't it?'

Patrick made no reply.

'And that's not all,' Myles went on. 'This time I'm going to chuck the drugs, and cut back on the booze—'

'Oh, yeah, right!'

'No, I mean it! This time I really do.' He paused. 'I've got to get things sorted out, Patrick. Toni's part of that. She'll keep me on track.' He took a long pull at the bottle. 'But I need you to help me, too.'

Patrick tensed.

Myles looked at him and said, 'I need you to take Nissa off my hands.'

Patrick stared at him. 'Jesus, Myles! Get real!'

'I am! What's the problem? She likes you. And you'd be helping me.' He took another pull, and Patrick saw how his hand trembled. 'With Nissa out of the way, I could concentrate on Toni. I could make it work. And then I'd be OK, I know it.'

Patrick rubbed a hand across his face. 'No, Myles. Uh-huh. Absolutely not. You got yourself into this, you get yourself out.'

Myles leaned back on his hands and gave a long sigh. 'I thought you'd say that.' He paused. 'All right, then. Tell me how I do it.'

'How you do what?'

'How I straighten things out with Toni.'

Patrick stared at the stars, and wished himself a million light-years away.

'I know what you're going to say,' said Myles. 'You think I should come clean with her about Nissa.'

Betelgeuse, thought Patrick, wherever the hell that is. Polaris sounds good, too.

'God, Paddy, you're absolutely hopeless! How the hell would it help if I told Toni about Nissa? What she doesn't know can't possibly hurt her—'

'But if she did, it would.'

'Which is hardly my fault, is it? It's *her* fault for being so fucking intense!'

'I thought it was her intensity which attracted you in the first place.'

'Fuck you, Patrick!'

I can't believe this is happening, Patrick thought. He felt dizzy, as if he was falling into the stars. 'I honestly think,' he said at last, 'that your best chance with a girl like Antonia is to come clean with her. If you told her yourself, she'd probably forgive you.'

Shakily, Myles took another drag. 'No way. I *know* her.'

Patrick flinched.

'In lots of ways,' Myles went on, 'she's frighteningly naïve. But deep down there's something strong about her. Something you don't want to mess with.'

Patrick was surprised, for he had felt that too.

'No, Paddy, she's not the forgiving kind. Nope. *Nyet.* No way, José.'

Patrick sighed. 'So what d'you want to do? You want me to go on covering for you while you go on two-timing your girl?'

Myles shrugged. 'Well yes, since you refuse to take Nissa off my hands. Although frankly, I'd have thought that was the least you could do.'

There was no reply to that. Myles never came out and said it, but at times he dropped a gentle reminder of what Patrick owed him.

Patrick said, 'You seem pretty sure that I'll play along.'

Myles's grin showed white in the moonlight. 'As sure as God made little green apples, Paddy me boy.'

'Why? I could tell Antonia any time I want. I could go up to her tomorrow and say—'

'Ah but you won't. We both know that.'

'Why won't I?'

'Because you're my best friend.'

Patrick went quickly to the other end of the terrace. 'You don't believe in all that loyalty crap,' he said over his shoulder.

'No, but you do.'

Patrick did not reply.

Myles came to stand beside him. 'You won't tell Toni,' he said quietly. 'Not a snowball's chance in hell.'

Oh, but Patrick had thought about it. For two weeks he had thought of little else. Why *not* just march up to Antonia and say, *Listen, you're wasting your time with Myles. He's been screwing Nerissa for months.*

What stopped him wasn't only Myles. Antonia would get hurt, too. For Patrick knew his friend. If Antonia chucked Myles, as she would if she found out from someone else that he was screwing Nerissa, he would turn on her. He would find a way to hurt her. And hurting people was Myles's one, true, God-given talent.

Not that one needed much talent to hurt Antonia. She felt things too deeply, and it made her vulnerable. Myles would have no trouble finding something to sink his teeth into. Her father, the dig, Cassius. And he would savage it to death.

Patrick glanced at his friend. What the hell did she see in him, anyway?

Ah, Christ, he didn't want to think about her with

Myles. It was only a matter of time before Myles tried to tell him what she was like in bed, and then how was he going to keep from smashing him in the face?

He said, 'Come clean with Antonia. It's the only way.'

'No.'

'Why not?'

Myles tossed the spliff into the garden, and they watched its red arc fade into the darkness. 'Because I'm not you, Patroclus. Sometimes I wish I were. But I'm not.'

Charles Hunt sat in pyjamas at his desk, and put his head in his hands. He was too tired to work, and too wound up to think of sleep. This was precisely what the doctors had cautioned him against, and already he could feel the warning signs. Not a pain, exactly. More a tightening in his chest.

He snapped off the desk light and let the moonlight invade the study. Perhaps that would make the tightness go away.

Through the open window he could see the eerie glow of the Sarac. There was one spot on the river to which his eye was always drawn: a point where the water foamed endlessly between two great boulders. That white foam. Endlessly obliterated, and endlessly renewed. He found it mesmerizing. It looked so ephemeral, yet it would always be there. Long after the dig was over. Long after he was dead.

He kneaded his temples. Two more weeks, and he would know for sure what he already knew in his heart: that this dig, the first and last he would ever supervise, was a total failure.

He knew what they would say at the faculty. '*No luck, eh, Charlie? Oh, what a shame! And after trying so hard!*' Then the smiles turning to derision as they learned the truth: that the Roman villa he had been so sure of finding was not on the main site after all, but securely buried beneath the modern house *adjacent* to it. The beautiful little house with its elegant paved terrace, whose elderly Parisian owner only visited for a couple of weeks every year, but had been so cooperative about letting him excavate her adjoining wasteland.

That house. It had no *right* to be there, directly on top of the find which would have established his reputation at last. And what made it so much worse was that he had uncovered just enough to confirm his worst fears: that a Roman villa did indeed lie beneath the house, for ever out of reach. That was unquestionably the meaning of those tantalizing nine inches of mosaic which Toni had uncovered a few days before, extending from the concrete foundations of the terrace.

'*Have you heard Charlie Hunt's latest? It's absolutely priceless! He finally wheedles his own dig, then botches it by excavating right next door to a Roman villa!*'

He would be a laughing-stock.

Who was he fooling? He was already a laughing-stock. Even to his own family. Even to Toni.

God, she was talented. She seemed to know instinctively when she had found something, however minute or fragmentary. It was as if she had a sixth sense in her fingertips. Sometimes he hated her for that. As he hated her optimism, and her dogged insistence on continuing the search. Day after day she kept on at the Source. Never wavering in her belief that she would find some link between Cassius and this godforsaken valley which he had come to loathe.

Already she had succeeded where he had failed, simply by gaining permission to excavate the Source.

Until now, old Panabière had never let anyone touch it. It had been in his family for generations, he always said, why couldn't everyone leave it in peace? Then Toni had gone to see him, and 'just asked', as she put it, and the farmer had crumbled. Perhaps he had realized that at last he had met his match.

And to think that this complicated, intense young woman was the creation of Charles Hunt. His child. The same bawling infant he'd been terrified of picking up for fear of damaging her, whose every imperious whim had been his delight to satisfy. How was it possible that he and Evelyn – two of the world's Laodiceans if they ever existed – should have produced such a being as this?

And what a crowning humiliation if she *did* find something at the Source. '*Have you heard the latest? Poor old Charlie's dig came to nothing, but the* daughter's *has turned up trumps!*'

His skin prickled at the thought.

How ridiculous, to be jealous of his own daughter. Jealous of a part of himself.

And the real irony was that he wanted her to succeed. He would be so humiliated. He would be so proud.

Antonia, sitting at her desk on the entresol outside her room, heard the familiar creak of her father's study door, and saw his shadow cut across the downstairs light.

From where he stood at the foot of the stairs he couldn't possibly see what was on her desk, but nevertheless she drew a sheet of paper across her notes.

'Can't you sleep?' he called up to her, softly, so as not to wake Modge.

'Not just yet,' she whispered. 'I thought a bit of work might help.'

'Toni, it's nearly four! You ought to turn in.'

'I will. Soon.'

He didn't answer. Perhaps he took that as an implied comment that she was more dedicated than he. Lately, he had been touchy about things like that.

She waited until he had gone up and shut his bedroom door before uncovering her notes.

Her notes. Her secret. The one place where her thoughts had no limits.

It had started as a hobby, a distraction for a lonely undergraduate. Since she met Myles, it had become a necessity. And at times it felt like her only link with Cassius.

During the day, as she trod a wary path between Myles' moods and her father's insecurities, there were moments when her mind would flash back to Cassius, and everything would be all right. It was as if the past – *his* past – was a wonderful peacock-coloured storybook, just waiting for her to turn the page and shed its rainbow light upon the present.

Tonight, she needed Cassius more than ever. She needed him to stop her thinking about Patrick.

'I didn't want this to happen,' Patrick had told her just before he drove off.

What hadn't he wanted to happen? Did he mean waking her up at two in the morning? Or did he mean whatever was going on between him and Nerissa?

What did he mean?

It had been easier when she thought he disliked her. But now what was she supposed to think? His offer to help at the Source; that remark he had made on the terrace. 'You're always saying sorry, when you haven't anything to say sorry about.'

This is simply wounded vanity, she told herself

angrily. He's been avoiding you for a fortnight, so of course you can't stop thinking about him.

Then she remembered Myles, and felt bad. He was moody and impossible, but he needed her. He didn't deserve a girlfriend who disliked sex, and couldn't stop thinking about his best friend.

It was all getting too complicated. Things had been simpler at university, when she had no-one.

Gritting her teeth, she forced herself back to the poem she had been working on.

The page before her was a mess, a jumble of crossings-out and bubbles of text shunted all over the place. To help herself back into the mood, she flicked to the Introduction she had already prepared: a layman's guide to Cassius.

'*Gaius Cassius Vitalis,*' she read, '*was born over two thousand years ago, in 86 BC. The son of a prosperous farmer in the Roman province of Gallia Narbonensis, he grew up on an estate in the south-eastern foothills of the Pyrenees – an estate he later immortalized in his poems, and which has been tentatively located in the valley of the Sarac. Unfortunately, all attempts to find the site of his villa, or the shrine mentioned in his poems, have come to nothing.*'

Here the text broke off, and was followed by a blank half-page. Full of optimism at the start of the summer, she had left space for the results of the dig.

Some hope. 'Come to nothing' still summed it up. Even that mention of a tentative location was a stretch. No-one knew for sure if Cassius had grown up here. It was just supposition.

From the age of fourteen to eighteen he attended the University of Marseilles, where he met the diarist Lucius Faenius Plautius – who became a life-long friend, and an essential biographical source for future generations. The young Cassius then joined the army, and for the next thirteen years he served with Pompey in Syria and Anatolia, then with Caesar in Gaul, Britain and Germany. He rose swiftly, achieving rapid promotion and many decorations.

It was during the Anatolian campaign that he began writing poetry, and soon made a name for himself as a founder member of the Neoterici, *the New Poets, whose immediacy and directness breathed new life into a stagnating art. To Catullus and Propertius and those who came after, Cassius was the standard-bearer, the first man in antiquity to write seriously about a love affair, and to acknowledge openly that one woman had been the ruling influence of his life. That woman is known to us only as the 'Lycaris' of the Poems: a woman with whom he had a brief, passionate affair when he was thirty-three.*

Antonia sat back and studied the words on the page. To most people, they were heresy. They contradicted what she had been taught at university, and set her in head-to-head confrontation with every classicist she knew.

For the simple fact was, no-one these days believed that 'Lycaris' had ever existed. Everyone accepted that, like Ovid's 'Cynthia', and many other imaginary mistresses, 'Lycaris' had only lived in the poet's mind. She was a literary conceit, a creation of his imagery: a way for him to explore the meaning of love.

They were wrong.

Over the years, Antonia had had the argument with friends, colleagues, teachers, and her father. 'How can you say he made her up?' she would cry. 'He didn't write fiction, he wrote from real life! "Lycaris" – whatever her name really was – was a living, breathing, flesh-and-blood woman! And he loved her, even when she broke his heart. He spent the rest of his life trying to fall out of love with her, it nearly tore him apart! We know all that, it's right there in the Poems!'

The answer was always the same. 'That's all very well, Antonia, but where's your evidence? What you're saying isn't scholarship, it's daydreams. You want to believe it, but that won't make it true. Where's your evidence?'

Of course, she had none. Only a belief as strong as it was unproven – and which, if she was honest, had as much to do with her childhood memories of an invisible friend as it did with any scholarly deductions.

And yet, that belief persisted. Despite the harsh empiricism in which she had been schooled, it remained. And with it, the gnawing sense that in denying the existence of 'Lycaris', the world had devalued Cassius himself. It had degraded him to nothing more than a talented scribbler, who had fashioned a woman out of words, then fallen in love with his own creation.

Her eyes returned to the page.

About the rest of his life we know tantalizingly little. We know that the affair with 'Lycaris' ended in heartbreak. Most people interpret this as meaning that his Muse departed suddenly, and he experienced a period of writer's block. Whatever the truth, we know that he left Rome in 53 BC, and never returned.

Thirteen years later, he fell victim to the bloody Terror which attended the death throes of the Republic. For reasons that remain unclear today, he incurred the wrath of Octavian, and was exiled to his estate in south-eastern Gaul. There, to avoid the ignominy of the inevitable show trial, he took his own life.

His friend Plautius was with him when he died, and the old man's letter describing it is justly famous. 'When I'm gone,' Cassius said, 'I want you to make a libation to the Goddess. This must be for me and for Lycaris together, so that our spirits can meet after death.' Plautius asked how he might do this, for he didn't know Lycaris' true name – and without that, the Goddess would not hear the prayer. Then Cassius did an extraordinary thing. Instead of revealing her name, he set his old friend a riddle. 'In poculo veritas,' he said. 'The truth is in the cup.'

Today, the established view is that this riddle – which has baffled scholars for centuries – simply means that a poet must seek his inspiration in wine. This was a widely held belief in the ancient world, and one which Cassius is known to have shared. So the riddle has been taken to mean: 'I seek the truth about Lycaris when I'm drunk – and so should you.'

Antonia sat straighter, rubbing the back of her neck.

A bat sped past the window: a silent velvet shadow tracking a trail of darkness across the stars.

Cassius, she thought, must have looked out at just such a view on his last night on earth, as he composed his riddle.

Although if you believed the 'established view', it was nothing more than an ironic word-game. 'Look for Lycaris in wine,' it told posterity. 'You won't find her anywhere else, for she never existed. I made her up.'

No, no, *no*! The 'established view' was all wrong. Cassius was not the man to bow out of life concocting ironic trifles. He was too direct and unflinching for that. The riddle had been important to him. 'Lycaris' had existed, and Cassius had loved her with all his heart.

Even if he had never written another poem, the one he wrote at the beginning of their affair had surely been proof of that.

> *One long look, and I was brought down.*
> *She entered my blood. Although at the time*
> *I didn't think she'd have me.*
> *But when we met again,*
> *how much we said to each other by moonlight!*
> *The night wind bore our words away.*
> *Then at last her breath yielded to mine,*
> *and mine to hers. We were sheeted in fire.*
> *And now like Pegasus I ride the stars,*
> *I walk the spellbound moon.*
> *The horse of darkness treads the sky*
> *and I am with him, for I am immortal.*
> *And she sleeps: her face as pale as fresh-cut marble*
> *against my cloak.*

Antonia put down her pencil and stared into the darkness. Compared with a love like that, what was the pallid, edgy dependency she had with Myles?

How could she even think about Myles on a night like this?

Not Myles, and not Patrick, either. Especially not Patrick.

'Go to bed,' she said angrily, shuffling her papers into a pile.

In two weeks the dig would be over, and everyone would go their separate ways. She would no longer have to watch Patrick and Nerissa circling each other like a pair of beautiful cats, while she and Myles played out their sorry little power game on the sidelines.

Two weeks, and she would never see Patrick again.

Two weeks, and it would all be over.

CHAPTER EIGHT

A family tomb near the Porta Capena, Rome, 25 June
53 BC

In the darkness, Cassius made out the shadowy form of
Albia on the bench in the little garden outside the tomb.

He and Faenio, his slave, made their way towards her
through the cypresses. Although the moon was only in
its first quarter, they had no trouble finding the path.
After three months, they knew every stone.

Faenio joined Albia to keep watch, and Cassius made
for the tomb, whose doorway showed as a faint, flickering oblong of light.

As he left them on the bench, Albia gave him an odd
look, and he wondered why. An instant later he found
out. As he reached the porch, something hard exploded
against the doorpost, a hand's breadth from his temple.

He just had time to duck before another missile
whizzed over his head.

Straightening up, he brushed fragments of earthenware from his shoulders. The perfume of olive oil
floated towards him on the warm night air, and he
smiled. She had been throwing lamps. 'You'd better
not use the last one,' he said, 'or you'll never see to find
your aim.'

'*Bastard!*' cried a voice from the shadows. 'What's it to you whether I do or not?'

'Where are you? It's dark in here.'

'Why should you care where I am?'

'Tacita, what's this about?'

'As if you didn't know!'

'Well, no, I—'

'Exactly *when* were you going to tell me that you've been recalled to Gaul?'

So that was it. 'Tonight,' he said evenly.

'Liar!'

'No. I was going to tell you tonight. That's the truth. I only heard yesterday myself.'

As his eyes adjusted to the gloom he made out her mantle, which she had flung across the flags. She herself was at the far end of the chamber, furthest from the remaining lamp. She was pacing up and down like a caged lioness. He thought she looked magnificent.

'Tacita,' he said quietly. 'You know I have to go. You know that.'

'No I *don't* know it, because you haven't told me yet! I had to hear it from Albia's new man, of all people! A squid-seller!'

He bit back a smile. He wondered what galled her most: the fact that he hadn't told her sooner, or that she'd heard it from a fishmonger. 'It had to come some time,' he said, 'I've already stretched my stay in Rome far longer than I should.'

'I'm so very flattered.'

'They need me out there. I know the terrain.'

'Well, you would, wouldn't you? You're scarcely better than a peasant yourself.'

He went to her and drew her against him. He was surprised to find that she was trembling.

She turned, and wrapped her arms tightly about his waist and buried her face in his chest.

'I'll be gone for six months at most,' he said into her hair.

'No,' she muttered, her voice muffled by his toga. 'At *most*, you'll be gone for ever. Those savages will slit your throat in the mountains, and leave your bones for the buzzards to pick.' She drew a shuddering breath. 'And it's not even as if you *try* to stay alive! I've heard about the risks you take.'

That made him chuckle.

'What's funny?'

'You are. You berate me for taking risks, while trying to brain me with a lamp.'

'No jokes, Gaius. Not tonight.'

He tightened his hold on her. Gradually, the trembling ceased.

After a while she asked, 'How long before you leave?'

'A week. Maybe I can stretch it to two.'

He bent his head to take in the scent of her hair. Peppermint and almond oil from the lotion she used to make it shine.

She drew back a fold of his toga, and slipped his tunic off one shoulder. then she bent her head, and he felt her warm breath on his skin. Her soft lips traced the line of his collarbone.

She opened her mouth and bit him as hard as she could.

With a cry he thrust her from him, and she staggered back against the wall and nearly fell.

'*Never* do that again!' he exclaimed. 'Are you all right? Ah, you're lucky I didn't hurt you!'

Shakily she wiped her mouth with the back of her hand. 'As if you care!'

That gesture was pure Tacita: one moment a lady – and the next, as coarse as a street-girl. He loved her for that.

He put a finger to his shoulder, and it came away dark with blood. 'Why?' he said.

Her chin went up. 'Now I've put my mark on you. You won't forget me when you're on campaign.'

'I'm not likely to forget you,' he replied.

He reached for her and took her gently by the nape, tilting back her head to expose the throat. 'Maybe I should do the same to you.'

She stayed perfectly still. 'Go on, then. If you dare.'

He contemplated the whiteness of her throat. Then he sighed, and bent and kissed her pulse. 'You knew I wouldn't,' he murmured.

She twisted out of his grip. 'Coward. I should have branded you instead. That's what they do to cowards, isn't it?' She wrenched her seal-ring from her finger. 'I should have heated this in a fire and *branded* you!' She threw it on the flags, then turned away from him.

He put his hands on her shoulders. 'You're not going to lose me,' he said.

'Oh no? What if you're killed?'

'I won't be . . . But if I were, I'd still be with you.' He put his palm over her heart. 'In here.'

'Spoken like a poet! What good would you be to me there?'

He did not reply. She was in a strange mood tonight. Morbid and angry and vulnerable. It was his fault. The constant strain of the lies and the subterfuge was beginning to tell on her. No doubt his choice of trysting place hadn't helped, either. She was too young to meet in graveyards. To have death thrust upon her at every turn.

'I'm sorry,' he said. 'I should never have brought you here.'

'You didn't bring me here. I brought myself.'

'Next time I'll find somewhere else for us to meet. And soon we won't have to do this at all. No more skulking in the shadows when we're married.'

He felt some of the tension leave her body. 'How do you propose to achieve that?' she asked over her shoulder.

'I'll find a way.'

Quickly, so that he wouldn't notice, she wiped her eyes with her fingers. Then she put out her hand and touched the nearest funerary urn, like a talisman.

The tomb was an overblown family affair about which she often teased him. It had a pedimented doorway guarded by a relief of brooding ancestors, and the inside walls were honeycombed with urns. Each sat in a scalloped niche of bilious green porphyry, surmounted by a funerary portrait. A plaque beneath was inscribed with a precise statement of the incumbent's lifespan in years, months and days.

The niche which Tacita had touched was the last resting-place of a woman, one Procula Secunda. According to her portrait, Procula had been a matron of unflinching plainness, with a stringy coronet of hair tweaked as tight as a hawser, and an expression to match. Her urn was sumptuous and fussy, and almost obscured by family emblems. Clearly her husband – whose ashes had joined hers a few years later – had been one of the New Rich.

Tacita muttered, 'Trust you to find a place like this. You don't even have the taste to pick a decent tomb.'

He smiled. 'That's me. Back to my peasant roots whenever I get a chance.' He thought for a moment. 'If you want to know, I picked it because she reminds me of you.'

'Not funny. Try again.'

'*An exemplary woman,*' he read aloud from the plaque, '*whom the gods endowed with all the virtues. Obedient, even-tempered, parsimonious and docile –*'

He felt her suppress a snort.

'*Never was there a moment when she ignored her husband's wishes, or lost her temper, or berated him—*'

'All right, enough!' She twisted round to face him, and his heart leapt to see her laugh.

'Am I forgiven?' he asked.

'I don't know about that. Let's not rush things, shall we?'

He bowed his head in acceptance. 'That'll do for now.'

They kissed.

When at last they drew apart for breath, she touched the bite-mark on his shoulder. 'Does that hurt?'

'Yes.'

Slowly and deliberately she drew her fingernail through the congealing blood, to reopen the wound.

'Now it hurts more,' he said.

'Good. It serves you right.' With both forefingers she gently parted the lips of the cut, then bent her head to his shoulder. 'Relax,' she murmured. 'You're tensing like a stallion.' Softly she blew into the cut. Then she pressed the edges back together, and sealed it with her tongue.

It felt like being attacked by some small, strange, sharp-toothed creature of the night.

'There,' she whispered. 'Now part of my spirit will be

inside you for ever.' She covered the wound with her hand. 'It will make a fine scar! A crescent moon, just like my amulet. From now on, wherever you go, you'll carry me with you.'

'I'll do that without a scar.'

'Fine words, poet. But this scar will last.'

Frowning, he searched her face. 'What's wrong? This isn't only about me returning to Gaul, is it?'

She met his eyes, and suddenly she looked very young. 'Gaius, I'm scared.'

'Of what?'

'I don't know. That's why I'm scared.'

'Tacita. Make sense. Tell me.'

She turned back to Procula's urn. '*Oppius my husband,*' she read shakily, '*do not sorrow because I have gone before you, for I await you in a timeless bed.*'

'So? I don't understand.'

On the flags before the urn, someone had placed a tile with the usual offering of corn and salt, and a crust of bread soaked in wine. Cassius watched Tacita kneel and break off a piece of the bread. She sniffed, and wrinkled her nose. 'The wine's gone sour.'

Still on her knees, she looked up at him. 'Do you really believe that they'll let us grow old together? Like these two, like Procula and Oppius?'

He did not reply.

'Do you believe,' she went on, 'that when our time comes, our sons and daughters will put our ashes in a single urn—'

'Tacita—'

'– and say the proper rites for us, so that our spirits can be together for eternity?'

'Yes,' he said. 'I believe all that.'

'Then you're a peasant!' she burst out. 'You say you don't believe in miracles, but you do! Deep down, in your heart, you do!'

'Perhaps.'

'*How* is it going to happen, Gaius? How? Do you plan to charm my father with that silver tongue of yours? Do you plan to achieve the impossible, and make him welcome a low-born provincial as a son-in-law?'

He flinched. 'It happens.'

'Not in my family.'

He knelt beside her. 'It will happen,' he said again. 'I'll make it happen.'

A bee wandered into the tomb. They listened to it thudding furiously against the walls. 'Now that's a good sign,' he said with a slight smile. 'You can't argue with that.'

'Don't try to humour me.'

'I'm sorry.'

She picked at the stuff of her dress. Then she said in a low voice, 'What do you expect me to do while you're away?'

'I expect you to wait for me.'

'And you think I will?'

'I know you will. Just as I know that when I return from Gaul, I'll deal with your family, and we'll be married.'

She nodded. Wanting to believe it. As he wanted to himself.

'Promise you'll wait for me, Tacita.'

She threw him a look. 'Why do you need me to promise?'

'I need something to keep me going in Gaul.'

'Oh well, in *that* case,' she said drily, 'I quite understand. What a prospect, stuck out in the back of beyond with all those trousered barbarians.' She shuddered, and he knew that the worst was over. 'All right,' she said. 'I promise.'

He bent and kissed her gently on the lips.

'Come back alive,' she said against his mouth. 'You're no good to me as ashes.'

'I'll come back alive.'

CHAPTER NINE

Thursday, 22 September 1988

She's going to think you're crazy, Patrick told himself as he started down the street towards the mill. What do you think you're doing, seeking her out at the crack of dawn to apologize for something she's probably already forgotten?

But that kind of argument hadn't got him very far. It had been two days since the Panda had roared out of the courtyard in the early hours of the morning, and he could still see the look on her face.

When Antonia was at bay, she wore a particular expression: a smooth, closed look, as if she had taken herself out of the present, and back to some secret place where no-one could reach her. When she looked like that, he wanted to pull her into his arms and hold her tight, so that Myles and Dr Hunt and Nerissa couldn't hurt her any more.

But what, exactly, was he going to say when he found her? '*Listen, if you got the impression from Nerissa's little display the other night that I'm sleeping with her, you're wrong, and I really need you to know that.*'

Yeah, but *why* do you really need her to know that?

The noise of a car behind him shattered the early morning calm. In disbelief he watched the Panda inch down the narrow cobbled street. 'Myles?'

'I know, I know, you can't believe your eyes,' muttered his friend as he cut the engine. 'A Cantellow awake and dressed before eight, it's a fucking miracle. Though come to think of it, you're up pretty early, aren't you?'

Patrick shrugged.

'Look. Paddy. I need a favour. Take Modge for the day?'

'What?'

Myles jerked his head towards the back of the car, and Patrick saw the eight-year-old curled up asleep on the seat. She was still in her pyjamas. Myles must have scooped her straight out of bed, stuffed rabbit and all.

'Myles, I can't. Not right now.'

'The thing is, I've got to go to town.'

'Which town?'

Myles flashed him an edgy grin. 'Paris.'

'*Paris?*' Patrick was about to ask what the hell he thought he was doing, when suddenly he knew. There was only one thing that would get Myles out of bed before noon and take him all the way to Paris. He said, 'I thought you'd decided to kick that stuff.'

'It's *because* I have that I've got to do this! One last fling to get it out of my system.'

'Myles . . .'

'Go on. Be a friend and look after Modge.'

Patrick hesitated.

Down by the river a thin plume of smoke was rising from the mill chimney. That would be Dr Hunt, fixing his breakfast. Antonia would have had hers hours ago, before she went to the Source. Now she would be back where she always was at this time in the morning: in the pot-shed, sorting the finds. Another half-hour or so, and her father would finish his breakfast and wander out to join her.

He bit his lip. If he said yes to Myles, it would mean waking Modge and taking her with him to the pot-shed. And he really needed to see Antonia alone.

On the other hand, his friend looked terrible. His face was drawn and glistening with sweat, and his glance skittered away from Patrick's.

Patrick sighed. 'I've got a better idea. We'll leave Modge with Antonia, and I'll come with you to Paris.'

'Don't be ridic—'

'You can't go by yourself. In this state you'll crash the goddamned car.'

'I'm not in a state!'

On the back seat, Modge stirred. Myles threw her a glance. 'Poor little cow. What did she do to deserve me?'

'Myles, don't do this. You don't need to go to Paris. You can give up that stuff right now.'

'Look after her, Paddy. That's all I ask.'

Patrick found Antonia alone, as he knew he would.

The pot-shed was a long barn on the opposite side of the courtyard, which the Hunts had rigged with light bulbs strung between the rafters. Three old stone sinks had been installed along the sides for washing and desalination, with four large trestle tables down the middle. These were covered with drying racks, washing-up bowls, scrubbing brushes, find trays, and box files. The walls were covered in colour charts and noticeboards. The noticeboards were covered in lists.

Antonia sat at the far table in a shaft of dusty sunlight, gluing pieces of pottery back together. She wore emerald-green shorts and a sleeveless azure top of

Indian cotton edged in scarlet. Her hair ribbons were the colours of raspberry and mint.

A bird of paradise girl, thought Patrick, his heart pounding.

What the hell are you doing? said the voice of reason inside his head.

Modge, now thoroughly awake, called out, 'Antonia, look at me, I'm in pyjamas! And this is Star Rabbit.'

Antonia raised her head. Wordlessly she took in Patrick's presence.

I guess you didn't expect to see me here, he told her silently.

'Hello, Patrick,' she said. 'I'm afraid Myles isn't here.'

'I know,' he replied, disconcerted. 'I just saw him leave.'

'If it's my father you want, he—'

'No. In fact, I came to see you.'

She blinked.

They walked the length of the pot-shed to join her.

Say your piece and get out of here.

Instead he found himself asking if she wanted any help.

Again she blinked.

He repeated the offer.

Idiot. What do you think you're doing?

She gave him a puzzled look. 'Um – well. Thanks. If you like, you could label those shards over there.'

'Oh, good,' said Modge, 'I like labelling.' She fetched a tray, a stack of context sheets, the finds register, and a pot of white Indian ink. Patrick pulled up a couple of stools.

He struggled to concentrate while Modge showed him how to paint the context number onto each shard, and warned him sternly against labelling too near the edge, as that was *exactly* the place most likely to crumble – and once you'd lost the context number, that was *it*.

Across the table, Antonia went back to her reconstruction with the self-conscious absorption of a person who knows she is being watched.

Her movements were precise and delicate, and Patrick found them hypnotic. Carefully she dusted off each shard with a fine, soft brush. Then she painted the edges with a thin film of PVA adhesive, stroking it on in layers with infinite care. Then she slotted the shard into place, using a mound of sand on a tray as a support. Finally, she smoothed the join with her fingertips, gently blowing away the last of the dust.

Patrick's mouth went dry.

To break the spell, he asked her what she was working on.

She threw him an uncertain glance, as if doubtful that he really wanted to know.

'I really want to know,' he said.

'It's a lamp.'

'And – you found that at the Source?'

'Yes.'

He had seen lamps like this in books. A flat disc-shaped chamber to hold the oil, with a stubby little nozzle for the flame. But this must have been a pretty small lamp, for he guessed that when it was completed, it would fit comfortably into her palm. That thought made his heart start to race all over again.

'I think she's a goddess,' she said. She held out a shard for him to see, and traced the profile of a woman with her finger. Patrick saw a straight Grecian nose, a mass of crinkly hair, and a dreamy archaic smile.

'Looks like a goddess,' he said hoarsely. 'Which one?'

She frowned. 'Not sure. Probably the Great Mother, Cybele. Or some sort of amalgam of her and the Moon Goddess. They were both pretty popular down here in southern Gaul. Or she might be the *triple* Moon Goddess, because of the three branches she's holding.'

Modge leaned over his shoulder, making him jump. 'That means she's three in one,' she said, smelling of the *pain au chocolat* he had bought her for breakfast. 'Antonia told me. The Virgin of Spring, the Nymph of Summer, and the Crone of Winter. D'you get it? The new moon, the full moon, and the old moon . . . What's a virgin?'

'Uh . . .' said Patrick, 'a girl who isn't married yet.'

'Oh. Like me and Antonia.'

Antonia flicked him a glance, and smiled. It was not her usual polite social beam, but the genuine, heart-breaking smile she had given him on that first day up at the Source. It made him want to gather her to him and bury his face in the soft curve between her shoulder and throat.

She put down the shard, and went to the sink to wash her hands. Her bare feet made a soft whispering sound in the dust. Like a caress running the length of his spine.

Now was the time for him to leave. Mutter some excuse and get the hell out of here.

He cleared his throat. 'So – what else have you found up there?'

'Not much,' she said over her shoulder. 'Quite a lot of fruit pips – pears, mostly. Wild pears were sacred to the Moon Goddess, because of their white blossom. And they were the sort of thing the peasants round here could have spared. Oh, and some body parts.'

'*Body* parts?'

'Not real ones. Pottery.'

Modge said, 'Antonia found an ear and a bit of a foot. In Roman times if you had a bad foot you left a little clay one in the pool and the Goddess made your real one better.'

'Right,' said Patrick.

There was a pause.

'So,' said Antonia, still at the sink, 'where did Myles go?'

Patrick's head snapped up.

'You said you saw him leave. Where did he go?'

'– He went to Paris.'

She turned. 'Paris.'

'He – uh, he had to see a guy about something or other.'

He watched her take that in. She returned to her stool and sat down. 'You know,' she said, 'you don't have to cover for him.'

He coloured.

'I know about the –' she glanced at Modge – 'substances.'

'What substances?' said Modge.

'Champagne,' said Patrick.

Modge shot him a disbelieving look.

'That's why he went, isn't it?' Antonia said. 'He's trying to get up the nerve to quit, and he thinks one last binge is going to help.'

He sighed. Then he said quietly. 'Is that why you stay with him? To help him quit?'

She raised her head and looked at him. 'I don't know,' she said at last. Then she added in a low voice, 'Sometimes I wonder why he stays with *me*. I mean, I don't like any of the things he likes. And I'm no good at letting go, he's right about that.'

He watched her take another shard and start painting

the edge with adhesive. This time her lips were pressed together, as if she was struggling for control.

That bastard, he thought. *Christ*, what does she see in him? If Myles had been there, Patrick would have grabbed him by the throat and beaten him to a pulp.

'I've tried them too, you know,' she said, slotting the shard into place. 'The substances. A little of each kind, so I could tell him they're not worth it and get him to stop.' She paused. 'I suppose that was a bit naïve.'

'It wasn't naïve,' said Patrick sharply, 'it was dumb. Really, really dumb.'

Modge's jaw dropped.

Antonia flushed. 'No it wasn't. There was no risk of getting hooked. I didn't even like them. They just made me sick.'

He felt himself becoming angry. 'You shouldn't have tried that stuff at all! Not for Myles, not for anyone!'

'Patrick,' said Modge, looking scared. 'Don't—'

'Why not?' retorted Antonia. 'Because I'm not "cool" enough to handle it? I bet Nerissa does all the time, and you never tell her she's "really, really dumb".'

He did not reply.

'You know,' she said with quiet intensity, 'sometimes I hate my role. The good girl. The boring one, who keeps everyone else in line.'

It wasn't hard to see what she meant. Over the years, she had boxed herself in. She had become the hot-shot archaeologist, too focused on work to have any fun. Maybe she'd hoped that going out with Myles would change all that, but instead it had only made it worse. Because Myles had shown her how different she was from people like him, who lived for the moment and drove to Paris on a whim. And screwed around behind their girlfriend's back.

He was surprised that she could be so open with him. Exposing her insecurities like a child.

To get up and leave now was out of the question. Not while she was in this strange, angry, self-denigrating mood. A mood he had helped to create.

Alfonse nosed his way around the door.

'Modge,' said Patrick. 'Alfonse is looking kind of hungry. How about you take him to the kitchen and give him some breakfast?'

Modge snorted to indicate that she wasn't fooled in the least, but she scooped up the cat and staggered out. When she had gone, silence returned to the pot-shed like a settling of dust.

Antonia was gazing down at her tray of potsherds. She looked as if she was about to cry.

He moved his stool nearer to hers. 'You are not boring,' he said quietly. 'And you shouldn't feel bad just because other people act like jerks.'

She did not reply.

'And another thing,' he said. 'Forget about Nerissa.'

'– What?'

'Forget about her. She's the boring one. Not you.'

Before she could think of a reply, he got to his feet and took the labelled shards to the storage trays in the corner, and started putting them away.

If I was Nerissa, she thought, watching his back, I'd ask him what he's thinking right now. It's as simple as that. Then I'd ask him to stay and talk. *Patrick*, I'd say, *I don't want you to go. I want you to talk to me. About you. I want to know everything. I want to know.*

So why don't you just ask?

Because you're a coward. That's why.

And because of Myles.

She picked up a shard and went back to work.

But to her surprise, he didn't leave the pot-shed when he had finished, but returned with a fresh tray and sat opposite her, with a mutinous look on his face.

For five minutes they worked in uneasy silence.

Then she took a deep breath, and asked what had made him try for Oxford.

He glanced at her in surprise.

'You don't have to tell me if you don't want to,' she said quickly, feeling the heat rise to her face. 'I was just curious. So I thought I'd ask.'

There now. What's so complicated about that?

He thought for a moment. 'I was working evenings on a dude ranch, and one time I got talking to this guest. Air-conditioning salesman. His wife was a teacher. She told me about some scholarship, and said, why don't you have a go? She said it was for Oxford, and I thought she meant Oxford, Connecticut.' He coloured, as if unused to talking about himself. 'It was kind of strange, really, because until then I hadn't even thought about going to college in the States, let alone England. But she kept on at me, and in the end I thought, what the hell? So I went for it.'

Slowly she nodded. Then she risked it. 'I bet your father was proud.'

He looked down at the shard in his hands. 'He never knew. He died before I heard I'd got the place.'

'I'm sorry. I didn't know.'

'That's OK. He knew I'd applied, and I guess he was proud about that.' His eyes became distant, remembering. 'Yeah. I guess he was. He even gave me a present. Me! We never gave each other presents. But he did. Couple of days after I told him I was trying for it, he came back from work with this pair of football boots.

131

Top of the range, he said.' He shook his head. 'Poor guy. He really believed that. He thought they were the ultimate in cool.'

'And – they weren't?'

'Not even close. I couldn't wear them to football practice, because all the guys would have laughed at him.' He glanced at her. 'At *him*, you understand? It didn't matter about me. They'd be making fun of him. Their dads were mostly doctors and engineers. It was that kind of school. Another scholarship.' He paused. 'They knew all about his drinking, and that he worked on an assembly line making third-rate sports gear. Kind of stuff you buy when you can't afford Nike. Big laugh. I didn't want to give them something else to make fun of.'

'So – what happened then?'

'Oh, nothing much. He had to go into town, and he saw me on the field wearing my old boots, and he was hurt. He didn't say so, but he was.' He shrugged. 'That's it.'

She put down the shard she had been working on. 'But – did you explain?'

'Explain what? That he spent his life making crap?'

'No, that you were only trying to protect him.'

'No. I didn't tell him that.' He paused. 'I left it too late.'

'What do you mean?'

'Couple of days afterwards, he was standing in line at the canteen and he had a heart attack. End of story.' He forced a smile. 'So I guess the moral is, don't let the sun go down on a quarrel, huh?'

It was painful to see him trying to make light of it. 'It wasn't your fault,' she told him.

'That's what the doctors said.'

'I'm sure they were right.'

'Yeah.'

She watched him place the shard carefully in the finds tray, reach for another, and take up the paintbrush to begin painting on the context number. His hands were brown, with scratches on the backs from all the digging, and he held the brush at the slightly awkward-looking angle which some left-handed people adopt when writing or painting.

As he flexed his wrist, the light caught the thick, raised vein snaking up his forearm. That's his life, thought Antonia. His blood, coursing just beneath the skin.

It looked frighteningly easy to cut. She wanted to cover it with her hand to protect it. To feel its smoothness and elasticity and strength.

She raised her eyes, and found with a shock that he was looking at her. His eyes were very blue, and filled with light.

'Antonia,' said Modge from the doorway, and they both jumped. 'When are we going to the Source?'

Antonia turned her head and stared blankly at the eight-year-old.

Patrick got to his feet. 'I'd better go,' he said.

She looked up at him. 'Yes,' she said at last.

But he stayed where he was, frowning down at her. 'Listen,' he said. 'Could you use some help up there?'

She opened her mouth to speak, then closed it again.

'Oh, *please*,' said Modge. 'He'd make an *incredible* difference. We've still got to do that whole strip at the back.'

She bit her lip. This is not a good idea, she thought. Then she told him, yes, they could do with some help. 'But – I'd better stay down here,' she added belatedly. 'My father. And – everything.'

'Yeah. You'd better do that.'

'I can give you a lift in the jeep, though.'

'Can I come too?' said Modge.

'Sure,' said Patrick, without looking at her.

'Cool,' said Modge.

Antonia wiped her hands on a rag and looked about her as if she had never seen the pot-shed before. 'You'll need some context sheets,' she said dazedly.

'Right,' said Patrick. He picked up a pad of context sheets, a sieve and a jerry-can of water, and walked quickly out to the jeep.

Eight hours later, Antonia straightened on her stool and told herself for the hundredth time that she was *not* going up to the Source to see how Patrick was getting on.

All day she had forced herself to remain in the pot-shed, doggedly reconstructing the lamp. It was now as complete as it would ever be, and she was heartily sick of it.

She found her espadrilles under the table and went out for some air.

The courtyard was deserted. Simon and Nerissa had left an hour before, taking the jeep into Mazerans for a look at the little town, and a quiet dinner on their own. To judge from the clink of bottles coming from the kitchen, her father was already fixing himself a drink. She decided against joining him. He would ask about Myles, and she didn't feel like covering for him.

There was no sign of Patrick. Either he was still up at the Source, or else he'd finished for the day, and had gone back to Les Limoniers for a shower, and a peaceful evening on his own.

She wandered down to the river. Alfonse lay on his

side on a boulder, lazily scrutinizing the swallows. At her approach he raised his head an inch from the boulder, and twitched his tail like a miniature lion.

She sat on a boulder, and lobbed a pebble into the current.

He simply feels sorry for you, she told herself. That's why he said what he did about Nerissa. That's why he's up at the Source now. He feels *sorry* for you.

She clasped her knees and shut her eyes, and wished she was more like Nerissa. Nerissa wasn't boring. He'd only said that to make her feel better. Nerissa was beautiful and exciting, and adored sex. Nerissa would have gazed at him with her wonderful eyes, and bloody well *gone* for it.

But Nerissa, she reminded herself, isn't going out with Myles. Myles who's in Paris, getting up to God knows what. Myles who needs you.

Oh Christ, what a mess.

She heard a trickle of gravel behind her and turned to see Modge picking her way between the rocks. Her fingernails were semicircles of dirt, and she had a smudge of black on her nose. Antonia sighed. For once, she didn't want Modge around. She didn't want anyone around.

Modge came and sat beside her, and tickled Alfonse's paws with a blade of grass. After a while she said, 'I'm hungry. Can I go and see what's in your fridge?'

''Course you can.'

But Modge made no move to go. Plainly she wanted Antonia to go with her.

Antonia stayed where she was.

Eventually Modge got the hint and stood up, brushing the dust off her bottom. 'Patrick says, can you go to the Source as soon as possible?'

Antonia stared at her. 'What? You mean he's still up there?'

Modge nodded.

'But – didn't he bring you down? He can't have let you come all this way on your own?'

Modge shook her head. 'He came part of the way with me, then we met Monsieur Panabière on his tractor thingy and he gave me a lift the rest of the way, and Patrick went back to the Source. Monsieur Panabière is in the kitchen having a drink with Dr Hunt.'

'But – do you know what Patrick wants?'

Modge gave an exaggerated shrug. 'He just said could you go to the Source as soon as possible. He didn't say why.'

Antonia pondered that. He must have a pretty good reason to ask her to make a two-mile hike at six o'clock in the evening. But she couldn't think what.

Maybe he just wanted to see her? Her heart began to pound. But if that was the case, why didn't he come down to the mill?

Forty minutes later, she reached the Source. There was no sign of Patrick.

She went inside.

She found him on his knees at the back of the main chamber. He was using a small trowel to work a patch in the final section, and he looked as if he'd been at it for hours. In the silver-blue glow of the gas lamp the sweat gleamed on his shoulders. His dark hair flopped damply onto his forehead.

At her approach, he did not look up. 'I think we're on to something,' he said.

CHAPTER TEN

Afterwards, it struck Patrick as extraordinary that a discovery which would alter the entire course of his life should arrive without any kind of warning.

When his trowel first struck stone, he felt not the slightest premonition of its significance. It hardly rippled the surface of his thoughts.

He was working a patch of the cave floor about seven inches beneath the topsoil, and idly wondering what Myles was getting up to in Paris, when he came up against something hard. A rock, he thought absently. The cave was littered with them: debris from a glacier, tens of thousands of years before. Or maybe it was a Stone Age tool of some sort. Over the weeks, Antonia had found several, and his guidebook said that at one time there had even been a cave painting on the ceiling – until, that is, an eighteenth-century priest had taken offence at its depiction of a stallion covering a mare, and whitewashed it into oblivion.

Whatever it is, thought Patrick, whistling between his teeth, it'll sure make a change from lumps of clay.

Then he noticed how the complexion of the soil had changed. Instead of the heavy red dirt of the cave floor, he had reached a layer of dry mustard-coloured sand, which crumbled easily, like sugar.

Weird, he thought, pulling the lamp a little closer.

Some kind of localized deposit from the glacier?

No. Not a deposit. It was *too* localized for that, only about the size of a beer crate. Could it have been placed there by human hands?

That was when he stopped whistling, and the adrenalin kicked in.

He put down his trowel, found a paintbrush in his rucksack, and used it to remove a small patch of dirt. Smooth, rust-coloured stone gleamed through yellow sand. His heart began to pound.

The urge to plunge in his hands and yank the thing out was almost overwhelming, but he knew that would be a disaster. The precise orientation of the find – whatever the hell it was – and the position of any associated objects, however tiny or apparently insignificant, could be crucial to its interpretation. If he rushed it now, all that would be lost for ever. Antonia would never forgive him.

It was a physical effort to curb his eagerness: to uncover just a little at a time, then stop and take notes on the context pad. His progress was agonizingly slow. The brush kept slipping from his fingers, and his writing was all over the place.

He glanced at his watch. A little after five. Fortunately, Modge had wandered off for a rest at the mouth of the cave, and had no idea of what he had found. Some instinct prevented him from calling her over. Whatever this turned out to be, Antonia should see it first. But he needed to get Modge back to the mill with a message.

Half an hour later, he had torn himself away for long enough to put Modge safely into the hands of Monsieur Panabière, with strict instructions to tell Antonia to come as soon as she could. Then he returned to the cave and got back to work.

Gradually, a shape began to emerge from the sand. It was a vessel of some kind, about the size of a large whisky tumbler, and it seemed to be made of a hard, smooth, semiprecious stone. Maybe it was agate or chalcedony or cornelian, he couldn't tell which. And as he had first suspected, the vessel had been deliberately buried: laid on its back in a precise east–west orientation on a bed of honey-coloured sand, then carefully covered over with more sand.

An endless time later, he had brushed away enough sand to make out the complete outline of the vessel. It was a goblet, lying on its side. He made out a graceful convex bowl, mounted on a short, slender stem and a small foot. Twin handles extended the length of the bowl in an elegant curve.

He could not breathe. It was the most beautiful thing he had ever seen.

The uppermost surface was still sugared with sand. With trembling fingers he worked at it with the brush. Finally, the last grains whispered away. He caught his breath.

He was gazing down at the crisply cut relief of a young man. The young man walked like a prince, with his head held high. His lips were parted in a smile of great serenity and joy, and one arm was raised, the palm turned outward in the age-old sign of friendship. He looked as if he were welcoming whoever was on the other side of the cup – the side which still lay buried in the sand.

Patrick gazed on the proud young face which had lain undisturbed for perhaps two thousand years. A drop of his sweat splashed onto the young man's shoulder, and trickled down to where the *toga virilis* parted to reveal an athlete's biceps. The wet stone glistened like fresh blood.

Patrick sat back on his heels, and for the first time, pain gripped his shoulders in a vice. He realized that he must have been working for hours, for beyond the cave mouth the sky had dimmed to a delicate translucent mauve. Already the cicadas were singing their night song: slower, sweeter, more musical than their noonday rasp. And from the shadowy cleft behind him came the voice of the spring: a constant, mysterious flow of words, just beyond the edge of human understanding.

Somewhere above the cleft, a fragment of darkness moved. His heart jerked.

A bat, he told himself, it's only a bat. Not some revenant issuing from the doorway between the living and the dead.

He shook himself, and flexed his aching neck and shoulders.

Get a grip, Patrick. There's no-one here but you and the bats.

He went back to work.

Half an hour later, just as he was starting to dig down underneath the cup to free it, Antonia arrived. He put down his brush and wiped his forehead with the back of his hand.

When she saw the cup, her lips parted, but no words came. Silently she sank to her knees. He watched her put out a hand to touch it, then draw back. In the bluish light of the lamp her face was drained of colour, her lips chiselled in marble. Her face reminded him of the goddess on the terracotta lamp. He couldn't look at her for long.

He got up and went to the spring, stooping, for here the cave ceiling was low, and treacherous with stalactites. He caught water in his hands and splashed his face and chest. The water was ice cold, and tasted faintly metallic. A healing spring, he thought.

Antonia had not moved. Beside her he felt big and awkward, like an intruder. This place was meant for goddesses and high priestesses, not for men.

'I think it's some kind of cup,' he said softly, to break the silence.

'It's a *kántharos*,' she replied, without taking her gaze from it. Like him, she spoke in a whisper, as if she feared to offend whatever his discovery had awakened. 'A Greek wine goblet. The Romans revived the style around the fall of the Republic.' She drew a deep breath. 'The Latin name for it is *cantharus*. But I prefer the original Greek.'

'Should we dig it up now, or wait till it's light?'

'We'll do it now.' She glanced up at him, and her lips curved in a faint smile. 'I'll work all night, if that's what it takes to get this out of the ground.'

She would, too. Sometimes she didn't know when to stop. That was one of the things he loved about her.

He asked if she wanted to take over the digging, but to his surprise she shook her head.

'You do it. I'll take the notes.'

'Are you sure? It's your dig.'

'Positive. I don't dare touch it yet.'

In the end it didn't take all night, it took less than three hours. Gradually Patrick worked his way under the cup, until finally it was ready to be lifted from its bed of sand. He glanced at Antonia over his shoulder. 'Is there any special way I should do this?'

'No. Just lift it very carefully. And try not to let any

of the sand inside fall out, there could be more finds in there. I'll empty it once we get back to the mill.'

Still he hesitated. 'Are you sure about this? If I don't do it right I could break it.'

'I don't think so. I think it's made of sardonyx. Hard as nails.'

'Sardonyx?'

She nodded. 'The Romans used it for making signet rings. It's incredibly rare to find an entire cup made of it. I've only ever seen one, in a museum in Paris.' She leaned closer. 'Yes, that's sardonyx, I'm sure of it.'

As she said it, a strange expression came over her face, as if an idea had just occurred to her. He threw her a questioning look, but she only shook her head. Obviously she wasn't ready to share it yet.

The *kántharos* came away from the sand with a suddenness he found shocking. It was intact and perfect in every respect. Holding it in both hands, he carried it to the middle of the cave and set it on the wooden crate which held the magnetometer. Antonia brought the lamp and hung it from one of the iron hooks in the roof.

The side of the *kántharos* which had lain face downward was still crusted with sand. Carefully, Patrick began to brush it away. Antonia knelt beside him with her hands on her knees. He could feel the warmth of her body inches from his own. He could smell the faint minty perfume of her hair.

Little by little, he uncovered the polished relief of a horse. A splendid muscular neck. Taut, rounded haunches. Delicate chiselled hooves. The stallion trotted joyfully over a field of rippling acanthus. Its head was raised and its ears pricked, as if it was eager to reach the young man on the other side of the cup.

Then Patrick saw the great wings half-furled across its back. 'Antonia, look! It's Pegasus!'

He heard the sharp intake of her breath.

Gazing at the winged horse, he felt suddenly cold. He sensed a breathlessness in the air, a thrill of expectancy and awe – as if some blind power had awakened, after an ageless sleep.

He licked dry lips. 'I guess it kind of fits. Didn't they used to call this place the Spring of the Horse?'

From her expression, he saw that she had been thinking the same thing. 'Horses were sacred to the Moon Goddess, because of their crescent-shaped hooves. And Pegasus was sacred to the Nine Muses as well as to the moon. In Greece, on their magic mountain, he made a spring for them by striking the rock with his hoof.' Shakily she pushed a lock of hair behind her ear. 'The rock above us is called the Roc du Sabot. That means the Rock of the Horse's Hoof.'

Patrick swallowed. 'So I guess the story of St Pastou is just kind of an add-on?'

She nodded. 'Christians trying to kill off an ancient myth with a fairytale.'

He took a deep breath, but it only left him breathless. He gestured at the cleft from which the spring trickled. 'How would Pegasus have got all the way back there?' he said, trying to make light of it to dispel his unease.

She raised her shoulders. 'Maybe because he's magic.'

He wished she hadn't said that. In this ancient cave, such things were possible. He could almost hear the rough whisper of feathers as the moon horse folded its wings. He could feel the musky heat of its breath, see the sparks fly as its hoof struck the rock and caused a spring to flow.

Maybe Antonia picked up something of what he was

feeling, for suddenly she said in her normal archaeologist's voice, 'Let's check under the foot for inscriptions.'

He cleared his throat. 'Yeah. That's a good idea.'

'I'll lift it,' she said, 'and you take a look.'

'Shouldn't I do the lifting? It's heavy.'

'No, I'll hold it. I – can't bear to look. In case there's nothing there.'

Again he glanced at her. Her face was taut. Whatever she suspected, she still wasn't ready to share with him.

He put the lamp on the floor beside him, got down on one elbow, and started to brush the sand from the smooth, round base.

His hand froze.

The underside of the foot bore three words, beautifully incised in crisp, authoritative Roman capitals. He said hoarsely, 'How did you know there'd be an inscription?'

'Oh God. I didn't. I only hoped. What does it say?'

Slowly he read it aloud, stumbling a little over the unfamiliar Latin. '*Gai sum peculiaris.*'

She took that in silence.

Thinking that maybe she didn't understand his accent, he spelt out the letters for her.

Shakily she replaced the *kántharos* on the crate. Then she sank to her knees, her eyes distant and unseeing. 'Oh God, yes. Oh yes.'

'What? What does it mean?'

'What does it mean?' Her gaze shifted to him, and he saw that her eyes glittered with tears. 'It *means*, Patrick, it means: "I belong to Gaius".'

The hairs on the back of his neck stood on end.

'*Goddess,*' she quoted softly, as the tears ran down her cheeks, '*I stand before Your sanctum, and pour the sweet, fresh Calenian wine for Your sacrifice. From*

*the blood-red sardonyx flows the blood-red wine: a
fitting gift, I think. And around my drinking-cup trots
Your beloved horse. The horse with wings.'*

Patrick looked from Antonia to the *kántharos*, then
back again.

I belong to Gaius.

Gaius Cassius Vitalis.

'Oh God,' he said. 'It's his.'

Antonia stood at the mouth of the cave and watched the
moon rise above the gorge. It was of that peculiar hue
which is neither golden nor silver, but simply moon
colour.

Strange how her first sight of the moon always came
as a faint shock. She never expected it. Suddenly, it was
simply there.

Over her shoulder she watched Patrick moving about
the cave, gathering materials in which to pack the
kántharos for the walk back to the mill. The debate over
whether to leave the cup here or take it with them had
lasted all of two minutes. True, there was a slight risk
that in the dark he might stumble and fall, and it would
be damaged. But neither he nor Antonia could face
leaving it unguarded at the Source, even for the few
hours left until dawn.

I can't believe any of this, she told herself for the
hundredth time. It's too much. I can't take it in.

Her throat worked. Behind her eyes she felt the pressure of tears.

Patrick had wrapped the *kántharos* in a plastic bag to
keep the sand inside, then encased it in wadding plun-
dered from the magnetometer crate. Now he was easing
the bulky roll into his rucksack. He was absorbed in what
he was doing, and unaware that she was watching. In the

gaslight his face was thoughtful and grave. A face full of youth and certitude, like the young man on the cup.

But earlier, when Pegasus had first come to light, he hadn't been so assured. He had been deeply shaken. She loved him for that. He had tried not to show it, but she knew what he felt, for she felt it herself. A sense of something let loose, blowing through the cave.

She wanted to tell him how glad she was that it was he who had found the *kántharos*.

Cassius would have been glad too, she thought. Oh, he would have liked you, Patrick. I know he would.

She turned back to the moonlight. The sky was a deep, soft indigo glittering with stars, and beneath it the cliff face shone like steel. A hot wind wafted up from the gorge, smelling faintly of dust and thyme.

Patrick emerged from the cave. He left the rucksack and lamp by the oak tree and came to stand beside her. 'I'm glad that's over,' he said. 'It sounds dumb, but I got spooked in there. I don't think she likes men.'

'Who?'

He nodded at the moon. 'The Goddess. Cybele. Artemis. Whoever she is.'

She made herself smile. 'Oh, I don't know. She's the goddess of little children, which I suppose includes boys. And of childbirth, I think . . .'

'Yeah, and also chastity, and sudden death. And doesn't she have a habit of peppering her admirers with arrows?'

She knew what he was trying to do. Get her to talk, so she wouldn't bottle everything up.

He looked down at her. 'Are you OK?'

'I – will be. It's just a bit much to take in. I've wanted something like this for so long. Since I was Modge's age.'

'I know.'

She wiped her eyes with her fingers. 'Sorry. I'll be all right in a minute.'

'It's OK. Take your time.'

After a while he said, 'What's that star over there? The really brilliant one, very low down?'

She sniffed. 'Um. Venus, I think. Actually, it's a planet. – Sorry. You probably know that.'

He scuffed the dirt with his foot. 'You'd think I would, wouldn't you? Country boy and all.' His lip curled. 'Guess I just never learned.'

'Funnily enough, it was my mother who taught me.'

'Why funnily enough?'

'Well, it's not the sort of thing you'd associate with her.'

'What would you associate with her?'

'Oh. Tea at Fortnum's. A manicure at Harvey Nicks.' For a moment she wished she hadn't said it. Then she realized that it didn't matter. She no longer worried about him thinking her snobbish or over-educated or showing off. And it was amazing how much easier it was to talk to him in the dark.

Suddenly she had an idea. 'Look over there,' she said, touching his arm and turning to face south-east. The dark mass of the Roc du Sabot towered above them. 'Do you see that very bright star on the right, just above that line of trees?'

'No . . . Yeah. I've got it.'

'That's Vega. Now look across to your left, about the width of your palm when you hold it at arm's length. Just above the top of the cliff, to the right of that tree, do you see a big square made by four stars, one at each corner? The one at the top right is quite bright, but the other three are very faint, you've got to look for them.'

After a while he said, 'I see it.'

'That's the great Square of Pegasus. The square's his body, and he's also got legs and a neck and a head, I think. But they're too faint to see without a telescope.'

'What about the wings?'

She frowned. 'You know, I don't think he's got any.'

'I guess we're supposed to infer them, huh? I mean, he must have them, if he managed to get all the way up there in the first place.'

She smiled. 'I suppose so.' After a while she said, 'I've just remembered something amazing. This is absolutely the best time of year to see him. Another few weeks, and he'll be over the horizon.'

Beside her, he remained silent.

'Isn't it amazing,' she murmured, looking up at the stars, 'that you just happened to find the *kántharos* at this particular time of year, just when—'

Patrick kissed her.

He took her by the shoulders and spun her round to face him, and kissed her dizzyingly. His mouth was warm and strong and incredibly tender, and he tasted of spring water and salty sweat. She opened her eyes and saw that his face was grave and intent, the dark brows drawn together in a frown.

After the first long astonishment, she clasped her arms about his neck and kissed him back.

They drew apart for breath, and his eyes met hers questioningly. *Do you want this? Do you want me?*

With her finger she traced the line of his brow. Then she raised herself and kissed his mouth. *Yes. I want you.*

The kiss deepened.

Never had she felt so absolutely and unreservedly wanted. And it was so easy and so natural to kiss him back. She felt no hesitation, no fear of doing it wrong. This was right, because it was Patrick.

He bore her back against the cliff face. A rock dug into her shoulder, and she flinched. He felt her recoil and turned them round so that he was against the rocks instead of her. Then he put his mouth to the tender place on her shoulder and gently sucked.

At the same moment, they drew apart.

He leaned back against the rocks, and shut his eyes, and slowly shook his head.

She put her forehead to his chest. His heart was pounding like a turbine. 'It's Myles, isn't it?' she said in a low voice.

He took a deep breath. 'Yeah . . . It sounds crazy, but we have to tell him first.'

'I know.'

'The guy's my best friend. I'm living in his *house*, for Christ's sake. I can't do this behind his back. Ah, Jesus! I wish I could.'

'I know. I feel the same.'

As they talked, their hands kept up a different dialogue: smoothing, stroking. Learning the contours of muscle and bone, the feel of hair and skin.

He took her head in his hands and kissed her once more. Then he said, 'Come on, let's go. If we don't get moving soon, I'll forget what I just said.'

They spoke little during the long walk down, and when they did, it was in whispers. Somehow that seemed to fit. The night was hushed, with only the song of the cicadas and the warm wind in the sage, and the sudden frantic scurryings of lizards fleeing the beam of Patrick's torch.

A few hours earlier, Antonia thought, you were walking up this path and you were full of trepidation and self-doubt. Now you're back on the same path, and everything's different. You're not alone any more.

They stopped once, on the bridge across the Ravin de Verdura. Patrick's knee was giving him trouble after the hours of digging, and he needed to rest it for a while. Shoulder to shoulder, they leaned over the parapet and watched the river glow in the moonlight far below.

Antonia felt the warmth of his arm against hers, and the steady rise and fall of his breathing. She took in his smell of sweat and dust and sage. I love you, she told him silently. I love you, I love you, I love you.

At length Patrick said, 'We'll tell Myles as soon as he gets back from Paris.'

'He'll be back some time today,' she said. 'Bound to be. He'll probably come straight to the mill. I'll tell him as soon as he arrives.'

'No. I think I should do it.'

She turned to him. 'Why?'

'He – might take it out on you.'

'He wouldn't get rough, if that's what you mean. Not Myles. He's not like that.'

'Maybe not. But still. I should be there.' He studied her face. 'As soon as we've told him, we'll go away for the weekend. We'll take the jeep and just drive. Get the hell out of here.'

'Yes. Yes, we'll do that.'

His hand came up and traced the curve of her neck and shoulder. Lightly, as if she was made of glass. 'This is nuts,' he murmured. 'I can't believe we're holding back because of Myles. If the roles were reversed, he wouldn't think twice.'

She loved the way his lower lip thrust out when he was angry. She stood on tiptoe and kissed it. 'Only one day to go.'

'One day,' he said.

CHAPTER ELEVEN

By five o'clock the following afternoon, the *kántharos* had been cleaned inside and out, and Antonia was in the pot-shed doing her best to make a line drawing of the reliefs – just as she had done her best to sift through the sand inside, and look up the address of the French authorities whom she must notify of the find.

She had made scant progress with any of it. Where was Myles? He should have been here hours ago.

She and Patrick had agreed not to see each other until Myles got back. They couldn't face play-acting in front of Nerissa and the others. But they had not envisaged waiting longer than a couple of hours. Now the wait had dragged on for most of the day, and Antonia was beginning to get worried. She kept picturing Myles trapped in the wreckage of the Panda. Or lying in a coma in some hospital bed. Or maybe he had picked up some undercurrent between her and Patrick, and decided to disappear for a few days, to give her a fright.

Outside in the courtyard, the sound of Patrick's voice brought her back to the present. She went to the door.

He was standing on the kitchen steps, talking to her father. He wore his usual washed-out navy T-shirt and dusty jeans, and he was looking gravely down at the older man, as they discussed some detail about the dig. She remembered the hardness of his body against hers, and the moment when his T-shirt had rucked up, and she had put her hand on his back, and felt the hot, smooth ridges of his spine.

The first time she had slept with Myles, she had worried for days over whether she would do something wrong, whether he would keep the lights on, and whether her body was good enough. It was like waiting to go into an exam which she knew she would fail.

With Patrick she felt none of that. She just wanted to be with him.

But where was Myles? If something had happened to him, she would never forgive herself.

But if she had known the wait would last this long, maybe she would have acted differently the night before.

She and Patrick had reached the mill about two, and he had left her at the kitchen door. He had handed her the rucksack without a word, then put his palm against her cheek, and turned and walked away, without looking back.

She had gone into the house and switched on the light – and the kitchen sprang to life in all its shocking normality. The same old clutter of dirty mugs in the sink, the same mess littering the table. A grease-stained newspaper off which someone had eaten their supper, a trio of teaspoons encrusted with sugar and flies, and a blood-spotted coil of Elastoplast which no-one had bothered to throw away.

She didn't mind. Who cared? She was not alone any more.

Taped to the fridge was an ill-tempered note from her father. *Since you didn't come back*, it said tersely, *I gave the child a sandwich and sent her to bed in the spare room. When you finally decide to reappear, kindly TRY not to awaken me.*

Obviously not the product of a happy man, she thought dreamily, scrunching it up and tossing it in the bin.

She went to bed with Patrick's rucksack beside her, and fell into an exhausted sleep just before dawn.

The next morning she called her father, Modge, Simon and Nerissa into the kitchen, and showed them the *kántharos*.

Surprisingly, Simon was the only one to show unclouded enthusiasm. Nerissa said 'oh how lovely' in a bored voice, and didn't the young man look like Patrick? Modge was awestruck at first, but when she heard where Antonia and Patrick had found the cup, her face closed, and her lower lip thrust out. Clearly she felt left out. Antonia's father said nothing at all. He went down on his knees, and studied the cup in silence. Then he reached out a hand – only to withdraw it, as she herself had done the night before. His fingers covered his mouth, and she saw how they trembled. 'Magnificent,' he murmured, blinking furiously. The contrast between this miraculous object and his own dead-end dig was just too agonizing to bear. She felt more sorry for him than she ever had before.

Eventually he shook himself out of his daze, and announced that they must make a video of those reliefs – film would be the only way to get the sense of them in the round – and he would go immediately to Toulouse and borrow a camcorder from his friend Professor Meriot at the university.

Antonia agreed with alacrity. They had a brief argument over whether he should take the jeep, which she won, since he intended to stay for a couple of days, and not even he could justify depriving her of transport for so long. Then she drove him to the railway station at

Foix. It was a relief and a sadness to see him go.

She put down her pencil, and rubbed the back of her neck. It was no good. She couldn't concentrate on anything as precise as a line drawing today. Not with Patrick so close by, and Myles so unaccountably, infuriatingly, worryingly absent. She pushed the drawing aside, and lost herself in the smooth, flowing lines of the *kántharos*.

It stood in a shaft of sunshine beneath the skylight, glowing with the intensity of fresh blood.

There was something about it which inspired awe. She had noticed that neither Simon, her father, Modge, or even Nerissa, could bring themselves to touch it. Perhaps it was the perfection of its symmetry, its purity of line.

The reliefs were miraculous: cut with subtlety and discipline to make skilful use of the natural colour variations in the stone. Pegasus' mane was streaked with ripples of deepest amber, so that it seemed to be floating on the wind. Bellerophon's toga had a flowing line of dark mulberry down the side, gracefully emphasizing the young man's eager forward motion.

It was unquestionably the work of a master craftsman, and in Cassius' day it would have been of enormous value. He must have commissioned it specially, and it would probably have cost him his estate. Which in itself was a puzzle – for it was unlike Cassius to have squandered a fortune on such a treasure. He'd had little time for material things, and the *Poems* contained several wicked lampoons on the vanity of middle-aged collectors, and the avarice of city girls on the lookout for rich benefactors. So what had driven him to commission a prize such as this?

And how had it found its way into a simple peasant sanctum in the hills?

Was it possible that Plautius had put it there after his friend's death? Perhaps in his despair at failing to solve the riddle, the old man had done the next-best thing, and dedicated the poet's drinking-cup to the Goddess.

The riddle. It always came back to the riddle. *In poculo veritas*. The truth is in the cup.

Is it possible, she thought suddenly, that it doesn't mean what everyone thinks it means? Not 'seek the truth when you're drunk' – but 'the truth is, *literally*, in the cup'? In *this* cup. In Cassius' cup.

'The truth is in the cup,' she murmured, running her finger around the rim. She pictured Cassius drinking from it – from this cup – this one, that she was touching now. *Gai sum peculiaris*: 'I belong to Gaius.' She saw his face as she knew it from the marble bust in Rome's National Museum: thoughtful and high-browed, and frowning slightly, as if wrestling with some idea which needed all his concentration. She saw him standing at the mouth of the Source, pouring a sacrifice of blood-red wine from a sardonyx cup.

She felt a shiver of apprehension. Not merely anxiety or uncertainty, but something very close to fear.

But of what?

She tried to shrug it off.

This is what people mean, she told herself, when they talk about being overwrought. So much has happened, so quickly, that you can't take it all in. Besides, what do you expect, after only two hours' sleep?

But there was more to it than that.

'*When we love*,' Cassius had written two thousand years before,

We hope and fear in equal measure.
Loving someone, and knowing how easily

they can be lost, is terrifying.
That's why I make this request of You, Goddess:
out of simple fear.
Grant us a little more time together.
Lycaris is young, she won't be content with
    memories.
And neither will I.
What's a year or two – or ten –
To an Immortal One like You?

The door creaked, and suddenly there was Patrick. He looked as exhausted as she felt. His face was drawn, and the shadows beneath his eyes were more pronounced. 'Hi,' he said.

'Hi.'

'Are you OK? You look pale.'

She wrapped her arms about her waist. 'It's nothing. Ghost just walked over my grave.'

'I thought it was a goose.'

'What?'

'The expression. A goose?'

'Oh. Probably.'

They exchanged tentative smiles.

He tapped the table with his fingertips and glanced at the *kántharos*, then back to her. 'Did you find anything inside?'

She shook her head. 'Only sand. So much for "the truth is in the cup".'

He gave her an enquiring look.

'The Cassius riddle,' she said. 'At least, I think that's what it means.'

She badly wanted to touch him, and he looked as if he wanted it too, for although he stayed on the other side of the table, his fingers moved slowly up and down the grain of the wood.

'Myles still isn't back yet,' she said.

'I know.'

'What's *happened* to him? He should've been back hours ago. He rang this morning, from somewhere on the Autoroute, said he'd be back by noon at the latest. And it's past five now.'

'He'll be here,' he said. 'Listen, if he was in trouble, he'd have called. And if he'd been in an accident, we'd have heard by now. He's probably just playing games. You know what he's like.' But he did not sound entirely convinced, and his eyes betrayed the same concern that she felt herself.

He asked her what Myles had said to her when he called.

She said, 'Just that he'd be back by noon.' She decided not to tell him what else Myles had said. It would only make him feel bad.

It had been a rushed call from a petrol station, for as usual, Myles didn't have enough *jetons*. He had sounded breathless and urgent, and curiously young. 'Sorry I'm such a shit,' he mumbled. 'Sorry. And I wanted you to know – you're not frigid. And I really get off on you.' In the silence which followed, she heard his breath coming fast and shallow, as it did when he was high. Then he said abruptly, 'I'm beginning to think I can't do without you,' and rang off.

She had felt achingly sorry for him. She shrank from the thought of telling him about Patrick.

Patrick was studying her face with an unreadable expression, and she wondered if he guessed that she was holding something back. She stood up and walked round to his side of the table.

He said softly, 'I'll stay and wait with you here.'

'No. Better if you go back to Les Limoniers. If you stayed here, I'd want to touch you all the time.'

He bit his lip. 'Try not to worry. He'll be here soon. And listen,' he added, 'whenever the hell he does get in, call me. *Before* you tell him. OK?'

She nodded.

'Promise?'

'Promise.'

She touched his wristbone with her finger. Then she traced the thick, corded vein up his forearm.

He put a hand on the nape of her neck, and bent and kissed her. She closed her eyes. Took in the heat of his mouth. Smelt sage-dust and clean sweat, and a dry, potent smell that was simply Patrick.

Abruptly, he turned on his heel and left.

After he had gone, she remained standing in the middle of the pot-shed for a long time. Then she took the line drawing, rolled it up, and tucked it inside the *kántharos*. Then she locked the *kántharos* in the only cupboard with a key, locked the pot-shed, put both keys on a cord around her neck, and walked across the courtyard to find herself a drink, and wait for Myles.

That day, a Friday, had been purgatory for Patrick.

At seven in the morning he had awoken from a dream about Antonia to discover that he was alone at Les Limoniers. Myles wasn't back yet. He swore viciously, took a freezing cold shower, and made himself coffee he didn't want. Then he did his damnedest not to think about Antonia. What was the use, when he couldn't be with her till God knew when? Jesus, it was going to be a long day.

Unless, he thought hopefully, Myles comes back this morning, and we get everything out in the open – somehow avoiding a major meltdown – and get away soon, *soon*.

It didn't happen. By midday Myles still wasn't back, and Patrick was starting to worry that something might have happened to him. So to preserve his sanity, he threw himself into a punishing day's work on the dig. And punishing it certainly was. Around four, when the air usually became more bearable, it only went on getting hotter. The woman in the bakery said there'd be a storm soon, and until then it would be *étouffant*, which Patrick took to mean pretty damned hot.

He saw Antonia only once, in the pot-shed, around five. Her lips looked bruised and red from last night, and he caught the milky scent of her skin from five paces away. He wanted her so much it was a physical ache.

Why couldn't they just say to hell with Myles, and go for it?

He'd had all day to think about that, and the answer was always the same. This wasn't only about loyalty to Myles, it went deeper than that. Whatever he and Antonia had together, he wanted it to begin *right*. No lies and no deception. No sneaking around behind a best friend's back. This was too important to start off wrong.

He knew from his own parents how easily things could turn sour between two people. They had spent years sniping at each other. And yet, when his mother finally left, his father was gutted. 'She tore the heart right out of me,' he used to tell his son. Over and over, until it ceased to be a lament, and became both a warning and a threat.

With Antonia it wasn't going to be like that. With Antonia it would be different.

To Patrick's surprise, he found he believed that.

He thought back to that first incredible moment at the Source, when he pulled her into his arms and began to kiss her, and she gave a little start, and then began to kiss him back. That moment of elation and astonishment when he realized she felt the same way about him.

Now it was six o'clock, and the evening stretched before him like a wasteland. He couldn't face a long solitary wait at Les Limoniers. And going down to the mill would be unbearable. So to fill in the time he got a ride to Sainte Eulalie-les-Thermes in Monsieur Panabière's ancient *camionette*, then blew all his money on a room for the weekend at the three-star Michelin.

He knew it was ridiculous. The room had a four-poster bed, for Christ's sake. How over-the-top could you get? But he did it anyway. Not because he was trying to impress Antonia – how could he? – but because he needed to do something tangible to mark what had happened at the Source.

The woman in reception was a scrawny blonde with an orange face which contracted in disbelief when he and Monsieur Panabière appeared in her beautiful marble entrance hall: Patrick in dusty Levi's, ripped T-shirt, and boat shoes held together with string; Monsieur Panabière in ancient blue overalls, a virulent magenta cardigan crocheted by his wife, and his infamous olive-green nylon wig.

The old man had told Patrick that he'd gone bald in his thirties, and his wife had bought the wig from a mail-order catalogue to keep him warm in the winter. To begin with he'd only worn it to please her, but then the sun began to turn it green, and he started to enjoy its effect on people.

He liked Patrick because he spoke Spanish, and was the first person he'd met in years who wasn't fazed by the wig. Patrick forbore to mention that he'd seen far more bizarre get-ups in the Dubois liquor store on a Saturday night, when he was looking for his dad. Although not by much.

'Ça à l'air d'une Boche, ce phenomène-là,' muttered the old man under his breath, eyeing the receptionist. He entered into his role as translator with gusto, stabbing the air with a grimy finger as he repeated each word, for the benefit of the receptionist and the guests on the terrace. And when she demanded payment in full, and Patrick produced his wad of grubby notes, the old man laughed so hard that he nearly spat his dentures onto the counter. He was all for driving off to celebrate with a *pastis* or three at his friend the *pharmacien*'s, until Patrick reminded him about the tractor part which had been his original reason for making the trip, and they went to the *garagiste* instead.

They got back to La Bastide at eight-thirty, and Patrick found Les Limoniers in darkness, with no Panda in the garage. Bloody hell. Either Myles was still not back, or else he was already down at the mill. When Patrick thought about that, a shot of pure jealousy ran through him.

He called the mill, and Antonia answered on the second ring. 'He isn't back,' she said tautly.

'Shit.'

'I can't take much more of this.'

'Me neither.'

'I keep reminding myself that he's done this before

161

– gone AWOL for days, I mean. But I can't stop imagining the worst.'

He could think of nothing to say to that.

A pause. He could tell that she didn't want to ring off either. So he asked her what she was doing tonight. It sounded so much like a bad chat-up line that they both broke out in edgy laughter.

She said, 'I'm having supper in the kitchen with Modge and Simon and Nerissa. D'you want to come?'

He pictured himself sitting opposite her under the watchful gaze of Simon, and Myles' stepsister, and half-sister. 'No,' he said between his teeth, 'I really really don't.'

'I thought you'd say that.'

He told her about the hotel in Sainte Eulalie. 'I wonder now why I bothered,' he said. 'The way I feel about you, we'll never *reach* the bloody place. We'll end up in some lay-by, getting arrested for public indecency.'

She laughed. 'I don't think there's any such thing as public indecency in France. They'd probably give us a medal instead.'

Eventually, they rang off.

Having spoken to her, he felt much better. It was nine o'clock but he couldn't face food, so he had another cold shower, then wandered into the kitchen, took a Coke from the fridge, and went out onto the terrace.

It was stiflingly hot, even worse than at midday. Would the storm never break?

He lay on one of the loungers and stared up at the night sky, searching for the Great Square of Pegasus.

He stayed there for hours, but he never found it.

Modge couldn't sleep. She lay wide-eyed in the mill's spare room, staring at the luminous green face of the alarm clock which Antonia had given her for company. She wished Myles would come home, so that she could go back to her own room at Les Limoniers.

All day she had been feeling horribly lonely and left out, and when she went to bed, it only got worse. She felt like the last person left on earth, like the Little Prince in the storybook, standing alone on his tiny football-sized planet as it spun out into the darkness of deep space.

Patrick and Antonia had changed. She couldn't say exactly how, except that they were different. Even when they were right there in front of her they were really far away, somewhere together where she couldn't go.

Oh, they were still nice to her. They waited politely when she talked to them, and even made a stab at answering her. But they didn't really hear what she said.

She blamed that horrible cup thing which Patrick had dug up at the Source. To begin with, it had seemed like a miracle: so beautiful, and with Cassius' *name* on it. But when Antonia told her how she and Patrick had found it together at the Source, Modge knew in an instant that she had lost them both. It wasn't *fair*. She had been with Patrick at the Source to begin with, but then he'd sent her away without telling her about the cup, and made her fetch Antonia instead. And now she had lost them both, and it was all the fault of that cup thing. It had put a spell on them, and she hated it. She hated the way it looked, standing on the table in the pot-shed, sucking in the light and glowing like blood. She refused to believe that it had anything to do with Cassius. It was much too nasty for that.

She had spent a miserable day shuttling aimlessly between the main site and the pot-shed, getting in the way. She couldn't even find Alfonse. Finally, she had filled the kitchen sink with hot water and given Star Rabbit a bath, but even that had turned out to be a dismal failure, because to her horror, Star Rabbit didn't come up nice and clean but merely turned grey all over, and his insides went knobbly – an uncomfortable reminder that he wasn't really a rabbit from Outer Space, but only a toy filled with lumpy stuffing. She had wrapped him in a towel and gone to sit in the sun so that he wouldn't catch cold.

Now she lay watching the hot wind sucking the curtains in and out, wondering when it would cool down so that she could sleep.

Some time later she was woken by voices, and a door slamming downstairs. She ran to the window, just in time to see the headlights of the Panda turning off. At last Myles had come home. Maybe now they could get back to normal.

But something was wrong. She could tell from the urgent tone of Antonia's whispers, and the stumbling noises on the stairs. She stood in the middle of the room, her heart thumping. When she couldn't bear it any longer, she opened the door.

At the end of the corridor, weak light poured from Antonia's room. Modge padded towards it. When she reached the doorway she froze.

Myles, her glamorous, wicked, infuriating older brother, was curled up on the bed with his head on Antonia's lap, shivering and crying like a baby, and wearing nothing at all. Modge could see his thing, and it was small and pale, like Jason Pershaw's at school, when the older children pulled down his trunks and sprayed him with cold water from the hose.

She couldn't breathe. It was all wrong. Horribly, horribly wrong. She longed for Star Rabbit, but he was still outside on the line, where Antonia had pegged him up to dry.

In the lamplight Myles' skin was clammy and white – even his lips were white – and he was gasping, really gasping, as if he couldn't get enough air. 'Oh God, oh God, help me, Toni, I'm going to die, my heart's going like a fucking rocket and I can't slow it down, I'm going to have a heart attack and die! Oh God oh God oh God oh God oh God!'

All the time Antonia was talking to him, very low and soft, and stroking his arm and telling him to breathe into the brown paper bag she was holding to his lips. You're not going to die, you're going to be all right. Just breathe into the bag, like the nurse showed us last time, remember? Just breathe in and out.

That made Modge feel a bit better. At least Antonia knew what to do.

Gradually, as the brown paper bag crackled in and out, Myles' breathing slowed. His shivering lessened to an occasional spasm. Antonia pulled the bedspread over him and settled back against the headboard, still with his head on her lap, still stroking his arm.

'God, Toni,' muttered Myles, 'I need you so *much*. Don't ever leave me.'

Modge had never heard him speak like that before, and it frightened her more than anything, for she could tell that he really meant it.

And she could tell from the look on Antonia's face as she sat staring into the darkness, that she knew that he meant it too.

CHAPTER TWELVE

*A family tomb near the Porta Capena, Rome, 25 July
53 BC*

She should have told him the moment they met that
night, but she couldn't bring herself to do it. She needed
to make love with him one last time before she ended it
for ever.

And it would be for ever. At least she wasn't deceiving
herself about that – as she had deceived herself about so
much over the past few weeks.

Oh, she had been living in a fool's paradise! She saw
that now. Hoping that time alone would solve everything: would allow him to find some way – through
patronage, his own fame, anything – to make himself
acceptable to her family.

But time had turned out to be not the solution, but
the greatest enemy of all. It had waited for her like a thief
in an alleyway, and then robbed her of everything at a
single blow.

And now tonight – which was to have been their last
night before he left for Gaul – would be their last night
for ever.

She raised herself on one elbow to look at him.

He slept on his back as he always did, with his head
turned towards her, resting on the crook of his arm. His

face was serene and young-looking, his eyelashes trembling as he dreamed.

It was a hot night, so they had made love without a covering, and in the lamplight his body was the colour of burnished bronze.

She knew each one of his scars: its exact shape and feel and provenance. Once, for a joke, she had plotted him like a map. Parthia. Britain. Syria. Anatolia.

The bump over the right wristbone marked the fracture which had set so badly. The little ridges over the lower ribs showed where he'd broken them in a fall from a palisade. Then there was the deep puckered slash from the Syrian sword, which began above the left hip bone, and ploughed up to just below the nipple. And finally the long, still angry-looking spear wound down his inner thigh.

About that one she had made a particular joke, likening it to the scar on Odysseus' thigh which had blown his disguise to Helen, when he tried to infiltrate Troy. 'Just *what* did Helen think she was playing at?' she had demanded in mock indignation. 'The woman was supposed to be washing the man's *feet*, for Heaven's sake, not investigating his thighs! But then, I suppose that's just the kind of man Odysseus was. You started off washing his feet, and before you knew it' – a fatalistic shrug – 'what can a woman do?'

That had made him laugh. He laughed a lot when he was with her. She made him happy. He made *her* happy.

Why couldn't it be as simple as that?

And now here she was, about to inflict on him the biggest wound of all. A great stabbing slash across the spirit, which would never heal. She knew how it would be for him, because it would be the same for her.

When she tried to think of what her life would be

without him, she couldn't do it. The years stretched before her, a featureless blank.

But she could picture how it would be for him. He would ride away tomorrow on the long, hard road back to Gaul, not understanding why she had ended it between them. He would never understand. For she could never tell him the truth. That was the one certainty she clung to. If she told him, he would try to stop her, and get himself killed.

Maybe the gods would see him safely through the worst of it. Should she make a special plea to them? Would they listen if she did? She didn't know what to do.

Once, he had remarked that you should be careful what you asked of the gods, for they had a way of granting the exact opposite, simply for their own amusement. She didn't know whether he meant that or not, or even whether he believed in them at all. That was a side of him she found hard to fathom. When she asked about it, he would answer with a smile, 'I believe that they exist to make us their playthings. Though I often wonder why they bother. It's not as if we can offer much resistance.' Yet there were other times when she sensed in him a bedrock of belief, buried far beneath all the rationalism and wit. She hoped she was right about that. He would need it to see him through.

Lightly, she traced the new crescent scar on his shoulder, the one she had given him a month before. Had some part of her known, even then, that it would come to this? Was that why she had put the Goddess' mark upon him? To make sure that She would watch over him when she, Tacita, could not?

Or was that just her own cowardly way of making herself feel better for what she was about to do?

Her fingers lingered on the raised red crescent. She mustn't cry. Not yet. Time enough later. A whole lifetime for that.

Without opening his eyes, he stopped her hand with his.

'You don't like me touching it,' she said.

Still with his eyes closed, he smiled, and shook his head. 'On the contrary, I do. But right now I'm too lazy to do anything about it.'

She settled against him and listened to his heart beat. He ran his fingers slowly through her hair, gently drawing out each lock from roots to ends, then letting it fall across her naked back.

'Gaius . . .'

'Mm?'

She swallowed. No. She couldn't do it yet. Just a little longer. 'Why did you choose this place for us to meet?'

'What?'

'A tomb. Why a tomb?'

She felt a laugh shake his chest, heard the smile in his voice. 'I don't know. Maybe the link between love and death appealed to me. Poets like that kind of thing.'

He made light of it, but she knew that he was probably in earnest. He often mocked what he took most seriously. Sometimes it seemed that only in his poems did he let his true feelings show.

She told him so now.

He raised his head to look at her, suddenly grave. 'And to you,' he said. 'I show my feelings to you.'

She couldn't bear to meet his eyes. Quickly she got to her feet, snatching her under-tunic and dress from the flags and hastily pulling them on. With trembling fingers she fastened her belt in a slipshod knot. Then she went to the doorway and stood staring out at the road.

It was in the time of the moon's dark, so the marble tombs and urns along the Appian Way caught only a faint gleam of starlight. Albia was wise to bring extra lamps, she thought numbly. We'll need them on the way back.

The way back. The thought of it was like a cold stone in her belly.

Gaius caught her mood, as he always did. She heard him slipping on his tunic and coming up behind her. He put his hands on her shoulders, and rested his chin on the top of her head. 'I'll be back in three months,' he said.

She turned into his arms and he held her tightly, as she needed to be held. She pressed her face to his chest to keep back the sobs, and his breastbone was hard beneath her forehead. His skin carried a faint scent of wine from the lees he used for mixing his ink. The fingertips of his left hand were always stained purple, and smelt faintly of grape.

She shut her eyes tight, tight, and let him rock her like a child.

A few words from me, she thought, and all I'll have left is memories. A few words. A hinge on existence. I can't bear it.

She took a step back and raised her head and said, 'I'm going to marry Lucius Cornelius Verus.'

She watched his face go still.

She thought: now we can never go back to the way we were. Everything we had was before this moment. Now it's afterwards. Now and for ever.

'No,' he said calmly. He sounded as matter-of-fact as if she had confused herself with someone else – as if another Tacita were going to marry Lucius Cornelius Verus. Not her. Not *his* Tacita.

'Yes,' she said. 'It's all arranged.'

He searched her face, struggling to take it in. She watched his grey eyes darken, the blackness at the centre spreading outward, like blood staining a bandage.

She was cold. Her teeth were chattering. 'Lucius Cornelius Verus,' she repeated. 'The advocate.'

'No.'

'It's arranged. The betrothal ceremony was yesterday. The wedding's next week.'

His face was blank with shock. His hands hung at his sides. 'I don't—' he began, then broke off. Slowly he shook his head. 'Two weeks ago you promised to wait for me. What's changed?'

'The wedding is next week,' she repeated unsteadily.

Her father had been overjoyed when she agreed so quickly to the match. Astonished, but overjoyed. So much so that he missed the fact that she had suggested it herself. But why should he question her motives, when she would be marrying one of the Cornelii?

'Tacita. *Why?*'

This deep, deep coldness in her bones. If only she could get rid of this coldness. She said, 'My father's beginning to suspect that I have a lover.'

He took her by the shoulders. 'Look at me. No, *look* . . . You're lying.'

'No.'

'Yes. You can't meet my eyes.'

He was right. Her father suspected nothing. But he would. And soon, if she did not move fast.

'I'm doing this to save your life,' she said. That was the truth – for if her father and brothers found out that she had a lover, they would have him killed. And probably her as well.

He didn't believe her. 'You're frightened. That's it,

isn't it? You're frightened, because I'm going away.'

'I'm frightened for *you*.'

He paced the length of the chamber. Then he turned. 'Come with me to Gaul.' She caught a flash of what made him such a good soldier. Assess the problem, then go for the bold solution: the one nobody expects.

'I can't,' she said.

'Yes you can. Come with me tonight.'

'They'd come after us. It'd be easy on the road. His men would find us. They'd slit your throat in front of me.'

He knew she was right. The bleakness in his eyes told her that. It was unbearable to watch. 'Don't do this, Tacita. Wait for me, as you promised. You promised to wait. Three months! What's three months? I'll be back. I'll sort things out. Don't do this—'

'I already have! Didn't you hear me? The wedding's next week!'

Again he paced the tomb, and this time he prowled like a caged animal. She watched the anger starting to work its way to the surface. Surely anger was a good sign? Surely it would help him get over this?

'You can't do this,' he muttered.

'Gaius, I—'

'*Cornelius?* The man's over fifty! He's got false teeth, and a little bald patch which he gets his barber to dye with German herbs! No, it's impossible, absurd! Think what your life would be!'

'I don't care about that.'

He stopped and looked at her, and his face changed. As if he were seeing her for the first time.

She flinched.

He shook his head. 'I won't let this happen.'

'You can't stop me.'

'Then I'll beg,' he snarled.

'No.'

'Oh, yes. That's the one good thing about having peasant blood, as you insist on calling it. We have no pride, you see, no pride at all. I'm begging you, Tacita. Don't marry this man. Even if you never see me again, don't ruin your life. Don't do it.'

'I can't let them kill you!' she burst out. 'Hate me if you must, despise me for the rest of your life! But I won't let them kill you!'

She ran to where they had lain together, where his cloak was still spread out, rumpled from their love-making, and where hers was still rolled up as a pillow. Somehow she managed to throw it across her shoulders. 'Forgive me,' she said from the doorway.

'How can I forgive you? You're destroying our lives—'

'I have no choice—'

'– and you won't tell me why!'

'There isn't time, Gaius!' Her voice broke. 'We've run out of *time*!'

She ran out into the darkness.

CHAPTER THIRTEEN

La Bastide, Saturday, 24 September 1988

'Patrick?'

'Antonia? Is that you? – What time is it?'

'Seven in the morning. Sorry, did I wake you?'

'I – Christ, I guess I overslept! I was up all night.'

'Me too.'

'Is Myles . . .'

'He came back last night, very late.'

'I'll come down.'

'No. No. That's what I'm ringing about.'

'Why, what's wrong?'

'Nothing. It's just that – I haven't told him yet.'

'Good, I'll come down, we'll tell him together—'

'Patrick, listen. It's complicated. He was in a bad way when he got back. Really bad. Some kind of panic attack. It took me all night to get him over it.'

'Jesus. Is he all right?'

'He is now.'

'What about you?'

'I'm fine. Just a bit tired . . . Actually, it was awful. He kept saying he was going to die. At one point I thought he might.'

'You should have called me.'

'No. You couldn't have done anything. And I knew

what to do, it's happened before. Anyway, he's fine now, but he's still asleep. That's the point. He'll sleep for a few more hours, and then, when he's on an even keel—'

'Are you kidding? Myles? On an even keel?'

'I know it sounds stupid . . .'

'It sounds like prevarication. We need to wake him up and talk to him.'

'It's not prevarication. You wouldn't say that if you'd seen him last night. He was so vulnerable. I felt like a criminal.'

'Antonia, *listen* to yourself!'

'All I'm saying is, we need to wait a bit longer. Just a couple of hours till he's awake and feeling better. Please, Patrick, I can't kick him when he's down. I just can't.'

'Hey. Hey. I'm sorry. I didn't mean to yell at you – Antonia? Are you still there?'

'Sorry. Sorry. I'm just a bit tired.'

'Take your time. Listen, I don't want to pressure you. If it makes you feel better to wait, we'll wait.'

'Thanks.'

'– So. How long d'you think before he wakes up?'

'Some time in the afternoon, I suppose.'

'The afternoon. Mm-hm . . . So, uh – what are you going to do till then?'

'I don't know. Work on the dig, I s'pose. Sounds ridiculous, but—'

'– anything to fill the time. Yeah, me too. I'll see you there.'

As soon as Myles woke up, he knew without opening his eyes that he was in Toni's room at the mill.

He could tell from the creak of the bedstead when he stretched, and the roar of the river through the open window, and the way the pillow smelt of the peppermint shampoo she always used.

He couldn't be bothered to open his eyes just yet. God, he was exhausted. There should be a new word for the way he felt. Steamrollered. Drained.

And low. So fucking low.

He rolled onto his side, and a piece of paper crackled under his cheek. There was a note on the pillow: *Gone to the dig, back by noon. Orange juice etc. in fridge. Have some. Hope you feel better soon. Toni.*

Her handwriting sprawled across the page, encapsulating everything about her which he was not. Elegant, forceful, straightforward and clever.

And kind. He had never thought about that before, but now he felt the truth of it. Toni was kind.

He rolled onto his back and stared at the ceiling. He felt so mean and worthless that he could no longer hold back the tears. They spilled down his cheeks and trickled into his ears, the way they used to do at boarding-school.

Next to Toni, what was he, Myles Sebastian Cantellow? He was nothing. Not even bad enough to be truly *bad*. His only talent was to screw things up for other people. Look at him now, flat on his back because he couldn't even handle coke without screwing it up, while his girlfriend was out in the blazing sun making yet more epoch-making discoveries.

Last night she had told him about the find at the Source, talking to him in a low, soft voice as he lay with his head in her lap drifting in and out of consciousness, like a kid being lulled to sleep with fairytales. He had never felt so peaceful and looked-after in his life.

Thank God he had Toni.

As always, his next thought was about what would

happen when she left. A panicky sweat broke out on his forehead. He put his fingers to his throat and felt his pulse. Too fast. He checked the whereabouts of the brown paper bag. To his relief, Toni had left it prominently on the bedside cabinet.

Calm down. Don't think about her leaving. She won't leave. Like she said last night, the worst is over. You'll never touch the stuff again – and this time it's *true*, it really is. And because of that she'll stay, and you'll be fine.

He awoke some time later, feeling much more his usual self. A glance at his watch told him it was ten o'clock. He had only been asleep for a quarter of an hour, but what a difference!

He heard a noise at the door, and turned to see Nissa watching him from the corridor. She looked wonderful, in one of her floaty flowered dresses which only just skimmed the tops of her honey-coloured thighs.

'Hello, Nurse,' he murmured. 'Come to give the patient his morning blow-job?'

'Get lost,' she said amiably. She leaned against the doorpost with her hands behind her back, sticking out her breasts like a precocious schoolgirl. 'I hear you overdid it in Paris, even for you. You certainly look like crap.'

She sounded impressed, and he grinned. He was feeling better by the minute.

'Still,' she said, putting her head on one side, 'as a special favour – and *if* the patient asks nicely – Nurse might *consider* giving him a hand job to speed up his recovery.'

Coming from Nissa, that was a favour indeed. Normally she didn't like the mess.

He couldn't believe his ears when he heard himself

turn her down. But he really didn't want sex. God knew what it would do to his heart.

Again he checked his pulse. So far, so good.

To help Nissa over her surprise, he said, 'But Nurse, the patient could really murder a drink.'

She smiled. 'I thought you might say that.' From behind her back she produced a bottle of Côtes de Roussillon, two tumblers and a corkscrew.

'Nissa my darling, you are my angel of light.'

God, it tasted good. And alcohol slowed your heart, didn't it? So that was all right.

After filling her own tumbler, Nissa reached across his chest and deposited the bottle on the cabinet. Then she lay on her front beside him, sipping contentedly.

Looking at her made his pulse rise a couple of notches. He should probably send her away. But then again, she was nothing he couldn't handle. He could feel himself getting stronger all the time.

With his tumbler resting on his chest, he pulled down her panties and ran his palm lightly over her peachy buttocks, skimming the triangle of pale, deliciously rounded flesh left by her bikini bottom.

'Mm,' she murmured, 'that's nice.' She pressed her hips into the mattress and clenched, and a dimple appeared in each buttock.

'You must have been a cat in a former life,' he said, still working her with his hand.

'Yum. Definitely. I could do this all day.'

'*You're* not doing anything.'

'That's the point.'

After a minute he got bored and gave her a smack. 'Off you trot, stepsister. I want a shower.'

But she rolled onto her back and unbuttoned her dress and told him to do her front.

He flicked wine across her breasts. 'Too much of a risk, you little trollop. Toni could come in at any minute.'

She snorted. 'Right now, Toni wouldn't notice if she found us working our way through the *Kama Sutra*.'

He rolled the wine around his mouth. 'What's that supposed to mean?'

'Oh, I forgot. You've been away for the last few days, so you don't know about it.'

'About what?'

'First do my front, *then* I'll tell you.'

He reached over and tweaked her nipple so hard that she yelped. 'Stop fucking around and tell me.'

'It's not *me* who's been fucking around,' she said sulkily, sitting and buttoning her dress. Then, disconcerted by his silence, she added, 'Well, it was bound to happen sooner or later. It's not exactly front page news.'

'What isn't?'

'Toni and Patrick.'

Something inside him dropped like a stone. 'That's a fucking lie.'

'Why would I bother to make up a thing like that? I saw them yesterday in the pot-shed. They couldn't keep their hands off each other.'

He pressed his fingers to his throat. His pulse was racing. Toni and Patrick. Toni and Patrick. No no no no no.

'It must have started while you were in Paris,' she went on, 'because before then I never detected a thing, and I can always tell.'

He felt hot and prickly and cold. It was like lying on needles. He felt sick.

'You look awful,' remarked Nissa. 'Fish-white and

179

clammy. Shall I call Toni?' She pushed herself off the bed but he grasped her wrist so tightly that she cried out.

Poor Patroclus, he told himself. It wasn't his fault, it couldn't have been, he wouldn't do this to his friend. She bowled him over. Stands to reason, doesn't it? Rich English girl. Clever. Talented. Beautiful. Country boy like him never stood a chance.

Ah, Toni! How could you *do* this? How could you *do* this to *me*?

But she had. She'd seduced his best friend behind his back, and now he had lost her, and Patroclus too.

'Who's Patroclus?' asked Nissa, and he realized he'd spoken aloud.

He ignored her. He thought about how he'd pleaded with Toni last night. How he'd whimpered and begged her never to leave him. That made him shrink. He had been begging her not to leave him, but she already had.

No. Not possible. There must be some way to get her back. Reel her in, that was what he must do. He must reel her in.

He refilled his tumbler and took a long, icy, invigorating pull. The wine flowed through his veins like mercury. Or like – what was that stuff the gods had instead of blood? Ichor, wasn't it? Yes. Ichor. Presumably Achilles had that too, being half god and half human.

You're Achilles the Golden One, he told himself. Veins bulging with ichor, and getting better in leaps and bounds.

To his relief, the pulse in his throat was strong and even. A bit fast, but what did that matter? A fast, vigorous, steady pulse. Going like a train. He could handle this. He could handle anything.

Yes, definitely, it was time to reel her in. He had

stayed in Paris too long, and she had got the bit between her teeth; now she needed to be reminded who was boss.

Already he knew how he would do it. It was only a matter of working out the details. 'Where's Modge?' he asked suddenly.

Still sulking, Nissa pretended not to hear.

'Come on, Nissa. Where is she?' His grip on her wrist tightened. Not enough to hurt. Just a reminder of what he could do if he wanted.

'How should I know? Around. I think I saw her in the kitchen, stuffing her face as usual.'

Good. Good. He would need his little sister's help. She could go places where he could not.

He glanced at Nissa. He still didn't feel like sex, but that was beside the point. The point was, he owed it to himself to fuck Nissa right here on Toni's bed – to *prove* that Toni had no hold over him.

Besides, sex was a kind of a ritual, wasn't it? Warriors did it before going into battle. 'You can unbutton that dress,' he said.

'Actually, no. I thought for once I'd go and help Si on the dig.'

Still gripping her wrist, he moved his other hand up her thigh. 'Later,' he said.

'Myles – I don't want to. Really. And I'm sure you shouldn't. You look terrible.'

His hand slid under her skirt and he rolled on top of her. 'This won't take long.'

'I don't *want* to,' she protested. Then she heaved a sigh. 'Oh all right, then. But make it quick.'

Five humiliating minutes later, he pulled out of her with a sob. 'I can't, I can't!' he cried, curling up in a ball and hiding his face in his hands.

'I could've told you that,' snapped Nissa. 'God, what

a mess. You look like you're going to have a heart attack.'

She left him rocking and sobbing on the bed, cursing Toni and Patrick, and himself most of all.

At half-past eleven Patrick straightened up in the sweltering trench where he'd been trowelling, and decided he'd had enough of this lunacy.

'I've had enough of this lunacy,' he told Antonia moments later, hunkering down beside her.

She made no reply. She looked exhausted, her eyes shadowed and huge. What had he been thinking of, letting things drag on like this?

'I'm going up to the house,' he went on, 'to shower and sling some stuff in a bag, then I'll meet you back at the mill. I don't care if he's awake or not, but we're out of here.'

She nodded.

He was often to think about that afterwards. About how different their lives would have been if they had managed to get away in time.

It was a little after twelve when he reached the mill. The heat was intense, worse than he'd ever known. The land lay stunned into stillness, bludgeoned by the unrelenting sun beneath a sky the colour of pewter.

There was no-one in the courtyard, and he sensed immediately that something was wrong. The kitchen door was ajar, and he pushed it open. He dropped his rucksack on the tiles. 'Myles? Antonia?'

Nothing. Not even the cat.

He went upstairs and found Antonia's room. It was empty, like all the others.

He had never been in her room before, but he knew it from the rainbow pile of clothes on the chair, and the tangle of jewel-coloured ribbons on the chest of drawers. Her bed was a chaos of brightly flowered sheets. He didn't want to look at it. That was where she and Myles – *no*. Uh-uh. Don't even *think* about it.

Then he noticed that her bedside cabinet was skewed, the door ajar. Myles had told him about the notes she kept in there, her big secret. At the time he had found that touching, for it showed a side of her he wouldn't have expected. Now, with a twinge of apprehension, he saw that the lock had been forced and the cabinet was empty.

Oh, shit. If Myles had messed with her notes it would flay her alive.

He found her in the pot-shed, turning the place upside-down. Her hair was wild, her face taut. She looked like a maenad. For a moment when she saw him in the doorway he wasn't sure if she recognized him.

'He's taken everything,' she said dully.

He licked his lips.

'All the context sheets. From both digs. And all my – um – my papers.' She pressed her fingers to her mouth.

He remembered that she didn't know that he knew about her notes.

'He left a note.' Shakily she held it out to him.

Even for Myles, the writing was terrible. Something about a paper trail with a prize at the end.

An appalling thought occurred to him. He threw her a glance. 'The *kántharos*. He didn't . . .'

'Yes,' she said. 'He took that too.'

CHAPTER FOURTEEN

Myles' paper trail was insultingly easy to follow.

He had scattered the context sheets and the pages of Antonia's notes liberally along the track to the Source. Some were thumb-tacked to trees, others tied to bushes with twine, and some had been impaled on Monsieur Panabière's barbed-wire fence.

He wants us to know exactly where it leads, thought Antonia numbly. Which probably means that he's put the *kántharos* somewhere else.

The *kántharos*. She couldn't bear to think of it. What if he'd dropped it? What if it had tumbled onto the rocks and cracked? If anything had happened to it – her stomach dropped.

'We'll take the jeep,' Patrick had said between his teeth. 'You drive. I'll get out and collect the pages.'

'No,' she said quickly.

'Why not?'

'I'll do it.' She didn't want him to see any part of her translations, and particularly her Introductory Note – her pathetic, overblown, horribly personal theory about Cassius and Lycaris and the riddle. The thought made her cringe.

'Wretched thing,' she muttered ten minutes later, dripping with sweat as she scrambled down a precipitous goat track which clung to the side of the gorge.

'How could I fool myself into thinking he wouldn't find out?'

Myles had excelled himself. He had jumbled up the context sheets from the main dig with those from the Source, then used pages from her notes, neatly folded into arrows, to point the way. That must be why he had left the Panda at the mill and done the whole thing on foot. Driving would have impeded inspiration.

'D'you think he has any idea what he's done?' muttered Patrick when she got back to the jeep.

She didn't answer. Of course Myles knew. If even a handful of context sheets was lost, the whole dig would be ruined. Twelve weeks' work lost beyond hope of retrieval. To say nothing of the wasted funds, and the recriminations her father would face at the faculty.

Thank *God* he was safely in Toulouse. By ill luck he had rung just as they were leaving, wanting her to look up a detail on one of the sheets. She had lied to him, saying she'd locked herself out of the pot-shed, and would call back later.

Patrick wrenched the jeep into gear, and she threw him a glance. From the set of his mouth she could tell how angry he was. She only hoped he wouldn't lose his temper when they caught up with Myles. Time enough for a fight once they had the *kántharos* safe and sound. Then maybe she too could allow herself the luxury of anger. Right now, it would only get in the way.

An hour and a half later, they had found the last of the context sheets. The knot in her stomach loosened fractionally, and she began to feel a glimmer of hope. At least that was one disaster averted.

Patrick cut the engine. They had just passed the turn-off to Le Figarol, and beyond this point the track was too narrow for the jeep. They would have to continue to the Source on foot.

But to her surprise, he made no move to get out. Instead he sat drumming his fingers on the steering wheel.

'Aren't you coming?' she asked.

'What for? We've got all the sheets and most of your notes.'

'But the *kán*—'

'I say we turn round and go back right now.'

She stared at him. 'What are you talking about?'

'Antonia, this is not the way to find the cup.'

'What?'

He looked at her. 'Do you really think that when we get to the Source, we'll find it waiting for us, like the pot of gold at the end of the rainbow?'

She swallowed.

'He's got us where he wants us, Antonia. Halfway up a goddamned mountain, scurrying around like ants. He's angry and he's hurting, because he knows about us – God knows how – and he wants us to hurt too.'

'So what d'you think we should do?'

'Go back down and wait him out.'

'But—'

'We've got to show him he can't control us. When he knows that, he'll give us the damn cup.'

He was right. But what he suggested was impossible. 'I can't do it,' she said. 'I have to go to the Source. I have to make sure.'

He studied her face. 'OK. OK.'

He turned the jeep around, and parked in the usual place, just below the turn-off for the farm. Antonia put the context sheets on the passenger seat with a stone on top.

'Here,' Patrick tossed her the keys. 'You'd better hang onto these.'

She threw him a doubtful glance. 'You're not going to get into a fight, are you?'

'Who, me?' His lip curled. 'I'm just coming along to make sure *you* don't scratch his eyes out.'

Suddenly the whole exercise struck her as absurd. 'Try and stop me,' she muttered ruefully.

They rounded a bend and came upon three more pages of the Introductory Note tied to a juniper bush, and Modge.

She was stomping towards them down the track, red-faced and fuming. She looked like a small dusty goblin.

Antonia felt a twinge of guilt. She had completely forgotten about the eight-year-old. 'What's the matter, Modge?' she said. 'Where's your brother?'

Modge threw her a thunderous look. 'He told me to bugger off! He made *fun* of me! He says I can be his helper, then he's nasty and pretends it's a joke but it *isn't*, it's just a trick to make me cross so I'll go away! I wish somebody'd make fun of him for a change! Then he'd find out how *he* likes it!'

Her outburst confirmed Antonia's suspicions about how Myles had got into the pot-shed without breaking the lock. The upper window was too small for a man, but big enough for a child to squeeze through.

She asked Modge if Myles had taken the cup to the Source.

Modge glowered at the ground.

'Modge, it's OK,' Antonia said, 'I know it's not your fault. But we need to find the *kántharos*. The stone cup? He took it, didn't he?'

'We did a paper trail,' Modge said stubbornly.

Patrick threw Antonia a warning glance. 'Listen,

honey,' he said to Modge, 'it's no big deal, it's just some dumb cup, OK? We're going on to the Source. How about you come too?'

Modge glanced from him to Antonia, then back again. She looked as if she might burst into tears. Then she shook her head. 'Two's company, three's a crowd,' she muttered, and started off down the track.

Patrick made to go after her, but Antonia held him back. 'Let her go. We'll catch up with her on the way down.'

'Wait for us by the jeep,' Patrick called after Modge. She did not turn round.

They trudged on up the track. Although it was only mid-afternoon, the light was worsening as the storm approached. The sky had turned a dirty grey, and a hot wind had begun to blow down the gorge. The heat was stifling.

As they walked, the paper trail began to change. Obviously Myles had become tired of making arrows, and had amused himself with a schoolboy version of origami. A witch's hat, a double helix, a fan. If it hadn't been for the *kántharos*, it would have been funny.

As for the *kántharos*, Antonia told herself, not even Myles would dare do anything to that.

Patrick echoed her thoughts. 'He wouldn't do anything to it,' he said quietly, 'Not even he would go that far.'

She clung to that.

It's going to be all right, she told herself. It's going to be all right.

They came on Myles without warning. They rounded a bend and there he was, perched like a leprechaun on the slope above them. He was smoking a Montecristo, and swigging Veuve Clicquot from the bottle.

'*Hail, brother, and farewell!*' he called down to Patrick, raising the bottle in a mock salute. 'Haven't you done well, getting all the way up here in this heat? And what a *lovely* couple you make! Stupid of me not to notice that before!'

Antonia stopped to catch her breath. 'Stop this, Myles. Give us the cup.'

'She's always telling me to stop,' he complained. '"Stop it, stop it, you're hurting!" Sometimes you can't hear yourself fuck! But then you'd know all about that, wouldn't you, Paddy old son?'

His eyes were red-rimmed and swollen. Antonia wondered if he'd been crying.

Patrick stood looking up at his friend. 'I'm sorry, man,' he said quietly. 'I didn't want this to happen.'

For a moment Myles' face worked. Then he snapped his fingers. '*De nada!* What's a fuck or two between friends?'

Antonia heard Patrick's sharp intake of breath. 'Myles,' she said. 'Tell us where you put the cup. Then we can all go home.'

'Fuck off,' he snarled.

'Come on, Antonia,' said Patrick. 'This is just a bloody waste of time.'

'Ooh,' Myles rolled his eyes, 'a *blurdy* waste of time! Doesn't it sound amateurish when a Yank says "bloody"? *Blurdy! Blurdy!*' And what about "bugger"? *Burrger. Burrger.*' He took another pull at the bottle. 'No prizes for guessing why that one's not a big winner across the Pond. What potential for confusion with the staple diet of the Great American Unwashed! Bugger, burger, bugger, burger. "Eskewz me, suh, but wuz thay-ut tew burgers or tew *buggers* yew wuz ay-uftah? 'Cos y'unnerstan', the burgers are in front, but the *buggers* are in back – if'n'y'all take mah meanin'!'"

Patrick touched her arm. 'Come on. Let's go.'

'Not without the cup,' she said.

'Antonia. Come. Now.'

'That's what *I'm* always telling her,' remarked Myles. 'Come now, for Christ's sake, because I am, and I'm fed up with waiting – but does she listen? Does she hell. Mind you,' he took another pull, 'you didn't need much urging last night, did you, old girl? Jesus, that was one Godalmighty seeing-to I gave you, wasn't it? No wonder you're sore at me – as they say –'

'Ignore him,' she told Patrick, 'he's making it up. Myles, stop being an idiot and tell us where you put the cup.'

Myles didn't answer. Instead he raised the bottle in a mocking toast. '*A cup of wine for the afternoon,*' he quoted, '*and* don't *let the water-jug near it. The Bacchus from these cellars flows* neat!' Then he drained the bottle and lobbed it over their heads into the gorge.

Antonia turned to Patrick. 'I'm going to the Source.'

'I told you,' he said, his face stony, 'that's what he wants.'

'I don't care.'

'Well I do.'

'Patrick—'

'*Jesus*, Antonia!' he burst out. 'Open your eyes! Can't you see you're playing into his hands? He's screwing you over, just like he's been doing all summer!'

'Well, not *all* summer,' put in Myles. 'If you remember, Patroclus, I've also been—'

'Oh yes,' said Patrick, tapping his temple, 'I forgot, you've also been screwing Nerissa.'

190

Antonia froze.

'But you knew that, right, Antonia?' Patrick's face was taut and furious. 'I mean, you must have asked yourself why he only sleeps with you on certain days of the week? It's because the rest of the time he's screwing her brains out! And you know why? Because he gets *bored* with all that Cassius crap! Don't look like that. You think I didn't know about your notes until today? Your big secret? He told me, Antonia. Just like he told everyone else in the goddamned village! Christ, girl, open your eyes!'

She stood there in the blazing sun while he hammered away at her, and her eyes were huge and dark in a face drained of blood.

Once he had started he couldn't stop. He was so angry – with Myles, with her, but mostly with himself, for letting this happen. For not saying the hell with it when they still had the chance, and getting her out of here. If he'd ignored all that crap about best friends, none of this would have happened.

And beneath his anger was the worst feeling of all, a churning black doubt that what Myles had said about spending the night with her was not simply the ravings of a drunk, but true.

That's ridiculous, he told himself firmly; this is Antonia we're talking about.

So? whispered a snide little voice inside his head. *She's no different than the others. Remember those sheets on her bed? How'd they get so messed up, if all she was doing last night was sleeping? Who knows, maybe she never* intended *to break up with Myles at all. I mean, think about it. The guy's rich and British and upper-class. Compared to that, what are you?*

Stop it, Patrick told himself. I will not let this come between us.

A few feet away from him, Antonia stood on the track twisting the pages she had collected into a roll. Her knuckles were white, and she was doing her best to ignore them both.

He went to her and told her he was sorry. She looked up and gave him a strained smile. She was struggling to keep a grip, and it hurt him to see the effort it took. 'That's OK,' she said. 'It doesn't matter.'

'Yes it does. I got angry. I got carried away. I'm sorry.' He wanted to say more, but Myles was watching them, feeding on the havoc he'd created. Patrick was damned if he was going to give him something else to laugh about.

And suddenly Patrick knew that if he didn't get out of there that minute, he would run up the slope and start pummelling his friend, and not stop until he'd killed him.

Antonia must have seen something in his face, for she put her hand on his chest and gave him a little shove and said, 'Go and find Modge.'

He said, 'Come with me,' and she said, 'Soon, but first I have to go up to the Source. Please, it's just something I have to do. You go and find Modge.'

Then she touched his hand and smiled at him, and his heart leapt, for this time it was a real smile, and he thought, it's going to be all right. We're going to get through this mess. And tonight we'll be together in that big old four-poster in Sainte Eulalie, just like we planned.

After Patrick had gone, Myles came down the slope and sat beneath an olive tree with his head on his knees. If it hadn't been for the *kántharos*, Antonia would have pitied him.

'Well, Achilles,' she said. 'You've just had a lucky escape. Another minute and Patroclus would have brained you.'

'Fuck off,' he mumbled without raising his head.

Without another word she left him, and climbed the last few hundred yards to the cave. Patrick was right. The *kántharos* wasn't there. She had no choice but to go back to the jeep and drive home, and hope that Myles would get bored and return the cup.

She found him where she had left him under the olive tree, and passed him without a word. A few minutes later he drew level with her, his face sullen and defeated.

Serves you bloody well right, she thought. I hope you get the mother of all hangovers.

She felt shaky and sick, her eyes scratchy with fatigue. And she wished she could stop the thoughts churning in her head. Nerissa. The *kántharos*. All that 'Cassius crap'. She wondered if Patrick felt the same way about that as Myles.

Oh, but he didn't mean that, she told herself wearily. He's exhausted. You both are. It'll be all right. Everything will be all right.

But when they got back to the jeep there was no sign of Patrick or Modge, and someone had shut Monsieur Panabière's new aluminium gate and blocked the way home. The jeep sat demurely behind the gate, ready and waiting to head off downhill. But a hefty padlock and chain had put paid to that.

Monsieur Panabière, thought Antonia exhaustedly. Barricading his farm against imaginary invaders.

This was all she needed. Now she faced a long, hot

walk down to the mill, with a sullen Myles complaining all the way. And still no *kántharos*.

Myles ran past the jeep and gave the gate a furious shake. 'This is the last fucking straw! *Now* what do we do?'

Antonia snorted. 'I'd have thought that was obvious. We climb over and walk.'

'You walk if you like,' he snapped, 'I'm driving.'

'Oh, yes? and how do you propose getting the gate open?'

'I *propose* that you nip over to Le Fig and sweet-talk that stupid old fart into giving us the key.'

Antonia stared at him. 'Nip over? It's more than two miles! And why should I? I wouldn't even be here if it weren't for you. Besides, he won't be in. It's Saturday. He goes to Mazerans to play *boules*.'

'Then we'll break in and find the key.'

'No way.'

His eyes took on a dangerous glint. 'Right,' he snapped, 'I'll *drive* to the fucking farm. Give me the keys.'

'Don't be ridiculous! That's not a track, it's a collection of pot-holes! I'm not letting you ruin my father's jeep just because—'

'Give me the keys, you slimy little bitch, or I'll come and get them!'

'Fine,' she muttered, fumbling in her pocket. She chucked the keys at him, and he caught them in one hand.

She turned on her heel and made for the gate.

Behind her she heard him gun the engine hard, then yank the jeep screamingly into gear.

'Don't force it, you idiot,' she shouted over her shoulder, 'you'll wreck the gearbox!'

Without looking up, he flipped her the finger.

She watched him back up jerkily past the farm track, then wrench the steering wheel round to make the turn. Again the gearbox shrieked as he ground it into first. Again she shouted at him to go easy.

He yelled at her to fuck off, and stepped on the gas.

Instead of going forwards, the jeep stayed in reverse. In a single bound it lurched backwards across the track to the edge of the gorge.

A cry died in her throat. In disbelief she watched one rear wheel slide smoothly over the side of the cliff. Dust and gravel flew. The wheel span over nothingness. Then, with a soft crumbling of earth, the other wheel went over.

Myles raised his head and met her eyes.

His face was blank, utterly blank, and the look they exchanged lasted for ever. Then the jeep tipped slowly backwards and slid into the gorge.

She couldn't cry out. Her throat had closed. She heard the rattle of pebbles trickling into the gorge. She felt the hot wind buffeting her face. She saw the context sheets fluttering into the air where the jeep had been. They were dazzling white and weirdly peaceful as they twisted on the wind. Like white birds fluttering against a pewter sky.

Somewhere behind her, Modge began to scream. A high, thin, piercing sound going on and on for ever. Then Patrick was running up and vaulting the gate, gripping her shoulder so hard that it hurt, and shouting at her to stay behind with Modge. Then he was scrambling down a goat track so steep that she screamed at him to stop, but he had already gone.

From far below came a terrific booming thunderclap, then a crackling like a forest fire. Suddenly black smoke was boiling up into the sky. Thick, bitter, oily black smoke. And a stink of petrol.

And always the context sheets: dazzling white and weirdly peaceful, fluttering like doves over the gorge.

CHAPTER FIFTEEN

*17 Wilton Row, Belgravia, Monday, 24 October
1988*

On the morning of the inquest, the Passmores break-
fasted earlier than usual, and Patrick was the last to
come downstairs.

He had slept badly. Since the accident he always slept
badly. And he felt tired all the time. Tired and heavy and
slow. Was that grief? It didn't feel like grief. More like
disbelief. A deep-rooted sense that none of this was
happening.

Myles' mother and stepfather and Modge were
already in the beautiful blue and white breakfast room.
As Patrick came in, all three looked up at him and
smiled. Modge slid off her chair and went into the
kitchen to tell Nadja to bring his orange juice.

'You're looking rather peaky, old chap,' remarked
Julian Passmore. 'Are those wretched burns giving you
trouble again?'

'They're all right,' said Patrick. 'Thanks.' He took his
seat, and poured coffee awkwardly into his cup with his
right hand. These days he did everything awkwardly,
but this morning felt worse than usual because he was
in a suit and tie. He hadn't worn a suit since Finals. It
felt like a straitjacket.

'Isn't it about time that Dr Foster took another look at your hand?' said Debra Passmore.

Patrick glanced at her. 'It's fine. Thank you.'

'It's no trouble. I'll get Nadja to make an appointment.'

Patrick thanked her.

They resumed their breakfast.

Patrick drank his coffee, and watched Myles' mother buttering a slice of toast – to add to the two slices already on her plate, which she would also forget to eat.

He and Julian exchanged glances. Julian's square, shrewd face tightened with concern.

Debra pushed the toast to one side and started flicking through the stack of faxes at her elbow which her clerk had sent overnight.

Myles had nicknamed his mother the Queen of Sheba, and Patrick could understand why. She had imperious dark eyes in a finely sculpted face, and when she spoke, her jaw clenched so tightly that the muscles knotted.

She was well groomed in a way which indicated that she wasn't interested in her appearance, but made the necessary effort because it mattered to those around her. Her glossy auburn hair was efficiently bobbed, and she wore minimal makeup, and no jewellery except for plain pearl studs. Today, as always, she was dressed in a tailored suit, a slightly mannish striped blouse, and a matching bow tie. Modge had told Patrick that her mother had a dozen suits like this one, as well as two dozen striped shirts and two dozen bow ties.

From what little Myles had said about his mother, Patrick guessed that he had been in awe of her. He sympathized. He was in awe of her himself.

But she had been briskly kind to him, as had her husband. Much kinder than he deserved. When he had arrived at their house three days before, he had been astonished to be given an entire floor for his own.

Seventeen, Wilton Row, SW1. An innocuous address. How was he to know that Wilton Row would turn out to be a discreetly opulent line of stuccoed townhouses just behind Buckingham Palace? Buckingham *Palace*, for Christ's sake!

His room was a padded oasis of deep navy carpets, quilted chintz bedspreads, and overlong curtains shutting out the world. In addition to the bedroom, he had a palatial navy-tiled bathroom, a study, and a sitting room equipped with a flat-screen television, a VCR and a Bang & Olufsen CD player.

An entire floor. As if, instead of leaving tomorrow, he was staying for good.

Across the table, Julian Passmore frowned at his *Times*. He doesn't look like a judge, thought Patrick in bemusement. Although what do judges look like, anyhow?

He found himself wishing Nerissa was here to help him cope with all this. But Nerissa was in Paris with Simon, and would only be back for the funeral. Julian had remarked to Patrick with surprising sharpness that his daughter was probably staying away out of pique, because she hadn't been asked to give evidence at the inquest.

Lucky Nerissa, Patrick thought.

Looking at Myles' parents across the table, he felt more of an impostor than ever. No, impostor wasn't the right word. He felt worse than that. He was a *usurper*. He shouldn't be here. He didn't deserve any of this.

Again that sense of disbelief. How had he got here?

He remembered stepping out of the little police station in Mazerans just after signing his statement.

That must have been a couple of days after his release from hospital, and three or four after the accident.

He was standing on the pavement beneath a plane tree when it struck him that apart from the loose change in his pocket, he had no money. He had blown everything on the three-star Michelin in Sainte Eulalie. And now he was alone in Mazerans with no way of getting back to La Bastide. Julian, Debra and Modge had dropped him at the police station, then driven on to Perpignan to make arrangements for having Myles flown back to London. Antonia and her parents had returned to England the previous day, and Simon and Nerissa had already left for Paris.

But if the Passmores had been with him, he would not have asked for a loan. They were wealthy to the point when money was an irrelevance, and prodigal in their generosity. It was that generosity which would have ruled out a loan. That and Myles.

He had wandered out into the place de la Mairie and bumped into Madame Merou, the baker's wife, who gave him a lift to La Bastide in return for his answering a few casual but achingly curious questions about the accident. Back in the village, he bumped into Monsieur Panabière, who lent him a hundred francs. Patrick felt OK about taking a loan from the old man, who was curt and no-nonsense and fully expected to be repaid, which he would be.

After leaving Monsieur Panabière, Patrick went up to Les Limoniers and threw his stuff in his rucksack, then walked over the bridge and out onto the road, where he caught the bus to Toulouse.

It was all bizarrely easy, with the fluidity of a dream. Except that the bus was delayed on the freeway and he missed his plane, by which time there wasn't enough left of the hundred francs to buy a hamburger. So all in all, it took quite a few days to get back to Oxford.

He remembered letting himself into Myles' house in Norham Gardens, having hitched from Dover and slept rough in a bus shelter somewhere along the M40.

He had stood blinking in the hallway, breathing in the house's familiar dirty-sock smell. The utter *disbelief* of being there without Myles. His friend's clutter was everywhere: his rugby shirt draped over the banisters; his CDs littering the floor; his favourite Snoopy mug – still one-third full of scummy tea – perched halfway up the stairs. Beside it lay the copy of *A Brief History of Time* which Myles had bought when it became a best-seller, then conveniently forgot, in favour of the new Wilbur Smith.

Patrick had teased him about that. 'Myles, you're such a poser! You're never going to read that thing!' Myles had laughed, and chucked a beer can at his head, and called him a wanker.

Twenty minutes later Patrick moved out, and paid a month's deposit on a tiny room in Jericho with the help of a hastily arranged and exorbitant bank loan. He still had the money in the bank which he had set aside for Myles as 'rent', but the thought of using it filled him with horror. He would have to give it to Oxfam.

He remembered sitting on the sagging bed in Jericho, wondering how to find Antonia. He no longer had her address, having lost the scrap of paper she had given him before she left. And there were hundreds of Hunts in the phone book.

Then he wondered if he should get in touch with her at all. Did he deserve her, after what he'd done to Myles?

Two days later, Mr Passmore ('Oh, call me Julian, there's a good chap. "Mr Passmore" sounds like a bank manager') turned up unannounced. Patrick never found out how he had traced him. Modge came with her father, and when she saw Patrick she gave a little mew, and fell on him like a long-lost brother.

Julian didn't ask Patrick where he had been all this time, and he gracefully accepted Patrick's refusal of the house in Norham Gardens 'for as long as he liked'. To make amends, Patrick offered to help sort out the house and dispose of Myles' belongings.

That turned out to be a lengthier task than either of them had anticipated, for to their astonishment they found that Myles had hoarded *everything*, from cards inviting him to birthday parties a decade ago, to his prep school reports and O-level exam papers. The school mementoes struck Patrick as particularly bizarre, for Myles had hated school. Perhaps he had kept them because he knew that no-one else would.

All that had been, what? Just over a week ago? Only a week?

Now he watched Modge put down her orange juice and quietly ask her mother if she could leave the table. Debra let her go with a tightening of the lips. She had made no secret of wanting her daughter to accompany them to the inquest, but the doctor had pronounced it 'most inadvisable', and for once Julian had gone against his wife and insisted that Modge should stay at home with the housekeeper.

Debra had taken some persuading. It was as if she failed to see why her daughter should be spared the forthcoming ordeal, when she was not.

For Debra Passmore, grief was an angry business. Hers was a deep-burning anger which rarely surfaced, but nevertheless made the house crackle with tension.

And now Patrick was about to make it worse.

'If it's OK with you,' he began carefully, 'I'll meet you at the Coroner's Court just before the hearing? I've arranged to meet Antonia and her mother for a cup of coffee.'

Debra raised her eyes from her faxes to look at him. Then, in that clenched-jaw way of hers, she said the exact opposite of what she meant. 'Of course. What a good idea.'

'What time are you meeting them?' Julian asked with his genial smile, monitoring his wife from the corner of his eye.

'About eight-thirty,' Patrick replied.

'That's good,' said Debra. 'The hearing's at ten, so you'll have plenty of time. We'll see you in court at about, say, nine forty-five?'

'Fine,' said Patrick.

'Good,' said Debra, and flashed him a brief smile, to reassure him that however much she might deplore his seeing Antonia, she did not hold it against *him*.

Why, he wondered, has she taken so violently against Antonia, but not against me?

Right from the start, when she and her husband had stepped from the enormous rented BMW on the morning after the accident, Debra had loathed Antonia with a visceral, wrenching hatred that was beyond all reason or appeal.

That girl, she would call her, when the iron clamps on her grief had been loosened by wine. 'If *that girl* hadn't thrown him the keys when he was *obviously* unfit to drive, he would be alive today!'

Patrick couldn't bear it when she talked like that. He wished he had the courage to say to her, OK, Debra, so Antonia threw him the keys. But she never meant for anything bad to happen. None of this is her fault! And if you think she's to blame, what about me? I was his friend, and I took everything from him. I took his trust and his hospitality. I took his girl. That's why he was drunk, Debra. That's why he couldn't handle the goddamned jeep. That's why he died. Do you ever think about that? Christ, I do. Every minute of every day.

But how could you say such things to a woman whose only son has been crushed and incinerated beyond recognition? Whose only means of coping is to turn her rage outward on someone else?

Oh, how he longed for Antonia. Since the accident he had hardly seen her, and never once alone. She had been at her mom's house in Suffolk all this time, and they got by on stilted telephone calls in which she assured him she was fine, in that very British way of hers which could mean anything from 'genuinely OK' to 'teetering on the edge of a nervous breakdown'. She sounded so numb and flattened out that he wondered if she was on sedatives, but she said she wasn't, and he believed her. He guessed he probably sounded the same.

These days, she rarely returned his calls. At first that had worried him, but now he was beginning to accept it. Maybe that was how it should be. After what had happened, how could he ride off into the sunset with Myles' girl?

Debra shuffled her faxes into a neat pile and tucked them under her arm. 'I've got to call chambers.'

Julian glanced up from his newspaper. 'Darling, do you think that's wise? To work now – it's too much of a strain . . .'

'It'll be more of a strain if they botch things and I have to sort them out later,' she replied.

Patrick saw how she gripped the faxes. Maybe she needed them right now.

She turned to him. 'Patrick, I forgot to tell you. We've arranged to go to the church on Wednesday at three, to go over the music for the service. You'll come, won't you?'

Patrick blinked. Today was Monday. Tomorrow he planned to return to Oxford. He wasn't sure what he would *do* there – apart from trying to find some kind of job – and of course, he had to return to London for the funeral, whenever that turned out to be. But he was certain he had told the Passmores that he was leaving tomorrow.

Debra picked up his hesitation. 'You'll stay for another couple of weeks, won't you?'

'Say yes, old chap,' said Julian. 'It would mean a lot to us. In fact, I don't think we can do without you. Modge certainly can't.' He softened that with one of his charming smiles, but he meant every word.

Patrick glanced from one to the other. He tried to return the smile, but his face felt stiff. Maybe that was the burns. 'Thank you,' he said. 'You're very kind.'

Before he left the house, he climbed to the top floor to say goodbye to Modge.

She was in the playroom, crouching on the hearthrug before a low table on which two Sindy dolls were having a furious row. A model Range Rover was parked beside them, perilously close to the edge. A roll of white paper protruded from its open boot, as if the Sindies had just bought a new rug and were bringing it home.

'No, *you* drive!' muttered Modge, butting the dolls' heads together. Her face was pinched and anxious. She was not enjoying the game.

'Hi,' said Patrick, pulling a chair closer to the table.

'Hi,' mumbled Modge without looking up.

He nodded at the Sindy dolls. 'Those guys look as if they're pretty mad at each other.'

Modge tightened her lips. 'It'll be all right. They're going to make friends again.'

'Sure. But you know, it's OK for them to be cross with each other for a while. Doesn't mean they're not still friends, and all.'

Which he had to admit was somewhat lacking in subtlety.

Apparently Modge thought so too, for she ignored him.

For several days after the accident she had been as clingy and dependent as a five-year-old, never letting Patrick or Antonia or her father out of her sight, and having screaming nightmares every night.

Then, a week later, she suddenly got better. She 'put it behind her', as Julian said, with undisguised relief. Now she spent most of her time in the playroom alone with her dolls. Julian talked of finding her a different boarding-school, to help her make a complete break with the past: perhaps one where she would be allowed to keep the pony she had always wanted.

'Children are astonishingly resilient,' Debra assured Patrick briskly, on the one occasion when he wondered aloud if the eight-year-old was really getting over her brother's death, or simply bottling everything up. Debra was probably right. She was the kid's mother, after all. And what did he know about kids?

One of the Sindies was now behind the wheel of the Range Rover, which teetered precariously on the edge of the table. The other Sindy shoved a rigid arm under the windscreen and yanked the car back to safety. The roll of paper slid from the boot and dropped onto the rug.

'Whoah, they've lost their load,' said Patrick. He reached for it.

'No!' cried Modge.

Her hand came down on his. Her grip was feverishly hot. He wondered what the roll represented to her. The adored older brother whom she had seen fall to his death?

He offered it to her. 'Here you go. All safe and sound.'

But she wouldn't take it.

He turned it in his fingers, and three neat, pencilled initials caught his eye. 'AEH/88'.

Antonia Elizabeth Hunt.

Frowning, he slipped off the elastic band and spread the paper on the table.

He found himself looking down at Antonia's half-finished line drawing of the *kántharos* reliefs. There in front of him was Pegasus, trotting joyfully towards his perpetually postponed reunion with Bellerophon.

He felt as if he were seeing them through deep water. Once, he had gazed on this young man's face and been awed into silence. But that had been a million years ago. It had happened to someone else.

His voice was hoarse as he asked Modge where she had found the drawing.

She did not reply. She was pushing the Range Rover slowly round the rug, her face pale and taut.

Gently, Patrick asked if Myles had given her the drawing.

The Range Rover completed a full circuit before she gave a slight nod.

'So he – uh – he got you to help take the cup, did he? As well as the other stuff?'

Another long pause. Another almost imperceptible nod.

Oh, *Myles*. Getting your kid sister involved in something like this! The context sheets were one thing – but the *kántharos*?

'Any idea where he put it?' he asked quietly. 'The cup, I mean?'

A vehement shake of the head.

'Because you see, Imogen, it's gone missing. Dr Hunt has looked all over, but he can't find it. And he really needs it, and Antonia too. It matters a lot to them. So it'd help if you knew where it was.' He wondered if he ought to leave it at that. The last thing he wanted was to pressurize her. Then he thought of Antonia.

Feeling slightly ashamed, he tried again. 'Are you sure you don't know where it is?'

Her face became puffy. 'Cross my heart and hope to die.'

He winced at the grim schoolgirl oath. 'It's OK, honey, I believe you. It's no big deal.'

The Range Rover did another circuit, then pulled up. 'Patrick?'

'Yeah?'

'Don't tell on me.'

'About what, honey?'

'That I helped Myles steal the cup thing.'

'Hey, it wasn't your fault! No-one's going to blame you.'

The Range Rover started up again. 'If you tell on me, the policemen will come and take me away.'

'No they won't. Policemen don't take little girls away from their moms. That's the God's honest truth, I swear it.'

She raised her head and gave him an unblinking stare. 'They will,' she said flatly. 'They'll ask questions and find out.'

'Find out what?'

A long pause. 'I was cross with him.'

He remembered the furious red-faced goblin marching down the track towards them. It wasn't hard to guess the way her mind worked. She'd had a fight with her brother, and he had been killed. Therefore it was her fault.

Patrick knew about stuff like that. He remembered the night before his mom walked out, when he'd had a pitched battle with her about being allowed to watch some dumb TV show, and she'd sent him to bed, and he'd lain awake muttering extravagant curses. The next day when he came home from school she was gone. His dad said she'd gone back to England. Patrick never saw her again. It was years before he could shake off the conviction that his curses had sent her away.

He tried to tell Modge about that, explaining as best he could that bad thoughts can't hurt people, and that she hadn't caused the accident by being mad at her brother.

She didn't seem to hear him. So much for Patrick McMullan the would-be therapist.

The only thing that had any effect was when he rolled up the line drawing and put it in his pocket. For safe keeping, he said, if that was OK?

It was. In fact she seemed relieved that the drawing was no longer her responsibility. She sat on the rug looking more than ever like a small intense goblin, and fixed him with her long-lashed brown eyes. 'Promise you won't tell on me at the trial.'

'Honey, it's not a trial. It's an inquest. A kind of hearing they have when someone dies in an accident, to find out what happened. Nobody gets blamed. And no, I won't be saying anything about you, because none of this stuff will come up. They only want to know about the accident.'

She didn't even blink. 'Promise you won't tell.'

'If it makes you feel better, sure. I promise.'

The Range Rover was back on its rounds, but now it had become an ambulance. '*Bee-bor, Bee-bor*,' crooned Modge.

What had he been thinking of, letting an eight-year-old wander off on that hillside on her own? Surely he could have found some way to protect her from what she'd seen?

But she had been spared nothing, for he had caught up with her on a bend in the track which afforded a fine, clear view of the jeep's obscenely graceful descent into the gorge.

He shut his eyes.

The bitter stink of gasoline clogged his nose and mouth and throat, and the furnace heat came at him in waves: singeing hair, searing eyes, scorching face and ears. His lungs swelled to bursting point, and when he staggered back it felt so good – so *good* – to get out of the heat.

In that moment, as he staggered back from the heat, he was forced to acknowledge what part of his mind had known since he first saw the jeep go over the edge. That it was hopeless. He would never reach Myles at the heart of the fireball.

He stood there powerless, with the stench of gasoline in his nose and mouth and throat. And beneath it he caught another smell: a sweet, sticky smell like roasting pork, that would stay with him for ever.

That was when the storm finally broke. Rain stung his eyes. But it was a treacherously feeble patter, blown this way and that by the wind, and doing nothing to quench the flames. The promise of the thunderheads had been false.

Already his eyes were swelling shut with the heat, and he was half blind as he turned and lurched downriver towards the mill. Go, go for help, *go*. Through his T-shirt the fireball scorched his back, and he heard its roar above the thunder of the river and his own rasping battle for air. Lightning made the path a stroboscopic nightmare of crazily flaring rocks.

As he reached the mill, pain flared in face and neck and hands. His jaws clamped shut in an animal grind. His chest heaved with tearing gulps which only left him hungrier for air. He crashed into the kitchen and fumbled with blackened fingers for the phone. His right hand blazed with pain, but his left had gone mercifully numb. On first reaching the jeep, he had used that hand to yank open the door and get to Myles. All he'd achieved was to sear away his fingertips and a diagonal strip across the palm. He peered down at the mess of oozing red meat that was his left hand. Forget about it. It belonged to someone else. Focus on the phone.

It was the worst kind of anxiety dream, for he didn't know the number to call. What did you call for an emergency in France? Was there a single number, like 911 in the States? Or were there different ones for fire, ambulance, police? Ah Christ, Christ, where was the fucking *number*?

Then Antonia was beside him, her face the colour of concrete, and she grabbed the receiver and punched in the numbers and jabbered away in French. Her voice came from far and far away, and Modge was clinging to her breast and keening like a puppy.

Then his eyes swelled shut and he was blind, his world reduced to the agony in his hand, and the choking bitterness of smoke. Antonia pushed him down onto a chair and wrapped his face and neck in wet cloths, and rinsed his hands, and shoved them into what sounded crazily like plastic bags.

All the time she was talking to him as if to an animal, her voice low and shaky, telling him he was going to be all right. He hung onto the sound of her voice. But he knew without consciously forming the thought that from now on nothing was going to be all right, ever again. The fireball had seen to that.

Four weeks on, he could still taste the oily bitterness of smoke, still smell that sweet, sticky undertow. That smell. It clung to clothes and hair and skin and memory. He would never be free of it.

And now Modge, with a child's unthinking egotism, believed she had killed her brother. She had been angry with him and he had died. Therefore she was a murderer.

He stood up, feeling big and clumsy and useless.

Myles had asked Patrick to look after his little sister – and all he had achieved was to ensure that she was in exactly the right place to watch her brother crushed and burned to death.

He went downstairs slowly, feeling the guilt tightening around him like a straitjacket.

After Patrick had gone, Modge put the jeep back on the cliff and started all over again.

The blond Sindy in the jeep was the brother, and the Sindy with the brown hair was the little sister. The little sister was the rescuer, who only said *nice* things about the brother and thought *nice* thoughts, and opened the gate so that the jeep could drive off down the hill, instead of having to back up, and go over the cliff.

Patrick said wishes couldn't hurt, but Patrick was wrong. The sister knew better. The sister had been cross with the brother. She had wanted him to clamber over the gate and fall and maybe bump his knee, so that everyone would laugh at *him* for a change. And look what had happened.

Down in the street, a car door slammed. The sister gave a terrified start. She couldn't *bear* that sound. She pressed her fist to her chest, and waited for the thumping to slow down.

Bad car.

It was just as well that cars lived in streets and couldn't climb stairs. If she stayed up here, the sister would be safe. She would be safe as long as she stayed upstairs, and never went near cars.

The thumping was slower now. Time to start again. The sister and the brother and the jeep.

And remember, everything is the other way round. The sister only thinks *nice* thoughts, and is the *rescuer*, and the *opener* of the gate.

CHAPTER SIXTEEN

'No doubt you'll think me old-fashioned,' remarked Evelyn Hunt as she wove Antonia's hair into a thick French plait, 'but I can't help thinking that some of those old traditions really made *sense*. In my mother's day when someone died, one went into mourning. There were lots of complicated rules about what one could and couldn't wear, and one jolly well stuck to them. Of course the point was to keep everyone occupied after the death, but there was more to it than that. Mourning dress makes sense. It gives people an indication of what one's going through. People in the street, in shops, one's acquaintances. It's kinder to the bereaved, and so much less embarrassing for everyone else. These days, they have ribbons for everything, don't they? All those dear little ribbons for AIDS and breast cancer, and heaven knows what else – but nothing for simple mourning.'

Simple mourning. Mourning Myles. It sounded bizarre. And not simple at all.

Antonia sat at the dressing-table in her room in Montpelier Street and watched her mother's reflection as she fixed the plait which had defeated her.

These days, the simplest tasks were beyond her grasp. She felt numb, and slightly sick. And cold all the time.

But the deeper feelings – like sorrow and pity and grief

– eluded her. She couldn't feel them. She couldn't even cry. It was as if she was sleepwalking.

Surprise, though, was something she could feel. She felt it now, at the comfort she took from being bossed around by her mother.

Evelyn Hunt had flown out the day after the accident and taken everything in hand. She had closed down the dig, paid off a bemused and shaken Simon, and found him lodgings in Paris with a friend of hers. Then she had shut up the mill, and briskly flown her husband and daughter home. She took Antonia with her to Suffolk, and dispatched her husband to Caroline in Gloucestershire, where he stayed – before, during, and after his resignation from the faculty.

He had not been called to give evidence at the inquest, and would not be leaving his bolt-hole to lend Antonia moral support. He had told his wife that he was not well enough to attend the hearing, and she had accepted that with the slightly impatient tolerance with which she met most of his pronouncements.

But he did not fool Antonia. Since the accident, he could scarcely bring himself to speak to her. He blamed her for the wreck of his career. 'It's not that it was her *fault*,' he had complained to his wife during one of their brief telephone conversations, while Antonia eavesdropped on the extension in her room. 'But manifestly it was her *responsibility*. So typical of her. I go away for a much-needed break leaving her in charge, and look what happens!'

Curiously, it was not Myles' death which he found hardest to take, or even the ruin of the dig, but the loss of the *kántharos*. He seemed to have adopted it retrospectively as his own. It had become the Great Find which would have made his name. Until it had been lost through a daughter's negligence.

'Who was that on the phone just now?' asked Antonia.

Her mother's mouth set.

Antonia tensed. 'Not the police again?'

'Who would have thought the French would be so thorough?' She gave Antonia's shoulder a little squeeze. 'Don't worry, darling. It's just a small point in your statement which they want to clear up. I told them you'd call back after the hearing.'

The *kántharos* would have been a national treasure, for Cassius had always been hugely popular with the French, and the authorities were desperate to recover it. Her father had notified them of the find while he was in Toulouse, and when it went missing the following day, in circumstances which were, to say the least, obscure, it was hardly surprising that they should be suspicious.

They had taken pains to assure Antonia that they did not, of course, suspect her of anything improper. But still. Did she honestly have *no* idea where the cup might be?

The enquiry made her feel like a criminal, and she hadn't mentioned it to Patrick. What was the point in making him feel worse than he already did? Besides, it would all blow over. Wouldn't it?

'Your young man phoned while you were in the bath,' said her mother, securing the finished plait with a black velvet ribbon, and scrutinizing her handiwork with a critical eye. 'He said not to bother you, he just wanted to check that we knew which coffee shop to go to. I must say he sounds nice. Much less of an accent than one would expect.'

Antonia met her mother's eyes in the mirror, and pressed her lips together in the expected smile.

'And I do like the way he calls you Antonia rather than Toni.'

Antonia was surprised. 'So do I.'

'Finally!' Her mother rolled her eyes in exaggerated relief. Catching her daughter's enquiring glance, she added, 'Well, I've always wondered how long you intended to cling to that horrendous nickname.'

'What do you mean? I never even liked it.'

'Darling, you were the one who chose it! Don't you remember?'

Antonia shook her head.

'One day when you were five, you declared, "I'm Toni. Nobody call me anything else." So that was that.'

'I don't remember.'

'Trust me, it happened. You absolutely *loathed* your name. Well, you loathed anything "girlish". Dolls. Dresses. And – heaven forfend – puffed sleeves. I suppose it was because they reminded you of Caroline, and were therefore utterly beyond the pale.' She shook her head. 'I never could fathom you. Still can't. Caroline was always so much easier.'

And yet, her expression seemed to say, you're still my daughter, and you need me, so here I am.

Antonia's mother was a tall, slender, dark-haired woman who held herself as straight as a backboard, and was still crisply beautiful at fifty-two. In honour of the inquest she wore one of her beloved Margaret Howell suits: a short boxy jacket in navy worsted, with wide trousers cropped to reveal delicate ankles. Beneath it she wore a shantung T-shirt in a subtle heather and indigo fleck, with her favourite 'everyday' Theo Fennell neck-lace and earrings. The thick gold chain sat perfectly over the neck of the T-shirt, and discreetly picked up the gilt buckles of her Ferragamo flats.

She would be wildly overdressed for the Coroner's Court, but it wouldn't perturb her in the least. Evelyn Hunt had been educated at Benenden and 'finished' in Switzerland ('In my day, girls went to Geneva or Lausanne, one never *considered* Oxford or Cambridge'). As far as she was concerned, one dressed 'properly' for all public occasions, and that included an inquest.

For the same reason she had insisted on buying her daughter a sleek Gérard Darel trouser-suit in supple charcoal wool, along with a shawl-collared blouse in eau-de-nil silk, and narrow black Galliano loafers. She had been implacable about 'decent' makeup, and a manicure at Harvey Nick's.

Antonia had mounted a half-hearted protest, and then caved in. Now she was surprised at how much better she felt for being 'properly turned out'.

She said so, and earned a wry smile from her mother. Really, darling! It hardly takes an Oxford degree to grasp that being properly turned out bolsters one's morale, now does it? In fact, a degree rather gets in the way, don't you find?

Mrs Hunt glanced at her watch, and her eyebrows shot up. 'Nearly eight already! We'd better hurry or we'll be late.'

Antonia stood up, and in her stomach a host of butterflies lifted off. In half an hour she would see Patrick again. Patrick, her lifeline to reality.

In the weeks since the accident, she had moved in a perpetual haze. Voices, faces, her own thoughts, all came to her at one remove, as if observed through glass or under water. Only in her talks with Patrick did the world take on depth and substance: the colours seeping back, the photograph coming to life. She clung to the thought that some day, after all this ghastliness was over, they still had a chance to be together.

It had been terrible when he went incommunicado for those two weeks. She had been convinced that he was gone for good – that he had fallen off the edge of the world, like Myles. Even now, although she telephoned the house in Wilton Row every day, he didn't always call back. To begin with she had worried that he no longer wanted to speak to her, but recently she had begun to suspect that Mrs Passmore wasn't passing on her messages.

That struck Antonia as entirely understandable. After all, she had killed Debra Passmore's son.

In one of their less stilted telephone conversations, Patrick had told Antonia how he had taken the Underground to St James's Park to check out the Coroner's Court. 'A truly weird neighbourhood,' he had said. 'You come out through this bizarre kind of Forties-style shopping-mall, and there, bang slap in your face, is New Scotland Yard. How to feel like a criminal, or what?'

He was right, she thought, as she and her mother left the taxi a few streets from the coffee bar and walked the rest of the way to get some air. It was an odd neighbourhood.

'Neither fish nor fowl,' her mother declared.

Antonia took it in her stride. She was getting used to unreality.

It was chilly for October, and had been mizzling since before dawn. They passed a street market with half-built stalls, their plastic rain-covers flapping dismally. Then a tall glitzy office block with glass lifts gliding up and down, then a launderette, a run-down family planning clinic, and an exquisite little Georgian terrace dwarfed by enormous concrete offices left over from the pre-glitz era.

Myles would have hated it, thought Antonia. Especially the family planning clinic. '*Oh, yuk,*' he would have complained, '*how horribly Kevin and Sharon!*' She had the strangest sense that she would be seeing him later, and could tell him all about it.

She waited with her mother in the Italian coffee bar which Patrick had described on the phone. It was a light, pleasant office-workers' retreat, with brass-framed mirrors and gleaming green tiles, and pretty little marble-topped tables. Outside in the Horseferry Road, buses and taxis thundered past. On the pavement, a small pewter-coloured sapling with no buds dripped rain onto a pile of black plastic rubbish bags.

Suddenly Patrick was standing by the table, and her mother was smiling up at him and introducing herself, then serenely 'taking herself off' to find the court and wait for them there.

It was unbelievable to see him again. She had forgotten the light in his eyes, and how very blue they were.

He no longer wore the dressings on his face and neck, which now merely looked as if he had a mild case of sunburn down one side, though she noticed that his smile was a little lopsided, as if the scorching, or the memory of it, still caused him pain. His hair had been cut very short, presumably to get rid of the burnt bits, but his eyebrows and lashes no longer looked singed.

His right hand had the same smooth sunburn as his face, but the left was still encased in bulky dressings. The doctors said it was a serious burn, which might mean skin grafts, plastic surgery, and perhaps learning to write again. 'Boring stuff,' Patrick said, clearly reluctant to go into detail.

She watched him go to the counter to buy their coffee. He wore what she guessed must be the subfusc suit in which he had sat his Finals. She had never seen him in a suit before. It made him look tall and rangy and intimidatingly elegant, despite the badly ironed white shirt.

Something nudged her memory. The shoes – hadn't Myles told her some story about the shoes? Ah yes, she remembered. Before Finals, Myles had counselled his friend on what kind of black shoes he should buy to go with the suit. Myles had been adamant that Church's brogues were the only conceivable thing, but Patrick had said, hell no, not at sixty pounds a pair, and returned in triumph a few hours later with his Covered Market purchase. Myles had been appalled, and genuinely distressed at the imminent ruin of his friend's reputation. 'You can't wear *black suede loafers* with a *suit*! Honestly, Paddy, haven't I taught you *anything*?'

Patrick brought their coffee and sat down opposite her. 'You look incredible,' he said bluntly. 'Black suits you.'

'You too.'

They stirred their coffee. It smelt rich and strong. It made her feel sick.

She groped for something to say. 'Are you . . .' she began. 'I mean, is any of your family coming to the hearing?'

He looked at her blankly.

'I thought – your mother being English, she might come along? Or – you might have relatives here?'

He shook his head. 'My mom died a few years back. There's an aunt somewhere in the Midlands. I called her once, just after I came to Britain, but . . .' He shrugged.

She asked him how Modge was doing.

'OK, I guess. At least—' he broke off. 'To be honest, I don't know. I don't even know how *I* am. None of this is real.'

They sat for a while in silence. Then he put out his good hand and touched hers. 'I've missed you,' he said, without looking at her.

'Me too.'

With his thumb he stroked the back of her hand. 'You know, it's weird. I'm really nervous about this hearing. I don't know why. I mean, all we've got to do is tell the truth, right? But it feels like Finals all over again.'

'I know. Me too.'

'I wish we could get it over with quickly. Too bad there's another inquest before ours.' He frowned. 'I mean, before this.'

She swallowed. 'Coming second. He wouldn't have liked that.'

He gave her his lopsided smile. 'But I guess he'd enjoy all the attention, huh?'

Abruptly, she couldn't look at him any more. She bowed her head over her coffee and felt the tears welling up. Her throat closed. The tears wouldn't come.

It had been like that since the accident. She couldn't cry. Perhaps that was why she felt sick all the time.

'All I can think about,' she said in a strangled voice, 'is his face as the jeep went over. I dream about it every night. He looked so blank. So utterly blank.' She drew a shaky breath. 'Then after the jeep disappeared, there was the longest time till it hit the rocks. That endless silence while he fell. And all that time – all that *time* – he must have known he was going to die.'

Suddenly the coffee shop was unbearably hot. She couldn't breathe. 'I keep wondering when he lost consciousness. I tell myself it must have been when he hit the rocks. I mean, as *soon* as he hit? It would have been then, wouldn't it? Instantaneous. A blackout. He wouldn't have known . . . he wouldn't have – felt – anything. In the fire.'

He made no reply. He just went on gently stroking the back of her hand, while she sat with her head bent low, panting out her grief.

After a while she straightened and rubbed her dry eyes. Her head throbbed with unshed tears.

They sat together in silence, while office workers bought cappuccino and muffins, and the buses thundered past outside. Then Patrick said, 'Your mom seems nice.'

It sounded so absurd that she gave an unsteady laugh. 'She is. I don't think I realized it till now.'

He glanced at the clock on the wall. Twenty to ten. 'We've got to go.'

She stood up. 'Let's get this over with,' she said.

They said goodbye on the steps outside the Coroner's Court. The Passmores would be waiting for him inside, and they both knew that Debra's presence would make further contact difficult.

As he held the door open for her, she looked up at him and said, 'After the hearing, can we – still see each other, do you think? Can we?'

He looked down at her for a moment. He tried to smile, but it wouldn't come.

'I – I mean,' she stammered, 'if you still want to?'

He opened his mouth. 'I still want to,' he said at last.

He reached into his breast pocket and brought out a folded sheet of notepaper and handed it to her: quickly, as if he might change his mind and take it back. On it he had set out his address and telephone number in

Oxford, along with instructions on how to get there. He had been forced to type it, as his left hand was still in bandages. She pictured him hunched over a typewriter, tapping out the letters with one finger.

Shakily she folded the notepaper and put it in her pocket. 'I'll call you after the hearing.'

'After the hearing. Right.'

It was only later, as she waited with her mother to go into the courtroom, that she realized that his answer had been equivocal. 'I still *want* to see you,' he had said.

Not: 'we still can'.

CHAPTER SEVENTEEN

Scouting the neighbourhood before the hearing, Patrick had been astonished by the Coroner's Court.

He had expected something institutional and bland, but what he found was an incongruously pretty Victorian mansion: a gingerbread house of fancy stonework and fairytale turrets, with a brightly coloured crest above the door. Only the neatly printed sign, *This is NOT the Magistrates' Court*, confirmed that he had indeed located the court of Her Majesty's Coroner.

Stepping inside now was like entering a time-warp: not so much Hansel and Gretel as Anthony Trollope. The walls were freshly painted a restful lemon yellow, with glossy white dado rails, and polished mahogany banisters. The stairs were thickly carpeted in forest green, and overlooked by gilt-framed portraits of clever and kindly men.

On the first floor was a dinky little waiting room which everyone ignored in favour of the landing: Patrick and the Passmores, Antonia and her mother (the two groups as far apart as possible, and with the minimum of greeting), a fireman and two policemen, and three people who seemed to belong to the first inquest. These last looked as ill at ease as Patrick felt: two heavy middle-aged men with motorcycle helmets at their feet, and a plump, raddled woman in black leggings and high-heeled pumps. All three were chain-smoking, and swapping muted jokes to keep up their spirits.

From the corner of his eye, Patrick saw Antonia thread her way between the motorcycle helmets to the window. She gave the woman in the leggings a brief smile, and was rewarded with an edgy 'isn't it awful?' grimace.

After about ten minutes, a fat young blonde in a white blouse and black skirt threw open the courtroom doors, and everyone filed in.

The courtroom could have been a Victorian gentleman's smoking-room. It was carpeted in burgundy, with fresh cream walls, more oil paintings, a pretty vaulted skylight pattering with rain, and a flamboyantly ugly fireplace with an olive porcelain surround. The only sign that it was a courtroom were five rows of mahogany seats with burgundy plastic cushions, and the coroner's desk, mounted on a dais a modest four inches high.

It was all terribly quaint and English, and after three years at Oxford, Patrick should have taken it in his stride. But as he took his seat beside Debra Passmore in the second row and they waited for the coroner to appear, he was ashamed to find that his hands were shaking.

He had never been in a courtroom before, and his expectations derived from movies and television. All this cosy prettiness unnerved him, and emphasized the deep foreignness of this bizarre country. Or as Myles would have put it, 'In England we do things *differently*, old son. You're not in the US of A now.'

That was the problem. For Myles' sake, he wanted to

do this right. But he was painfully conscious of not knowing the rules.

The wait grew longer, and a pulse began to beat a tattoo in his throat. Then the fat blonde emerged from a door to the right of the desk, and commanded them to rise for Her Majesty's Coroner. Patrick's stomach turned over.

The coroner was a dapper, pleasant-faced man in his fifties, with crinkly mid-brown hair and tortoiseshell spectacles. He wore a charcoal business suit, immaculate white shirt, spotted burgundy tie, and a matching silk handkerchief frothing raffishly from his breast pocket. He took his place behind his desk too swiftly for Patrick to observe his shoes, but it was dollars to doughnuts they were Church's brogues. Belatedly, Patrick wished his were too. He should have listened to Myles when he had the chance.

'The first case we're going to hear,' said the coroner briskly, 'concerns the death of Joseph Phillip Younger, of . . .' He gave the address and a brief description of 'the deceased' in a calm, well-modulated voice which projected an easy efficiency without sounding offhand. Now and then he flicked through his file to recall a detail, but never faltered or interrupted his flow. He spoke slowly and clearly, for the benefit of the clerk at the table in front of his desk, who was tapping notes into a laptop.

It was a polished performance by a man who clearly enjoyed his work. If the silk handkerchief betrayed a touch of vanity, perhaps that was understandable.

Patrick tried to concentrate on Joseph Phillip Younger's death – it seemed callous not to – but he found it hard to stay focused. Beside him Debra

Passmore sat very straight, her hands clenched in her lap. He couldn't see Antonia, as she was across the aisle. He wished he was sitting with her instead of the Passmores. It had been a mistake to let Debra come between them. But had she? He could not recall her saying or doing anything to keep him by her side. It was he who felt obligated.

A policeman was giving evidence. Unlike the courtrooms of Patrick's imagination, there was no witness box as such. Just a low dais to the right of the coroner's desk, on which the chair seemed to function more as a marker than a seat. Apparently the witness was expected to stand unless told otherwise.

The law book which Patrick had borrowed from Debra stated that 'an inquest is not concerned with allotting blame or liability. It is simply an enquiry into a death, the purpose of which is to determine the identity of the deceased and the cause of death, and if possible, to seek to prevent such deaths from occurring in the future.'

This is not about blame, he told himself. Blame and causation are not the same thing.

Yeah, right.

Joseph Phillip Younger's inquest was proceeding speedily to its conclusion. Mr Younger, a seventy-five-year-old alcoholic, divorced and in poor health, had hanged himself because he no longer wished to live.

His relatives picked up their motorcycle helmets and shuffled out, looking relieved. End of Joseph Phillip Younger, and on to the next one.

The coroner shifted in his chair, as people do to mark a fresh stage in the action.

The pulse in Patrick's throat started up again.

'Now,' said the coroner, 'we move on to the death

228

of . . .' he consulted his file, 'Myles Sebastian Cantellow of 17 Wilton Row, London SW1: a death which occurred in France, but over which I have jurisdiction, as the body now lies in my district . . .'

Bizarre to hear Myles' address given as the house in Belgravia, when in the three years that Patrick had known him, he had spent perhaps as many nights under his mother's roof. And strange too, to hear 'Cantellow' mentioned after weeks of Passmores. On his mother's remarriage, Myles had chosen to retain his father's surname – not as a mark of affection, but simply to irritate Julian, whom he disliked marginally more than his own father. It seemed that Sheridan Cantellow felt the same way about his son, for he had not come down from Edinburgh for the inquest. According to Debra, he had 'asked to be informed' of the outcome, and hoped to be able to attend the funeral. 'Hoped to attend'? Jesus Christ. Poor Myles.

'. . . I have it in mind to admit eight items of documentary evidence,' said the coroner in his smooth consultant's voice. 'The statements of Monsieur Clovis Panabière (a local farmer), the French gendarme who was called to the scene, the representatives of the emergency medical and fire services, Dr Roger Gilbert (the pathologist), Dr Antonia Hunt, Patrick McMullan, and Nerissa Passmore. I take it that no-one objects?'

Beside him, Patrick felt Debra twitch. She seemed uncomfortable in the role of passive observer.

'Good,' said the coroner, flicking her a wary glance. 'Then can we go first to Patrick McMullan.'

Patrick stood up and the usher showed him how to take the oath. That at least was exactly as it was on TV, and he was relieved that his voice didn't shake when he read the words on the card. But it bothered him to be swearing 'by Almighty God', since he didn't believe in God. It felt like a lie, and gave him the uneasy sense of having got off to a bad start.

The coroner read out Patrick's name and his new address in Oxford, and Patrick confirmed that they were correct.

'Now,' said the coroner. 'Before we tackle the issues, I just want to clear up a technicality. I understand you weren't available, Mr McMullan, to provide a supplementary statement between the 29th of September and the 12th of October. Would you tell me why?'

The question took Patrick completely by surprise. He thought he'd explained that to the British police. Hadn't they passed it on? 'Uh – yes, sir. I was trying to get home. I mean, back to England.'

The coroner raised his bushy eyebrows and waited for him to elaborate.

'I missed my flight. It took longer than I expected to get back.'

'It took two weeks to catch another flight?'

'No, sir.' Damn, but the guy was thorough. Patrick had been hoping that no-one would get to hear about this. He found it embarrassing. 'I couldn't get another flight because I didn't have any money. So I got a job on a building site in Toulouse till I had enough for the ferry. Then I hitched the rest of the way.' The bushy eyebrows rose a fraction higher. Perhaps the coroner didn't understand what hitch-hiking was. Patrick started to explain. 'That is, I thumbed a—'

'Yes, yes,' said the coroner, with the ghost of a smile, 'I'm familiar with the term.'

Patrick saw Debra and Julian shaking their heads in consternation. *If only we'd known! We could have advanced the poor boy the money! For heaven's sake, he could have come with us!* Which was kind of the point, though it would be hard to explain that to the Passmores.

'Well, that seems in order,' the coroner went on evenly. 'Now we can turn to the question of identity. I don't think this need detain us long, but I must ask one or two questions, as the dental evidence is inconclusive. I understand, Mr McMullan, that you were the first on the scene, having watched the jeep go over the cliff with the deceased behind the wheel?'

'Yes, sir.'

'Now. As I understand it, you ran back up the track to assure yourself of Dr Hunt's safety, then took a narrow and extremely precipitous track down the face of the cliff to reach the jeep. There you tried to rescue the deceased but were beaten back by the heat, sustaining some injury to yourself in the attempt.' His eyes flicked to Patrick's bandaged hand. 'Is that a fair summary of what happened?'

A fair summary?

Patrick had followed the coroner's account with difficulty. The man's words were so divorced from his own experience that it was like listening to an account in Serbo-Croat and having to perform a simultaneous translation.

The truth was, his memory was a patchwork of disjointed images. The jeep sailing into the gorge. White paper fluttering against an iron-grey sky. Then nothing until he scrambled down to the bottom. The crunch of broken glass under his shoes. Boiling black smoke and yellow flame. Twisted metal and dark sticky runnels of melted Plexiglass. The smell.

The jeep had hit the rocks on its rear, and concertinaed. A cartoon crash, straight out of *Tom and Jerry*.

He remembered putting his hand on the door handle, then a wall of heat throwing him back onto the rocks.

Then for an instant the wind had parted the flames, and he caught a fleeting, never-to-be-forgotten glimpse of something black and *shiny* sitting behind the wheel.

That vision was etched on his retina. He saw it when he closed his eyes. He saw it in his dreams. He was seeing it now. *Is that a fair summary of what happened?*

Everyone was waiting for him to answer. 'Yes, sir,' he said at last. 'That's how it was.'

The coroner nodded.

Seems I get ten out of ten, thought Patrick sourly, beginning to dislike the man for no better reason than that he was thorough, and seemed to enjoy his ghastly job.

The coroner handed the usher a sheaf of papers and she gave a set to Patrick: two sheets of A4 stapled together, each bearing two glossy black and white photographs. 'We'll be discreet about these,' the coroner said, studying his own set, while Patrick struggled single-handedly with his. 'They're available to those who wish to examine them, but relatives of the deceased are warned that they may find them distressing. Now, Mr McMullan,' he said without raising his head, 'these were taken by the police after the fire had been extinguished. Clearly the deceased was terribly badly burned, completely unrecognizable, but does this approximate to what you saw when you arrived on the scene?'

Patrick focused on holding the pictures steady and keeping his features expressionless. He was damned if he was going to give this prick the satisfaction of seeing him flinch.

He recognized part of the jeep's door, and something

behind the wheel. The 'something' was more wizened than when he had seen it, and less shiny. It looked flaky, like charred paper. As if a gust of wind would blow it away.

He nodded.

'For the note, Mr McMullan—'

'Yes. Sir. It's what I saw.' Maybe he should have said *he*, not 'it'. But the thing in the photographs was very definitely an 'it'.

'Very good,' said the coroner, which struck Patrick as surreal. 'So to recap. You saw the jeep go over with the deceased in it, and you saw him *in* the jeep when you reached the bottom of the gorge?'

Patrick said yes.

The coroner nodded. 'I think that's as far as we need go on identification. Usher, you may take back the photographs.'

There was a general breathing out while the fat blonde waddled down the aisle. There had not been many takers for the photos: just the policeman from the first inquest, who seemed to have stayed out of professional curiosity, and two sallow young men at the back, whom Patrick supposed to be reporters.

He glanced at Antonia. She looked startlingly unfamiliar in black rather than her bird of paradise colours, and with her hair tightly confined in a plait. But she caught his eye and gave him a slight smile, and though he didn't smile back, he could tell that she knew he would if he could. Suddenly he felt much less isolated.

'Let us pass to the cause of death,' said the coroner, scanning his file. 'Given the state of the body, the pathologist's report is naturally heavily qualified in many respects, but what emerges is that this was a young man of twenty-four, in good physical health, save for the fact that what remained of the liver showed signs of alcohol abuse . . .'

The liver. Jesus, did he *have* to put it like that? Patrick had been looking at Debra while the coroner was speaking, and he saw her sag and age before his eyes. Someone had placed her son on a table and chopped him up like a slab of charred meat.

'. . . blood alcohol,' continued the coroner, reading from the report, 'could not be established with any accuracy, but was estimated at significantly above the legal limit of 80 mg per 100 ml.' He sounded severe. Plainly, Myles was being docked points for bad behaviour. 'Now, Mr McMullan.' The coroner glanced up and fixed Patrick with serene brown eyes. 'About half an hour before the accident you saw the deceased consume an entire bottle of champagne.'

'Yes.'

'And in her statement, Ms Passmore tells of having seen him consume the better part of *another* bottle of wine that morning. Moreover we know from the statement of Dr Hunt that the deceased had consumed a considerable amount of cocaine the night before. To your knowledge, did the deceased habitually make use of proscribed substances?'

Patrick licked his lips. He felt the heat of Debra Passmore's gaze. 'Yes,' he said at last.

'And was he also in the habit of combining them with excessive amounts of alcohol, or would that have been unusual for him?'

He cleared his throat. 'It was not unusual. Although he had recently made up his mind to quit the—'

'Confine yourself to the question, Mr McMullan. If you please.'

Patrick felt himself colouring.

'And had you ever seen him drive in this condition?'

'Yes, sir.'

'Often?'

'A few times. I guess.' And I never tried to stop him, either. I figured it wasn't worth it, he wouldn't have listened anyhow. Yeah. And now I've got to live with that too.

'So where does this take us?' asked the coroner with a touch of the amateur dramatics. 'We know the deceased was well over the legal limit when he got into the jeep, and we know that he was seen first to *reverse* in order to make the turn, and then to attempt to move *forwards* in order to drive off down the hill – but instead, he remained in the wrong gear and backed over the cliff edge. I understand he had made a similar error once before in the same vehicle?'

'Yes, sir. Those gears could be sticky, I'd noticed it myself when I drove it.'

And in her first incandescence of grief, Debra Passmore had screamed for hours about suing the Hunts for letting her son drive a defective jeep. Days later, an indefatigable Julian had at last persuaded her to drop the idea.

'So it would seem that the deceased repeated an earlier mistake, his faculties being impaired by alcohol and cocaine. Would you agree?'

'Yes, sir,' murmured Patrick.

'Well, that all seems in order. Now finally on the medical evidence, it's clear that trauma from the crash was the principal cause of death, but it may not have been the *only* cause.' He flicked through several pages, and again Patrick sensed that he was enjoying ferreting out the clues. 'Ah, yes. Now I just wanted to clear up whether, when you first reached the burning jeep, you

235

saw any sign at all that the deceased was still alive?'

'S – sir?' Patrick stammered.

'Because you see,' went on the coroner, implacable, 'the autopsy detected the presence of carbon monoxide and cyanide in the tissues, so we know that he was still alive at least when the fire started.'

The ground tilted beneath him. Dimly he perceived movement on the benches. Heads bent to knees, hands pressed to mouths.

The coroner noticed nothing, for he was still scanning his file. At Patrick's continued silence, he raised his head and shot him an impatient glance.

'No, sir,' said Patrick. His voice sounded distant. 'I saw no indication that he was still alive.'

'Thank you.'

Patrick drew a ragged breath.

'And so we come to the surrounding circumstances,' said the coroner, 'namely, *how* the deceased came to be driving, in his state of intoxication, halfway up a precipitous mountain track. Again I shall summarize from the statements, and you will please tell me if I've omitted anything material. You and Dr Hunt – the girl-friend of the deceased – had recently formed an "attachment"' – Patrick flinched – 'of which the deceased had become aware – we know not how – and which prompted him to take revenge on Dr Hunt by laying a kind of paper trail up the mountain track. There an altercation ensued. A fair summary?'

'Yes,' said Patrick.

'Now. After the altercation, Dr Hunt suggested that you go off in search of the deceased's eight-year-old sister, who was also on the mountainside at the time. This you did.'

'Yes.'

'And on your way you passed the jeep, and noticed that a farm gate which had been open when you drove up the track was now closed and padlocked, thereby blocking the jeep's exit.'

'Yes.'

'Now I want to ask you this. When you and Dr Hunt arrived earlier, why did you choose to park *uphill* from the gate, where you were at risk of being blocked in, if the gate were shut?'

Patrick blinked. 'There wasn't anywhere else to park, sir. We always parked there. It was the only place where the track was wide enough to let Monsieur Panabière – he's the farmer who—'

'I know, I have his statement—'

'To let his tractor past, if he came by.'

'I see. And before you parked, you turned the jeep round so that it was facing downhill. Was that also something you always did?'

'No,' he said uneasily. 'I guess that was the first time I did that.' Jesus, it sounded suspicious. Like he'd done it on purpose.

'So why did you do it this time?' The genial brown eyes were slightly less genial.

'Because I knew we'd be tired when we got back to the jeep. Neither of us had slept much the night before –' oh boy, how good *that* sounded – 'and I thought it'd be safer if we didn't have to do it on the return trip when we'd be even more tired.'

There was a silence while everyone thought about that, and Patrick wished he'd used any word in the dictionary but 'safe'.

'Now back to the gate. Did it strike you as odd that it should be closed and padlocked?'

'Perhaps a little. Though it had happened before. I

237

mean, not the padlocking, but it had been closed once or twice.'

'You see, Monsieur Panabière says in his statement that he definitely did *not* close *or* padlock the gate when he and his wife drove by at about two o'clock. Monsieur Panabière speculates that the gate may have been shut by hikers, as some kind of prank. He says he had encountered this problem before. Did you see any hikers that day?'

'Not that I recall.'

'And do you have any idea who shut and padlocked the gate?'

'No, sir, I don't.'

The coroner nodded. 'Well, I don't think we can take that any further. There doesn't seem to be anything out of the ordinary, no evidence of foul play. So,' he frowned at his papers, 'after climbing over the gate, you found the deceased's sister some distance further down the track, at which point you chanced to glance back, and caught sight of the deceased with Dr Hunt.'

'Yes, sir.'

'According to Dr Hunt's statement, after you left her she had a further altercation with the deceased, who demanded that she give him the keys of the jeep. Did you see this altercation?'

'I couldn't see Anto— Dr Hunt, but I could see Myles.'

'But you say in your statement that you *saw* her give the keys to the deceased.'

'I saw him catch them, but I couldn't see her. There were bushes in the way.'

'Ah yes, quite so.' The coroner checked his file. 'She says in her statement that she *threw* the keys at the deceased.'

From the corner of his eye, Patrick saw Debra Passmore stiffen. 'I guess so,' he said reluctantly. 'But if she hadn't let him have them, he would have taken them from her anyway, so—'

A quelling glance from the coroner. 'Then you saw the deceased get into the jeep.'

'Yes.'

'And the jeep went over the edge.'

'Yes.'

'And we're back where we started. Very good.'

Patrick swayed. His back ached from standing for so long, and his left hand throbbed. If the coroner said 'very good' one more time, he didn't know how he'd keep from reaching over the desk and smashing his face in.

'I'm reaching the end of my questions, Mr McMullan,' said the coroner in a kindly voice which made Patrick feel ashamed. 'But I have to ask, and this is important so I want you to take your time, did the deceased at any time seem excessively upset or depressed over what he had just discovered about your attachment with Dr Hunt?'

'Sir?'

'To the extent that he might have taken his own life, or been reckless as to whether he lived or died?'

Debra Passmore put her hands to her mouth.

How could he possibly answer that? He opened his mouth to speak but no sound came out. He swallowed. 'Myles,' he faltered, 'Myles *was* reckless. It's who he was. But that doesn't mean he—' he broke off. Started again. 'He would never try to kill himself. Absolutely not. He had too much to live for.'

Suddenly he had a picture of Myles hooting with laughter at the cliché. '*Too much to live for? Jesus*

Christ, Patroclus, where did you get that one?
"*Eastenders*"?'

They would have a laugh about that afterwards.

Then it hit him, as it was always hitting him, that he would never have a laugh with Myles again. The blood soughed in his ears. The courtroom misted over. 'I knew him,' he said. His voice cracked. 'He would never kill himself. He was my best friend.'

This time the coroner did not admonish him to confine himself to the question. He regarded Patrick in silence, as if mildly intrigued by this evidence of grief. Then he said, 'One last question. The deceased's younger sister was with you at the time of the accident, and witnessed it too. Understandably, she is too distressed to be questioned. But I must ask you. To your knowledge, could she add anything further to what we've heard today? Anything at all?'

Patrick thought about that. He thought about Myles enlisting his sister's help to take the *kántharos*. He thought about the eight-year-old's pinched little face as she re-enacted the accident with her Sindies. He thought about his promise that he wouldn't 'tell on her', and his promise to Myles to look after his sister. 'No, sir,' he said. 'She couldn't add anything.'

'Thank you, Mr McMullan, that will be all.'

It was only when he had resumed his place next to Debra, and shut his eyes and taken a couple of deep, slow breaths, that he felt something crackle in his jacket pocket, and drew out Antonia's line drawing of the *kántharos* reliefs.

He had intended to give it to her in the coffee bar, but somehow he'd forgotten all about it.

Suddenly he wondered if he had made a mistake by protecting Modge just now. For the first time it struck him that so far, nothing had been said about the *kántharos*. Surely that was a bit odd? Shouldn't he have said something?'

Ah, but what good would it have done? It would only have meant all kinds of questions for poor little Modge, and what was the point? She didn't know where Myles hid the goddamned cup, so what was the goddamned *point*?

He put back his head and gazed at the rain streaming in little grey runnels down the skylight. He felt more drained than ever before in his life.

Cassius, the riddle, the *kántharos*. What did any of that matter now?

He stuffed the drawing back in his pocket.

The coroner went over the same ground with Antonia as he had with Patrick, but at greater speed.

She did her best to answer, but found it hard to follow what he was saying. As a result her delivery was halting, and she frequently had to ask him to repeat the question. She suspected he found her uncooperative, perhaps even evasive. She couldn't help it. All she could think about was the fact that Myles had been alive when the fire broke out.

But surely he wasn't still conscious? Or was that just another of the tidy little lies which people tell themselves in order to sleep at night? '*At least he didn't suffer.*' '*It would have been instantaneous.*' '*He wouldn't have felt a thing.*'

The coroner had asked her another question. Something about the paper trail. She apologized and asked him to repeat it, which he did with slightly laboured patience.

'Yes,' she said, 'by the time Patrick and I reached the

turn-off for Le Figarol, we had already collected all the context sheets.'

Her voice sounded cold and flat, as if she were talking about the weather. She realized how she must appear to him. A hard, unfeeling career woman who had ruined the friendship between two young men, coolly lied to her own father, thrown a tantrum and hurled her car keys at her recently spurned and horribly drunk ex-boyfriend, then stood and watched him fall to his death without lifting a finger to help, while his best friend risked his neck to save him. No wonder the two reporters in the back row were scribbling furiously.

And no wonder Debra Passmore was giving her that basilisk stare.

'. . . so why,' said the coroner, 'did you then think it necessary to leave the jeep, and continue the search on foot? Since you now had all the papers, why did you not simply turn round and go home?'

She gazed at him in puzzlement. 'Why?'

'Yes. Why?' Impatience made the kindly voice a touch less kindly.

'Because,' she began, 'we still had to find the *kántharos*.'

'The – ?' The coroner frowned, and flicked through his papers. 'I don't recall anything of that name being mentioned in the statements. Please explain.'

What does all this matter now? she wondered wearily. 'It was an artefact,' she said. 'A stone cup. Roman. Patrick found it a few days before the accident.'

'Roman, you say? Was it valuable?'

'Oh, yes. Because of its associations, it would have been – well, priceless.'

The two reporters sat up straighter on their seats and exchanged knowing 'here it comes' glances.

'And why were you trying to find this artefact?'

'Well,' she said reluctantly, 'because Myles had taken it.'

An eruption in the Passmore camp. Julian looked aghast. Debra's face was an ivory mask.

'Dr Hunt,' said the coroner in the voice of a consultant rebuking a slipshod nurse, 'I can find nothing in your statement about such an artefact, Roman or otherwise.'

'Really? I – I'm very sorry. Maybe I wasn't asked. I mean, the police only wanted to know about the accident.'

It was all so confusing, what with the local gendarmerie pestering her for details of the accident, and the French heritage authorities who were only interested in the *kántharos*. She had assumed that the two would have talked to one another.

The coroner wore a considering look. 'Very well,' he said at last. 'So now you say that the deceased had *taken* this item. How did you know this? Had he admitted it to you?'

'Not as such, no. But we knew he had.' She glanced at Patrick, but he had his head down, staring at the floor. 'There wasn't any doubt about it—'

'This is outrageous!' cried Debra. 'The girl's lying! She's trying to use my son to cover up her own negligence – because he's dead and can't protect himself! She's unbalanced! My son was not a *thief*!'

'Mrs Passmore,' said the coroner firmly, 'I'm sure I don't need to remind you, of all people, of the penalties for disrupting court proceedings.'

'But she's calling my son a thief! And where's her evidence?'

'I shall be addressing that.'

'I'm not calling him a thief,' said Antonia stubbornly,

'and I'm not lying. I'm only saying that he took it, and that's why we didn't go back when we had the context sheets. We should have gone back, I know that now. But we didn't. Because he took it. Oh of course he *meant* to give it back. He wasn't a thief. But he did take it. I'm certain of that.'

After the mother's outburst, the coroner briefly considered clearing the court.

He had been watching Mrs Passmore, and in his professional opinion if anyone was unbalanced, it was she.

Oh dear oh dear oh dear. Such an unfortunate disturbance, and over a point with no more than a tangential bearing on the case. Except, of course, that if it were true, it would at least explain why these unfortunate, overwrought young people had stayed on that mountain in the sweltering heat, instead of behaving like sensible mortals, and returning home before someone got hurt.

But since when have people in love behaved like sensible mortals?

He took off his glasses and polished them on his pocket handkerchief, and longed for lunch.

The eternal triangle, he thought wearily, permitting himself a brief pause in which to collect his thoughts.

To his left, the girl stood rigidly straight, her face set and defiant. He thought her features a little too forceful for true beauty, but she was undeniably attractive. Strange that she seemed unaware of it herself.

It was the boy who was beautiful. The coroner, a happily married man, felt slightly queasy about using such a word to describe another male, but there it was. The boy had that magnetic, changeable quality which fascinates both sexes. No wonder he looked so drained.

The eternal triangle. Oh, dear.

It was all too easy to picture how the whole thing had come about. A trio of intelligent, privileged, neglected young people, unwisely left to their own devices in a remote and rather overheated corner of the South of France. Drink and drugs and sex. It never varied. And nine times out of ten, no permanent harm was done.

But in this case, a chain of minor errors and missed chances – each one innocuous in itself – had led to a death. And now the mother was baying for blood, and perhaps the press would be too, if they thought the story juicy enough – which they might, with this theft 'angle' thrown in. And then God help that poor young woman.

But the truth was, even if the dead boy *had* stolen the wretched thing, no-one was to blame. It was simply an accident.

Oh dear oh dear oh dear. The hearing had been going so well. But he could hardly close the case while this silly, niggling point remained unexplored. He had a reputation for thoroughness to uphold. Besides, leaving a point unresolved would give him indigestion.

Reluctantly, and wondering if he was making a mountain out of a molehill, he instructed the usher to recall and re-swear the boy for further testimony. In the pause which ensued, he made a mental note *not* to ask the next of kin if they wished to cross-examine the witnesses. For a woman like Mrs Passmore, to do so would be a red rag to a bull. He only hoped she was too overwrought to think of it herself.

The girl was dismissed and went back to her seat, and the boy took the stand again. He appeared dazed by the sudden turn of events. The coroner had seen that happen dozens of times before. The witness relaxes after his initial testimony, never dreaming that he can be recalled to clear up further points.

'So, Mr McMullan,' the coroner said, noting with pleasure the authoritative timbre of his voice, and the way the boy's shoulders loosened fractionally under its spell: 'just to clear up this small point for us. Did you gather from anything the deceased said or did that he had taken this – artefact?'

The boy's eyes were fixed on a spot on the ground just in front of the coroner's desk. He frowned, then drew his thumb across his bottom lip. In a low voice, without looking up, he said, 'No, sir. I did not.'

The coroner watched the colour drain from the girl's cheeks. She looked as if she had been struck across the face.

The boy flicked her a glance and added, 'I mean, I don't know if he took it or not.'

'Just to be clear. You can't confirm that he took it?'

'– No, sir. I can't.'

The coroner was astonished. The boy was quite clearly lying, and up till now he had been scrupulously truthful. Indeed, it had been painful to watch him struggling to leave nothing out, however unflattering it might be to himself. So why tell a falsehood now, on a point of only peripheral relevance? Perhaps, after all the damaging revelations he had been forced to make about his dead friend, he could not bring himself to brand him a thief as well.

Technically, of course, it was perjury. But in twenty-five years of serving Her Majesty, the coroner had learned when to tolerate the odd white lie. Clearly this was one such occasion. He had done his best and discharged his duty. And of course, it would make no difference to the outcome.

Time to wrap this one up and go to lunch. He tidied his papers and prepared to deliver his finding. Accidental death caused by trauma, burning and fire fume inhalation.

Which would be no help whatsoever to all these tortured people. They would leave his court as he had seen hundreds of others before them: blaming themselves and others, in a desperate urge to make sense of the senseless. He bit back a yawn. It was all too familiar.

Odd about that lie, though. He wondered why the poor boy thought it necessary to lie.

CHAPTER EIGHTEEN

Upper Missenden, Suffolk, five days later

Antonia was changing her clothes for the fourth time when the crunch of wheels on gravel told her that Patrick had arrived.

She froze. Stared in panic at the mess of clothes on the bed. Told herself she was being ridiculous, it didn't *matter* what she wore. That was the least of her worries.

She grabbed the topmost jersey on the pile: a scratchy concrete-coloured crewneck which reminded her of school. It had shrunk in the wash, and only just reached the waistband of her jeans. She scrambled for her loafers beneath the bed. Tried to find a hair ribbon, failed, and scraped back her hair with an elastic band snatched from her desk.

Heart pounding, she ran out onto the landing, and the mirror at the top of the stairs stopped her short. A gaunt, unstable young woman stared back at her: cavernous dark eyes in a chalk-white face. *Like piss-holes in the snow*, Myles used to say.

'So,' said the coroner, 'you can't confirm that he took it?'

'No, sir,' said Patrick. 'I can't.'

She still couldn't believe it. She kept reliving the moment when he glanced at her across the courtroom,

248

and the lie crackled between them like static.

The irony was, everyone believed him, and thought *she* was the liar. '*As to this question of the missing artefact,*' the coroner had said in his winding-up, '*I am by no means satisfied that we have heard the whole truth. However, I shall say no more about it, as I don't believe it was material to the death of the deceased, which I find to have been accidental.*' 'By no means satisfied that we have heard the whole truth . . .' The coroner had been careful not to look at anyone as he said it, but Antonia had felt all heads turn towards her.

Why did they believe she was the liar? Was it just a question of appearances? Did they prefer Patrick to her, simply because he was able to show his feelings, while she could not? Whatever the reason, the real question buzzed inside her head like an angry wasp. Why did he do it?

There must be some reason she had overlooked. He would explain it as soon as she opened the door. He would take her in his arms and apologize, and tell her he was going to sort it out. And she would say, oh of *course*. Now I understand. Now everything will be all right.

When she opened the door, he was standing with his back to her, looking out over the carriage drive. He turned. 'Hi,' he said. He glanced briefly at her mouth, but made no move to kiss her. He didn't even touch her arm.

'Hi,' she replied.

He wore jeans, a skiing jacket, hiking boots, and an indigo cotton shirt that she hadn't seen before. She wondered if Debra Passmore had bought it for him.

'So you found us OK?' she asked.

'I wondered if I'd got the right place. The cab driver

said there's a Holt Place, and a Holt Grange. I couldn't remember which one was your mom's.'

'We're the Place. The Grange is a converted barn on the other side of the village. Well, of course you'd know that, since you're here and not there.' She was talking too fast, but she couldn't slow down. Her jaw was clenched tight. She wished one of them would have the courage to touch the other.

He glanced up at the old house. 'It's some place you've got here.'

She was surprised. 'Is it? Um. Yes. I suppose it is.'

The blue shirt turned his eyes to cobalt. She wanted to put her arms around him and feel his hard warm chest against her, and smell the spicy scent of his skin.

But still he made no move towards her, and she could not bring herself to go to him. If he flinched she wouldn't be able to bear it.

A cold weight settled in the pit of her stomach.

She stepped back into the hall and he followed her, and she closed the door. 'The house is a bit dark on a day like this,' she said, sounding absurdly like a tour guide describing a stately home. 'So I thought we'd go into the garden. As long as the rain holds off.'

She grabbed a Barbour from the stand and led him across the echoing entrance hall, and through the drawing room and the french windows onto the terrace. He looked about him in that silent, watchful way he had when he felt unsure of himself, and she realized that asking him to Holt Place had been a mistake.

Feeling more and more like a tour guide, she led him through the rose garden and the heather garden, then down the steps and across the lawn to the river. He walked beside her with his hands in his jacket pockets, and for the first time since she had known him, she detected the slight limp which Myles used to tease him about in France.

'Thanks for coming all this way,' she said awkwardly.

He glanced at her. 'I wanted to see you.'

She swallowed. 'I thought it'd be better to talk face to face. The phone's impossible. These days, Debra just cuts me off.' She threw him a glance to see how he had taken that, but his face remained carefully blank. 'I can't face London at the moment,' she added. 'This place has become my bolt-hole.'

'Sure is some bolt-hole,' he murmured.

Unhappily she surveyed the grounds, her mother's pride and joy. The day before, the gardeners had come in force, and there was not a leaf out of place. The lawns were a preternatural emerald on which a single perfect catalpa tree glowed golden against a dark-grey sky shot through with shafts of sunlight. Beyond the lawns, the massed waves of heather were aflame in the afternoon sun. Raindrops glittered on the rose-covered terraces. In the honey-coloured light, the old stone house was at its most stately and imposing.

Even the river conspired against her. Beneath the trailing willows, Geoffrey, their ancient asthmatic swan, chose that moment to sail past them, arching his ebony neck with imperious scorn.

What had she been thinking of, summoning Patrick to a place like this? *The Princess will give an audience at three. Commoners are kindly requested to arrive on time.*

'My mother's not here,' she said by way of damage limitation. 'She's gone to town with my father, so we've got the place to ourselves.' She coloured. That sounded like a come-on. Or worse, as if she was condescending to put him at his ease. 'They're seeing a cardiologist,' she added. 'My father's not well.'

'Is that so.'

'At first I thought he was making it up, but it turns out he's rather ill. Some sort of weakness in his heart.' She bit her lip. 'Actually we're quite worried.'

Slowly he nodded.

It stung her that he made no pretence of sympathy for her father. Suddenly she wanted to shake him. Here she was, making awkward one-sided conversation, hating herself for gushing and saying the wrong thing, when it was he who had created the distance between them. 'I suppose,' she said, 'you saw what they wrote about us in the newspaper?'

He turned to her. 'What?'

At last, a response. She felt a sick satisfaction. 'Tuesday's *Daily Mail*. Our cleaning lady brought it. It was just a couple of paragraphs. "Goings-on of the *jeunesse dorée* on the French Riviera". That kind of thing. Wildly inaccurate, of course, but quite entertaining. As long as it's not about you.'

'Antonia, I—'

'They made me sound like a cross between Medea and Lady Macbeth. Ruthless treasure-seeker purloins priceless artefact for private sale . . .'

'*What?* They said you *stole* it?'

'Oh, not in so many words. But you know how good they are at innuendo.' She paused. 'They seem to think I took it, then tried to pin the blame on Myles, because he's dead.'

'Christ.'

'You came out of it pretty well, though. A sort of latter-day Gary Cooper, riding to the rescue of your dead friend by proclaiming the truth.'

He flinched.

'There's irony for you, don't you think?'

'Antonia, listen, I never expected—'

'Of course no-one actually *believes* all that nonsense. But you can see them thinking about it. No smoke without fire. And when all's said and done, the wretched thing *is* missing, and I did royally screw up both digs. There's no getting away from that.'

'Myles did the screwing up. Not you.'

'I was in charge. That's what counts.' She snapped off a slip of willow and started stripping the sharp-scented bark. 'Oh, and I didn't get the Cambridge job, after all. They're giving it to someone else.'

'What? I thought you had it in the bag.'

'So did I, until all this came along.' She tossed the twig into the river and watched it glide off downstream. 'It doesn't matter. I've got something else lined up.' She didn't add that the 'something else' was gofering for a suspiciously unheard-of assistant professor in Tucson, Arizona, whose only claim to fame was a passion for neolithic shell middens too obscure to interest anyone else. 'Doesn't sound very Roman,' had been her mother's only comment, which pretty much summed it up.

'I'm so sorry,' he said in a low voice. 'I had no idea this would happen.'

She started on another twig. 'You can't imagine what it's like, reading lies about yourself in the paper. And d'you know the really horrible thing? It's the fact that I'm worrying about it at all. Worrying about myself, and my father, and our bloody careers, when Myles isn't even buried yet.'

'Antonia—'

'It makes me feel so mean and grasping. So *dirty*.' Suddenly she burst out, 'I just want to know why!'

'Why what?'

'Why did you lie?'

His face closed. 'I didn't lie.'

She was aghast. 'Patrick. Come on. This is me!'

'At no time did Myles say he'd taken it. At no time.' He sounded as if he'd been over it a hundred times in his head.

'But—'

'You were there, Antonia. You know that as well as I do.'

'How can you say that? Everything he *did* – the way he looked, what he *didn't* say, what he *didn't* do – it all shouted the fact that he'd taken it!'

He turned his head and stared at the river.

'Patrick. Please.' She struggled to keep her voice steady. 'It's your word against mine, and they prefer yours. After all, I had a reason to lie, didn't I? At least, that's how it looks. I mean, the bloody thing was my responsibility, and it disappeared, so obviously I needed to cook up a story, so obviously I blamed Myles. When you think about it, it actually does have a sick kind of logic. Can you imagine how it makes me feel?'

He hacked at the leaf mould with the heel of his boot. At last he said, 'I honestly had no idea it would turn out like this. But I had to think about Modge.'

'Modge? How does Modge come into this?'

He frowned. 'If I'd told the coroner that Myles took the cup, think what would have happened.'

Bewildered, she waited for him to go on.

'They'd be beating a path to her door. The police. The press. Hell, maybe her own parents: "So the kid helped the brother take it, did she? Well, hey, let's go question her! And if that only pushes her further into her traumatized little shell, gee, that's just tough, ma'am, we're only doing our job." And for what, Antonia? What good would it do? She doesn't know where it is.'

'That's not the point.'

'Then for Christ's sake, what *is* the point? What do you want me to do?'

'Tell the truth.'

'The truth. The truth. Jesus Christ, Antonia, she's only eight years old. Right now the truth is the last thing she needs!'

'What about me? What about what I need?'

He sighed. Then he turned and met her eyes. 'I'm sorry,' he said at last. 'He asked me to look after Modge, and I can't just walk away from that. Not even for you.'

Despite the warmth of the sun, she began to feel cold.

The river had turned his eyes a changing greenish blue, and at his back the water slid by, a satiny stream of silver willow leaves. It seemed to her that he was drifting with it, carried further and further away from her on the current.

She realized that she had lost him.

'This isn't about Modge, is it?' she said quietly. 'Or what you said at the hearing. It's about Myles. You've come to say goodbye. Because of Myles.'

His face was bleak.

Something sharp lodged in her breast. 'Patrick, it was an *accident*! It wasn't your fault.'

He would not look at her. 'If it hadn't been for us, he'd be alive.'

'But—'

'I'm sorry, Antonia . . . I'm sorry.'

Despite the sun, she felt chilled to the marrow. Her teeth began to chatter.

'I'd better go,' he said in a low voice. 'I'll miss my train.'

She stood looking up at him. His face was bereft and young, and she wanted to say something – anything – to make things better. But there was nothing left to say.

In silence they retraced their steps along the river walk and across the lawns, past the heather and the roses, and the swimming pool and the tennis courts, and through the kitchen garden at the side of the house. At last they reached the carriage drive.

'So I guess you'll be coming on Tuesday,' he muttered. 'For the funeral.'

To stop her hands from shaking she jammed them into her pockets. 'No,' she said. 'I won't. Debra wrote and told me to stay away.'

He turned to her. 'What?'

'She doesn't want me there. She made it very clear.'

He shook his head. 'She didn't mean it. She's not herself, she doesn't know what she's—'

'Oh please!' she cried, unable to bear it any longer. 'Spare me the excuses for Debra Passmore! I don't *want* to come. All right? I don't want to slink around in dark glasses dodging the *Daily Mail*! I don't *want* to arrive late and leave early to avoid a showdown with that awful woman! And most of all, Patrick, I don't *want* to have to sit there and watch you turning into their surrogate son!'

He flinched as if she had struck him. The blood drained from his face.

It began to rain, a light, furtive pattering among the shrubs bordering the drive.

'I'm . . . sorry,' she said at last. 'I shouldn't have said that. I just – I can't come. That's all.'

He opened his mouth to speak, then closed it again. Then he glanced up at the big stone house behind her. 'I've got to go.'

She felt sick. 'I'll give you a lift to the station.'

'No. That's OK. I'll walk.'

'It's four miles.'

To soften his refusal, he forced a smile. 'Thanks. I'll be OK.'

The rain was coming down hard now, making the rhododendrons bob and droop.

She pressed her lips together and nodded. 'I'll walk with you down to the road.'

Halfway down the drive, he turned. 'Go back in the house. You're shivering.'

She shook her head. She had to clench her jaws to stop her teeth from chattering.

'Go on,' he said again. He put his hand on her shoulder and gave her a little push. 'Go back in the house. You're getting soaked.'

In disbelief she watched him turn and walk away. She watched him until he disappeared from sight. He did not look back.

Six o'clock on a dank Tuesday afternoon in Belgravia.

Someone, thought Patrick, should write a book about What to Do After the Funeral. That's the crunch time. When you've done all the administrative stuff and the running around, and there's nothing left to do. *Absolutely fuck all*, as Myles would have said.

You can't read, you can't watch TV, you can't even get warm. If you go for a walk in the streets you feel like a Martian. All you can do is sit in your 'guest sitting room' and contemplate the walls. And you feel so bleak. So goddamned bleak.

Yeah. What do you do after a funeral?

Of course, now would be the perfect time to call Antonia. Great excuse. Tell her about the service. The enormous echoing church. The cold hypocrisy of the speeches, including your own. The pathetically small clutch of people who bothered to turn up. And the dawning realization that you had been his first and only friend.

'Didn't you know?' Nerissa had asked him coolly at the reception. She had arrived that morning, looking wonderful in something new and black which she'd obviously picked up in Paris.

'No,' he'd said, holding a glass of champagne which he didn't want, but felt obliged to drink, for Myles. 'I didn't know.'

So all things considered, now would be a good time to call Antonia. And when he was done telling her about the funeral, he could ask her why she hadn't changed her mind and come.

All through the service he had kept turning round to see if she was there. He kept hoping, right up until everyone started filing out into the rainswept churchyard. Until it hit him. She wasn't coming.

Not that he could blame her for that. Not after what she had told him about the newspapers, and Debra's note. Not after the way he had behaved in Suffolk.

The surrogate son.

Ah, God, the way she had said it.

He leapt to his feet and prowled the room. Surely, *surely*, she didn't think he was sponging off the Passmores? Surely that wasn't what she meant?

Although maybe it was. With a background like hers, maybe she encountered that a lot.

No, it was good that he hadn't chickened out and called her, and he mustn't weaken now. A clean break, that was the thing. It was only what he deserved.

He moved to the window and stood looking down at the street.

Now you're free, he told himself, squaring his shoulders. Free to pursue your goal. Whatever the hell that is. But you'd better think of something fast, boy – because you sure can't be a therapist now. Helping people doesn't seem to be your thing.

The way she had looked at him as he walked away down the drive.

Ah, *shit*, why can't you stop thinking about her? It's over. No going back now. Put the whole stupid mess behind you and move on.

God, he needed a drink. A whole goddamned row of them, lined up and awaiting execution until he was blindly, paralytically drunk. What was it Myles used to say? *Absolutely rat-arsed.* Yeah. He wanted to get absolutely rat-arsed.

A knock on the door. He jumped.

'Do you mind if I come in?' said Debra. 'I was sorting the last of Myles' things, and I found something you should have.'

She wore one of her stripy shirts, with crisp Armani jeans. The minute they had returned from the church she had run upstairs and changed, ignoring Julian's plea that she should lie down for a while.

She never lay down. Patrick wondered when she slept. Her life consisted of wall-to-wall tasks. If he or Julian offered to help, she would give them her brittle, sleep-walking smile, then go right back to work as if she hadn't heard a thing.

As soon as he saw what lay in her palm, he recognized it, and his stomach turned over.

It was the Roman coin which she had given Myles

when he started at Oxford. A perfect silver *denarius*, with a profile of Constantine on one side, and a trireme slicing the waves on the other. Myles had kept it proudly on his desk, for he loved 'intellectual' things. And although he never said as much, he had clearly been flattered that his mother thought him capable of appreciating such a gift.

Once, he and Patrick had translated the inscription round the edge. *Fel. Temp. Reparatio.* A Return to Happier Times. It was the inscription which made Patrick recoil in horror. Perhaps Debra did not know Latin. Or perhaps she had never examined the coin closely enough to notice it.

He cleared his throat. 'I'm sorry. I can't accept this.'

'Please. I insist.'

'No. I'm sorry. No.'

'I want you to have it.' She paused, and he saw the muscles of her jaw clench. 'For what you said at the hearing. You stood up for him. You told them all that he wasn't a thief.'

Patrick stared down at the coin lying on her palm. *Felix Temporum Reparatio. A Return to Happier Times.*

Take this magic talisman, quoth the wicked witch, *and you shall be my chosen one, and I will give you riches beyond price* . . .

If Antonia could see him now, what a chance for her to say, I told you so! The surrogate son being offered his reward for lying through his teeth. For giving her up.

His gaze moved to Debra's face.

The skin around her eyes was pinched, and her lipstick had faded into little plum-coloured creases. She was not the wicked witch, or the surrogate mother. She was merely a brittle, brilliant woman whose carapace of anger had not yet grown thick enough to hide her pain.

She looked exhausted. Maybe, like the rest of them, she had been playing the 'if' game. If only I'd spent more time with him. If only I'd got to know him better. If, if, if . . .

Well, all *right*, then, thought Patrick. From now on, this is the way it's going to be. You can't change it. You can't go back and start over. Myles is dead. You've got to live with that.

He took the coin from Debra's hand, and the metal felt hot and heavy in his palm. 'Thank you, Debra,' he said.

At six o'clock on the day of the funeral, Antonia finished clearing out her room at Upper Missenden.

She carried a large cardboard carton of papers down to the incinerator behind the rhubarb patch, along with a box of matches, a can of Bar-B-Blaze, and the other half of the bottle of Pinot Grigio with which she had drunk a toast to Myles when the service was due to begin.

She was thinking about lighting the fire, and wondering hazily where she'd dropped the matches, when her mother's face appeared above the rhubarb.

Mrs Hunt glanced at the bottle in her daughter's hand, but made no comment. 'You're not still sulking because of what your sister said, are you?'

Antonia flashed her an unsteady grin. ''Course not! The last time Caroline got to me was when I was eight.'

'Good. Because when you've finished incinerating the vegetable patch, I need you to help with supper. Your nephew's being more than usually vile, even for him, and you're the only one he listens to.'

'That,' said Antonia, taking another swig from the bottle, 'is because I wallop him if he doesn't.'

'Well, do please feel free, you'd be doing us all a favour. And don't be too long.'

'I'll be through in a minute.'

Her sister had arrived unannounced with her three undisciplined and worryingly foul-mouthed children shortly after five. 'Swamped,' Mrs Hunt had murmured with a fatalistic shrug, and started ransacking the freezer.

Just then, Caroline had wandered into the kitchen and started telling Antonia from the heights of three weeks of 'Volunteer Counselling – a Facilitational Nexus' that she ought to have gone to the funeral to 'achieve closure' with Myles. 'You have to *work* for resolution, Toni. It won't come without a struggle.'

Behind her back, Antonia had pulled a face at her nine-year-old niece, and stuck two fingers down her throat – which got them both into trouble when Caroline turned round too soon.

Caroline was wrong. Going to the funeral would have achieved nothing except a public showdown with Debra Passmore. It certainly would not have achieved 'resolution', whatever the hell that meant. Though she had to admit that it sounded nice. *Resolution*. It had a smoothness to it. Like sugar dissolving in warm water.

'Still,' she muttered, fumbling in the grass for the matches, 'it's a bit bloody soon for that, I reckon.' She didn't want to resolve things with Myles. She wanted to throttle him for landing them in this shit.

Poor, selfish, insecure, *stupid* Myles. Now she would never get the chance to ask him why he had felt it necessary to creep around with Nerissa behind her back, instead of just coming out and telling her about it. She wouldn't have minded half as much as he seemed to think – because the truth was, she had never felt for him a tenth of what she felt – sorry, had felt – for Patrick.

Poor Myles. If only he had known. Or maybe it was better that he didn't. God, it was all such a mess.

She took another pull at the bottle. 'No,' she told the rhubarb soberly. 'If Caroline wants to see *closure* at work, she should come outside and get a load of this. The final stage in the makeover of Antonia Hunt. Stage One: chuck out entire wardrobe and deposit with Oxfam. Stage Two: write smarmy Uriah Heep letter to Assistant *Perfessor* What's-His-Name, grovellingly accepting his crumby job. Stage Three: the Grand Finale. Assemble assorted Cassius crap, convey to garden, add assorted combustibles, stand well back – and *whoosh*. Adjust to desired temperature and leave till completely consumed.'

She upended the cardboard box over the incinerator, and books and papers tumbled out. First came the famous Cassius manuscript, including all copies and diskettes; then her entire collection of the *Poems*, in all known English translations: twelve, the product of years of trawling through secondhand bookshops.

Burn it. Burn the whole bloody lot.

A fire would do her good. It would be nice to be warm for a change. God, she was cold. Her teeth were chattering again. It felt as if they hadn't stopped chattering since she had stood in the drive in the pouring rain, watching Patrick walk away.

At that moment, she had understood what it meant to be sick at heart. She had felt as if someone was inserting a pair of steel plates in her breastbone, and slowly drawing them apart: crunching back the ribs to expose her heart to the cold, raw air. That feeling had not gone away. It had stayed with her for days. It was with her now. And she couldn't get warm any more.

But last night, in a dream, the solution had come to her.

She had been riding a white horse along a low ridge covered in snow, cantering effortlessly into the distance – which was pretty strange, because in real life she was terrified of horses. As she watched herself getting smaller and smaller she felt snow settling on her face like a caress: a fine, soft, soothing blanket of snow.

When she awoke, she knew exactly what to do.

A clean, bare hillside covered in snow. A clean start. That's what you need. Chuck away all this rubbish and start again.

At long last she found the matches under a dock leaf. Tucking the Pinot Grigio awkwardly under her arm, she emptied the Bar-B-Blaze into the incinerator, struck a match with an unsteady flourish, and dropped it in. Orange flames whumped into life, and nearly took off her eyebrows.

'Way-hay!' she cried, staggering back. 'Welcome to the new Antonia Hunt!'

She sank to her knees and settled down to watch.

The heat on her face felt good. And the sweet, sharp scent of the damp grass, and the sour smell of the burning books, they were good too. A nettle brushed her hand. Its sting felt clean and cauterizing, and that was good as well, for it was burning away the old Antonia Hunt.

She was glad she had resisted the temptation to call Patrick. What was there left to say? What was the point in thinking about him, when it only meant thinking about Myles, and her father, and Cassius, and the *kántharos*, and so on and on, until you were right back to Patrick again.

He had made his choice. He had chosen the Passmores over her. There was nothing left to say. And let's face it, Antonia, it was never more than a bad case of puppy love in the first place. OK, twenty-four is a bit late for puppy love, but you always were a slow starter, there's no getting away from that.

So bite the bullet and tell the truth. You were desperate for love. Poor Myles made you feel worthless and frigid, till you just couldn't take any more. You'd have fallen for anyone. Then along comes this handsome Yank and, wonder of wonders, he actually pays you some attention – and *whammo*, you're hooked! Stands to reason, doesn't it? But that doesn't mean it was love!

'Anyway,' she muttered, waving the bottle at the fire, 'it's all over now. Patrick McMullan, I hereby consign you to the flames.'

She took another swig, and nearly choked.

All over now. From now on, the *work* is the thing. Your lodestone, your guiding star. As it was in the beginning, so shall it be for evermore. Now and for ever, unto the ending of the world. Amen.

She leaned forward, peering through the holes in the incinerator at the orange flames. 'Yup. From now on, the work is the thing. Stick to that, and you can't go wrong.'

She finished the bottle and chucked it into the fire.

To her disappointment, it did not explode, but merely thudded onto the crackling books, and lay there hissing like an unexploded bomb.

The flames died down as swiftly as they had arisen.

The embers threw out a feeble warmth, then turned grey and began to float away on the breeze.

She sat back on her heels.

In her breast, the steel plates shifted painfully. Her shoulders sagged. Her head drooped.

After five weeks, the dam finally burst. Great wrenching sobs tore through her. She beat the ground with her fists. She tore at the nettles.

And all the time the steel plates were grinding away inside her breast. She wondered if they would ever stop.

PART TWO

CHAPTER NINETEEN

City of Perusia, February 40 BC

Tacita awoke in the freezing darkness before dawn, huddled in her cloak of sour-smelling homespun on the cold stone floor of the Etruscan tower. She felt frozen and stiff, and so weak with hunger that when she grasped the window ledge and hauled herself to her feet, the blood roared in her ears, and pinpricks of light darted before her eyes.

All night long, the north wind had raged about the great beleaguered city, and the harsh song of the wolves had echoed through the frozen hills. All night long, Tacita had begged the Goddess for an answer. Should she try to get a message down to Gaius in the enemy camp, imploring him to help her? Or should she cling to her pride, even if that meant condemning herself and her family to death?

But seeking his help would be such a risk! They had not spoken in thirteen years. And he was the enemy now.

Pulling her stool to the window, she sat and watched the darkness leach from the sky. Below her, the city of Perusia slept its uneasy sleep, bathed in the peculiar, hushed radiance which reigns after a heavy fall of snow.

Their rooms were on the fourth storey of the north

tower of the Etruscan Gate, looking east across the plain towards the mountains. A thousand feet below, a sea of blue mist cloaked the valley of the Tiber. And beneath the mist, the enemy waited for Perusia to die.

She had not been surprised to learn of Gaius' presence in the besieging camp. It struck her as entirely natural that one day they should find themselves on different sides in a war: he fighting to crush the old Republic and establish a new order; she – or rather, her husband – siding with the republicans. What surprised her was that it had taken thirteen years to reach this point.

Ah, *what* was she to do? Seek his help? Or starve?

If it were only for herself, she would not dream of asking him. But there were others to think of. That was the dilemma.

And she was running out of time in which to decide. Two days earlier, her slender store of barley had finally given out, and she'd bartered the last of her pearls for a pair of bull's horns to render into broth. She had done amazingly well to get the horns at all, for after five months of siege, anything animal, however inedible, was as precious as rubies. But she had discovered an unexpected talent for haggling – much to the disgust of her husband, who had refused even to taste the glutinous mess, until she snapped at him like a fishwife and ordered him to eat.

Two days from now, even the broth would be gone. And she was running out of things to sell.

Every time she thought about asking Gaius for help she flushed with shame. Surely at best it would prove a humiliating waste of time – and at worst, a catastrophe. Once he learned that she was in the city, what might he not do? She knew from his poems that he had not forgiven her. Surely this would only give him the perfect opportunity for revenge?

Rationally, she could not believe that he was capable of such cruelty. But a man could change a great deal in thirteen years. How could she play dice with her family's lives?

Besides, why *should* he help her – the enemy – when to do so might put himself in danger? Surely Octavian would not tolerate treachery in one of his own commanders? Not when the success of the entire campaign hinged upon crushing Perusia.

Although if anyone could talk himself out of trouble, it was Gaius. And Octavian was known to be a fervent admirer of his poems. So maybe he would get away with it after all.

Dawn was breaking. In the rosy light, the grim old hill town looked almost benign, its ancient walls a soft terracotta, its shattered buildings forgivingly cloaked in snow.

With its enormous walls of Etruscan stone, Perusia could never be stormed, and Octavian knew it. He also knew that all he had to do was wait. It wouldn't be long now. Another few weeks, and those still alive inside would be too weak to spit at him. Already people were calling it the 'Perusine War', which probably suited him very well. Waging a war sounded so much more heroic than waiting patiently with an army of several thousand while a few hundred men, women and children slowly starved to death.

Far below her, the mist cloaked the enemy's fortifications, but through it their presence could still be felt: a vast, deadly ring, several miles around, of palisades and ramparted towers, and trenches filled with stakes.

Despair seized her. Even if she decided to send a

message to Gaius, how would it ever get through? Cleon, her slave, had assured her that he had spied out a way. But how was that possible?

The sun was gathering strength. She must decide now. Cleon would need the mist for cover, on his journey down to the enemy camp. It would be a ridiculously dangerous mission, but if anyone could carry it off, it would be him. He knew enough about soldiering to pass himself off as a legionary who had got separated from his unit. And he would risk his life for her without a thought.

If only she could decide. But still the Goddess withheld Her guidance, and as Tacita stared out of the window for a sign, all she saw was mist and sunlight: confusion and clarity in equal measure.

Perhaps the Goddess had been offended by the paltriness of her sacrifice: a handful of dried trefoil leaves, two wizened black olives, and a few drops of *posca*. There wasn't even any oil for a proper prayer-lamp. Oil? If she'd had oil, it would have gone into her family's mouths, not into some lamp!

She thought longingly of all those incredible, long-ago meals in Rome. The sea-bass – her husband's favourite – with that special sauce of pounded cheese and chicken livers and cumin. The fruits from their estates: great bowls of mulberries and figs and pomegranates. Why, even the potions she'd smeared on her face would have fed her family for days. Honey and milk and almond oil, and those little blocks of sea-salt with which Albia used to buff her shoulders before a party.

So yes, perhaps the Goddess *was* offended by the meanness of her sacrifice. But what did She expect after five months of siege?

In the early days of her marriage, it had astonished

Tacita that she had stumbled so easily upon the solace of worship, when she had spent her girlhood earnestly debating the theory and finding it wanting. Then she realized it was simply a matter of desperation. A woman needs something to fill a void.

Not that her husband was a bad man. Not really *bad*. Clever in a narrow-minded way, unimaginative, infuriatingly pedantic, and mendacious when it suited him. In short, a lawyer.

But at least he had left her alone after the twins were born, and had the good sense to take a freedwoman as a mistress. In recent years he had made much of his wife's spotless reputation, which was indeed a rarity in their circle. Her brother called her a minor miracle: a pretty young matron with an elderly husband, who never gave in to temptation. If he had known how little she was tempted, perhaps he would have been less impressed.

No, her husband was not a bad man. Merely a clever fool who had allowed ambition to lead him by the nose, and put them all in danger by backing the losing side. It was she who had seen disaster coming, and sent the twins to her brother's.

She realized that her mind was wandering. It was becoming harder and harder to focus.

She shuffled to the table and poured herself a couple of fingers of *posca*, mixing it with snow from the windowsill to freeze out the vinegary taste, and swigging back the slush in a single practised gulp.

She set the beaker on the table quietly, so as not to awaken her husband in the next room. At sixty-five he still had the ears of a cat, and had developed a healthy streak of avarice since their money was swallowed by taxes. It was no coincidence that the downturn in their fortunes had been accompanied by blossoming relations with her brother, who was far more adept at political manoeuvring than he.

She wondered if Gaius knew she was in the city. Surely he must? Octavian's spies were said to be everywhere. And Gaius was now a general, after all. Perhaps he had known for months that she was here. Perhaps he approved of her incarceration. Perhaps to him it seemed no more than a fitting punishment for what she had done.

She, on the other hand, had only learned that he was part of the besieging forces four days before. Cleon had heard it from a scout who had just returned from the Flaminian Way. Thankfully, Cleon had had the good sense to tell his mistress privately, rather than blurting it out in front of her husband. Tacita had been astonished that the slave had known about her and Gaius at all, for she had never told anyone. It turned out that Albia had entrusted him with the secret a few weeks before she died.

In all their years apart, she had seen Gaius only once, seven years before, when he had given a reading in Rome. It was six months after the twins were born: a desperate time for her, when she lay and stared at the walls, and there seemed no point in carrying on.

Then, one leaden afternoon in early February, she could bear it no longer, and recklessly decided to attend the reading. She told her husband where she was going – it would have been folly not to – but she doubted if he took it in. He was drafting his closing arguments for a particularly difficult case. Besides, what was it to him if his wife attended a poetry reading? For a lady of quality that was an entirely suitable diversion. And naturally, given their position, the poet in question had to be the best in Rome.

She had worn a heavy veil so that Gaius couldn't possibly recognize her.

He had not aged, so much as hardened. The vertical lines at the sides of his mouth were now deeply etched, and sun and soldiering had burned him a dark bronze. It made his light-grey eyes more startling still, and hard to look upon for long.

She noticed that he moved with less of the easy grace she used to love. Once or twice he flexed his left shoulder as if to keep it from stiffening, and when he walked to the lectern she saw how he limped. Perhaps that old spear wound was still troubling him.

During the reading he did not smile once. Not even when the little poem about the socialite and the gladiator convulsed the audience in fits.

But it was miraculous to see him again. Miraculous.

His voice was the one thing that hadn't changed. And he still had the ability to lose himself in the words, and let the feelings through.

Near the end, he gave them a new poem which hadn't yet been published. As he read it, it seemed to Tacita that the audience fell away, and he was speaking to her alone. They were back in the old days, in the moonlit tomb by the Porta Capena, lying together on his cloak.

I asked the gods to heal me,
but they only laughed. 'What, and spoil
all our fun? Come, Cassius, you
profit from this anguish as much as we!
Where would your poems be without Lycaris?
How would you earn your immortality?
Admit it, poet: she has been both

the summit and ruin of your life.'
And of course they're right.
But how strange that I
cannot write her out of my heart.
I've tried for years, but it can't be done.
I'm branded.
She's seared into that stubborn, beating muscle.
I cannot cut free from this love.

She had sat with the tears streaming down her cheeks. Was it possible that after all these years, after what she had done to him, he still loved her?

The final poem he had read cast that neatly into doubt: a brilliant and extremely black comedy of manners about the wedding night of a young patrician girl and an octogenarian with no teeth.

So maybe 'I cannot cut free' dealt only with past feelings which he had long since put aside?

And yet, even if that were true, there was no denying his pain. Year by year in the poems, she had watched him work his way through anger and bewilderment and contempt, until all those had burned away, leaving only the pain. He couldn't understand *why* she had left. She should have thought of that. She should have realized that for a man like him, not knowing would be slow torture.

She couldn't bear it.

So the next day, she wrote him a letter. She spent the whole morning on it, scribbling her way through several dozen drafts before finally arriving at a courteous, beautifully turned request for an interview. Of course she couldn't tell him anything in the letter itself, in case it fell into the wrong hands. It was simply a respectful expression of good wishes, such as any well-educated

Roman matron might send to any famous poet.

The letter was returned the same afternoon, with the seal unbroken.

She was devastated. She lay for weeks, staring into space. Not eating. Not sleeping. Unable even to find solace in her children. Her husband put it down to the melancholy which sometimes seizes women after giving birth, and sent her to the country for a change of air. Albia went with her, and dosed her with white poppy seeds to make her sleep.

She did not even have the comfort of pretending that he hadn't known who the letter was from, for she had used her signet ring to seal it. He would have recognized her seal instantly. He used to pluck the ring from her finger and hold it just out of reach, and make her buy it back with kisses.

She wore it still. That, and the little crescent amulet which her mother had given her when she reached womanhood, were the only jewels she had left. A few more days, and she would not even have those.

'So you'd better hurry up and write the wretched letter, hadn't you,' she muttered under her breath, 'or you won't be able to seal it properly!'

Hmm. Apparently, she had made her decision without being aware of it. Maybe that was the *posca*, putting new heart into her. Or maybe the Goddess had spoken, after all.

She dragged the stool to the table, then went to her cot and pulled out the small reed carton of writing materials which she had hidden beneath it. This time there could be no botched drafting. She must succeed at the first attempt or not at all, for she had just the one sheet of paper – of horribly poor grade, fit only for wrapping fish. It seemed strangely appropriate that the sludgy ink at the bottom of the jar should stink of cuttle-fish instead of wine.

She took up her knife and cut a fresh nib. In the harsh light of morning her hands looked as cracked and red as dried venison. Twenty-nine years old, but with the hands of a crone.

Appalled, she put down the quill. If by some miracle Cleon managed to get the letter to Gaius, and if – by an even greater miracle – Gaius deigned to open it, and took pity on her, and somehow contrived to spirit her and her family out of the city – what would he think when he saw her? Would he even recognize her? How could she bear to see the dawning horror in his eyes, as he realized that this wizened ruin was his own Lycaris?

Before the siege she had been proud of her looks. Still slender despite the child-bearing, still with all her own teeth, and her own abundant black hair. But now! Her clothes hung on her. Her hair was as coarse and dull as hemp. Her skin was the colour of dirty snow.

'Oh, stop it,' she muttered crossly. 'You're not doing this so that you can amaze him with your beauty. This isn't about *you* at all! Just remember that, you silly little fool, and get on with the wretched letter!'

Recklessly she poured herself another half-beaker of *posca*. She let two drops fall for the Goddess, then tossed back the rest in a single gulp and chased it down with snow, as deftly as any hard-bitten legionary. A favourite verse slipped into her mind. *'The horse with wings sometimes comes to me in my dreams – and that's not just when I'm drunk. But when I am, you should see how Pegasus flies!'*

'That's the spirit,' she muttered, as the warmth of the *posca* stole through her. 'You're not dead yet, now are you, my girl? So get to work. And when you've finished,

278

you can have a bath as a reward. That'll set you up for the day. A good, brisk, invigorating scrub with a whole bucketful of snow.' To her husband's disgust, she was becoming almost as skilled at snow baths as she was at haggling.

She dipped her quill in the inky sludge and began to write. Quickly, before the *posca* wore off and she changed her mind.

CHAPTER TWENTY

Chalk Farm, early February, the Present

Antonia sat over a mug of coffee in her best friend's tiny kitchen, and tried not to mind the furious whispering out in the hall.

'I don't want breakfast when *she's* there,' hissed Kate's nine-year-old, Emma. 'She's all in black, and scary, like a *witch*.'

'Don't be ridiculous,' retorted her mother crisply. '*Emma* – come back. *Emma!* Come back!'

Footsteps thundered up the stairs.

Across the table, Kate's husband Phil gave Antonia a rueful grin.

She forced herself to return the smile.

She always hoped children would like her, but they rarely did, and Emma was no exception. Antonia had been at Erica Gardens for five days – ever since burst pipes had rendered her own tiny flat uninhabitable – and Emma hadn't eaten a single meal in her presence.

Slowly she turned the mug in her hands. *There was once a witch who lived all alone, in a horrible run-down little flat with a leaky roof, and dressed in black, and never had enough money or a proper job, and scared little children without meaning to.*

On any other day she would have laughed that off,

and told herself not to wallow in self-pity. This morning, with the envelope at her elbow waiting to be opened, she felt vulnerable and sad.

She glanced around her at Kate's bright orange kitchen, packed with all the paraphernalia of togetherness. A tottering pile of Phil's paperwork; Emma's latest 'project' – a Norman motte and bailey made of loo rolls; the fridge, covered in dinosaur magnets and shopping lists, and the little notes which Kate and Phil left for each other when they were working late, which was always.

Her hands tightened on the mug.

Kate came back into the kitchen, red in the face from an unsuccessful tussle with her daughter. She glanced at the envelope at Antonia's elbow. 'Aren't you going to open it?'

'Mm,' Antonia said.

From the postmark, they both knew what it was: the letter from the solicitor, telling her how much she had inherited from her mother.

At best, she might get a half-share in the flat in Tooting, which was all that remained after the Lloyd's fiasco. It wasn't much, but a godsend all the same: as the insurers had refused to pay up for the repairs, she had precisely seven hundred pounds in the bank for her old age, and no job, once she finished ghosting poor old Professor Edgeware's monograph on pots.

But still she hesitated. She felt mean and grasping to be thinking of her mother in such a way. This was her *mother*. Her last link with the past. A cold white envelope on a plate.

'Go on,' said Kate, more gently.

Antonia picked up the envelope and tore it open. Rapidly she scanned the contents.

Outside, cars revved, children slammed garden gates,

and Mrs Wrigley's Jack Russell launched his daily salvo at the postman.

Antonia's hand went to her throat.

'What?' said Phil and Kate together.

'She's – she's left the flat to my sister.'

'*What?*' said Kate. 'The whole thing? To Caroline?'

Antonia nodded.

'Jesus,' breathed Kate. 'Is that coals to Newcastle, or what?' Antonia's sister was married to a property developer who had made a fortune in the Eighties, and managed to hang on to it through the recession.

'There's more,' said Antonia. She dropped the letter on the table and put her head in her hands. 'I get the mill at La Bastide.'

There was silence in the kitchen.

The *mill*? What had Mummy been thinking of? To leave the flat to Caroline, who didn't need it, and the great run-down white elephant to her. How exquisitely the wrong way round. What had Mummy been thinking of?

Come to that, how had her mother still owned the place at all, when Lloyd's had swallowed everything years ago? Perhaps it was in some kind of offshore trust which they couldn't get their hands on?

Suddenly she felt contrite. Her poor mother probably hadn't been thinking at all, just floating in a haze of anti-cancer drugs. She'd probably simply wanted to get the will out of the way quickly, and muddled up her daughters' names.

And of course, Antonia told herself, Mummy didn't *owe* you a thing. You were the one who ran away to Arizona and scarcely kept in touch. Didn't even come home for Daddy's funeral. Mummy wasn't to know that you didn't have the fare. Not when your postcards told her breezily that you were 'doing fine'.

The mill. The mill. Oh, bloody hell.

You'll have to sell it, she told herself. Immediately, and from a distance. No point going over there. No point. No way.

Kate said, 'It could be worse. A place in the sun.'

'It's January,' muttered Antonia. 'There is no sun.'

'So? Nice and quiet. No tourists.'

'There aren't any tourists at La Bastide, even at the height of summer. Unless they're lost.'

'Well, just think,' said Kate, with a glance at Phil that Antonia was supposed to miss; 'we can descend on you in the school holidays. I mean, if you haven't sold it by then.'

Antonia had a sudden vision of the hand-painted *à vendre* sign which had adorned the butcher's window for as long as anyone could remember. 'I'll be lucky to sell it by *next* summer,' she said. 'You're welcome to descend whenever you like, but you'll have to do without me.'

'So you won't be going out there yourself.'

Antonia shook her head.

Kate looked relieved, which irritated Antonia more than she would have imagined.

'So the next step,' Kate said briskly, 'is to find you a lawyer. Know any good *notaires*?'

'No,' Antonia replied. Then she added, 'But I know a man who does.' It was about time that her brother-in-law came in useful.

Kate pushed the phone over to her. 'Go on, then. No time like the present.'

Antonia threw her a glance.

Dear, bossy, over-protective Kate. She had a pile of faxes at her elbow screaming for answers, but she gave no sign of impatience, and would be cross if Antonia tried to shoo her away. Antonia wished she had half her balance, generosity and kindness.

They had met during Antonia's first month in Arizona, when Kate was an embryo television researcher, and Antonia badly needed picking up off the floor. Kate had rolled up her sleeves and got on with it. Mrs Tiggywinkle to the rescue.

Sometimes Antonia wondered if her friend consciously fostered her resemblance to a hedgehog. She was naturally spherical, with beady dark eyes and a short sharp nose, and razor-cut black hair which bore an uncanny resemblance to spines. Perhaps it was a look which helped in her work. Perhaps it distracted people, and made them easier to manage.

And Kate *adored* managing people. Although maybe that was understandable with a husband like Phil, a diabetic physicist who sometimes forgot his jabs, and subsided in a wan heap on the laboratory floor. Perhaps Kate's need to manage people stemmed from a secret worry that if she didn't, they would subside in a heap, like Phil.

Half an hour later, Emma had been driven to school, Phil despatched to his lab, the worst of the faxes neutralized, and Kate swept back into the kitchen just as Antonia slammed down the phone and decided to murder her sister. 'This,' Antonia said between her teeth, 'is too much.'

Kate pulled up a stool.

'I've got to go out there,' Antonia said.

'What, to the mill? Oh I don't think that's a good idea. Oh no.'

'Oh yes.' She paced the kitchen. 'Apparently I *can't* sell the wretched place from here because it's full of

284

"family stuff" which I've got to sort out first.'

'What? But I thought no-one ever went there, after—'

'So did I, but it turns out I'm wrong. It turns out that about seven years ago, Mummy and Caroline had some ridiculous idea of doing it up and renting it out. So they took over some "rather good" pieces of furniture to make a start. Then Lloyd's happened, and Mummy got ill, and moved in with Caroline, and Caroline had her hands full – oh, yes, she managed to slip that in, how she coped single-handedly while I was in America – "single-handedly" I *don't* think: she had about ten dozen nurses at her beck and call—'

'Antonia—'

'– and of course since then she's been so *horrendously* busy that she's never got around to bringing it all back. Obviously the real reason is that she lost interest, because in fact it isn't all that "good" – but of course now it's suddenly become a pile of priceless antiques which I've got to go and retrieve. Oh, this is so *like* my sister!'

'But – can't she go herself?'

'Oh, darling, of *course* not!' Antonia snarled in an exaggerated Knightsbridge accent. She knew she was over-reacting, but she didn't care. 'How could she possibly *spare* a couple of days, when she's got two au pairs and a live-in housekeeper to supervise? Not to mention her husband, whom she can't leave for five minutes without the poor sweetheart going into a decline! But then *you* wouldn't understand that, would you, Toni darling, because you're single, and childless, and unemployed, and—'

'Antonia,' Kate said firmly, 'stop it or you'll burst a blood vessel.'

Antonia came to a halt in the middle of the kitchen.

'Sorry. Sorry. It's amazing. She gets to me every time.'

Some things never changed. The same old patterns, laid down years ago and endlessly repeated. The stay-at-home sister sharpening her claws on her 'career woman' sibling – and vice versa – like some eternal game of poker. *'I'll raise you one husband, three kids, and an enormous house in the country.' 'I'll see you an Oxford PhD and a career.'* It didn't matter that the career was moribund to the point where euthanasia was becoming a serious option. The pattern had been set decades ago, and now the responses shuttled merrily along like model trains.

Antonia disliked the thought intensely, and slammed the lid on it hard. 'Sorry,' she said again.

Kate refilled the kettle and switched it on.

'Forget coffee,' said Antonia. 'You've got a meeting to go to.'

'Forget that,' snapped Kate.

They made coffee.

'Actually,' said Antonia, 'it really isn't Caroline's fault. She's always been well-off, so it's impossible for her to imagine what it's like not to have money.'

Kate threw her a dark look. 'Don't try too hard. Tolerance was never your thing.'

'You're right. My sister's a cow.'

'That's better.'

Antonia kneaded her temples. 'But there's no getting away from it. I've got to go over there.'

'I really don't think that's a good idea.'

'Neither do I. But I'll manage. I've got enough for a cheap flight and a few days' car hire. Four days. Five at the most.'

Kate's hedgehog face became grave. 'I wasn't thinking

about the money. It'll be the first time you've been back since the accident.'

Antonia stared at her. 'Good Lord, Kate, I'm not worried about *that*! I'll be fine! I *was* thinking about the money!'

'Really?'

'Of course! Listen, all that was twelve years ago. I'm a different person now.'

Kate studied her in silence.

'I'll be fine,' she repeated. 'Maybe I'll even get in a few days' work while I'm there. And besides,' she added slyly, 'it means I won't have to keep dodging calls from Simon.'

That hit home, and Kate's small mouth puckered with displeasure. She didn't like Simon Toynbee, but she approved of him as an appropriate match for her friend, and made no secret of wanting to see them get together. True, in an unguarded moment she had once admitted that he wasn't what she *herself* went for in a man – but that was beside the point, because she'd been in her twenties when she married Phil, and still young enough to play the field. At thirty-six, Antonia should take what was offered, before someone else did.

Antonia gave herself a mental shake. Jesus, she was in a bad mood. If even Kate was beginning to irritate her, it was high time she had a spell on her own.

She picked up the phone and called Trailfinders, and five minutes later had a budget ticket to Toulouse for the first flight out on Friday morning.

'But that's the day after tomorrow!' said Kate.

Antonia gave her a tight-lipped smile. 'The sooner I go, the sooner I'll be back.'

*   *   *

The journey to France was like an anxiety dream, but Antonia was so relieved to be on her own again that it only made her laugh.

Arriving at Gatwick at the crack of dawn, she realized she'd forgotten all about the skiing season. The terminal was packed with an uneasy blend of laddish youths on package trips, and middle-aged couples clumped defensively about their carry-ons, like musk-oxen protecting their young.

As usual, everyone except her was either with someone, phoning home, or buying presents for partners and children. A few years ago that would have depressed her. She used to call it 'Airport Loneliness', when she would walk into a crowded departure lounge and feel like a Martian among all these busy, connected people. Now she no longer cared.

After a delay of nearly two hours they finally boarded the plane, and as she shuffled along the first-class aisle, a first-class child calmly and deliberately poured Ribena down her jeans. Its mother, a Prada-clad Frenchwoman with leathery skin, gave Antonia a coldly accusing stare. Antonia ignored the mother and glared at the child, who turned mottled purple and began to wail. Antonia walked on. Sometimes, scaring children had its compensations.

The airline must have added a couple of extra rows of seats, for only by sitting sideways could she accommodate her knees. She didn't mind. She took a highlighter and the latest *Pottery Review* from her briefcase, and settled down to work.

Normally she could work anywhere, but to her annoyance, an image of the mill kept cutting across her thoughts, like someone coughing at a concert. To chase it away, she took out her notebook and scribbled a To

Do list. Collect car; shop: bread, butter, cheese, eggs, apples, tea, coffee, long-life milk, detergent, loo paper, wine. Make bed & drink; bath; food; sleep. Next am: make Task List. Writing 'make list' on a To Do list made her smile, but she did it anyway. Lists kept her focused and in control.

The thing to remember, she told herself, is that you're only there for five days at the most. And who knows, by then you might even have a purchaser.

Her efficient-sounding *notaire* had already put the searches in hand, so that a sale could be pushed through in a matter of weeks. 'Il faut se depêcher, monsieur,' she had urged him, 'j'ai fort besoin de l'argent.' She could almost hear the Gallic shrug down the line: the French equivalent of 'Sure, lady, but first you gotta find some schmuck to *buy* the dump.'

A pair of twenty-something lovers stopped in the aisle and beamed down at her hopefully. Would she mind swapping seats, so they could sit together? She sighed, gathered her papers, and shunted over to the window. The girl moved in and curled up with her head against her boyfriend's shoulder and her bare feet against Antonia's Ribena-soaked thigh. Antonia didn't mind, for they were clean feet, the toenails painted apple green. But she did wonder what the girl thought she was doing, wearing open sandals in January. Perhaps she expected it to be hot in the South of France.

At last the plane took off, the stewardess came round with the drinks trolley, and Young Love clicked plastic tumblers of Bulgarian Shiraz, and gazed hungrily at each other's lips. The boy was not bad-looking in a meaty way which wouldn't keep, but the girl was dough-faced and dumpy, and kept tugging her sweater over her ample buttocks.

Dimly, Antonia remembered being as self-conscious as that. In her teens she'd tried every diet known to magazines. She'd even drunk vinegar, because that was how Madame Bovary had kept slim. In her twenties, she had found still more reasons for self-consciousness: she was too naïve, too academic, not enough fun. And of course, poor Myles hadn't helped. Then, as she approached thirty and finally gained some assurance, she stopped caring. There's irony for you. You spend your entire youth wishing you were more confident, and when you finally get there, it doesn't matter any more.

The boy ran his chubby fingers through his girl-friend's hair, and several strands floated down and alighted on *Pottery Review*. Brushing them off, Antonia felt about a hundred years old. It occurred to her that it had been three years since a man had touched her as this youth was touching his girlfriend. In fact, it had been three years since a man had touched her at all, apart from her hairdresser and her GP.

The thought amused her so much that she startled the stewardess by calling her back and ordering a Bloody Mary.

Things began to get better as soon as they landed at Toulouse.

Some good fairy had reminded Antonia to reserve a hire car in advance, and at the Budget desk she enjoyed the petty triumph of collecting the last Renault Clio under the envious gaze of a throng of hungover lads and their sour-faced girlfriends.

She decided against the motorway, and took the Route Nationale south. It was a clear day, crisp and sunny, and her spirits rose as she headed for the hills.

She had forgotten how suddenly the Pyrenees reared

into sight. One minute you were trolling along through Vernet, obediently watching out for hanging traffic lights, and the next, there they were: a great, shining white presence on the far horizon.

The Romans, she remembered suddenly, had loathed mountains. What appealed to Romans was Nature tamed and cultivated: gardens and vineyards and tidy little lakes. Not great chaotic peaks which were hell to cross, and only good for harbouring rebels. In fact, the Romans had taken so little interest in their mountains that they never even bothered to work out that the Pyrenees ran from east to west, not from north to south.

Strange. She hadn't thought about that in years.

In the rear-view mirror, the skiing fraternity took the turn-off for Andorra and disappeared. Suddenly hers was the only car on the road.

The countryside became harsher. She remembered it from her childhood. These white Roussillon cattle. These neat terraces of vines. These tiny silent villages clinging to the jagged hills.

It was all so familiar – and yet, seen for the first time in winter, disturbingly different. The earth was bare, the vines reduced to bizarrely twisted stumps from a Van Gogh painting. It was slightly shocking. Like seeing an old friend for the first time without her makeup.

When she reached the supermarket outside Quillan, she knew she had arrived in Catalonia. The good-looking boy at the checkout bade her a singsong *bonjura*, and chivalrously carried her box of *pang* and groceries out to the car. He had a Spaniard's velvety eyebrows and direct, chocolate-coloured gaze, and when she smiled at him, he flushed as dark as a nectarine. Ah, yes. It doesn't take much to lift the spirits at thirty-six.

She reached La Bastide around two. Stopping the car on the bridge and stepping out into the teeth of an icy north wind, she was assailed by the scent of woodsmoke – a scent so familiar that it brought the tears to her eyes, and her childhood surging back.

Everything was as she remembered. Smaller, of course, and greyer, for the Catalan sky was now heavy with cloud. But there on the hill was the same blocky little church where Mass was said once a month, when the travelling priest came through. And high above the village, there was the Castel Sarac, which she had once believed was inhabited by elves. And down on the main street she could just see the sign for the *depôt de pain*, where she had once trotted, a self-important eight-year-old, to buy baguettes for her father.

An image of another eight-year-old superseded the picture. Modge in her tight yellow shorts, skipping in puppyish circles around Patrick as they walked down the rue de la Clouette. Firmly, Antonia closed the lid on that. Climbed on her white horse and cantered away across the snow-covered hillside.

She got back in the car and eased it gingerly down the track towards the mill.

The last time she had been on this road had been when her mother drove them to the airport the day after the accident. Then she had been shocked, in a daze.

Too dazed to remember much about it, she discovered to her relief. She heaved a shaky sigh, and realized that she had been holding her breath.

The past has no dominion, she told herself.

She had read that in a magazine at the hairdresser's. So it must be true.

She parked in the courtyard and found the key under the stone where Monsieur Merou, the *gardien*, had said it would be, and let herself into the house. Another wave of relief. She inhaled only the mustiness of stale air, damp and cobwebs. The mill was free of ghosts.

It had the dead coldness of a house which has stood empty and unheated for years, and it was *dark*: she had forgotten how tiny the windows were – designed for retaining heat, rather than admitting light. At the height of summer, that had never mattered: on the contrary, they had welcomed the cool and the damp. Now it was like being in a grave.

A cold grave. Monsieur Merou had obligingly started the generator and lit the ancient boiler the day before, but the radiators were still struggling to get above blood heat. She turned up the thermostat, and down in the uncharted depths of the cellar, a boom like a nuclear explosion told her that the boiler was lurching into a higher gear. Monsieur Merou had warned her about that noise on the phone. As long as it stopped after five minutes, you were OK. He hadn't said what would happen if it did not.

The kitchen was appalling. Grey crocheted curtains rotting where they hung. Stained brown linoleum. Dismal yellow light from a lonely forty-watt bulb. The kitchen table had lost a leg and was leaning drunkenly, and beneath it, something small had once crawled to die. Antonia thought of Alfonse, and wished she hadn't. She scooped up the powdered remains in an old newspaper and carried them out into the courtyard.

Back inside, she told herself firmly that she had been in shabbier digs in her career, so stop complaining. But she revised her stay from five days down to three.

No wonder her mother and sister had lost heart. It would take at least fifty thousand pounds and several years of nervous exhaustion to haul this decayed ruin into the twentieth century – and then who would want it? She might as well kiss goodbye to any thought of a rapid sale.

She went to the sink to wash her hands. After an alarmingly long time, the tap finally spat out a jet of rusty water. She rinsed her hands, then went outside and brought the groceries in from the car. Miraculously after its Rip Van Winkle sleep, the fridge-freezer was still shudderingly alive, although for how much longer she wouldn't like to bet. It didn't matter. If it packed in, she could survive on French toast.

She went upstairs, walked straight past her old room, and put her bag in the spare room. Her old room contained too many memories of Myles. Ghosts or no ghosts, there was no point in tempting fate.

She unpacked her laptop, and made her bed in thirty seconds by shaking out the sleeping-bag she had brought from her flat. Then, pulling on an extra fleece, she returned to the kitchen, found an old *Star Trek* mug under the sink, and half filled it with supermarket wine. OK, it was only two-thirty in the afternoon, but that meant it was one-thirty back in England, so this counted as a lunchtime drink.

The wine was so vile that it made her gag. She examined the label. Oh, bloody hell. In her haste she had grabbed the cheapest thing on the shelves, and was the proud owner of two litre bottles of industrial-strength *vin doux*: syrupy pink Grenache with a red plastic prise-open top and a blatantly mendacious label. If this was *naturel*, Bhopal was a lemonade factory. No wonder it only cost eighty pence a litre.

Tumbler in hand, she made a swift review of Caroline's 'good' pieces. They comprised two mahogany side-tables and an inlaid armoire in the dining room, and a reproduction Tudor desk in the sitting room. The whole lot would probably cost more to ship home that it was worth. *Damn* Caroline. Damn her to hell.

It was still only a quarter to three. Another long swallow of petrol put fresh heart into her, and on impulse she decided to take the bull by the horns and walk up to the Source.

'La Sourça, La Sourça,' she sang defiantly as she attacked the slope. But the track was steeper than she remembered, and she soon stopped singing and concentrated on the climb.

The noise of the river fell away, and her footsteps were loud in her ears. She passed frost-blackened rosehips, bare brambles, and shrivelled sage. The hillside was hushed and still, save for the eerie rattle of last year's leaves on the oaks fringing the track. It was as if winter, with a single frosty breath, had blasted them on the bough.

She heard no birds or lizards, and caught no spicy scent of herbs. It was a land forsaken by everything but winter.

She realized with a shock that she had not trodden this path since the day of the accident. But to her enormous relief, it too harboured no ghosts. The past had happened to someone else. She felt as if she were on some tour, ticking off the sites from a long-ago fairytale.

Here, at this turning in the path, a boy once had an accident and died. And here, on this narrow green bridge above this tributary gorge, another boy once stood shoulder to shoulder with a girl, and made plans with her in the moonlight. And here, by the mouth of this cave, the boy took the girl in his arms, and kissed her for the first time.

A glance inside confirmed the cave's non-spectral status. It smelt faintly of urine, and the floor was littered with crushed beer cans and condoms. The voice of the spring reminded her of a loo cistern which wouldn't stop running.

'Nope,' she said aloud. 'No ghosts in here.'

Incredible to think that once she had believed this was a magic place. Incredible to think that Cassius himself had worshipped here.

And incredible to think that all that had ever mattered to her.

The walk up to the Source had taken longer than she'd expected, and by the time she got back to the mill it was five o'clock, and already beginning to get dark.

As she let herself into the kitchen, the stillness engulfed her like a tomb. Her breath steamed. Clearly, the radiators had done all they could.

She decided to build a fire in the sitting room. She fetched wood from the ancient stack outside the pot-shed, with vine twigs for kindling. The fire flared briefly and without heat, giving off billows of bitter brown smoke which stung her eyes and sucked the air from the room. Then it died.

She flung open the windows, shut the doors, and retreated to the kitchen, where she could still see her hand in front of her face. It was either that, or die of carbon monoxide poisoning.

So OK, the fire had been a bad idea.

Head pounding from the fumes, she thought about food and decided against it in favour of a second mug of petrol. Then she *must* make a start, or she'd never get the place sorted out in three days.

The kitchen cupboards yielded nothing that wouldn't benefit from a spell in a landfill site. The same went for the hall and the dining room. The understairs cupboard contained a pre-war vacuum cleaner, a crate of empty wine bottles thick with dust, a decade's worth of mouse droppings, and two boxes, neatly labelled in her father's small, crabbed hand. One was a large tea-chest entitled *Main dig finds, grids A035 to Z728*. The other was a cardboard carton of *Antonia's things*.

Antonia's things?

But she hadn't left any things. Had she? She tried to remember, but the days after the accident were a blur. Maybe she hadn't packed too carefully. That wouldn't surprise her, since she couldn't remember packing at all.

Frowning, she carried the carton into the kitchen, placed it on the table, and stood staring down at it.

The mystery solved itself as soon as she summoned the courage to lift the lid. Inside, meticulously packed in cotton wadding, were the finds from the Source. Until now she had completely forgotten them. Fragments of earthenware; blackened fruit pips left by Gallic peasants two thousand years before; a couple of Palaeolithic axe-heads; and, in a shoebox all to itself, the little Cybele lamp.

Her eyes misted over. Her father must have packed everything when he returned after the accident to make a last, fruitless search for the *kántharos*. He had packed it with care, indexing the finds on a neat, handwritten list taped inside the lid.

'Oh Daddy,' she murmured. 'If only I'd known.'

She hated to think about him now. After the accident she had put him to the back of her mind, vaguely believing that one day she would make her peace with him. Then, in the spring of her fourth year in Arizona, his heart had given out while he was hurrying across the concourse at Waterloo to catch a train. Now when she thought of him at all, it was with a grinding sense of guilt. A guilt which could never be assuaged.

At the bottom of the carton she found a red cardboard wallet labelled *Cassius Notes*.

Her mouth went dry.

But she had *burnt* all that. Miss Scarlett did it in the rhubarb patch with the incinerator. And yet here was a cardboard wallet full of God alone knew what, tidily labelled by her father. Frowning, she sat down on one of the rickety kitchen chairs and drew out the contents of the wallet.

Her pulse steadied. It was harmless. A pocket Latin dictionary; a battered paperback edition of the *Poems*; a sheaf of jottings on the dig, still gritty with bronze-coloured dust; and an A4 page of handwritten 'Thoughts on the Cassius Riddle' – pompous title – penned by her twenty-four-year-old self.

The Cassius riddle.

In poculo veritas.

God, she hadn't thought of that in years.

'*The truth is in the cup*', she declared, raising her mug in a toast. 'Cassius, you never spoke a truer word!'

As if in reply, a postcard slid from the papers onto the floor, and suddenly Cassius was staring up at her.

With a yelp she pulled her feet up under her – as if the postcard might at any moment sprout legs and scuttle across the floor.

She broke out in a chilly sweat. She hadn't looked upon that face for twelve years, and now here he was, gazing up at her – and from a *postcard*, too. As if despatched from the Underworld by some malevolent little demon.

Heart thudding against her ribs, she met the

thoughtful marble eyes across two millennia.

It was a photograph of the bust which Plautius had commissioned at the time of his friend's death, and which was now in the National Museum in Rome. It was in the Republican style, which meant it was an accurate portrait, not an idealization.

He had a broad, clear forehead, slightly furrowed by the drawing together of the vigorous arching brows; a wide mouth, firmly shut; a solid jaw. The modelling of the face was wonderful, the expression one of intense concentration, as if he were striving to work something out. One could tell that he had been a soldier. The hair and beard had been clipped pragmatically short, and the throat and shoulders were strong and muscular.

As was customary with portraits of the time, he was dressed in the manner of a Greek orator: bare-chested, with a mantle flung across one shoulder. The other bore a small crescent-shaped mark just below the collarbone.

Down the centuries, that mark had been the focus of much scholarly debate. Was it some kind of ceremonial scar – perhaps a dedication to Luna or Cybele? Or was it a war wound, or a birthmark?

All of this flashed through Antonia's mind in the seconds while she crouched on her chair, staring down at the postcard on the floor.

At last she uncurled her legs. Then she reached down and picked up the card by the edges. She turned it over. On the back, the Antonia of twelve years before had copied out two lines of Latin verse.

ossa tibi iuro per matris et ossa parentis . . .
me tibi ad extremas mansurum, vita, tenebras.

She hadn't thought about that poem – about any poem – in years, but now the card index in her brain clicked into operation and threw up the translation.

I swear by the bones of my parents that I will be yours, my life, until the ultimate darkness.

Suddenly she wanted to tear up the postcard into a thousand pieces.

'What the bloody *hell* possessed you to copy that out?' she cried. Her voice echoed bleakly in the empty kitchen. 'Surely you didn't actually *believe* all that rubbish? Christ, what a little idiot you were!'

She pushed the card, face down, into the middle of the sheaf of papers, and crammed the whole lot back in the wallet. Then she buried the wallet at the bottom of the box of 'Antonia's things', shoved the box back in the understairs cupboard, and slammed the door.

CHAPTER TWENTY-ONE

She woke up the next morning with a pounding headache, and a strong desire to call Kate.

Not feeling feisty enough to do battle with the shower, she splashed rusty water on her face, and pulled on yesterday's jeans and fleece before setting out for the phone booth in the place de la Mairie.

It had rained during the night. Clouds shut in the village and beaded the cobwebs on the woodpile.

Walking past what had once been the site of the main dig, she saw that the little house which had blighted her father's hopes had changed hands. The 'café' curtains and wrought-iron window screens had given way to sleek white shutters and Venetian blinds, and the front door was flanked by a pair of elegant bay trees. The changes spoke of money and taste, as did the shiny black Land Rover Discovery parked outside.

Much too posh for locals, she mused. Must be week-enders from Bordeaux or Nice. Her hopes of a quick sale spluttered feebly back to life. Maybe the new owners had rich, stupid friends who were longing to sink their money in a ruin.

She walked on past terraces of naked earth, criss-crossed with vines and the stark ashen skeletons of last year's fennel. A muddy grey horse raised its head and gave her a baleful stare.

La Bastide's narrow streets were deserted and unwelcoming, all the windows securely shuttered. At her back a shutter creaked open, then rattled shut. The Catalan version of twitching net curtains.

Searching her pockets, she realized with a spurt of irritation that she'd forgotten to buy a phone-card at the airport. Oh well. It was one way of getting reacquainted with the locals.

The Bar-Tabac in the rue Bayadère was still run by the Vassals family, and had hardly changed. The same shelves of dusty plastic toys and curling magazines, the same fog of cigarette smoke and coffee.

At the back of the shop, two women studied magazines. At a table by the window, three old men in blue jackets nursed sticky *coups de rouge* and crumpled roll-your-owns. As Antonia came in, they turned stiffly and gave her moist phlegmatic stares. She murmured 'Bonjour, messieurs', and was rewarded with the briefest of nods.

So the rules haven't changed, she thought wryly. The outsider still makes the first move.

Vassals *fils* was serving at the till: a soft-shouldered young man with whom she had once played a hilarious game of tag in the cemetery when they were ten. When he saw her, he registered astonished recognition, but said nothing. She bought her phone-card in disconcerted silence.

For the first time she wondered what the village would think of her. Would they welcome her as the daughter of once-regular visitors? Or had the accident changed all that? Who knew what garbled version had been handed down? And the Passmores had always been more popular than the Hunts. Far bigger spenders, even in the old days.

She dismissed such thoughts as paranoia. She was probably irrelevant to La Bastide.

The women by the magazines were staring at her. Annoyed, she turned to repay the compliment, and found herself looking into the blankly astonished faces of Nerissa and Debra Passmore.

Of the three of them, Nerissa recovered first. '*Antonia?* Antonia Hunt?'

Antonia stood in the middle of the shop, blinking stupidly.

Nerissa came forward. With a brief smile she put her hand lightly on Antonia's arm, then leaned over and brushed her cheek with her own.

'– Nerissa,' said Antonia dazedly. 'And – um, Debra. How are you? Both?'

'My God,' said Debra Passmore. 'My God. How extraordinary.'

Antonia could think of no answer to that. She felt obscurely as if she had been caught doing something wrong.

At the table by the window, the old men were sitting back in their chairs to enjoy the show. This, Antonia thought grimly, is probably as much fun as they've had all winter.

'Have you been here long?' Nerissa asked, sounding bizarrely as if they had just met at a cocktail party.

'Since yesterday. And – you?'

'The same. We arrived last night. Horribly late.' She opened her mouth to say something more, then seemed to think better of it, and flashed a wide smile instead. 'It's amazing to see you. You haven't changed a bit.'

Antonia could think of nothing to say to that, for it was manifestly untrue in her own case, and unnervingly accurate in Nerissa's.

'Are you staying at the mill?' Debra asked. She spoke with her jaws tightly clenched, as if they were wired together. Antonia remembered that from before.

'For a couple of days,' she replied hoarsely. 'I came out to sell the place.'

'Oh really?' Some of the tension left Debra's mouth. 'Well, I'm sure you'll find a buyer in no time. Such a wonderful location.'

Antonia mustered a wry smile. 'Nice of you to put it like that. I'm afraid it could most charitably be described as a picturesque ruin.'

Nerissa said, 'Someone told me you went to the States.'

Antonia told her she'd worked there for eleven years before returning to England, and they lapsed gratefully into comparing Arizona with the Home Counties.

Antonia hadn't seen Nerissa since the day of the accident, but she hadn't changed at all. Not for her the depredations of sunburn and fatigue, the monthly hormonal rollercoaster and general loss of looks. Her skin was still smooth and honey-coloured, and she still wore that air of serene assurance which Antonia had once so envied.

Although perhaps that had something to do with the spectacular diamond solitaire on her engagement finger. It was a little surprising that finding a husband had taken Nerissa so long, but from the size of the stone, he was probably worth the wait.

Debra, on the other hand, had changed enormously. All traces of softness in her features had burned away. The ivory skin was stretched like parchment over too-prominent bones, and the bridge of the nose looked painfully sharp. She reminded Antonia of a picture in *National Geographic* which used to fascinate her as a child: the well-preserved mummy of a redoubtable, once-beautiful Egyptian queen.

Nerissa asked if Antonia ever bumped into Simon Toynbee, and she said yes, in fact they'd worked together in Tucson, until he'd given up archaeology for television journalism. Then, because she saw no reason not to, she added that she'd gone out with him for a year, before eventually calling it a day.

'Really?' Nerissa's eyebrows rose. It wasn't clear whether she was surprised at Antonia for having had a relationship with Simon in the first place, or for being the one to have finished it.

'Yes,' said Antonia. 'Really.'

'Simon always was a bit intense,' said Nerissa.

Antonia nodded sagely, wondering what she meant. She asked Nerissa what she had been doing with herself.

'Oh, this and that,' said Nerissa. 'Some television work. That sort of thing.'

Antonia gave a polite nod. 'I did a little myself a year ago. Just a schools programme. Nothing much.'

Nerissa gave her a considering look.

'Well,' Debra said briskly. 'We ought to be going. Lunch at Sainte Eulalie. And you know what dragons they are about arriving on time!' Again that tight smile, but warmer now. 'It's been extraordinary to see you again, Antonia. Extraordinary. And I do wish you luck with the mill.'

Surprisingly, she sounded as if she meant it. Antonia was touched by her effort at friendliness.

To put some distance between them, she stayed behind to buy a newspaper. When she emerged onto the street, the clouds were closing in fast. The Castel Sarac had all but disappeared, and soft rain was beginning to make her hair frizz.

The encounter with Debra had left her feeling shaken, but curiously empowered. She had been right to assure Kate that returning to La Bastide held no terror for her – and now here was the proof. She'd just had a friendly, civilized conversation with Debra Passmore.

It occurred to her that perhaps her mother's legacy had not been as mistaken as she thought. Perhaps it hadn't sprung from a mix-up over names, but a desire to show her daughter that the past has no power to hurt the present. *The past has no dominion.*

If you can handle Debra Passmore you can handle anything, she told herself, and walked straight into Patrick.

The ground tilted beneath her. She slid back into the past. It was 1988 and she had slipped away from the dig to buy bread, and suddenly here he was, down from Les Limoniers on the same errand.

'Hello, Antonia,' he said calmly.

He looked incredibly, agonizingly the same. The dark hair was still thick and shining, the blue eyes still full of light. They even had the same bruised-looking shadows beneath.

And he appeared completely unruffled. As if bumping into her was an everyday occurrence.

She opened her mouth, but no sound came out. Cleared her throat, and started again. 'What – are you doing here?'

He blinked at the baldness of the question. 'I have a weekend place here. The first house in the village? Down by the bridge.'

Dear God. They were neighbours. At least, for the next couple of days. 'So – you're the new owner?' she floundered. 'I – was just admiring it. Looks like you've made some changes.'

'That wasn't me. That was Nerissa.'

Nerissa. She felt a falling sensation in the pit of her stomach. Nerissa. The engagement ring. Of course. Suddenly she knew why he wasn't surprised to see her. He had been forewarned. Nice of Nerissa not to do the same for her.

She pressed her lips together in a smile. 'Well. Congratulations. When's the wedding?'

'She didn't tell you?'

'We didn't talk for long.'

He nodded.

'Well,' she said again. 'She's done it beautifully – I mean, the house. Vast improvement on what it was before.'

'Thanks.' He was giving her the detached appraisal of someone who has just come across an old book which they enjoyed in their youth but can't imagine reading now. It made her feel sharply aware of her lack of makeup, and her unwashed hair scraped back in an elastic band.

'You must have done well for yourself,' she said, thinking of the weekend place and the diamond solitaire.

A slight lift of the shoulders. 'I'm a barrister now.'

'A *barrister*?'

His lip curled. 'Ain't that a blast? Me, with a tenancy at Hammond's Inn.'

Hammond's Inn. That was Debra's chambers.

He noticed that she noticed, and for a second his features contracted slightly.

'So what kind of law do you do?' she asked.

'PI,' he said. At her blank face he added, 'Personal injury litigation.'

She nodded, unable to think of a comment.

He certainly looked like a barrister. He had changed from a rangy and rather scruffy youth into a slender, confident man of unstudied elegance. Fishing jersey, cords, expensive skiing jacket, and an edge of striped City shirt which reminded her disturbingly of Myles.

'How about you?' he said. 'Are you still—'

'An archaeologist. Oh, yes.' She dug at the cobbles with her boot-heel. 'Freelance, actually. Just about scraping by. In fact, that's why I came out. I'm selling the mill. I need the money.'

She decided that was all she would tell him about her career. Compared with 'PI', it wasn't breathtaking. Three years in shell middens, two terms as an assistant professor with no tenure at the end, then years of digging on other people's digs, writing up other people's research, and lecturing to bored tourists on cruise ships. Recently, Kate had pestered her to do another TV slot, but she'd turned it down. They wanted her to do a feature on Hadrian's Wall, but as far as she was concerned, Roman history was out of the question. Besides, she wanted the security of tenure. She wanted a roof over her head which didn't leak.

None of which she felt like sharing with this coolly elegant man standing before her. He wasn't interested. He hadn't even asked the obvious question: where did all the money go? Of course, there was no reason why he *should* ask, but she found his lack of curiosity dismaying.

Down by the bridge, a car hooted. He turned and raised a hand in acknowledgement. That would be Nerissa in the Discovery, chasing him up for 'lunch at Sainte Eulalie'.

Sainte Eulalie. God. Did it *have* to be there?

'Gotta go,' he said.

'Of course.' She squared her shoulders, and borrowed Debra's line. 'Well, Patrick, it's been extraordinary to see you again.'

He gave her an unsmiling nod. 'Goodbye, Antonia.'

'A large glass of wine,' she muttered between her teeth as she headed back to the mill. 'A *large* glass. Then straight to work. The sooner you get out of this hellish place the better.'

She had given up all thought of calling Kate. She would not be able to hide her disarray from her friend, who would be on the first plane out. Kate loathed Patrick. True, she had never actually met him. But that had never stopped Kate.

It was all so surreal.

She had always assumed that Debra would have sold Les Limoniers years ago. And yet here they were, playing Happy Families. And with Patrick.

The surrogate son.

God, how he had changed. The romantic boy who had dreamed of becoming a therapist and helping people had morphed into a barrister. She wasn't sure what 'personal injury' was, but she was willing to bet it didn't have much to do with standing up for the underdog. At least, not at Hammond's Inn.

It was impossible to believe that such a man had ever memorized passages in the *Poems*, or been struck with superstitious awe on finding a stone cup in a cave. '*Spooked. So I guess the Goddess doesn't like men, huh?*'

She hadn't thought of that in years. Now it only made her sad.

Astonishing how people changed. No more *Poems*. No more *kántharos*. A barrister.

And yet, why should that surprise her? She had watched plenty of men go the same way. They got through all the girlie emotional stuff in their twenties, then buckled down to what really mattered. Getting ahead.

It was just that somehow, she had never imagined that happening to Patrick.

Letting herself into the mill, she was met with an exhalation of pure cold. It was like walking into a deep-freeze. She put her hand on the nearest radiator. It was glacial. Cursing aloud, she grabbed her torch, found the key to the cellars, and climbed down the near-vertical steps to find the boiler.

As she did so, she had a childish sense of transgression, for her father had always kept the cellars locked. They honeycombed the entire area beneath the mill, and were a lethal playground of broken bottles and ancient milling machinery.

Fortunately, she did not have far to look. The boiler crouched at the bottom of the steps: a copper monolith the size of a small submarine. It had the menacing stillness of an unexploded missile. Judging from its temperature, the *syncope* had been fairly recent, but she did not dare try resuscitation.

She shone the torch on her watch. A quarter-past twelve. No point going back up to the phone booth and trying a plumber, not until three o'clock at the earliest. No plumber worth his Catalan salt would answer the phone during the siesta.

For a bleak moment she stood in the freezing darkness and thought of Patrick and Nerissa having lunch at Sainte Eulalie, then returning to their beautiful, well-lit, efficiently heated little house.

'*Stop* that!' she muttered angrily. 'Stop it right now.

Fetch wood, get the range going, and you'll be *fine*. Hot coffee in no time.' Her voice sounded thin and shaky. An unconvincing display of bravado if ever there was one.

She was in the courtyard backing away from the woodpile with an armful of vine stumps, when she stepped on a rake which clanged against an old watering-can, and startled a monster in the pot-shed. She screamed, the monster squealed, she fell backwards, and the vine stumps went flying. In the instant before the monster escaped, she saw flailing hooves, a mane as coarse as rotten straw, and horrific wet mauve flesh where an eye should have been. Then the monster kicked up its heels and clattered out of the courtyard.

Bruised and shaken, she sat where she had fallen on the muddy cobbles, fighting back the tears.

First Cassius, then Patrick, and now *this*. A monster horse hiding in the pot-shed.

She screwed up her eyes and forced herself to take deep, slow breaths. Stop it. *Stop* it. Tears won't achieve anything.

'Are you all right?' said a well-bred English voice a few feet away.

She opened her eyes, and saw Julian Passmore looking down at her with an expression of concern on his square, genial face.

'Not really,' she muttered unsteadily. 'I've just been attacked by a rabid horse.'

Smiling, he reached down and pulled her gently to her feet. 'You know, I don't think horses get rabies. That was only Monsieur Panabière's little cart-horse. His name's Hippolyte. You mustn't mind him. He had an altercation with a Percheron last year – hence the eye, or lack thereof – and since then he's been a tad grouchy.'

'Grouchy? He came straight for me!'

'Poor little fellow was probably startled.' He eyed the scattered vine stumps. 'I think I'd better bring those in before they get wet, don't you?'

She sniffed. She was embarrassingly glad to see him.

She had always liked Myles' stepfather. When she was a teenager he would sometimes come down to the mill and share a bottle of wine with her father, and ask her interesting questions about books, and listen to the answers. Even during the ghastliness of the accident he had been resolutely kind to her.

He's much too nice to be a judge, she thought, watching him calmly picking up vine stumps. Although maybe he's retired by now.

Accurately assuming that she had never made the Girl Guides, he suggested that he might just help her get the range going, if that was all right? She said it was. She also agreed when he suggested that he might just pop down into the cellar and take a look at that boiler – 'My dear girl, I insist. We had one just like it for years. These contraptions and I are old adversaries!' And when he'd got it going again in a humiliatingly short time, he suggested that he might just help her boil some water for tea, and she agreed to that too.

'This is incredibly kind of you,' she said humbly, cradling her steaming mug and feeling about twelve.

He smiled. 'You looked as though you could do with a helping hand. Besides,' he paused, 'I dare say it was something of a shock, bumping into Debra like that.'

His directness surprised her. But that was one of the things she had liked about him as a child. 'A shock for her too,' she said. 'I should imagine.'

He sipped his tea and made no answer.

'You know,' she said carefully, 'I had no idea that any

of you were still here. Frankly, I'd have thought this was the last place you'd ever want to come.'

His face became grave. 'On the contrary. We spend all our spare time out here. Debra's converted one of the spare rooms into an office. Faxes, computers, scanners. I suppose for her this valley is . . .' he searched for words, 'it's where she feels closest to him.'

Antonia contemplated her tea. Despite the fact that they were sitting in her own kitchen, she felt like an intruder. 'I hadn't thought of that.'

He put down his mug and spread his hands on the table. They were good hands, with wide palms and short strong fingers. Hands for petting Labradors, and reassuring frightened horses. 'I'm afraid I have a rather difficult favour to ask of you,' he said.

She waited, wondering what was coming next.

'Every year around this time, we give a little drinks party for the village. A sort of belated *réveillon*. Everyone's invited, and quite a few even turn up. It's tomorrow at seven.'

She looked around wildly for an excuse.

He raised a hand to ward off her protests. 'Before you say no, please hear me out. Reason the first: everyone else has been invited, so it would be jolly odd if you weren't too. Reason the second: there'll be hordes of people besides us, so you needn't fear an Inquisition. The Passmores will be thoroughly diluted.' An apologetic smile of genuine warmth, which made Antonia swiftly revise her opinion of his abilities as an advocate. 'And reason the third – which if I'm honest, is the only one that counts – I think it would help Modge enormously to see you.'

'Modge,' she echoed blankly.

'Imogen. Our daughter.'

313

'Yes, I – I remember her, of course. But I don't . . .' she trailed off.

His eyes crinkled in a smile which was painful to watch. He was ten years older than his wife, which must put him in his mid to late sixties, and suddenly he looked his age. 'She's had a bit of a rough time over the past few years. I don't know exactly why. Adolescence, I suppose. A phase. At least, that's what one hopes.' She could tell he didn't really believe it. 'Patrick's been marvellous. He's the only one she'll talk to.' Again that smile. 'Of course, her mother and I are *completely* beyond the pale. Though I suppose that's natural enough at twenty. Isn't it?'

He looked at her doubtfully, as if seeking reassurance. She was touched that he should appeal to her, a woman in her thirties who had never had a child.

'I don't know what I could do,' she said helplessly.

'I just thought,' he went on, 'that as you're someone she's always admired – and liked, enormously – it might do her good to see you again.' He sighed. 'She always feels so terribly out of place at these events. Sometimes I think it might be better if we just let her stay upstairs with her videos and her computer, and whatnot. But I suppose Debra's right, and she's got to learn.'

Antonia had a sudden memory of her teenage self – lumpen, greasy-nosed, and on the edge of tears – standing on the landing listening to her parents debating her fate. 'But honestly, Evelyn, if the child doesn't *want* to attend this wretched tennis party, is it really necessary to compel her?' 'Yes, Charles, it really is. She's got to learn.'

History repeating itself. Poor Modge.

A drinks party at Les Limoniers with Debra and

Nerissa and Patrick. Dear God, what would Kate say when she heard?

Julian Passmore spotted her hesitation and pounced. 'So you'll come?'

She raised her head and gave him a smile which she hoped didn't look too forced. 'Of course I will,' she said.

CHAPTER TWENTY-TWO

'I can't *believe* you'd be so stupid,' said Debra for the hundredth time. 'To ask that woman here, to this house, for a drink?'

Still in her bathrobe, she was charging about the bedroom, ripping sheets from the bed and tossing them on the floor. The bathroom had already succumbed to the purge, and was submerged in a maelstrom of towels, most of them unused. Tomorrow the whole lot would be bundled off to the laundry in Mazerans.

Julian subsided into an armchair, and kneaded his temples. The priestess purifying the sanctum, he thought wearily. He wondered if the curtains would also fall victim to his wife's cleansing rites. And after that, what? A purge of the sitting room? A complete redecoration? Perhaps the mere mention of Antonia Hunt had tainted the entire house.

'I couldn't very well not invite her,' he said mildly. 'We've asked everyone else.'

She ignored that. 'Have you forgotten what she did to my son? Have you forgotten that she branded him a thief?'

'Of course not.'

'To ask her *here*. To this house. It's an outrage. A – a desecration.'

'No,' he said firmly. 'It's civilized.'

'Oh, *civilized*!' she returned with scorn. 'And was it

civilized of her to come back here after all these years? Here, to our haven? Where we've been so happy?'

Julian made no reply.

Debra kicked a path through the bedding, and sat down at her dressing-table. She wrenched open her makeup drawer. 'I don't know what you were thinking of. You spend years urging me to put everything behind me. "Put it behind you",' she mimicked, snatching a lipstick at random and stabbing at her mouth. 'Then you invite that creature into my house. I'd have thought the inconsistency would be obvious even to you.'

Julian studied her rigid back. 'I thought it might help Modge. I still think so. She used to adore Antonia.'

'Modge,' she snapped, 'has nothing to do with anything.'

He leaned back and closed his eyes, and let the silence grow.

'You think I'm over-reacting,' she said at last.

'I think you're upset, and it's my fault, and I'm sorry. But I'm not about to disinvite her now.'

'You're disappointed,' she said, as if he hadn't spoken. 'You hoped I'd got over it.'

'Hush.'

She was staring down at her makeup. 'One never gets over it. One never gets over losing a child.'

'I know.'

'No. You don't.' She raised her head and stared bleakly at her reflection.

He saw that she had misapplied her lipstick, blurring the outline of her mouth. With her smudged lips, and the short, damp hair feathering round her ears, she looked absurdly young. Like a child caught plundering her mother's things.

He went and sat beside her on the stool. 'This thing

tonight,' he said. 'You don't have to come down. You know that. I'll tell everyone you're ill.'

She lifted her chin and met his eyes in the mirror, and he saw with relief that the steel was back in her gaze. 'I shall be perfectly fine,' she said. 'God knows, if I can be civil to my own appalling clients day in and day out, I can be civil to that creature for a few minutes.' She reached for a tissue and deftly removed the offending lipstick. 'I shall be gracious. I shall be *civilized*. I shall even smile at her. I did it yesterday, so I can bloody well do it again.'

'That's my girl.'

A corner of her mouth went up. 'You patronizing bastard.'

He smiled. 'I love it when you call me names. It makes me feel mad and bad and dangerous to know.'

She gave a snort of laughter. 'Go and deal with the caterers, and leave me in peace! I've still got to call chambers and stop them buggering up those skeleton arguments, and then I've got to sort out all these sheets.'

'Leave them. We'll take the spare room tonight. Suzanne can deal with everything in the morning.'

She nodded, willing to be persuaded.

He wished she was as biddable when it came to the important things. But then, he reflected, if she were, she wouldn't be Debra. And he wouldn't adore her so.

He put his hands on her shoulders and gave her a little squeeze. 'It'll be over soon. "That creature" will be gone by tomorrow. She told me. All you've got to do is hold on till then.'

'I thought you'd already read this one,' said Nerissa, picking up the glossy hardback thriller from the chest of drawers.

Patrick, sitting on the bed surrounded by faxes, put his hand over the receiver. 'I left it somewhere. Got another at the airport. – Hello? Ms Wilkes?'

His instructing solicitor came on the line, and launched into a litany of woes. He took a deep breath and began to calm her down.

It was the usual weekend panic. Another exhausted young assistant in a big City firm, left cradling a pre-trial injunction while her boss went skiing. Everything had been ticking over nicely until Friday night, when the other side lobbed in a ton of new evidence and ran for cover. Suddenly faxes were scudding like missiles, clients screaming for reassurance, and previously rock-solid witnesses getting cold feet. Poor Ms Wilkes had battled single-handedly all weekend, before finally calling in the cavalry, which was shortly to receive a hundred and fifty pages of draft evidence 'for review'. And since Ms Wilkes had probably had about four hours' sleep in as many days, the cavalry would have to do a complete re-draft by tomorrow morning.

So far, so ordinary.

It would have been easy, if Nerissa hadn't kept wandering around, distracting him. He knew she was doing it on purpose, to get him off the phone. She had only come out to La Bastide to help Debra with the drinks party, and she was keen to get started.

A stab of lightning behind his eyes made him wince. Oh, terrific. Another headache on the way. He reached for the extra-strong painkillers on the bedside cabinet, and his fingers connected with bare wood. Suddenly he remembered the red and yellow packet sitting serenely on his desk in chambers, waiting to be scooped up.

Oh, fuck. *Fuck*.

Nerissa was frowning at the blurb on the back of the

book. 'Insurance fraud in the City. I'd have thought you got enough of that at work.'

He covered the receiver. 'I work with drug companies,' he told her. 'Remember?'

She shrugged.

He returned to Ms Wilkes. 'Sure, Helen, fax me the drafts, I'll get back to you tomorrow morning.'

'That's what happened to Antonia's parents,' said Nerissa: 'insurance fraud. Did you know that?'

Patrick flicked her a glance and nodded. 'No problem, Helen. Talk to you later.' He rang off and lay back on the bed, pressing the heels of his palms into his eyes to make the lightning go away. It didn't work.

The doctors couldn't find anything physically wrong with him, and the shrink had said that it was his subconscious trying to tell him something and it would take months to find out what. Which had been the end of the shrink.

It was probably just this fucking case. If there was any justice in heaven, the other side should win – but they would not, because their solicitors were too busy talking to the press to ferret out the smoking guns in the documents. So it would be yet another win for Hammond's Inn. Another case of shooting fish in a barrel. And this time the 'fish' were twenty-four middle-aged women whose brittle-bone therapy had put them in wheelchairs. So what was new?

Nerissa climbed on the bed and curled up beside him. 'She *says* she's done some TV work.'

'Who?' he muttered, picking up the latest fax from the clients and beginning to read.

'Antonia. But she didn't say what. And I've certainly never seen her in anything.'

She had her back to him, but he could tell she was

upset. He felt a twinge of guilt. He hadn't been paying her much attention lately. And it was tough that her acting career had never taken off. She had tried hard to begin with, but it had come as a shock to her that she hated talking in front of an audience. These days she pretended to go along to auditions, but her agent said she hadn't been to one in months. Patrick wondered what she did instead. And whether she knew that he knew.

'Maybe,' Nerissa said, 'she's making it up about her TV work.'

'Maybe,' he replied, stroking the back of her neck, and continuing to read.

'And did you know,' she went on, 'that she actually went out with Simon Toynbee?'

He put down the fax and stared at her. 'Simon?'

The phone rang.

It was Ms Wilkes again: sorry, *sorry*, it had slipped her mind, but would he mind terribly sorting out a glitch on jurisdiction, which had just raised its head, and was clearly scaring the hell out of her?

'Sure, Helen,' he said, 'why don't you run it past me now?'

Simon Toynbee?

'Simon Toynbee,' Nerissa repeated with satisfaction. 'They got together when they were in the States, and it lasted a year. At least, that's what she said.'

Jesus, thought Patrick, slipping into autopilot with Ms Wilkes. Antonia and Simon Toynbee?

All he remembered of Simon was a carroty ponytail, a pair of skinny knees, and an irritating habit of pinning the blame on other people. What the hell had she been thinking of, going out with a jerk like that?

Christ, but this was turning into a bad weekend.

321

Seeing her again had been horrible. It was as if the last twelve years hadn't happened at all. As if he was back in her mother's driveway in Suffolk, looking down at her as she stood shivering in the rain.

Clearly she had felt the same way, for her face had been naked and appalled. She couldn't hide it. She didn't have a barrister's training.

She had been wearing almost the same clothes as when he last saw her, right down to the elastic band holding back her hair. No makeup, not even lipstick. And she had scarcely aged. Her face was still pale and unlined, and she still had that straight-backed, slightly over-worldly Minoan look.

And yet, *something* about her had changed. He recalled that on the dig she had always been apologizing for something, as if to pre-empt criticism from her father or Myles. She didn't look as if she apologized any more.

But why had she come back? Why, now, after all this time?

Everything she had said seemed to have a barb in it. '*Yes, still an archaeologist. Just about scraping by.*' In other words, I've stayed true to the dream. What about you? '*A barrister?*' A sell-out.

And that pointed little hesitation when she heard that he was in Debra's chambers. As if a tenancy had just fallen into his lap, instead of being earned by years of damned hard work.

He had been tempted to tell her what it had really been like. How, after the inquest, he hadn't even *seen* the Passmores for several years – for despite their protests, he had dropped out, and gone bumming around South America on his own. Always on his own. He needed that. As he needed the harshness and the danger, and the sense of being on a different planet, a world away from Myles, and Wilton Row, and Antonia.

But then one day about three years later, he woke up and thought, OK, so I'm not dead yet. So what do I do now? The most natural thing would have been to go back to the States. But that would have been too easy. He wanted the odds stacked against him. Really stacked against him. So he thought, why not go back to England and be a barrister? What could be more perverse than that?

To his surprise, he found that he liked it. And was good at it.

Ending up in Debra's Chambers had been unintended. A coincidence. Hadn't it?

He had wanted to tell Antonia all that, but what was the point? She probably wouldn't even believe him. She'd just think it was lawyer-speak.

Or maybe he was being paranoid. After all, he could hardly blame her if she felt that life had dealt them uneven cards. The Lloyd's thing must have hit her pretty hard.

Ah, but what was Julian *thinking* of, asking her up to the house?

Ms Wilkes was purring a heartfelt thank-you down the line. He said goodbye, and rang off.

Nerissa had found his present for Modge on the chest of drawers and was holding it against herself, her features a picture of mock horror. It was an X-*Files* T-shirt, Extra Large. When he told her it was for Modge and to leave it alone, she rolled her eyes and replaced it with exaggerated care. 'Oh, for *Modge*! Are you sure it's big enough?'

He ignored that.

In the next room the fax clicked into life, and the first of the drafts began to come through.

Nerissa said, 'Well, I suppose that's one person who'll be pleased to see Antonia.'

Oh, God. Modge. He should have thought of that. What was Antonia's return going to do to Modge?

Nerissa caught his expression and her lip curled. 'You know, if my half-sister wasn't such a godawful mess, I'd think seriously about becoming jealous.'

Patrick collected the first pages of evidence from the fax, threw himself on the bed, and reached for a pen. 'She's just unhappy, is all,' he said.

'I would be too,' said Nerissa, 'if I looked like her.'

Modge snatched her overshirt from the clothes pile, and pulled it over her head. Then she wriggled into her leggings and squeezed her bare feet into the black stilettos.

There, she told her hateful reflection in the mirror. Now you're not just ugly, you're spectacularly ugly.

She crammed on as many rings as each finger would take, but couldn't find her choke-chain anywhere. Oh well. The ear-studs would have to do.

It was a pity she hadn't had the courage to have her eyebrows pierced, but every time she thought about combing her hair and snagging the comb on the stud she wanted to throw up. Which only showed how uncool she really was, because people who pierced their eyebrows never combed their hair at all.

She pulled the shirt away from her cleavage and put her head down and sniffed. Good. She hadn't washed her bra for a week, and she smelt like Gorgonzola cheese. That was only what she deserved.

She heard Nerissa's voice downstairs in the hall, and her defiant mood evaporated. She sank to the floor with her back against the wall, and clutched her knees.

Nerissa would look amazing. She would be wearing that short Sixties-style dress she'd picked up at Prada, which made her into a cross between Cindy Crawford and Claudia Schiffer. No wonder Patrick fancied her.

She moaned, and covered her face with her hands.

You're a joke, she told herself, rocking from side to side. A fucking joke. You're *twenty*, for fuck's sake. You're not sixteen or seventeen, when it's OK to be a total mess. You're *twenty years old*. You should be leaping about in Gap khakis and a stretchy top that doesn't reach your belly button. You should be back-packing with a boyfriend, or going to university, or driving fearlessly around in a new car, or having *kids*, for Christ's sake.

Instead, *look* at you. A pathetic, stay-at-home, retarded, failed-all-your-exams-*twice*, size sixteen freak. No wonder you're still a virgin. A twenty-year-old virgin who can't even drive.

Maybe you should sneak out and get a bus some-where, and pretend to be a prostitute, to get some experience. But you'd only screw it up. You'd get cut up by a pimp, or arrested, and rescued by Daddy.

And this drinks thing tonight! *God*. All those people staring at you. Smiling to your face, then shaking their heads behind your back.

Then she thought about seeing Antonia, and she felt hot and prickly, as if she was going to throw up.

Antonia had been with them on the hillside when it happened. Modge knew that because Daddy had told her, but she couldn't remember it herself. She couldn't remember much of what had happened that day. She remembered helping Myles take the cup thing, and lay the paper trail – but after that there was nothing, just a big blank until she was standing with Patrick, watching the jeep sail out over the gorge. That single frozen moment. Those white papers fluttering against the grey sky.

Sometimes she wished she *could* remember. She knew Mummy resented it that she didn't. Mummy seemed to take her lack of memory as disloyalty to Myles. Myles the paragon. No-one was allowed to forget anything about him.

She brought herself up short.

What a cow you are to say a thing like that. And remember, if the thought of seeing Antonia again is getting to *you*, just think what it's doing to Mummy!

Oh, but she wished she could stay up here in her room. It was the only place where she felt safe.

Her room was an exact replica of the one at Wilton Row, with the same black walls and black curtains permanently drawn, and the same black foam mattress, and tea-chests painted black. Her computer cast an eerie green glow on the only picture, her life-size Marilyn Manson poster. She could sit and stare at him for hours, losing herself in the pure white planes of his face, in his dull black eyes. He looked so dead, so perfect.

The poster had perplexed Daddy when she first put it up. 'Marilyn? But that's a girl's name. Looks like a chap to me.' At the time she had thought that was kind of sweet, though of course she had called him a moron to his face.

That had been the last time he entered her room. Mummy never did.

Suddenly she felt exhausted. She wanted to curl up and sleep for ever. Maybe that's why people kill them-selves, she thought. Not because they want to die, but because they want to sleep for ever.

Will it always be like this? she wondered. Trapped in

this horrible body, with no-one to love you except Patrick, who's going to marry Nerissa. And always this grinding feeling that Mummy can't bear to have you around. That she'd rather you had died instead of Myles.

Won't someone help me?

But how could they? It was hopeless. It was no *use* going on a diet, because even if she lost stones and stones and became miraculously pretty, *and* got into university *and* learned to drive, Patrick would still marry Nerissa, and her mother would still resent her – for not being brilliant and successful and dead.

For not being Myles.

'"And Daniel was cast into the lions' den,"' Antonia muttered as she waited on the Passmores' porch, '"but he felt no fear."'

Or something like that.

Easy for Daniel to say. He'd had a Supreme Being at his back.

Just remember, she told herself grimly. After tonight, you'll never have to see any of them again.

Then the doors were flung open and Julian was enveloping her in a bear hug – 'You are a *darling* for coming' – and pressing a large glass of ruby Merlot into her hand. 'Let's pitch right in and see if we can find Modge,' he murmured, shepherding her smoothly upstairs into a sea of noise and faces.

She had left it as late as she could, and the house was full. As they wove through the throng she recognized Vassals *fils* and the butcher's adopted daughter, and Monsieur Panabière, looking surprisingly small and frail without his formidable wife, and Madame Merou from the *depôt de pain*. The old lady had dyed her hair russet, but it was growing out in a broad grey stripe down her centre parting, which made her look like a badger. A disconcertingly bad-tempered badger. She studied Antonia sourly, then muttered something to her husband from the corner of her mouth.

Antonia found such blatant rudeness unsettling. She wondered if her paranoia in the Bar-Tabac might have been justified. Certainly, none of the villagers made a move to welcome her.

She took a sip of her wine. Then another, with more appreciation. She had forgotten that Julian knew his wines. She told him so, and he looked quietly pleased. She rolled the Merlot round her tongue, letting it wash away Madame Merou's poisoned glance and the chemical Dutch courage she had gulped down before leaving the mill.

Across the room, Debra nodded at her and smiled, stick-brittle in a plum-coloured silk shirt and black woollen slacks. Nerissa raised a hand from a doorway. To Antonia's relief, there was no sign of Patrick.

Julian read her mind with startling ease. Something had come up on one of Patrick's cases, he said. He'd be along later.

She made a mental note to be gone before 'later', and to take a circuitous route home. She didn't want a moonlit encounter in the rue de la Clouette.

They moved into the next room, which in Myles' day had been a dumping-ground, but was now a rather grand dining room. In honour of the party, the table had been moved back against the wall and piled with drinks, dispensed by uniformed staff of uniform youth and beauty.

Les Limoniers was startlingly different from what it had been twelve years before. It had been redecorated with expensive designer simplicity, and was now a haven of muted Etruscan reds, soft pooled lighting, and restful tropical plants, with tall pieces of abstract sculpture as focal points. The effect was serene and welcoming.

Definitely not Debra, thought Antonia wryly. Then she remembered the older woman's kindness in the Bar-Tabac, and felt mean.

'Here she is,' murmured Julian, propelling Antonia into a corner behind an enormous date palm, where a plump black-clad figure was staring out of the french windows. Although the girl must have spotted their approach in the glass, her back remained resolutely turned.

Oh, great, thought Antonia. Someone else who isn't exactly overjoyed to see me. What the hell am I going to say to her?

Julian was no help. With the ease of a seasoned party-goer, he had already evaporated.

Then the girl turned, and Antonia forgot herself in pity.

It was like meeting herself in a parallel universe. At that age she could so easily have become like this, if she hadn't thrown herself into work as an escape. There had been times when she too had been tempted to say, to hell with everything, I'm sick of trying all the time and getting nowhere. I'm already fat and ugly, so why not be *really* fat and *really* ugly?

The girl who stood blinking at her in the lamplight was unrecognizable as the quirky little goblin who used to dog her footsteps at the Source. She looked like a tart. Tight black leggings over bulging thighs, and an enormous black rayon overshirt smeared with makeup round the collar. Her face was white and puffy and pitted with blackheads, the eyes ringed with kohl beneath vestigial pencilled brows. The greasy shoulder-length hair had been dyed dead black, and was flecked with dandruff which she obviously picked, for her parting was dotted with fresh scabs.

Antonia remembered how she had loathed false jocularity at that age. 'You've grown up,' she said flatly.

Modge blinked. 'Well, I've certainly grown.' She spoke with a nasal twang, in the estuary English often affected by well-heeled youth. 'You've changed too. What happened to all the bright colours and the parrot earrings?'

'I ditched them years ago. I'm not much into jewellery any more.' As she said it, she noticed the cheap silver-wire rings crammed onto the plump fingers. Modge caught her glance and raised a pencilled brow.

'Too expensive,' Antonia explained. 'I've got to watch the money.'

Another snort. 'Dad said that's why you're here. To sell the mill.'

'If I can. How about you?'

'How *about* me?'

'Why are you here? Do you like coming back to the valley all the time?'

Modge rolled her eyes. 'Did you, at my age?'

'At your age I didn't like anything.'

Modge threw her a suspicious glance to see if she was being humoured.

There was an awkward silence. Suddenly Antonia sympathized with all those thankless people who had tried to engage her in conversation at that age. She had no idea what Modge liked or disliked, and there seemed little point in trying to find out. She would only be met with a brick wall of mistrust. Damn Julian. What

330

did he think she was, a social worker?

'Did you know,' Modge said casually, 'that Myles is out here too?'

Antonia took that without blinking. At least, she hoped she did.

'It's true,' Modge said, watching her face. 'Mum brought his ashes back and chucked them in the gorge. So just think. When you're down there in that old mill, busily dusting away, you're actually brushing off little bits of my brother.'

Antonia took a long swallow of Merlot. 'I never dust,' she said.

That earned another snort, slightly less belligerent than the last.

So Julian had meant it literally when he said Debra felt closer to her son at La Bastide. Myles was back in the gorge. Myles. In the gorge.

She felt hot and breathless, as if she was about to faint. Suddenly the din was deafening, the Etruscan walls bearing down on her.

A waiter passed with a tray, and she grabbed fresh drinks for herself and Modge, and downed most of hers in a single gulp. She was angry with herself for having succumbed to Julian's emotional blackmail. Who was he, that she should expose herself to this? And what gave any of these people the right to make her feel like an intruder? Here, in this valley which she had once loved?

'*Antonia Hunt, how extraordinary. What brought you back? How long are you staying? Never thought we'd see you here.*'

Why the hell not? She had as much right to be here as they. It wasn't as though she'd committed some crime.

As if summoned by her dark thoughts, Patrick

appeared in the corner of her vision. He was talking to Monsieur Panabière, stooping to bring his head level with the old man's. He wore cords, and a thick poloneck of some muted sea-green fleck, and he looked tired. He was blinking as if the light hurt his eyes.

Time to go.

Unfortunately, she could see no-one within spitting distance on whom to palm off Modge. She couldn't just abandon her. She remembered only too well the glaring horror of being left high and dry at a party.

'You know,' said Modge, 'Mum's absolutely desperate for you to leave.'

'Really?' she said, with exactly the same false jocularity which used to make her own hackles rise. 'I was just thinking I might.'

'Not this *drinks* bollocks,' said Modge with another roll of the eyes. 'The *village*. She wants you out of the village.'

Antonia gave the girl her full attention.

'She's been on the rampage all weekend,' Modge went on. 'Tearing up the house, and calling you "that creature". Is that because you slagged off my brother at the inquest?'

Antonia looked down at her empty glass. 'Probably.' She grabbed another drink, and knocked it back in one. She thought about Debra wishing her well in the Bar-Tabac, then 'tearing up the house' and calling her 'that creature'.

'People are such fucking hypocrites,' said Modge.

'Who's a fucking hypocrite?' said Patrick with a smile, as he moved to join them.

'Not you,' said Modge quickly. 'I didn't mean you.' When she looked at him, she shed a decade. It was painful to watch.

So that's one thing which hasn't changed, thought Antonia. She's still got a massive crush on him.

She turned, and gave him what she hoped was an easy smile. 'Apparently you've got special status,' she remarked.

He did not return the smile. 'Hello, Antonia.'

He never used to drink, but now here he was knocking back the Merlot. Something else that had changed.

She watched him making Modge laugh with an account of a gibbering solicitor. He's done well for himself, she thought, no doubt about that. Weekends in France with the Head of Chambers. Engaged to a judge's daughter.

According to Julian, Patrick was a rising star in his own right: one of the most highly regarded 'senior juniors' in his field, whatever that meant, and tipped to take silk in a couple of years.

She still couldn't believe it.

'I still can't believe you became a lawyer,' she said, when Modge had left them to go to the loo. 'You were going to be a psychologist, and help people. What happened?'

He gave her a lopsided smile. 'Sold my soul to the Devil.' He sounded as if he was only half joking.

'Do you enjoy it?' she asked.

He shrugged. 'Does anyone enjoy their work all the time?'

'God, you really *are* a lawyer,' she replied. 'That was a perfectly meaningless answer.'

He studied her. 'Why'd you come back, Antonia?'

That brought her up short. She had forgotten how direct he could be.

'I told you,' she said. 'To sell the mill.'

'Is that all?'

'Of course.'

He nodded.

She was annoyed to find herself becoming angry. 'I had no idea *you* were out here, if that's what you're thinking.'

'Just curious. That's all.'

She gave him an ill-tempered smile. She could feel her control slipping by the minute – which was hardly surprising, given the amount she had drunk.

Nerissa wandered over and gave her a brief smile, then glanced up at Patrick. 'Glad you could make it,' she told him. 'At last.'

'I've got to go back in a minute,' he replied.

'What, so soon?' She gave Antonia a long-suffering girlfriend grimace. 'He works *all* the time. It's such a bore.'

'I'll bet,' Antonia said, earning a sharp glance from Patrick.

Nerissa leaned against him with easy intimacy.

Antonia felt out of place. Time had stood still for her, with her potsherds and her shell middens. But for Patrick and Nerissa it had moved on to grown-up things, like doing up houses and getting engaged.

God, she really had overdone the wine. It was time to leave before she smashed something.

Unfortunately, her hostess chose that moment to appear at Nerissa's elbow. 'I'm so *glad* you decided to come!' she said to Antonia, with a warmth which made what Modge had told her doubly surreal. 'From what Julian says, we're lucky to catch you at all! Apparently you're off tomorrow?'

Perhaps if Debra hadn't said that, everything would have turned out differently. Perhaps Antonia would have mouthed a few pleasantries, then made an excuse and slipped away. And perhaps next morning she would have flown meekly home, and never seen any of them again.

But it was the way Debra said it. With such calm certainty. The Queen of the valley, serenely assuming that the inconvenient intruder would go quietly, with the minimum of disruption to her realm.

Suddenly Antonia knew just how Monsieur Panabière felt, defending his farm from imaginary invaders. She understood his need to take pot shots at people. She felt like doing it now. 'Not quite,' she told Debra crisply. 'I'm afraid I've changed my mind.'

Patrick's glass stopped on its way to his lips.

Nerissa watched her narrowly.

Debra did a wonderful job of looking faintly surprised. 'Oh? So you're not leaving tomorrow?'

Antonia shook her head. 'I thought that as I'm here, I might as well stay a couple of weeks. In fact,' she smiled, 'I thought I might see if I can find where Myles put the *kántharos*.'

CHAPTER TWENTY-THREE

A military camp outside Perusia, February 40 BC

'I should've had you flogged!' roared Cassius, as his fist connected with his adjutant's jaw and sent him flying.

Around them, rankers stared slack-jawed with amazement. It wasn't often they saw their general lose his temper. And they'd never seen him strike an officer before.

At least someone's enjoying this, thought Cassius grimly. He flexed the fingers of his left hand, which were already beginning to throb.

Quintus Fabius Valens sat blinking in the snow, blood streaming from a broken nose.

'You bloody fool,' said Cassius, standing over him. 'I wonder why I bothered to save your life. I should've had you executed instead of cashiered.'

He ordered a legionary to take the lad away. Then he turned and started walking back to his tent. At his side, his other adjutant, Acilianus, pursed disapproving lips. No doubt he was itching to tell his general that pampering traitors set a bad example for the men. Especially if the traitor was an officer, who should have known better.

Cassius bit back a weary smile. Fabius and Acilianus were both bright, well-bred, ridiculously young, and forever bickering. They reminded him of two small boys vying for their father's attention.

But in their different ways, both interested him, and he was sorry to see Fabius go. Acilianus was a prig and an intellectual snob, but he had a keen mind and an original turn of thought – when he dared to express it. Fabius, on the other hand, was too soft-hearted to be a soldier. He had an eye for the poetry of war, but no stomach for its mechanics. And he was a hopeless leader of men.

The boy had been hauled before Cassius an hour before, having been caught 'red-handed', as Acilianus gleefully put it, sending a note to his sister-in-law in the city. He'd been trying to wrap it round a slingshot, of all things. The oldest trick in the book.

Perhaps, thought Cassius, it was the lack of originality as much as the treason that had infuriated him. 'What in *Hades* do you think you're playing at?' he'd roared when the lad was brought before him. 'Throwing away your career? Jeopardizing your very life? Yes, your life, you idiot! If I was Octavian, you'd be crow-meat by now!'

He had been deliberately coarse, outraging the young officer's feelings in order to drill some sense into him. It hadn't worked.

Fabius had raised his head and given him a proud unrepentant stare, like a Spartan hero facing down the Persians. He'd probably got that from some play. 'I'm sorry, sir,' he said, 'but I had no choice. She's my wife's sister.'

'What sort of excuse is that?'

'Forgive me, sir, but a valid one, I think.'

'Oh, really?' Cassius stared the boy down.

'If you'd ever had a wife,' Fabius muttered with his eyes on the ground, 'you'd understand.'

That had brought Cassius up short. He could hardly chastise the boy for impertinence when he positively encouraged his juniors to voice their opinions. But this shocked him. Was that how they saw him? As a hoary old general who'd never had time for women?

'It's your wife and child I was thinking of,' he growled. 'You don't seem to realize, but attitudes have hardened since the siege began. This idiocy could have got you killed.'

Luckily for Fabius, Octavian was away in Spoletum consulting oracles, so he'd got off lightly. Which was why Acilianus' nose was out of joint.

Cassius flicked the young man a sideways glance. 'You think I was too soft on him.'

'Not my place to comment, sir,' was the crisp response.

'It is if I tell you it is,' Cassius retorted.

A stubborn silence.

'It was a *note*, Marcus. Not a parcel of food or weapons or, Heaven help us, a plan of escape. A note. Advising his poor, silly sister-in-law to do the honourable thing and slit her own throat before we do it for her. It's a little hard to see the treason in that, don't you think?'

The adjutant's long sharp nose went pink at the tip. 'I'm sorry, sir, but you ordered me to state my opinion, so I'm obliged to inform you that I cannot agree.'

Cassius blew out a long breath.

The morning was wearing on. The sun had long since burned off the mist, and a thousand feet above the camp, the walls of the beleaguered city glowed a peachy terracotta. The grim bulk of the Etruscan Gate looked almost benign.

'Tell me,' said Cassius thoughtfully as they crunched

338

through the snow towards his tent. 'Doesn't our task here sometimes strike you as a little bizarre?'

Acilianus' shoulders slumped.

Again, Cassius bit back a smile. His adjutant hated it when he became contemplative. It made him uneasy. He didn't seem to understand that Cassius only did it for amusement. To relieve the tedium of five months of siege.

'No, sir,' Acilianus said severely, 'not at all.'

'I mean,' Cassius went on, warming to his theme, 'here we are, two provincials, supporting the heir of Caesar, the greatest patrician of them all, by sitting on our backsides waiting for *another* lot of patricians to starve to death.'

A dogged silence. Eventually Acilianus said, 'I do wonder about the outcome, though.'

'Mm?'

He looked uncomfortable. 'I mean, what will happen when it's over. Not just to Perusia. To – um, everything.'

Cassius gazed up at the doomed city. A veil of cloud had passed across the sun, and the Etruscan Gate had lost its peachy glow. Now it was merely a great grim block of stone manned by a handful of dying people. 'One thing's for sure,' he murmured. 'When all this is over, we won't have a republic any more.' He thought for a moment. 'Maybe an empire. Of a sort.'

Outside his tent, the sergeant on duty put a letter into his hand. 'Arrived early this morning, sir. From the city.'

'The city?' Cassius frowned. 'Are we due a report from any of the agents?'

'Don't think so, sir,' said the sergeant.

Cassius turned it over to inspect the seal.

The sounds of the camp abruptly fell away. The snow beneath his boots tilted up to meet him.

It was her seal.

No. It couldn't be. She couldn't be up there. Not in that doomed city which he would soon be razing to the ground.

Her husband could not have been so *stupid*! Surely he'd had enough sense to stay away? To stick like a limpet to her brother, that consummate survivor, who had slithered unscathed through years of civil war.

He became aware that Acilianus and the sergeant were watching him curiously. He folded the letter so that they couldn't see the seal, and asked the sergeant if he knew who had delivered it.

A ranker from another unit, he answered. Or maybe a spy. They weren't sure which.

'Hold him,' Cassius ordered, and drew back his tent-flap.

'Sir,' said Acilianus, preparing to follow him in, 'I was thinking that now would be a good time to go through those lists of—'

'Later,' said Cassius. 'I'm not to be disturbed. On any account.'

'But sir—'

'Later,' he snapped, and went inside.

She's in the city, he thought in disbelief.

Faenio had stoked the brazier before he left, and Cassius could feel its heat on his face, but it gave him no warmth. He was cold. So cold.

He wondered how she kept warm up there. An idiotic thought. One did not keep warm in a siege in the middle of winter. He knew, for he'd been in one himself. He remembered the constant cold, which sapped the will and thickened the thoughts like ice-

340

water. And the hunger: a fierce, corrosive pain in the belly.

Ah, no, what was her husband *thinking* of, dragging her into a nightmare like that? Better if she were dead.

Her letter was propped up on the table against a bowl of dates. He hadn't summoned the courage to open it yet, and had turned it round so that he couldn't see the seal. That seal brought back too many memories. Images he had believed were long gone.

Damn her to Hades.

And damn her husband, for bringing her to this.

Lucius Cornelius Verus. The last time he'd seen the man had been on the night of her wedding. He had watched, drunk and invisible behind a raucous throng of wedding guests, as the procession made its way to Cornelius' house.

It had been a big, showy, traditional affair. All the trimmings, no expense spared. The sacrifice, the spelt-cakes, the torchlit procession through the streets.

As tradition demanded, two young boys, probably her cousins, led her by the hand, and a third, wide-eyed and solemn, lit the way with a whitethorn torch. Her head remained downcast and closely veiled as she took the wand and daubed the ceremonial lard on the doorposts of her new husband's house.

Cassius couldn't see her face. He watched her hands winding the posts with the requisite strands of wool. The long sweep of her flame-coloured wedding veil, shocking against the glaring white of her tunic. Like blood on snow.

It was all impeccably proper and old-fashioned. Her family had seen to that. And how like them to go for the harshest, most irrevocable form of marriage. The form which made educated women spit, and mutter about enslavement.

He had wondered what she thought about that. He was forever wondering. What was in her mind? What did she think she was doing? Why, why, why?

The husband stepped out from the throng and made a speech welcoming his guests to his house: a tall, spare man in his fifties, with a sharp nose and no lips, and a thin pasting of red hair across a high freckled skull.

It was commonly believed that red hair was unlucky in a groom, but presumably she felt she could safely disregard that. Cornelius was too rich and too noble for it to present a problem.

Cornelius reached the end of his self-serving little speech, and a hush fell. The crowd parted, the torch-bearer raised his arm, then cast the torch in a high flickering arc down the street.

Cassius held his breath.

According to superstition, this was the last chance for a bride to get out of an unwanted marriage. If she retrieved the spent torch and placed it beneath the marriage bed, her new husband would not live out the night.

Of course that was no more than an old wives' tale, a half-remembered charm from ancient times, which no-one took seriously. No-one except Cassius. Tonight he was with the old wives for all he was worth. This was her last chance. Surely she had bribed someone to retrieve the torch?

Through a haze of cheap wine he watched it roll and clatter across the cobbles. No-one made a move to collect it. No discreet slave in the pay of an unwilling bride. The crowd started cracking jokes again, eager to get inside and begin the wedding feast. He watched the last sparks splutter and die. Bitter smoke stung his eyes. He tasted bile.

The new husband surveyed his guests with a tight little smile, then turned and led the way into the house. She bowed her head and followed him. Clearly, Cornelius wasn't going to exert himself by carrying her over the threshold.

The house swallowed her up.

Cassius didn't remember anything more about that night, or about the days and nights which came after. His good friend Bacchus saw to that. Took him by the scruff of the neck, and hauled him drunkenly through that first terrible confusion of loss.

'Why did you do it?' he whispered to the embers in the brazier, as he had cried out so many times before. Why? *Why?*

Did you ever love me? Or was I just a novelty for you, a bit of rough trade from the provinces? Or perhaps you saw me as a challenge, a famous name to add to your list of conquests?

But how could that be, when she hadn't *had* a list of conquests? He had been the first. He was certain of that.

And it wasn't as if she had been forced into the marriage. Tacita was not a girl to be browbeaten by her family into a match she didn't want. She had gone ahead with it willingly. She had wanted it.

Ah, but there was no point in going over all that again. He had never understood why she did it. He never would.

He turned on his heel and whipped back the tent-flap, to let the icy air slap some sense into him. The startled sentry nearly dropped his spear.

After a minute or so, Cassius went back inside and picked up the letter.

How easily memories revived. One glance at her seal, and all the pain, the anger, came flooding back.

So much for getting over things.

He had thought he'd managed it at last. He remembered sitting up in bed one afternoon – he couldn't recall which afternoon, or whose bed – and putting his pounding head in his hands and telling himself to *stop*.

Stop playing the lovelorn fool. So you've lost her. So what? You're not the first man to lose a woman. The world won't come to an end because of this. Make a clean break. Soldier on. That's what they're paying you for.

And now here he was, right back where he started. And all because of her.

Once, several years before, he had received another letter from her. He had been in Rome, it was winter, the morning after a reading, and a note had arrived, bearing her seal. He knew it instantly. He guessed without opening it that she had been in the audience the day before. She had sat there and listened to him pouring out his heart. He found that peculiarly humiliating. Especially when he remembered the poem he had read. '*I cannot cut free from this love*'.

How she must have enjoyed that! *So he still loves me*, she must have thought smugly, as her litter carried her back to her husband's house.

It had been no effort at all to return the letter unopened. He had scarcely thought about it, and never regretted his decision. He had no regrets now. It had been the right thing to do. The right thing. What in Hades did she expect?

And now here was another letter, just like the first.

He stood in the middle of the tent, looking down at the letter in his hand. Then, quickly, he broke the seal.

It did not take long to read. It was short, and obviously penned in haste. A bald request for him to help her and her family escape the siege.

Short and to the point. How like Tacita. No sentimental harking back to the past, no 'if you ever loved me, think of me now'. She was too proud for that. Her letter did not refer at all to what had once been between them, except for the two little words with which she addressed him at the start.

Mea vita, she began. My life.

Anger curdled inside him. How dare she address him like that after all these years? How *dare* she?

Mea vita. My life.

She used to call him that as they made love in the old tomb by the Porta Capena. She would whisper it against his chest. My life, my life.

He would feel her hands on his back. Her fingers digging into his shoulder-blades. The moist warmth of her breath on his skin. *Mea vita, mea vita*.

He tore up the letter and threw it on the fire.

CHAPTER TWENTY-FOUR

La Bastide, early February, the Present

What a truly bright thing to say, thought Antonia, as she stood in the phone booth nursing a hangover.

'You told them *what*?' yelled Kate.

'I was angry. And drunk. And she acted like she owned the place.'

And you should have seen her face as I said it. Just that one tight little smile. It was terrifying.

'Besides,' she added as an afterthought, 'it's about time I had a crack at finding the wretched thing myself.'

Kate gave a disbelieving snort.

'What's that supposed to mean?'

'It means, how much of this is about a dead Roman, and how much is about Patrick McMullan?'

'Oh leave off, Kate! He's got nothing to do with it. He won't even be here most of the time.'

'I thought you said they were staying the rest of the week.'

Antonia cooled her forehead against the side of the phone booth, and fought down a rising tide of nausea. She wished her friend wasn't quite so relentless.

'I just think,' said Kate, relentlessly, 'you need to be clear about why you're staying. If it's to set the record straight about that cup thing and vindicate you and your dad – fine. If it's to give the Passmores and that man a bloody nose – *not* fine.'

Antonia told her not to be melodramatic, and rang off.

Two hours later, she sat at the kitchen table with her chin on her hand, contemplating the red cardboard wallet of Cassius notes. She had got as far as taking out the postcard of Cassius and sticking it on the fridge, but she still couldn't bring herself to make a start.

A start on what, exactly? she asked herself. What on earth do you think you're doing?

To prevaricate, she cleaned the kitchen as best she could, moving cautiously to avoid stirring up the needles in her skull. Then she washed some bras and pants in the sink. She had almost run out of putting-off tasks, and was taking a bucket of water to the pot-shed in case the rabid horse returned, when Modge appeared in the gateway.

She wore the same black leggings as on the night before, with trainers and a heavy man's sweater – black, of course. Her skin was flaky with several days' makeup, and her eyes were slitted against the wind.

With a grimy thumbnail she dug at the gatepost. 'Mum's pissed off with you,' she said.

'*I'm* pissed off with me,' Antonia replied.

Modge threw her a glance. 'Why?'

'I drank too much last night, and I feel terrible.'

Modge snorted. 'Patrick's pissed off with you too.'

If he was, he hadn't shown it last night. When she'd blurted out that she was going to find the *kántharos*, his face had been a careful study of non-response. God, he was self-controlled.

'He's all right, you know,' said Modge, picking up her train of thought. 'When I was at school he used to send

347

me postcards from court. Sometimes he'd do a sketch. The judge snoozing, or something. He said I was the only one who could read his writing. He's got awful writing, he had to learn all over again when he burnt his hand.'

For Modge it was a speech of epic proportions. She caught Antonia's glance and flushed. Then she nodded at the bucket. 'What's that for?'

'Hippolyte. He and I got off to a bad start.'

'He's just jumpy because of his eye.'

'That's what your father said. It made me feel bad. Hence the bucket.'

'I thought you didn't like horses.'

'I don't,' said Antonia, surprised that she remembered. 'But still. He was here first.'

'It's in the wrong place.'

Antonia threw her a look.

Modge bridled. 'It's true! He'll never come back now that you're here. And if you want to know, horsenuts would be better than just water.'

'Horsenuts,' repeated Antonia, wondering what they were.

There was an awkward pause. For something to say, Antonia asked Modge if she liked horses.

She shrugged. 'They're all right. 'Least they don't order you about all the time.' After a pause she added, 'That's what I want to do, work with horses. There's this course at Newmarket. But I'll never get in.'

'Why not?'

'Mum wants me to go to Oxford – like the paragon.'

It took Antonia a moment to realize that she was talking about Myles. *Myles?* A paragon? Surely Debra hadn't done some kind of posthumous whitewash on him? Poor Myles. He would have hated that.

348

'What was he like?' asked Modge abruptly.

Antonia bit her lip. Then she said, 'Sometimes he could be a real prick.'

Modge lost her seen-it-all cool, and gasped.

'But the thing about Myles,' Antonia went on, 'was that he knew it. And when he was in the right mood, he could laugh at himself. He had a terrific sense of humour. Very black.' She paused. 'I always liked that about him.'

Modge was pretending not to listen. She had gone back to attacking the gatepost with her thumbnail.

Antonia picked up the bucket. 'So where should I put this, then?'

Another shrug. 'I dunno. Just not so close to the mill.'

'Show me.'

Modge heaved a sigh. They left the mill. At the bridge, Antonia turned and started up the track towards the Source. Modge drew back. 'I'm not going up there,' she said accusingly, as if Antonia had tried to lure her into a trap.

'Why not?'

'I never go up there.'

Antonia glanced up the track.

Suddenly she remembered an eight-year-old clutching her breast and keening like a puppy. 'Modge, I'm sorry. I should have thought.'

'Who *cares*?' Modge glowered. 'I don't even remember it.' At Antonia's surprised glance, she rolled her eyes. 'Well why should I? I was only eight.' She paused. 'I s'pose you do. I s'pose you remember everything.'

'I – try not to think about it too much.'

'Then why'd you come back? That doesn't make sense.'

Antonia thought about that. Modge was right.

Modge pointed to a spot about twenty paces further up the track beside a clump of evil-looking hellebore. 'Put it there. It's as good a place as any.'

Antonia crunched up the track and set the bucket in position. Modge had stayed where she was. Antonia called down to her, 'I'm going on for a bit. Why don't you just come part of the way?'

'I *told* you,' Modge shouted, 'I *never* go up there!'

Antonia sighed. She'd had about as much as she could take of maladjusted youth for one morning.

She was almost out of earshot when behind her Modge called out shrilly, 'Antonia! Did you mean what you said?'

'About what?'

The girl's face was white and pinched. 'You know what I mean! Last night. Did you mean what you said about looking for – that *thing*?'

Antonia stopped. 'Yes,' she said at last.

At least, she thought, I meant it then. But what about now?

She walked on up the track, and a chill north wind whipped her cheeks and rattled the dead leaves on the trees.

Kate was right, she must decide why she was staying. And if she was staying at all. Was it for a belated stab at finding the *kántharos*? Or simply because the Passmores – and Patrick – so plainly wanted her gone?

She felt too tired and hungover to sort it out now.

She heard horse's hooves above her on the track. She froze. The crisp *clip-clop, clip-clop* was approaching fast. Monsieur Panabière's little cart-horse trotted round the bend. When it saw her it came to a cartoonish stop – front legs splayed, nostrils dilated – and fixed her with a baleful one-eyed stare.

Mexican stand-off, she thought faintly. Her heart began to thud.

He was much smaller than he had appeared in the pot-shed, and extremely muddy. He had a square, ugly head on a very thick neck, and knobbly Thelwell legs.

Warily he watched her through a matted forelock. One front hoof was tilted, ready for flight, and though he was a good thirty feet away, she could see how it trembled.

He's frightened, she told herself. Just like me.

She forced herself to stay calm. He's just a pony. More scared of you than you are of him.

But that had never worked in the past, and it didn't work now.

They continued to stare at each other. Her mind skittered in all directions. Woman and horse, she thought. On the way to the Spring of the Horse.

Without warning, she was up at the Source on a moonlit night, and a boy's voice, rough with emotion, was saying, 'Didn't they used to call this place the Spring of the Horse? Kind of fits, huh?'

The hairs on the back of her neck stood on end. A tightness which had nothing to do with the hangover gripped her stomach. Where had *that* come from?

She thought back to when she had last walked this track, full of alcohol-induced bravado three days before. *The past has no dominion.* How empty that sounded now.

The past has no dominion? It's all around you! It's down there in the gorge, where Debra Passmore scattered her son's ashes on the wind. It's here on this track, where Patrick's fingers once brushed your arm, and his breath heated your temple as you planned your first weekend together.

Shakily she sat down on a boulder, and put her head between her knees. She forgot about the pony, she forgot about everything except the shock-waves crashing over her.

She stayed with her head between her knees for a long time.

'Are you OK?' said a man's voice in front of her.

Blearily she raised her head.

It was Patrick.

Think of the Devil and he appears, she thought numbly. Only he's not the Devil. He's just a man you once loved, who's become a stranger.

It was a bleak thought, and it made her feel worse.

'You're very pale,' he said, looking down at her. 'Is it the horse?'

Hippolyte was still there, watching them doubtfully, and swishing his tail from side to side.

She licked dry lips. 'Yes,' she muttered. 'It's the horse.'

She watched Patrick amble up to the pony and fondle its ears. Hippolyte nuzzled his chest, leaving a trail of green slobber across his jersey. Patrick didn't seem to mind. He gave the pony a slap on the rump and said, 'Go on, boy, she doesn't want to see you right now,' and the pony tossed his shaggy head, swung round, and trotted back up the track.

Patrick returned and sat on the boulder next to hers. 'Better?'

She nodded. But she wasn't, and he looked unconvinced.

For twelve years she had thought she'd put everything behind her. But all it took was a horse to bring it flooding back.

The wind freshened. She buried her chin in her coat-collar. 'For what it's worth,' she said at last, 'I regret what I said last night. I mean, the way I said it. About Myles. It was insensitive . . . I don't suppose Debra would accept an apology if one were offered?'

'I wouldn't even try.'

'That's what I thought.'

They sat in silence for a while. Then he said quietly, 'I just don't see what you think you can achieve.'

She glanced at him.

'I mean, you can't seriously hope to find that thing after all this time?'

He waited, but she did not reply. He was right. She didn't seriously think that. Did she?

'And why now, Antonia? If you were going to do it, I'd have thought you'd have tried years ago.'

He spoke calmly and without rancour, in the quiet, searching voice he probably used for cross-examining witnesses.

She said, 'I haven't thought about this stuff in years. I've been in the States.'

'Doing what?'

How to answer that? How to tell him what it had been like at the beginning? *'Antonia Hunt? Oh yes. Quite a good brain, but wasn't she involved in something rather ghastly out in France? A boy was killed, wasn't he? And something valuable went missing, under dodgy circumstances? She was in charge, you see. That's the point. Frankly, I don't see how we can have her on the faculty.'*

That sort of thing had followed her around for the first few years. After that she had given up.

She said lightly, 'I made quite a name for myself in shell middens.'

'That sounds a long way from Roman history.'

She hacked at the dirt with her boot-heel. 'It's what I wanted.'

Again he looked at her. 'I thought you wanted Cassius.'

I did, she thought bleakly. Tears pricked her eyes. Probably just the wretched hangover making her weepy. Out loud she said, 'I gave up on him years ago.'

'What do you mean?'

'I got rid of all that stuff. Books. Notes. The lot.'

His face went still. 'When?'

'Just after the inquest. I didn't want anything to do with it.' She forced a smile. 'So melodramatic. The sort of thing you do at twenty-four.'

'It's not melodramatic. It's crazy.'

She shrugged. 'It's all over now.'

A thin rain began to fall, hissing in the dead oak leaves and spattering the track. It occurred to her that so far, neither of them had mentioned the accident – although they were only a few hundred yards from where it happened.

'You know,' she said carefully, 'it took me years to accept that the accident – was just that. An accident. Just something that happened.'

He got to his feet and went to the edge and stood looking down into the gorge. 'So you've made your peace with him,' he said tonelessly.

'I think so, yes.'

He turned. 'Then why are you here?'

She blinked.

'What good is this doing, Antonia? God knows, that was a bad time for all of us . . .'

She flinched.

'Don't go dredging it up again.'

354

'Are you trying to persuade me to leave?'

'I'm trying to persuade someone I once cared about not to make a mess of her life.'

Someone I once cared about.

Again she recalled that moonlit night twelve years ago. If their twenty-four-year-old selves could have known how things would turn out – that they would be standing here now, confronting one another as strangers – how could they have borne it?

'You're exaggerating,' she said evenly. 'A couple of weeks' holiday in the South of France is hardly—'

He raised a hand. 'Don't lock horns with Debra over this. It's a really bad idea. Believe me. I know her.'

She swallowed.

'Go back to London, Antonia. Put this behind you.'

She got to her feet. 'It's because I've been doing that for the past twelve years,' she said, 'that I need to tackle it now.'

That night, Modge had the nightmare for the first time in years.

She was in Highgate Cemetery surrounded by pigeons, and their fluttering wings were all around her, filling her with terror. The only way out was down a flight of vertical steps into some kind of underground chamber, but she couldn't go down there because something small and malevolent was waiting at the bottom.

The fluttering filled her head. Her heart swelled with panic. She screamed, and jerked awake.

Still in her sleeping-bag, she wriggled off the mattress and crossed the floor to the window.

During the night, clouds had rolled down from the mountains and invaded the village. She watched them creeping up the rue de la Clouette: a silent, stealthy visitation from another world. She wondered if she was really awake, or still in the nightmare.

She was filled with an awful confusion of guilt: a hazy sense that she had once done something terrible, and would do anything not to remember what it was.

But what did Highgate Cemetery have to do with that? She'd never even been there.

Once, she'd looked up the nightmare in a book on dreams. The book said that dreams were messages from the subconscious, and often used word-games to disguise their meaning. Which didn't help at all.

She would give anything to be back in Wilton Row, where she could creep down to the breakfast room and huddle with the dogs till it was light. She used to do that when she was eight, when she was having the nightmare every night.

Now a picture opened up inside her head, as if someone had loaded a slide in the projector and clicked it into place. A memory from nowhere.

The *kántharos* stood on the table in the pot-shed. It sucked in the sunlight and throbbed a deep ruby red, as if filled with blood.

She wriggled back across the floor and snapped on the light. 'What's happening?' she whispered, and in the stillness her voice sounded terrifyingly like someone else.

Antonia's back, she thought. That's what's happening.

As soon as she had heard that Antonia was back, she had felt the first prickle of unease. Something awful was opening up beneath her feet, like a lava crust splitting to reveal the churning chaos underneath. And in some way that she didn't understand, the cup was part of it.

She had hated it almost on sight, because after Patrick

and Antonia found it they had changed – and the day after that, Myles took it, and was killed.

Apart from Patrick, she had never told anyone about Myles taking the cup. After their talk in the nursery they had never spoken of it again. She couldn't. She had a superstitious fear that if she did, he would be forced to leave, like in a fairytale.

But it gave her a sick satisfaction to know that at any time she could go to her mother and say, 'Antonia was telling the truth. I know. I helped him take it.' That had a terrible attraction about it, like standing on a cliff thinking, what if I jumped? Because she knew that if she told, her mother would hate her for ever.

That cup, that horrible cup. It all came back to the cup. Patrick and Antonia had dug it up, and everything had gone wrong. And now Antonia wanted to dig it up again.

She huddled deeper in her sleeping-bag.

Outside, the clouds pressed against her window, cutting off the house from the rest of the village. Nothing was real any more. The nightmare was seeping into the waking world.

Julian had been woken by Modge crying out in her sleep.

Debra hadn't stirred, but he knew she was only pretending to be asleep.

By rights, she ought to be asleep. After the fiasco on Sunday night she had thrown herself into an eighteen-hour day of conference calls and fifty-page faxes, in a vain attempt to push away the thought of that poor silly girl down at the mill.

He got up quietly and went out into the corridor to listen at his daughter's door. All was silent.

Twelve years ago, he would have gone in and sat by

the bed till dawn. Three years ago, he would have called out softly to check if she was all right. These days he knew better than to do anything. She would only resent it, and call him patronizing. Perhaps she got that from her mother.

He went downstairs to make tea. The kitchen was warm and welcoming, but he missed the dogs. The Merous' cat sometimes wandered in, but it wasn't the same. Julian admired but didn't at all understand cats, and they could tell.

Standing at the window waiting for the kettle to boil, he saw that down in the valley a light was burning in Patrick's study. His shoulders slumped. God alone knew what Antonia's return was doing to Patrick. He wished he'd never invited her up to the house.

What had he imagined it would achieve? It hadn't done Modge any good. On the contrary, she was having nightmares for the first time in years. And now his poor boy was being deprived of sleep.

His boy. His 'son in law'. He smiled slightly, as he always did at the well-worn joke. Although soon – as soon as Patrick could be persuaded to name the day – it would come true.

Julian had been elated when the engagement was finally announced. It was what he had always secretly longed for but never thought possible, for deep in his heart, he didn't believe Nerissa was good enough for Patrick. An odd thing to think about one's own child, but there it was. He loved Nerissa, but he didn't *like* her. He had caught her lying too often to feel comfortable with her.

Sometimes he wondered if she needed help, if he ought to do something about it. But he never did. If she wanted to pretend that she went to all these auditions, then let her. In time, Patrick would find out. Patrick would deal with it.

Julian loved Patrick. He loved his driven nature and his kindness and romanticism. And he loved the times when he would look at Patrick and see not the polished barrister, but the heartsick boy blinking back the tears on the day of the funeral.

That had been such a ghastly afternoon: dark and cold, with everyone alone in their rooms, wondering what to do next. That was when Julian had wandered onto Patrick's floor, and found the boy standing at the window, looking lost.

'Debra's going out with Nerissa,' Julian had said, feeling suddenly awkward with this silent, intimidatingly young American. 'Sort of a girls' night out.' He paused. 'We can't very well stay in. Too ghastly to contemplate. So I wondered. I know a little bar where they serve the most enormous brandies. D'you care to come along?'

Later, in Saldi's, he had turned from the bar and seen Patrick sitting in the booth, blinking owlishly at the snifter and the Montecristo which the waiter had set before him. Plainly they were the first of either he had encountered, and he was unsure how to tackle them. He looked drained, his blue eyes glassy with unshed tears.

In that moment, Julian's heart went out to him. There was no other way of putting it. His heart actually tightened and strained outwards.

He sat down beside the boy and showed him, without showing him, how to take the tip off the cigar. Then he dropped in what he hoped was a casual-sounding warning against inhaling. 'It's not like, er – pot, d'you see?' At the time he had thought that was rather good, a deft contemporary touch – but afterwards he learned that one no longer called it 'pot', but 'dope' or 'ganja', or some such term. Typically, Patrick had had the grace not to point that out.

He had responded so *gratifyingly*. Within minutes the colour had returned to his cheeks, and his eyes had lost their saucer look.

The kettle was boiling. Julian tore his gaze from the window and made tea.

This was all his fault. He had invited Antonia Hunt up to the house, and now look what had happened. He was to blame for his daughter's nightmares. He was to blame for his poor boy's lack of sleep.

How the devil was he going to get her out?

Modge's nightmare had woken Debra, but she was damned if she was going to check on the girl. She was twenty years old, she had to learn. *Twenty!*

My God, she thought, at that age I'd just had Myles.

Every time she looked at her daughter she felt angry. She was forever reminded of her first thought on hearing the news about Myles.

Why wasn't it Modge?

A terrible thing to think. What sort of mother would think a thing like that?

She would never forget the way she heard the news. It was Saturday evening. Julian was away at some dinner, and she was in the clerks' room in chambers. They had a five-week trial starting on the Monday, and the solicitors had ballsed up the evidence yet again. Strange how precisely she recalled the details.

She was standing at her head clerk's desk, ranting down the phone at the other side's Junior Counsel, when suddenly she glanced across the room and saw Julian standing in the doorway in his dinner jacket, looking at her. Their eyes met over the heads of the clerks, and she knew instantly that something was terribly wrong.

Afterwards, she learned that Patrick had spent hours on the phone in the hospital at Mazerans, tracking down Julian at the dinner, rather than calling her directly at chambers. He had wanted her to hear the news from her husband, not from some policeman, or from an American she'd never met.

For that she would be grateful to him for the rest of her life. She couldn't have borne it if Julian had not been with her when she heard.

She thought about that moment every day when she woke up.

Why wasn't it Modge?

She couldn't remember the funeral at all, and most of the inquest was a blur, except for Patrick telling the coroner that Myles had been his best friend. *His best friend*, she had thought numbly, at the time. *I never knew any of his friends. I never knew my son.*

But what else could you have done? You never planned to have children. They were a mistake.

She had never imagined how much time a baby took up. And the law was implacable. It stopped for no man, and certainly not for a woman with a child. Within a month, she had given him to a nanny.

I never knew my son.

And now that girl was back. Resurrecting her lies. Calling Myles a thief again.

She sat up quickly, pushing her hair behind her ears. No more agonizing. You've lain in bed doing nothing for long enough. It's time to act.

A glance at her watch told her it was five o'clock, which meant four in London. Her clerk would be overjoyed to be woken at this hour. Well, tough. He could make himself useful for once, instead of messing up her diary.

She rang him at home and told him to drive to chambers and fax her the details of the six best notaries in France. Now.

Time to get moving.

Time to get that girl out of here.

Down in the valley, Patrick had woken at four with the same headache he'd had when he went to bed. Fortunately, his restlessness had not disturbed Nerissa, who was a heavy sleeper.

He pulled on jeans and a sweater, and went downstairs to his study.

'I got rid of all that Cassius stuff . . . Just after the inquest. I didn't want anything to do with it.'

The way she had looked as she said it.

He remembered the way she used to talk about her work, falling over her words in her eagerness to explain. The warmth in her brown eyes. The uncertainty. The need to be loved.

She used to wear coloured ribbons in her hair, two or three together. He would place bets with himself as to which ones she'd be wearing next. Mint, raspberry, lemon, grape. Today on the hill, she had worn a dark-blue scarf wound several times about her neck. It contrasted shockingly with the extreme pallor of her face.

He went to the window and stood watching the clouds invading the village.

She was playing with fire, taking on Debra! It was like watching a puppy toddling along the edge of a cliff, and being unable to help.

He had tried to warn her, but it hadn't done any good.

He had known it would not. Once Antonia got her teeth into something, she wouldn't let go. She didn't know how. That was Antonia.

He snapped on the desk light, and began to search the drawers. He couldn't remember where he had put the bloody thing.

At last he found what he was looking for, in a small drawer behind the pigeon-holes. He took it out and cleared a space on the desk, and unrolled Antonia's line drawing of the *kántharos* reliefs.

It was scarcely yellowed after its long incarceration in his desk. It looked just the same as when Myles had given it to Modge for safe keeping.

Patrick had not looked at it in twelve years. Not since the night he'd returned from Suffolk.

He gazed down at Pegasus trotting with flying tail and tilted head towards Bellerophon. The young man's face was serenely joyful, confident in his own strength, and in the justice and goodness of the world.

Slowly, Patrick rolled it up and put it back in his desk.

He had loved her once. When she walked into a room and said his name it was as if no-one had ever spoken it before, as if she made him a new and better person just by saying it. And sometimes, when they were drinking on the terrace and Modge said something funny or Myles acted up, there would be an instant when he would meet her eyes, and know that she felt what he did. Whatever it was – affection, impatience, amusement – she was feeling it too. He wasn't alone any more.

He got up swiftly and went into the kitchen. Stuff like that only happens in your twenties, he told himself. Then you grow up. You put away childish things.

Four hours later, Nerissa came sleepily downstairs, to find him packing up his papers.

'I thought we'd go back to London today,' he said over his shoulder. 'If that's OK with you.'

'Whatever,' she yawned. 'It'll give me a chance to prepare for that audition.'

'Fine,' said Patrick. 'I'll call the airline and change our flights.'

The day after her encounter with Patrick, Antonia moved the kitchen table back against the wall, dragged in the mock-Tudor desk from the sitting room, and set up a workstation.

Then, still restless, she drove to Mazerans for supplies. She had already returned the rental car, but Vassals *fils* had surprised her by coming forward with the loan of a clapped-out Citroën which had been gathering rust in his barn for years.

The drive to Mazerans was a mistake. She had forgotten the narrowness of the roads, and the kamikaze tendencies of the locals. By the time she got back, she was white and shaking.

As she opened the door, she was engulfed in the subterranean stillness of the mill. Streaming walls, a musty smell of mouse, and the dispirited glimmer of the forty-watt bulb. To warm herself up, she spent half an hour running a bath, which was cold by the time it was three inches deep. Around four, she wandered up to the bridge.

Patrick's house was in darkness, the shutters closed, the Discovery gone. In the Bar-Tabac, she had learned that he and Nerissa had cut short their trip and gone back to London. Well, fine, she thought. At least you won't have to picture them wandering around in nearly married bliss.

She leaned over the parapet and gazed down at the foaming white water. How strange, she thought. You spend hours trying to work out what you're doing here, then you blurt out the truth to Patrick without even thinking.

'It's because I've been putting it all behind me that I need to tackle it now,' she had told him.

She saw now that it really was as simple as that.

She brought out the postcard of Cassius, which she had taken with her for good luck on the drive to Mazerans. Looking down at the beautiful, searching face, she thought of what she had lost when she had given him up. She remembered how she used to feel about her work – really *feel*. All that beauty and imagination and joy. All that fizzing optimism. *She* was going to be the one to solve the riddle, just as her father had said. *She* was going to show the world what Cassius was really like, to prove that Lycaris was not some dry poetic construct, but a living woman whom he had loved with all his heart.

She had been going to do all that. And now look at her. Her life was reduced to shell middens, and Professor Edgeware's monograph on pots. She had let everything she cared about slip away. She had stood back and watched it happen. If she gave up now and went back to London, none of that would change. She would have nothing but shell middens and monographs for the rest of her life. She would disappear into the woodwork. She might as well be dead.

This was no longer about defying the Passmores, or Patrick, or even vindicating her father and setting the record straight. It was too late for any of that. This was about regaining what she had lost.

Again she glanced at the dark, shuttered bulk of Patrick's house. It was good that he had gone. Much better without him.

She studied the postcard in the gathering dusk. 'From now on, Cassius,' she said, 'it's just you and me.'

CHAPTER TWENTY-FIVE

A week later, the impossibility of finding the *kántharos* began to sink in.

The two favourites, the mill itself and the Source, had turned up nothing after extensive searches. Which meant that after a week Antonia had narrowed it down to anywhere on the cliff between the mill and the Source. Or in other words, half a mountainside. Unless of course Myles had jumped in a car and driven out of the village, in which case it could be just about anywhere.

She pushed back her chair, went to the range for her tenth mug of coffee that morning, and wondered what to do now. Then she poured the coffee down the sink, flung on her jacket, and let herself out into the teeth of a blustery north wind. Maybe a blast of cold air would clear her thoughts.

She walked fast to keep warm, and by the time she reached the slope above the mill her head was spinning and she had to stop for breath.

Automatically she checked Patrick's house for signs of life, but it was still dark and shuttered.

No reason for it to be otherwise, she told herself. Get back to the problem in hand.

You can't find the cup, and there's a good chance that you never will. So what do you do now?

The choice was a stark one. Either accept that the

search was hopeless, pack her things and go home, or – what?

Do what you've been longing to do all along, said a voice in her head, and tackle the riddle. No more delays, no more putting off. Let's solve this thing.

In poculo veritas.

The truth is in the cup.

Again she glanced at Patrick's house. Returning to London would mean that the Passmores – and Patrick – had won. So the choice turned out to be no choice at all.

Back at the mill, she found her battered copy of Plautius' *Letters*, and turned up the old man's account of the riddle.

'*We sat outside his house in the warm spring sunshine,*' wrote Plautius, allowing himself a rare touch of lyricism,

and Cassius turned the razor in his fingers so that the light caught it, and said, 'When I'm dead, I want you to make a libation to the Goddess. This must be for me and for Lycaris together, so that our spirits will be joined after death. This is important, my friend. I need to know it will be done.'

At this I became greatly agitated. 'But how can I do this,' I said, 'for you've never told me her true name! You must tell me, or the Goddess won't hear the prayer.' Cassius gave a slight smile. 'That's a problem. But I'm afraid it's impossible.'

Thoughtfully, he went to the edge of the terrace, pausing to admire his favourite wild pear tree, which was just coming into bloom. Then he turned back to me and said, 'What I can do is set you a riddle, which will only reveal her name when she too is gone.'

He raised his splendid new drinking-cup to his lips and drank, and said, 'The truth is in the cup.' Then he smiled again, and said, 'Not very clear, perhaps. But if the Goddess wills it, you or someone who comes after will solve it, I think.'

Antonia sat back in her chair and gazed at the post-card on the fridge. Realistically, Cassius must have known that there was little chance of poor old Plautius – an octogenarian by then – outliving Lycaris and solving the riddle. So he must have been counting on the old man's pedantry as a lawyer to record his exact words, thereby giving posterity a chance.

'Because you *wanted* someone to solve it,' she told the postcard. 'Didn't you? "This is important . . . I need to know it will be done." You needed to know that someone, some time, would uncover the truth and make the libation, and bring your spirits together. Will it be me, Cassius? Will you help me to help you?'

Impassively the marble eyes gazed back at her, giving nothing away.

'*The truth is in the cup.* Or maybe it's *on* the cup. If only I had the bloody thing I might be able to work out which.'

She strained to picture it. She saw it in the pot-shed as it had looked on the afternoon before the accident.

Patrick touched the table with his long brown fingers, and glanced from her to the kántharos. '*Did you find anything inside?*'

She shook her head. '*Only sand. So much for "the truth is in the cup".*'

He gave her an enquiring look.

'*The Cassius riddle,*' *she said.* '*At least, I think that's what it means.*'

369

She stood up quickly, knocking over her chair. The clarity of the memory was breathtaking.

This isn't *about* Patrick, she told herself. He's just getting in the way. Slam the door. Shut the lid. Get back to the cup.

The cup.

How it had glowed in the dusty sunlight. Like rubies, or fresh blood. How beautiful Pegasus had looked as he trotted joyfully towards Bellerophon.

It seemed entirely natural that Pegasus should feature on a poet's drinking-cup, for to the Romans he had been a potent symbol of inspiration. And Pegasus was also sacred to the Moon, which gave him another link to the Source.

'The Spring of the Horse,' she murmured.

Could there be any significance in *where* the cup was found? Could that tell her anything about Lycaris?

The Source had been an ancient shrine to some sort of moon goddess, or perhaps to Cybele the Great Mother, or possibly an amalgam of the two. And Cybele had been Cassius' favourite deity – the goddess he had trusted to reunite his spirit with Lycaris. Could Lycaris have been a priestess of Cybele? Or perhaps a fellow-worshipper, whom he'd met at some ceremony honouring the Goddess?

But that was mere speculation. There was nothing in the *Poems* to support it.

Unless, she thought suddenly, unless you've been on the wrong track all along – and Pegasus himself is the key? Maybe the truth is, *literally*, in the reliefs?

She dredged up everything she could remember about the Pegasus myth.

Bellerophon had tamed the magical horse, and over many adventures, a bond of love had grown between

370

them. But then Bellerophon had become arrogant, and stormed Olympus, so Zeus had ordered Pegasus to topple his master from the skies and leave him to his fate. For the rest of his life, Bellerophon had wandered the earth alone – blind, crippled, yearning in vain for his miraculous companion.

So why, Antonia wondered suddenly, are Pegasus and Bellerophon reunited on the *kántharos*?

Wait. Wasn't there another version of the story? A lost play – known only from a few lines quoted in Ovid – in which, after many years, man and horse are joyfully reunited?

Feverishly, she ransacked the cupboards till she found the mildewed copy of Ovid in her father's old room.

A crushing disappointment. The dates were all wrong. According to the footnotes, the play had been written in the decade before Christ: a good thirty years *after* Cassius died.

Still nagged by a sense that she was missing something, she prowled round the kitchen table. Perhaps it was some tiny detail in the reliefs which had slipped her mind. If only she had the line drawing, she would have a chance. Damn Myles for taking that too.

Still circling, she became aware that the room was going round faster than she. She sat down, and a few seconds afterwards, the room came to a halt. She glanced at her watch. It was three in the afternoon. Had she had breakfast? Or lunch? She couldn't remember.

The fridge contained half a chicory, three rashers of iridescent bacon, and an egg. She made herself another mug of coffee.

Again she struggled to picture the *kántharos*.

But Patrick was back in the pot-shed, and although he was keeping to his side of the table, she knew that he wanted to touch her, for his hand was moving slowly up and down the grain of the wood.

She walked round to him. Put her fingertips to his wristbone. Traced the thick corded vein up his forearm.

He placed his warm hand on the nape of her neck and drew her to him, and bent his head to—

The phone rang.

She jumped.

Heart pounding, she started at the new phone which had been installed only the day before.

No-one had her number except for Kate, who was incommunicado on location for the next two days. So who could it be?

Debra? Nerissa? Patrick?

Warily she got to her feet and picked up the receiver. 'Hello?'

'Wow,' said Simon Toynbee, 'I must be out of touch. I thought it took months to get a phone in Europe. What'd you do, sleep with a phone engineer?'

She breathed out. 'Hello, Simon,' she said. 'I suppose Kate gave you my number?'

'Uh-huh.'

She had forgotten his love of Americanisms. That was one of the things which had irritated her towards the end.

'So what's with the phone?' he said. 'You planning to stay out there awhile?'

She told him about Kate's threat to invade if she didn't get a phone, and Vassals *fils*' brother-in-law in France Télécom. She did not volunteer that Vassals *fils* had felt obliged to pull strings for her out of guilt at the coolness of the other villagers.

Simon was telling her about his latest 'project'. She searched her memory for what Kate had said in her last Simon update.

'He's working in London now,' Kate had told her. 'Freelancing, but going all out for some job at Timescape Productions. Assistant producer of documentary features. I'd be amazed if he got it, but then, he always did aim high.' After a pause she added, 'He asked after you, which I thought was rather nice. I mean, not bearing a grudge or anything, when you dumped him like that.'

'I didn't "dump" him,' Antonia had replied. 'I simply told him I didn't think we should go on seeing each other. We agreed from the start that it would be low-key.'

'Yes, I'm sure it was all very rational and PC. But still, it's nice that he took it so well.'

She wrenched her mind back to the present. Simon was still talking about his 'project', and as she had no idea what it was, she opted for silence rather than trying to make the right noises. Simon had a keen ear for when someone wasn't listening.

As always when she spoke to him, she felt a twinge of guilt. They had got together in Arizona because they were the only English people in the Archaeology Department, he fancied her, and she had been alone for so long that she needed to know that that was still possible. Moreover he posed no threat to her, for there was never any danger of getting emotionally involved. Which was hardly fair on Simon – a fact he had been at pains to point out when they split up.

That had been three years ago. Since then, they had talked on the phone from time to time. As Kate said, 'All very rational and PC.'

She realized he had asked her a question. Something about a conference in Bordeaux? 'Sorry,' she said, 'the line's awful at my end, what was that?'

'I said, the conference is in a couple of weeks, so if you're still there, how about I drive over and we have dinner, for old times' sake?'

She winced. 'Oh, I don't know . . .'

He gave a hollow laugh. 'Can't even commit to dinner, huh? Same old Toni. And I really thought we'd made some headway with that isolation thing of yours.'

She did not reply.

'So what are you doing out there, anyhow?' he said.

'Oh, this and that.'

'Kate says you're after that cup thing. But that can't be right. Right?'

'Why not?' she asked, nettled. 'That cup thing' was a deliberate trivialization, designed to get under her skin.

'Jesus, Toni. I thought you got rid of that fixation years ago!'

'It's not a fixation, and can we please talk about this some other time? Why don't you give me your number and I'll ring you back?'

'What's this, "don't call me, I'll call you"?'

'Come on, Simon, give me a break. I've got work to do.'

That shut him up. He was sensitive about her work, and always on the lookout for signs that she was ahead of him – even though he had quit archaeology years ago for TV journalism.

He gave her his number and rang off.

Carefully, she replaced the receiver. Bloody Kate. Just as well that she *was* incommunicado, or she'd get a bollocking down the phone.

She wondered if Kate had told Simon about Patrick.

On the whole, she thought not. Simon had always loathed Patrick. If he had known that his old rival was back in the valley, he wouldn't have been able to resist a comment.

Bloody Kate. Bloody Simon. Bloody Patrick.

'Bloody hell,' she said.

Two weeks passed, and she never did call Simon back.

The Passmores came for weekends, but left her alone, and Patrick's house stayed empty and dark. He couldn't spare the time, said Modge, when Antonia bumped into her in the place de la Mairie. The girl looked worse than ever, pasty-faced and tired, and her eyes wouldn't meet Antonia's. Modge pointedly did not ask about her progress with the *kántharos*, and Antonia didn't volunteer an update. Besides, there wasn't much to tell.

For two weeks she had gone back to basics, and re-read all she could find on Cassius. She'd haunted the museums and libraries of Narbonne, Toulouse and Béziers. She'd immersed herself in the *Poems*. And every day she wished that she hadn't incinerated her notes.

So far, all she had come up with was a clearer sense of the social gulf between Cassius and Lycaris.

> *Your suitors can give you ropes of deep-glowing*
> *emeralds and yellow topazes.*
> *I can't offer you anything.*
> *Except perhaps immortality.*

Yes, Lycaris had definitely been an uptown girl. But what *kind* of uptown girl? In Rome at the end of the Republic there had been quite a range. Was she already married when she met Cassius? Or a divorcée? Or an innocent? Or a high-class prostitute?

375

'Rule out the first,' Antonia said, circling the kitchen table, 'because reading between the lines, she and Cassius split up when she *got* married – to an older and richer man. And rule out the last, because if she'd been a whore, you'd have said, wouldn't you, Cassius? You were never one to mince your words.'

Which left either a divorcée or an innocent.

She stopped circling and rubbed her eyes. It was half-past one in the morning, but there was no point in going to bed, for she wouldn't sleep. As soon as her head touched the pillow her brain would go into overdrive.

She sat down and closed her eyes. Snatches of poetry drifted into her mind.

'Her breath yielded to mine, and mine to hers . . . We were sheeted in fire . . . My heart went up and sang in the sky . . . And now like Pegasus I ride the stars, I walk the spellbound moon . . .'

Her eyes snapped open.

Wait. You're missing something. You've got the lines jumbled up. 'My heart went up' is from a different poem.

But why does that matter?

Her pulse quickened. She didn't know why it mattered. Just that it did.

Feverishly she flicked through the *Poems* till she found the line. It was where she least expected it. In the *last* poem. The one Cassius wrote on the day he killed himself. How could she have forgotten something as important as that?

Last night I dreamed of you again.
Beneath my eyelids you appeared for the final time,
and my heart went up and sang in the sky.
Now my death will not be bitter,

I won't drown in the river of darkness.
And when your own time comes, Beloved,
may the Goddess grant our plea,
and breathe your spirit into mine,
and mine into yours, for eternity.

That final poem, so famously different from the others he had written after the break-up with Lycaris. It was as if at last he had vanquished all the anger and the pain. As if he had finally come out into the light.

'To most modern readers,' one Cambridge classicist had written, 'such joy on the day of one's own death is impossible to comprehend – but the Roman was different. To him, death was not the end, but a door into another life, to be welcomed with rejoicing.'

Another classicist – this time from Oxford – had arrived at precisely the opposite conclusion. 'The last poem is not, as some misguided commentators have claimed, about *embracing* death, but *defying* it. It is a magnificent refusal to countenance the dying of the light.'

What if, Antonia wondered, they're both wrong? What if the answer is both simpler and more mysterious than that?

For if Lycaris had caused the dark fatalism of the later poems, might she not also have caused the miraculous lightening at the end?

'You're on to something,' she breathed. She knew it. She had the same prickling sense of connection as she did in the moment before making a find, when a current seemed to ripple from the earth into her fingertips.

Think. *Think.*

Somehow, Lycaris had brought about a turnaround in Cassius – an alteration so profound that he had sat down and written that last, extraordinary poem. Then, *on the same day*, according to Plautius, he had opened his veins.

Therefore, there must be some connection between his death and Lycaris. Therefore, the key was to find out *why* he killed himself.

Once again, she turned up the old man's account in the *Letters*, but it gave no clue. Not even Plautius seemed to know why. All he could suggest was that his friend had suffered a catastrophic fall from grace and taken the honourable way out, rather than face the dishonour of a sham trial.

So far, so Roman. But why? What had Cassius done to bring such disaster on his head? And why couldn't he have found another way out? By all accounts he had been a resourceful, highly experienced officer, who had for years successfully navigated the perilous political waters of the dying Republic. So why had he given up and taken his own life? It just didn't seem like Cassius.

But clearly this was the question she must answer if she was going to solve the riddle.

Filled with new energy, she made another cup of coffee, and settled down to re-read everything she'd gleaned over the past three weeks. It was two-thirty in the morning, but what the hell. At least the phone wouldn't ring.

To her surprise, she realized that in all her years with Cassius she had never focused on his death. Nor, it turned out, had anyone else. They had all been content to look no further than Plautius' account. And in a sense, why shouldn't they? No-one had ever regarded the poet's death as the key to Lycaris.

Three hours later, she had found nothing to add to the *Letters*, except for a vague recollection that somewhere in her old notes – the ones she'd incinerated in the rhubarb patch – there had been an obscure reference which might be of use. She shut her eyes and struggled to dredge it up. She remembered a note scribbled in green ink in her copy of Frontinus' *Stratagems* – a first-century compendium of underhand military tricks in which Cassius had been cited with approval. But infuriatingly, she couldn't remember what it said.

By six o'clock, just as the first chickens in the village were beginning to complain, she knew what she had to do. She had to retrace her steps: go back to Frontinus, review what she had once known about Roman military tactics, and hope that something in the trawl would jog her memory. The only place where she could do that was the British Library.

She had to go to London. There was just enough credit left on her card to cover a ticket, and she could stay in Erica Gardens to save the heating on her flat. Kate wouldn't mind. In fact, she had been pestering her to take a break. She would be delighted.

Kate wasn't. Kate was horrified.

'Exactly how much weight *have* you lost?' she demanded as soon as she opened the door. Then she reached out and unceremoniously pulled down Antonia's lower eyelid. 'I knew it,' she snapped. 'You're anaemic. Which is hardly surprising, when you're living on nothing but bread and wine.'

'No wine,' said Antonia, dropping her bag on the rug and collapsing onto the sofa. 'It may surprise you to learn that I haven't had a drink in three weeks.' Which was only because she'd forgotten to buy any, but Kate didn't need to know that.

Kate ignored her. 'And what sort of visit do you call this?' she demanded. *'Two days?'*

'A practical one,' Antonia replied. 'I need to get back, I've got work to do.'

Kate took the chair opposite, and crossed her arms over her bosom. 'I still can't believe you're letting that man ruin your life all over again.'

'This is about *regaining* my life. Not ruining it. And "that man" has nothing to do with anything.'

Kate studied her with narrowed eyes. Then she gave a theatrical shrug. 'If that's the way you want it. To change the subject, a letter came for you yesterday, by courier. I think it's from that French lawyer of yours.' She held it out. 'I was going to call you last night,' she said, watching Antonia open it, 'but your line was busy.'

'Mm,' said Antonia, scanning the letter.

'Well? Is it good news?'

'Mm,' said Antonia again. 'You were right, it is from the notary . . . It seems he's found a buyer for the mill.'

'What? But that's *amazing!'*

Antonia nodded, and handed Kate the letter. She sat back in the sofa, closed her eyes, and wished she didn't feel so exhausted and let-down. Maybe Kate was right about the anaemia. She watched her friend reading the letter under her breath, ticking off the good points with little jerks of her spiky Mrs Tiggywinkle head.

A company owned by a consortium of Swiss tax exiles was looking for a site in the area to develop as a hotel. If the venture proved profitable that would be fine, but if it didn't that would be fine too, as they could offset the losses against their other gains. The money they were offering was more than generous, and they would let her stay on rent-free for a month or so to complete her research, provided she committed to the sale immediately – which the *notaire* clearly believed she should, for with his letter he had enclosed the papers for her to sign.

Kate was right, it was amazing news. Incredible, far better than she could have hoped.

'So why aren't you over the moon?' said Kate.

'I am,' said Antonia, still with her eyes closed.

She heard Kate's exasperated sigh. 'What did he *say* to you?'

'Who?'

'Patrick McMullan.'

'I told you, this has nothing to do with him.'

'So why the dull-thud reaction to the purchaser of your dreams?'

Antonia opened her eyes and stared at the ceiling. Please, Kate, don't cross-examine me. Not now. Out loud she said, 'Because I want to stay at the mill and solve the riddle.'

'But it says here that you can stay on for another month—'

'It could take longer than that.'

'So? You can continue when you're back in London.'

'No I can't.'

'Why not?'

Antonia bit down on her irritation. Come on, she told herself, don't snap. This is the only friend you've got. 'I don't *know*,' she said at last. 'I just know that I need to be there. That's all.'

There was silence. Then Antonia said, 'Now, Kate. To change the subject again. Let's talk about Simon Toynbee.'

How like Antonia to make herself ill, thought Patrick as he watched Nerissa making her way towards him through the crowded restaurant.

'Acute anaemia,' the madwoman had ranted on the phone. 'The poor girl's making herself ill, and it's your fault for victimizing her.'

He had tried to tell her that she was mistaken, but he hadn't got very far. 'Ms Walker—'

'Don't give me that *Miz* rubbish! It's *Mrs* Walker to you, thank you very much—'

'Fine,' said Patrick wearily. '*Mrs* Walker. I'm afraid I don't know what you're talking about. I haven't seen *Miss* Hunt for the past three weeks, and the one time we did speak, I tried gently—'

'*Gently?*'

'Gently – to talk her out of it. So while I'm sorry that she's ill, it really has nothing to do with me.'

'Tell that to your horrible Marines,' snapped the madwoman, and rang off.

Heads turned as Nerissa came towards him, and two waiters hurried up to make sure she could manage her chair.

'How was the audition?' he asked.

She made a face and shook her head.

He wondered when she would get around to telling him what she actually did when she was supposed to be at these auditions. It never seemed the right time to ask her. Maybe she had a lover. He found that he didn't really care. And instead of making him angry, that only made him feel sorry for her.

He ought to care. This wasn't fair on her. Or on Julian, or even on Debra, who, although she regarded her stepdaughter as an alien species, clearly approved of the engagement. Perhaps she saw it as some kind of dynastic coup.

'Excellent wife material,' he could imagine her saying. And she was right. Nerissa looked stunning, could run

382

his social life superbly, and would no doubt give him beautiful children – while leaving him free to get on with his work. He was a bloody lucky man, as his colleagues were fond of telling him.

Suddenly he felt exhausted. He wondered if that was the headaches, or the Anderson case, or Antonia.

Probably Antonia. Why couldn't she just give up and go home? Because of her, Modge had retreated further and further into her frightened little shell, and Debra was punishing herself even more than usual and grinding the rest of chambers into the ground, and Julian was wandering around like one of his Labradors, looking lost.

Nerissa was telling him something about her latest audition, but he couldn't hear, for the restaurant was the usual high-decibel nightmare.

He longed for the peace and solitude of the valley.

It was the beginning of March, so the first signs of spring would be softening the jagged edges of the Fenouillèdes. Great splashes of yellow broom would be lighting up the hillsides, the rosemary would be swarming with bees, and the almonds and mimosas would be bursting into bloom.

He longed to be there.

And he needed to make sure that Antonia was all right.

Unfortunately for Antonia, Kate wasn't only correct about the anaemia. Two days turned out to be far too short to complete the research at the British Library.

What had she been thinking of? Did anaemia muddle the brain? It took her two whole days just to track down the reference which she had scribbled on Frontinus – and then it turned out to be only a footnote in an obscure German text on Roman military strategy, which didn't advance things very far. All it contained was a cryptic reference to Cassius' legion having been involved in the Perusine War of 40 BC, the five-month siege which had marked a critical phase in the Civil War.

From Plautius, she knew that Cassius had been on active service throughout that time, so it was safe to assume that he had been with his legion during the terrible climax of the siege, when the city was torched, and three hundred republicans massacred.

But that was as far as she could get – except for a throwaway reference to another, still more obscure German monograph on siege tactics, which might possibly contain something more promising.

That reference, the pretty young librarian told her, was in off-site storage, sorry, it would take a couple of days to retrieve. Antonia explained that she didn't *have* a couple of days, as her plane ticket was a budget one and couldn't be changed, nor could she afford to buy another. The librarian thawed slightly. For a small fee, they could post her a photocopy in France, or maybe she'd like to try the pilot e-mail scheme? Antonia chose the post. The mill's electricity was erratic. Her laptop had crashed twice already.

By now it was five o'clock. She went out into the Charing Cross Road and bought a bottle of iron pills and, on impulse, a small black nylon rucksack for Modge, along with two big fluorescent green plastic hair-clips. She tucked one inside the rucksack with a note scribbled on the receipt: *I'll wear mine if you wear yours*. Maybe it would persuade Modge to wash her hair.

Unfortunately, that left no time to look for a horse outfitter's, or whatever kind of shop might sell the 'horsenuts' that Modge had suggested for Hippolyte.

Standing in the middle of the pavement amid a heaving throng of shoppers, Antonia suddenly had an acute attack of loneliness. She felt like a time traveller, moving unseen and unheard among people inhabiting a dimension other than her own. Backpackers stared through her with the sulky arrogance of youth. Families broke and flowed round her and re-formed, secure in their little bubbles of connectedness.

Her spirits plummeted. Everything was hopeless. She would never solve the riddle. Her life stretched before her as an endless round of pointless research and 'To Do' lists and self-imposed deadlines, which were really nothing more than a pathetic attempt to invest her life with meaning – when the truth was, no-one except Kate cared if she ever got out of bed again.

She wondered where Patrick was, and what he was doing. Probably working late at chambers after a heavy day in court, beating up old ladies in the name of multi-nationals. A bleak thought. It made her feel worse.

It was half-past five, but she couldn't face the family togetherness of Erica Gardens, so she took the Tube to Finsbury Park and went to check on her flat. She needed to go there anyway for more clothes; and the answer-phone would come in handy, too. Kate had been pestering her to take it over. 'It's bad enough your being all alone out there without ignoring my calls whenever you like.'

To her dismay, the flat was in almost exactly the same state of disrepair as when the pipes had burst a month ago – right down to the patch of plaster shaped like Africa which had landed on her Weetabix on that fateful morning when she had nipped out for milk, and the ceiling fell in.

'This is beyond a *joke*,' she muttered, subsiding into a chair and feeling ridiculously close to tears.

So what do you do now? Stay on for a few more days, and put a bomb under the builders?

That would be the logical, the practical thing to do. But how could she, when the envelope from the British Library would soon be winging its way to La Bastide?

She decided to write the builders a stiff note, and leave it at that.

But she couldn't find any paper. Not a single sheet, not anywhere in the flat. Then she remembered that when the ceiling came down, she had salvaged all her books and papers and moved them to the safety of Kate's loft.

'Beyond a *joke*,' she repeated, ransacking her bag for something to write on, and coming up with nothing, not even a till receipt.

Eventually, in her ancient filing cabinet, she found a grubby pack of Post-It notes which had slipped down between the suspension files. It would have to do.

But she never got to write her note, for something else had also fallen between the files. It was a small sheet of white paper, carefully folded into four. She recognized at once.

It was the slip of paper on which Patrick had typed his Oxford address just before the inquest. He couldn't write in longhand because of the burns on his hand, so instead he had typed it, including painstaking directions, so that she wouldn't get lost.

They had been standing together on the steps of the Coroner's Court, and he had reached into his breast pocket and brought out the paper and handed it to her – quickly, as if he might change his mind and take it back.

'I'll call you after the hearing,' she had told him, pocketing the note.

He nodded. 'After the hearing. Right.'

He had been ill at ease in his unfamiliar suit: young and grave, and far too thin. He had looked down at her with those vivid blue eyes, and her heart had swelled with sudden happiness, for she had believed that everything would turn out all right. She had truly believed that nothing – not even the accident – could come between them.

Angrily she crumpled the note and shoved it in her pocket. What a fool she had been to keep it all these years. What a stupid, pathetic, sentimental *fool*.

She searched her bag and brought out the number Simon had given her two weeks before. Then she called him, and arranged dinner at La Bastide.

CHAPTER TWENTY-SIX

As soon as they entered the little restaurant in Mazerans, Antonia knew that dinner with Simon was a mistake.

It wasn't his fault. He was just the same as always: clever, insecure, amusing and intolerant. But this seemed to be one occasion when the wrong company was worse than no company at all.

That made her feel bad about having got him to drive all the way from Bordeaux, and she redoubled her efforts to be nice. But as she watched him patronizing the waiter, she did wonder what she had once seen in him. He was good-looking and he fancied her. Was that all it took?

People meeting Simon for the first time were often struck by his resemblance to Vincent Van Gogh, although they soon decided that Simon was better looking. He had pale, deep-set eyes fringed with blond lashes, a severe mouth, and an aquiline nose. To underline the resemblance – of which he was secretly proud – he wore his sandy red hair in a brush-cut, which presumably also disguised the thinning on top.

He dressed to emphasize his tallness and his zealot's face, and tonight he wore a black shirt, black jeans, and black elastic-sided paddock boots. If monks' robes had been in fashion, he would have worn one of those too.

Twelve years ago, Patrick had nicknamed him the Grand Inquisitor. The name still fitted.

'So,' he said when the wine had arrived, been sent back, and replaced to his satisfaction. 'Who have you been seeing since we split up?'

She threw him a look. 'That's a bit direct, isn't it?'

He shrugged. 'You know me. That's my way.'

She took a sip of her wine. After three weeks on the wagon it tasted wonderful, and she took another, longer pull. 'Actually,' she said, 'I haven't been seeing anyone.'

He looked pleased. 'In three years? Jesus. Am I a tough act to follow, or what?'

Her lip curled. Let him think that if he wanted.

He leaned forward. 'It was your own fault, you know. You were the one who couldn't commit.'

She raised her glass in a silent toast. Then she asked him about his work.

He told her about his latest project, a ground-breaking new concept for documentaries which he was trying to place with Timescape – 'kind of Tarantino meets *Horizon*' – but he couldn't say more about it, as it was 'still under wraps'. Then he moved on to the insularity of the British TV scene, and how no-one in the States ever called it 'schools television', it was all just TV, the UK was so stratified.

Finally he asked about her progress with the Cassius riddle.

Damn Kate's big mouth, she thought. But she saw no reason not to tell him. Briefly, she explained her idea that the key to the riddle lay in the poet's death.

He raised an eyebrow. 'I'm not sure how far that'll get you. I thought there was some theory that he was caught with his hand in the till.'

She tried not to show her irritation. She had forgotten

how much he adored nettling people. He called it being provocative. 'That "theory",' she said, 'was discredited in the Twenties. It was devised by an alcoholic wife-beater who pretended to be a professor from Heidelberg University, and in fact turned out to have no Latin what-soever and only a dim idea of who Cassius actually was.'

That came out more sharply than she'd intended, and his eyes gleamed. Damn. The wine was affecting her more than she'd anticipated.

Simon said, 'I hear what you say, but still, isn't it a terrific concept for a feature? Debunking sacred cows makes fantastic issue TV.'

'He's not a sacred cow. He's a poet.'

'Whatever. I still think it has potential. Maybe I'll do a treatment, see how it pans out.'

'Go ahead,' she said, attacking her *cassoulet*.

He grinned. 'God, it's easy to get a rise out of you, Toni! Always was.' He reached over and lightly stroked her hand.

His fingers on her skin were warm, and it was a moment before she withdrew her hand. In fact, she told herself muzzily, it really felt quite good. She couldn't remember the last time a man had caressed her hand. Or any part of her, for that matter.

For a moment she toyed with the idea of letting him stay overnight. It would make a change to have some-thing in her bed apart from a hot water bottle.

'Le contact d'un epiderme sur un autre epiderme.' Wasn't that how someone had once defined sex? Either Voltaire or Pascal, or some other breathtakingly cynical Frenchman.

She stared down at her *cassoulet*.

'The contact of one skin on another.' Is that all there is?

Another glass of wine helped, and she concentrated on the food while Simon calmly and seamlessly blamed everyone but himself for the sluggish progress of his career. He blamed his parents for bringing him up in Ewell – '*Ewell*, for Christ's sake!' – his ex-wife for being an overachieving attorney who had messed with his head, and Channel Four for failing to spot his potential and give him a job.

Antonia thought of Patrick, who blamed himself even when things weren't his fault.

Suddenly she wished that was Patrick sitting opposite her now.

She pulled herself up short.

No you don't, she told herself. You wish it was the Patrick of twelve years ago. The Patrick of today is a barrister who's going to marry Nerissa.

'So,' said Simon, 'I hear Patrick McMullan's back in your life.'

She gasped, inhaled a flageolet bean, and nearly choked.

When she was breathing normally again she said, 'Patrick is not "back in my life", and I haven't seen or spoken to him for over three weeks.'

Simon grinned. 'I have to tell you, you are a glutton for punishment.'

'What do you mean?' she said crossly.

He spread his hands. 'Isn't it obvious? The guy's engaged to Nerissa.'

'Thank you, I do know that.'

'Of course,' he went on, 'he always wanted her, even way back when she was with me. So I guess persistence finally got its reward.'

She reached for her glass.

'I saw her the other day in London. Still as gorgeous

as ever. What'd he do to get a woman like her?'

'It's hot in here,' she said. 'Can we go?'

Again he grinned. 'Why not?'

The moon was up by the time they reached La Bastide. It was a clear, cold night, and in the steely light the mill looked mysteriously beautiful.

'I enjoyed tonight,' said Simon as they stood by his car.

'Good,' said Antonia.

'So. Decision time. Shall I stay?'

She looked up at him. The moonlight suited the severe planes of his face. And it would be cold in the mill.

Le contacte d'un epiderme sur un autre epiderme.

'I don't think that would be a good idea,' she said.

His lip curled. 'What's the matter? Forgotten how?'

She forced a smile. He was uncomfortably close to the truth. And he knew it.

'Hey, no problem,' he said. 'But d'you mind if I use your bathroom before I go?'

'Be my guest.'

While he was upstairs doing battle with the plumbing, she checked the answerphone, and was astonished to find that she had a message.

'Antonia?' said Kate. 'It's Kate. Pick up the phone. You can't be out. You're never out. Pick up. Please.' She sounded agitated, and far less assured than usual. 'Listen, I did something OTT even for me, and I'm sorry – I rang your barrister and gave him a bit of an earful. About you. Yes I know I shouldn't have done it, and I'm really sorry. Actually he was quite nice about it, considering. Anyway, sorry. God, I hate these machines. Call me. Bye.'

Oh, *Kate*.

She glanced at her watch. Ten o'clock. Nine in

London. There was only an outside chance that he'd still be in chambers.

She rang Enquiries and got the number of Hammond's Inn, and to her surprise, the clerk put her straight through to 'Mr McMullan'.

'Antonia?' he said quickly. 'What's wrong? Are you OK?'

'I'm fine. Listen, sorry to bother you at work, but I just called to apologize for Kate . . . My friend, Kate Walker? I understand she gave you a bit of a hard time.'

'Are you sure you're OK? She said you're ill.'

'I'm fine. Really. Kate always exaggerates.'

'Uh-huh.' He didn't sound convinced. 'She said the mill's barely habitable.'

'Ah well, that depends,' she said lightly.

He waited for her to elaborate, so she told him about the Boiler Monster in the basement, and the Russian roulette experience of taking a shower, as the water was either boiling or freezing, or not happening at all.

That made him laugh.

There was another silence. She said, 'You're working late for a Friday, aren't you?'

'Not really. I've got a trial coming up.'

'Would that be the Anderson thing that's been in the papers?'

'Right.' He sounded wary. As well he might. The press was giving his clients a roasting.

She heard Simon coming downstairs. 'Well,' she said awkwardly. 'I'd better let you get on.'

'Listen, Antonia . . .'

'Yes?'

'. . . uh – if you need help out there, will you call me?'

For a moment she was too surprised to reply.

'Please.' He sounded as if he meant it.

'OK,' she said at last. 'Thanks.'

When she hung up, she found that she had been clutching the receiver so tightly that her knuckles were white.

Simon was standing in the doorway watching her. 'I presume,' he said drily, 'that was the Patrick who isn't back in your life.'

She did not reply.

He gave a small, pained smile. 'You know, I'm not sure you should have let me come all this way just to make me a pawn in your own private little game.'

There was just enough truth in that to make her feel guilty. Which of course was exactly what he wanted. She took a deep breath and counted to ten. Then she said steadily, 'I think you'd better go. You've got a long drive ahead of you.'

Silently they went out into the courtyard. He turned to her. 'D'you know why I really came out here tonight?'

'You said it was for old times' sake.'

He shook his head. 'I was worried about you. Kate told me about Patrick and I thought, oh no, there she goes again, on her Miss Havisham trip.'

She knew better than to ask him what he meant.

'Look at you, Antonia. You're right back at square one! Grubbing around trying to make some dead Roman into a hero when all the evidence points otherwise—'

'"All the evidence?" How can you possibly—'

'– while that Yank you always had the hots for is back in London playing Happy Families with Myles' mummy and daddy, and Jesus, even with his ex-girlfriend! How can you live like this? Do you have any idea how isolated you've become?'

'Actually yes, as it happens, I—'

'You're all alone, Antonia. You've been alone for years. It's a cold way to live. That's why I came to see you tonight. Because I hate to see you do this to yourself.'

'And that,' she said, her voice shaking with anger, 'is bollocks. You didn't come tonight because you care about me. You came because you're still angry that I chucked you before you could chuck me. You wanted to set the record straight, didn't you? You wanted to screw me one last time, then chuck me in the morning.'

In the moonlight she saw his features contract, and she knew she had guessed correctly.

'You're still hung up on him,' he said softly. 'I should have known.'

'Get out,' she said.

When he had gone, she slammed the door behind her with such force that she shattered the fanlight. Glass tinkled onto the linoleum, and a blast of cold air curled round her neck. Then the house settled back into silence.

You're still hung up on him.

Bastard.

She longed for Kate. She went to the dresser and poured herself a mug of the cheap red wine she had bought on her way from the airport, and drank it straight off. It tasted vile, but somehow she managed to keep it down. She refilled the mug and stood at the kitchen window, looking out into the courtyard.

A wind got up, and stirred the dead leaves on the cobbles into a dreary little dance. She remembered standing on the porch in her green kimono twelve years before, berating Myles and the others in the Panda. They had laughed at her. The nagging shrew. Perpetually on the sidelines. Perpetually alone.

You're all alone, Antonia. Just like you've always been.

And Patrick's going to marry Nerissa.

She drained the mug and snapped on the light. It barely enlivened the gloom.

'Fuck it,' she said. She drew back her arm and smashed the mug against the wall.

She picked up the bottle and threw that too: it shattered like a rifle shot, spattering glass and sticky red wine all over the wall. Then she wrenched open the fridge and yanked out a bottle of white wine, and smashed that too.

When she'd run out of things to smash, she came to a panting halt in the middle of the wreckage. Black spots darted before her eyes. Her palms were sticky and hot. She felt sick.

She was shaken by the depths of her violence. She had thought she had everything nicely under control, yet all along, this murderous *alter*-Antonia had been crouching inside her like a time bomb, waiting to cry havoc and let slip the dogs of war.

A wave of nausea shot up her throat. Clamping her hand over her mouth, she stumbled upstairs. She only just reached the bathroom in time, and retched into the loo till her stomach ached.

When it was over, she subsided shivering onto the floor. She pulled a towel off the rack, curled up underneath it, and passed out.

She dreamed she was back in the restaurant with Simon. But this time Patrick was at the next table, with Nerissa.

Then Simon and Nerissa faded away, and Patrick came over to her, and she rose to meet him. He put his warm hand on the nape of her neck and drew her to him, and bent and kissed her mouth. She put her arms around him. She felt the scratchy warmth of his sweater, and the softness of his black hair. But to her dismay, she couldn't feel his mouth at all.

She awoke huddled on the bathroom floor, sobbing uncontrollably. She was freezing and stiff, and her head was thumping like a pile-driver. From the cardboard texture of her cheeks, she had been crying in her sleep for hours.

The bathroom was in darkness. The luminous hands on her watch told her it was five o'clock. She guessed it must be five in the morning rather than the afternoon, but she had no way of knowing for sure, and that frightened her.

Draping the towel around her shoulders, she shuffled downstairs. The dream followed her, imbuing everything with a desolate sense of loss.

The kitchen looked as if it had been vandalized. The linoleum glittered with broken glass, and the walls were streaked with red wine: a dismal parody of Grand Guignol.

Fortunately, the coffee jar and her tooth-mug had escaped the orgy of destruction. She brushed broken glass off a chair, and sat down with her head in her hands to wait for the kettle to boil.

Gradually the throbbing in her temples eased. She felt exhausted and drained. There was a faint, persistent ache in her breast, as if something deep inside were shifting painfully.

She thought about Patrick in his house in London, getting up to start the day. Lights would be blazing, faxes already clicking away. Nerissa would be in the kitchen, looking wonderful in some *peignoir* from Harvey Nicks, as she made him breakfast and helped him forget all about that crazy obsessive woman at La Bastide.

Antonia wondered how things would have turned out if she had tried again with him twelve years before. What if she had tried once more to reach him, to make him see that despite the accident, they could still be together? What if they had both tried again?

Once more, she felt that faint nagging pain in her chest. Like a wedge of ice, working its way to the surface.

Maybe if they had both really tried, they would be married by now. Maybe they would have children.

The kettle was boiling. She got slowly to her feet. No use thinking about that now. The music had stopped too soon, and they had ended up with the wrong people. Or rather, he had ended up with Nerissa, and she had ended up with no-one.

Cradling her steaming mug in her hands, she let herself out of the house, and wandered down to the river. Sleet stung her cheeks, and the towel did nothing to keep out the cold, but she lacked the energy to go back for her coat.

Dawn was not far off, and the stars looked very cold and distant and unforgiving.

She reached in her jeans pocket, and drew out Patrick's note. Then she crumpled it and tossed it in the river, and watched till it disappeared from sight. Then, moving like an old woman, she went back into the house.

It was cold in the kitchen. No, it was *freezing*. And eerily quiet. It took a moment to work out what had changed. The familiar nuclear hum of the boiler had stopped.

Now this, on top of everything else.

With spanner and torch she descended into the cellar. Half an hour later, she knew it was hopeless. The boiler had finally given up the ghost.

When she got back to the kitchen, there was a message on the answerphone.

'This is Debra Passmore,' said a crisp, clenched voice. 'You'll shortly be receiving a letter from your lawyer, but I thought, for the avoidance of doubt, that I ought to ring and make sure that you understand the essentials.' She sounded friendly and calm, as she had done on that first day in the Bar-Tabac. 'It will no doubt come as a surprise to you to learn that I'm the majority shareholder in the company which is buying the mill. No doubt you'll be aware from the papers you've just signed that completion is set for the 24th of March. Which means that on that date I shall own the mill. And I'm sorry, Antonia, but I won't be able to let you stay. So do make sure that you're out by midnight on the 23rd at the latest. Without fail. Thank you so much. Goodbye.'

Antonia stood blinking down at the machine, struggling to take it in. Somehow, the friendliness of Debra's tone made it worse. *Do make sure that you're out by midnight on the 23rd at the latest. Without fail.*

The 23rd was ten days away. By then, the British Library's photocopy might not even have reached her. Or proved any use at all.

So that's that, she thought numbly.

She pressed the REWIND button and erased Debra's message. Then she sat on the kitchen floor and began to cry.

CHAPTER TWENTY-SEVEN

A military camp outside Perusia, 21 February 40 BC

It could hardly be a coincidence, thought Cassius, listening to the night wind howl about his tent, that the day on which he had reached the crossroads of his life should also be a public festival honouring the dead.

Was that just another instance of the gods' unfathomable sense of humour? Or was it a sign from the Goddess, pointing the way?

He didn't know. He didn't know.

But that was the gods for you. Whatever guidance they gave – whether through the most venerable oracle in Rome, or the grubbiest street-corner seer – it could always be taken several ways. The gods did not deal in certainties.

The only thing he knew for sure was that the road before him was forked. If he took one fork and ignored Tacita's letter, she would certainly die in the siege. If he took the other fork he might succeed in rescuing her, but then he would be a traitor to his own side, and *he* must die.

Of course, when she wrote her letter, she couldn't have known about that. Doubtless she assumed that as a general, he was above punishment. She couldn't know how Octavian's attitude had hardened over the months, as he perceived that this starving city was the last obstacle between him and absolute power.

'Not one of them shall remain alive,' he had declared in his dull, methodical monotone. 'Not one, my friend. They are the enemies of Rome.'

Outside, the storm intensified. The walls of the tent bulged inwards with the weight of drifting snow.

Cassius looked about him, and all he could see were the symbols of death. A horse's head painted on a bowl of dates; a sky-blue cloth draping the table; even his signet ring, which he had slipped off and left on the pallet, as he always did before making an offering.

All the signs pointed to death. But whose death? Tacita's? Or his?

His throat tightened with sudden anger. What *right* had she to ask this of him? What right had she to ask anything at all?

'She has no right!' he cried aloud.

A corner of the tent-flap twitched, and Faenio put in his head. 'You called?' he said brightly, knowing very well that Cassius had not.

Cassius dismissed him with a jerk of the head.

'Seeing as I'm here,' said the slave, with a familiarity born of forty-five years of service, 'I thought I might bring you a bite to eat.'

'I don't want anything to eat.'

'Just a little porridge and cheese to keep out the chill. Or some of those sesame cakes—'

'I said no!'

Faenio blinked.

'Wine,' muttered Cassius. 'Bring me wine. And Faenio – not the usual. Break open a cask of the Calenian.'

Faenio's grizzled eyebrows shot up. He glanced at his

master's black-glazed libation bowl, which stood ready on the table between two small prayer-lamps.

From the old slave's mobile face, Cassius could guess what was passing through his mind: *Two prayer-lamps, if you please. And the vintage stuff as well. Must be a pretty special offering to warrant all that.*

But fortunately for Faenio, he had the good sense to leave without voicing his surprise.

A short while later he returned with a flask of the Calenian, a pitcher of water, and his master's *kántharos.*

Cassius waved away the water. 'Tonight the wine stays neat.'

Again Faenio could not conceal his surprise. On campaign Cassius always took his wine well-watered. Always, without fail. 'Neat wine in wartime,' he would tell his new recruits, 'is the quickest way to defeat that's yet been invented.'

Well, for once, thought Cassius, I shall break my own rule. And I'm damned if I'm going to explain myself to my slave.

Faenio was hovering unhappily by the tent-flaps. 'Now *please*,' he began in the cajoling tone he used to employ when his master was ten, and wouldn't eat his beetroot, 'at least let me bring you a dish of flatbread. You've been in here since morning without taking a bite, and it's nearly midnight now! Even Acilianus is worried.' He said that as though it rendered his case unanswerable, for it was no secret that Faenio, a hot-blooded Cretan, regarded the young adjutant as the coldest of cold fishes.

'I told you,' growled Cassius, 'I don't need food. And as for Acilianus, tell him to go to bed, he isn't on duty.' After a pause he added, 'Tell him he can come to me at first light tomorrow.'

Surely by then, he thought, I'll have reached a decision? Surely the Goddess will have shown me the way?

He turned to the slave. 'And you,' he said in Greek, so that the sentries wouldn't understand. 'Come to me two hours before first light. Alone. I may have work for you.'

'You – *may*?' The slave looked bemused.

'That's what I said,' he snapped. 'Now get out. And no more interruptions!'

But to his astonishment, the old Cretan hovered unhappily by the door.

'Didn't you hear me?' said Cassius between his teeth.

The slave swallowed. 'You'll be angry, but I must say something.'

'What?'

Again Faenio swallowed. Then it came out in a rush. 'Whatever you decide to do, I think you should see her one last time. Find out why she left. For your sake. I really think you must.'

Cassius went very still. 'What in Hades are you talking about?' he said, in the soft, quiet voice which his men had learned to fear.

'I – I recognized her seal,' stammered the slave. 'I guessed the rest. I'm sorry. I should be flogged. But this is too important, I had to speak out.'

Cassius stood in the middle of the tent with his head lowered like a bull. 'A flogging, you say? You're lucky I don't break your neck. Now get out. Before I change my mind.'

When the slave had gone, Cassius remained in the middle of the tent, clenching and unclenching his fists.

See her one last time. Find out why she left.

That is the one thing, he told himself, which I will

never do. It would be too painful. And what would be the point?

But this was taking him nowhere.

He went to the table and poured wine into the libation bowl. With his foot he drew back a corner of one of the hides covering the ground, and carefully poured a ruby stream onto the cold rust-red earth.

Wine for the Great Mother. Drink deep, Goddess. It's the best I have. Then show me what I must do.

Next, he let a few drops fall upon the little mound of salt, wheat and green olives which at dawn that day – before ever he received Tacita's letter – he had placed by his pallet as an offering to his forebears.

Wine for the dead.

Finally, he pulled a chair close to the brazier, drew his bearskin cloak about him, and took a long swallow for himself.

Wine for the – how should I describe myself? The soon to be dead? Or the merely living? Which is it to be?

Ah, but she had been clever in that stark little note! She had not spelt out the consequences if he refused her extraordinary request. She didn't need to. They leapt from the page. *'Don't let us die like dogs in the street,'* she had written. *'I know you can find some way to help us to safety.'*

For if you don't, Gaius, continued the unwritten message beneath the words, *you must stand by and watch me butchered by your men. You might as well take your own sword and slit my throat yourself. Anything else would be cowardice.*

But what gall she had, to make this request of him! What did she imagine he owed her, that she could ask such a thing?

And what, he thought suddenly, was to stop him

rescuing only her, and leaving the husband and whelps to their fate? Had she thought of that?

Ah, but it would never work. Even if he managed to dodge the charge of treason – which he might if it were only a matter of stealing a woman – it would not end there. She would never forgive him for letting her children die. And no doubt her brother, that reformed rake turned self-righteous patriarch, would be outraged at seeing his sister forced into concubinage by an upstart provincial. He would probably do the decent thing for the honour of the family, and have her poisoned.

So what it amounted to was this. Unless he, Cassius, rescued the whole lot of them, it wouldn't work. And she knew that. Ah, but it was a cunning little note!

He flung off the bearskin, put his elbows on the table, and pressed his brow to his clenched fists.

No, it wasn't cunning. There had been no guile in that hastily scribbled message. She was desperate. That was all. Doubtless she loved her children, and probably her husband as well. From what he had heard, it had been a happy marriage. Three healthy children, no rumours of divorce, and never a whiff of scandal to sully her name. These days in Rome that was something of a miracle.

So why, asked the small insistent voice inside his head, did she call you *mea vita* in that note? *Mea vita*. My life.

'To remind you, you fool,' he muttered, 'of what we once meant to one another. That's all it signifies. The poor girl's desperate. She only wants to live.'

Who could blame her for that? She must be – what? Twenty-nine? Only twenty-nine. She was still so young. Too young for all of this.

She had always been too young. That was the trouble. He should never have started with her. Small wonder

405

that she hadn't had the strength to carry on, that she'd panicked and run back to her family. How could you expect anything more from a sixteen-year-old girl?

The wine began to steal through his veins, caressing his thoughts with warm perfumed fingers. He leaned back and closed his eyes.

Beneath his eyelids an image appeared, small and clear and bright. Tacita on the night of her wedding.

But this time, something about the picture was different. Something had been added to the memory.

He was standing in a doorway about thirty feet from her new husband's house. It was dusk, and the street was only dimly lit by the torches of the wedding guests.

She had just finished daubing the doorposts with lard, and was passing the wand to her maidservant. She wore the traditional wedding robe of snowy muslin fastened beneath the breasts with a girdle of twisted wool. And for the first time since Cassius had known her, her long dark hair had been put up: twisted as custom dictated into a tight, hard cone transfixed by six vicious wooden fillets. From these descended the wedding veil, a startling ankle-length sweep of flame-coloured silk.

The wooden spikes, the rigid cone of hair and the ritual shock of silk combined to make her appear remote, primitive, and at the same time savagely confined. It made him deeply angry. Was *this* what she had wanted all along? Was it to *this* that she had run from him? Where was all her talk of freedom? Where was his wild girl now?

But as he watched, the evening breeze lifted the veil for an instant, and beneath the brilliant drifting silk he caught a glimpse of the nape of her neck. It was pale and slender and very young: almost the neck of a child. A narrow white stem offered for sacrifice.

His pain and anger peeled away, and in their place was nothing but pity. She was too young. Too young for any of this.

A gust of wind shivered the tent-flaps. Slowly, Cassius opened his eyes and gazed into the glowing heart of the brazier.

So the Goddess had answered him, after all.

Not once in thirteen years had he remembered that glimpse of her neck, or the tearing pity which it had evoked. Not until now, when the Goddess had given it back to him. How could he have forgotten something as important as that? Or was it that he had *needed* to forget? That it had been too painful to remember?

He picked up the flask, and poured a finger of wine into the *kántharos*.

It didn't matter why he had forgotten. Just as it didn't matter what – if anything – she still felt for him. What mattered was that he still loved her. He saw that now. And loving her, he must do everything in his power to save her. No matter what the cost.

Turning the *kántharos* in his hands, he studied the play of light on the plain, smooth Corinthian bronze. Then he raised it to his lips and drank.

Smoke from the brazier stung his eyes.

Promptly at first light, Acilianus presented himself outside his general's tent, wondering what on earth this was all about.

Faenio, that insolent no-good Cretan, was nowhere to be seen, and it was the general himself who drew back the flap.

He looked tired, as if he hadn't slept at all, and as he walked to the table his limp was more noticeable than usual. The thigh wound must be giving him trouble again, as it sometimes did in bad weather.

The general pulled up a chair and motioned Acilianus to do the same.

Surprised, Acilianus sat. He was surprised, not because the man before him was a general and he was only an adjutant, for this particular commander rarely insisted on protocol – but because he, Acilianus, was not a man who evoked friendliness in others. People did not warm to him. Long ago he had convinced himself that he didn't mind.

'Do you speak Greek?' the general asked abruptly.

Startled, Acilianus replied that he did.

'Good,' said the general in Greek. Then, without further preamble, he calmly proceeded to outline a plan to rescue four magistrates and their families from the siege. Acilianus' part would be to collect the little group from a meeting-point in the chestnut woods north-west of the city, and lead them five miles across country to a cluster of deserted farm buildings on the old road south of Lake Trasimenus. Thereafter, Acilianus' role would be at an end. The general was very clear about that.

When he had finished, the general snapped his fingers, and a slave – not Faenio, Acilianus noticed in a daze of astonishment – brought bread and olives and a pitcher of hot water for the wine. The general dismissed the slave, then calmly poured wine into two cups, placed one in front of Acilianus, and suggested that he help himself to water.

Acilianus sat slack-jawed, with his hands between his knees. The analytical part of his brain couldn't help noting the excellence of the general's plan. It had all the boldness and cunning which made him so admire this man. But the *aim*! Had the general taken leave of his senses? Had staying up all night inflamed his brain? Or was it the fault of that mysterious letter which had arrived so unexpectedly yesterday morning?

And yet, the general didn't look deranged. In fact, for all the lines of fatigue, his face was curiously serene.

Apparently, the same could not be said of his own. 'Marcus,' said the general with a curl of his lip, 'you look utterly bemused. Is there anything about your orders which you don't understand?'

Acilianus swallowed. 'Um – no, sir.'

'Good.'

'But—'

'Yes?'

'But – but *sir*! What you're ordering me to do – what *you're* planning to do – it, it . . .'

'– contravenes what we're here for, yes I know.' Calmly the grey eyes met his. 'The point is, will you carry out your orders?'

There was a pause. Acilianus squared his shoulders. 'I take my orders from you, sir. Nothing's changed about that. Of course I'll carry them out.'

'Good.' The general stood, and dusted off his hands. Clearly as far as he was concerned, the conversation was at an end.

Acilianus did not move.

The general shot him a glance. 'Was there something else?'

He bit his lip, uncertain how to begin. 'I – I feel it my duty, sir, to point out – not as a soldier to his commander, but as one man to another – that this has no chance of remaining a secret for long. I don't mean that *I'll* tell anyone, because I won't, your orders are very clear on that. But sooner or later it will come out. It's bound to.'

'I'm sure you're right,' agreed the general. 'We can

only hope that it will be later rather than sooner.'

'But – don't you see, sir? This will have . . .' he searched for words, '– this will have consequences.'

'Of course,' said the general crisply, 'and I've provided for that.' He picked up a letter which had been propped against a bowl of dates, and handed it to Acilianus. The letter bore the general's personal seal. 'This,' said the general, 'absolves you of all responsibility in the affair. It makes clear not only that you were merely following my orders, as you are obliged to do, but that you knew nothing of the identities of those you were told to accompany. With this letter you'll be all right, you can be sure about that. I wouldn't put your life at risk over this. Indeed I wouldn't get you involved at all, except that I myself can't get too near the city, or I'd be recognized, and scupper the whole thing.' He frowned. 'And there are – reasons – why I can't have any dealings with the individuals concerned.'

Acilianus was almost beside himself. 'No no *no*!' he cried. 'I wasn't thinking of me! I was thinking of you! The consequences for you!'

Again the grey eyes met his, but this time they were curiously distant. 'As regards myself,' the general said, 'I am aware of the consequences.'

Normally Acilianus wouldn't have dreamed of persisting. But this wasn't a normal conversation. 'But – sir,' he said unhappily, '*are* you aware of them? Yesterday you had Fabius cashiered for – for writing a letter! How do you think Octavian will take this? You, one of his most trusted commanders! I know he admires you, sir, but – I don't think your poetry's going to protect you in something like this!'

To his bewilderment, the ghost of a smile appeared on the general's lips. 'Oh, I'm pretty sure it won't!'

'There'll be a trial. You'll be convicted. You'll be—'

'There will be no trial.' The general spoke with such quiet certainty that Acilianus blinked. Then understanding dawned. His jaw went slack.

'It's only common sense,' said the general testily. 'If I lived, I'd be forced to reveal where they've gone, and then the whole bloody thing would be pointless, wouldn't it?'

'But they couldn't make you talk, sir. Not you.'

'Oh yes they could. At my age one has very few illusions left – least of all, I hope, about oneself. I doubt that I'd display any more fortitude under torture than the next man.'

'But . . . what will happen?'

The general rubbed a hand over his face. Suddenly he looked exhausted. A man of forty-six who had lived a hard and often dangerous life, and was now confronting the reality of his own imminent death. 'I think the most I can hope for is to be allowed to return to my estate, and end things honourably there, by my own hand. I think he might grant me that. Yes,' he murmured to himself, 'I think he might. If not for the sake of my poetry,' he added with a wry glance at Acilianus, 'then for the sake of my family honour. As you know, family is very important to our leader.'

The adjutant had never heard the general speak of family before. Shyly, he enquired about these hitherto unknown relations.

The general's smile broadened into a grin that was almost boyish. 'I'm afraid it's not much of a dynasty! An older sister whom I haven't seen in years, and two thick-headed nephews whom I dislike, and who no doubt dislike me back.' He paused. 'But it'll be good to get back to my valley. I've only a small place there, you know, it's hardly more than a farmhouse. But it has a fine view of the river. And there's a wild pear tree just below the terrace—' He broke off, his eyes distant, remembering. 'Ah, you should see the yellow broom at this time of year! The hills are aflame with it.'

'I know,' said Acilianus quietly. 'I'm from Nemausus myself.'

'Really?' The general looked delighted. 'Well then, you know what I'm talking about.'

There was a moment of silence between them.

Acilianus fingered his wine-cup. He couldn't believe this was happening. Absurdly, he felt like bursting into tears.

The general tapped the tabletop with his fingertips. 'It won't be such a bad death, you know.' He sounded almost apologetic.

'I don't see why you have to die at all!' retorted Acilianus. He was seldom moved to anger, but now he was furious. He told himself that it was simply the waste of a talented commander which offended his sense of order.

But apparently the general was not deceived. 'Why, Marcus,' he said with gentle mockery, 'I do believe you have more in common with our soft-hearted young Fabius than you care to admit.'

Acilianus felt himself colouring.

The general laughed. He actually laughed.

'I don't understand any of this!' Acilianus burst out. 'Can't you – can't you at least tell me *why*?'

The general studied him. 'Perhaps I can. Yes, I think I owe you that.'

He slipped off his signet ring and turned it in his fingers. It was of fine Alexandrian workmanship: a green chalcedony intaglio of a coiled serpent which

Acilianus had often admired. Snakes often featured on signet rings, and could be symbols of death, or rebirth, or healing. He wondered what this one meant to the general.

'A long time ago,' said the general, still studying the ring, 'someone very close to me did something which hurt me. I never understood why they did it. I still don't.' He frowned. 'And now I never will. That made it – somewhat hard to get over.'

Acilianus guessed that he was talking about a woman, perhaps the 'Lycaris' of his poems. But as the general seemed reluctant to mention her directly – no doubt to protect her if she was still alive and still married – he decided to keep his supposition to himself.

'I spent the next thirteen years being angry,' the general went on. 'Trying to hate others, but really only succeeding in hating myself.' He shook his head. 'Perhaps that's the way of these things. I don't know. But yesterday, quite unexpectedly, I was given the chance to . . . to make things right, I suppose. Or at least, to make them as right as they can be after all this time.'

He glanced at Acilianus, and the light in his eyes was hard to bear. 'You see, Marcus, I've been presented with a choice. Either I cancel those orders I've just given you, and when we break the siege and the prisoners are brought before me, I take my sword and kill them with my own hand. Or else your orders stand.' A corner of his mouth went up. 'So there we are. Not such a hard decision after all.'

CHAPTER TWENTY-EIGHT

La Bastide, 16 March, the Present

You should not be here, thought Patrick, as he leaned over the bridge and watched the dark-green water sliding by. This isn't fair on Nerissa. Or Antonia. Hell, it isn't even fair on Debra – although since you're here *because* of her, it's all getting pretty complicated.

He rubbed a hand over his face. The first twinges of a headache jabbed his temples.

Five o'clock on a Thursday afternoon, and already it was getting dark. He turned up his collar against the wind and started towards the mill.

He had not been down this track in years, and had forgotten how much he hated the place. He could never think of the mill without reliving his headlong dash along the river to the phone. The panic as he realized he didn't know the number for the emergency services. The pain in his hands and face. That sweet, sticky smell clogging his nostrils.

How did Antonia stand it?

A battered little Citroën was in the courtyard, and the kitchen lights were on, but when he knocked on the door, nobody answered. Cautiously he went inside. There was no-one about.

The kitchen was appalling, worse than anything he

had imagined. And it looked as if it had been vandalized. Broken glass crunched underfoot, and the walls were splattered with what smelt like wine, or maybe some kind of cleaning fluid. It was smeared in places, as if someone had made a half-hearted attempt to wipe it off, then given up. It looked like a road-kill.

In the weak yellow light from the single bulb, the ceiling was a dismal patchwork of mould. Musty swathes of cobwebs festooned the empty shelves, and a pervasive smell of rot emanated from the curtains thumb-tacked over the windows.

And it was freezing, actually *freezing*. His breath steamed, and when he put his hand on the ancient radiator, it was dead cold. 'Jesus, Antonia,' he murmured, 'can't you look after yourself better than this?'

Surely she could not be used to conditions such as this? And if she was, what on earth had her life been like?

He went to the foot of the stairs and called, but there was no answer, so he returned to wait in the kitchen. She could not have gone far.

Twelve years ago, the mill must already have been pretty run-down, but he had never noticed. It had been the height of summer, and they had lived outdoors. The mill had merely been a haven of coolness and shade for when the midday glare got too much.

He remembered how there always seemed to be food upon the great oak table in the kitchen, and in the evenings everyone would simply take what they wanted, and wander out to eat by the river. He remembered their long, wildly enthusiastic discussions, heated by bottle after bottle of cheap, rough *vin de pays*, and fuelled by great wedges of crusty village bread and wild boar pâté, and creamy local cheese, and apricots still warm from the sun. He remembered tossing olive stones far out into the river, and watching the sky turn from lilac to deep sapphire to indigo, and the stars come out, as the little powdery brown moths dashed themselves to tatters against the Calor Gas lamps.

What had happened to all that? Where had it gone?

He wandered over to the fridge, which was feathered with yellow Post-It notes. In their midst, a postcard of Cassius frowned thoughtfully into the distance.

The Post-Its bore cryptic messages scrawled in Antonia's elegant spidery scrawl: *Perusia: C's earlier posting – signif? Milk, Dried apricots, Horse nuts (what are they? where find?), Chocolate.*

At least she still likes chocolate, he thought. I guess that's something.

The noticeboard in the pot-shed had looked like this: an eclectic mix of shopping lists and colour-charts and dig rotas, arranged around a reconstruction plan for the little Cybele lamp.

The Cybele lamp. He hadn't thought about that in years. Now he remembered sitting on a bench while Modge instructed him severely on the proper way of labelling finds. He remembered watching Antonia work. He remembered being unable to breathe. The slow strokes of her brush as she painted the edges of each shard with adhesive. The gentle precision with which she fitted each piece into place. He hadn't wanted it to end.

He turned sharply away.

The kitchen table had lost a leg, and been unceremoniously upended against the wall. Dammit, Antonia, you shouldn't have tried that on your own; what if it tipped over? Do you think you're invincible? Or have you forgotten how to ask for help?

In place of the table, she had dragged in a heavy antique-looking desk, God alone knew how. Unlike the domestic chaos of the rest of the kitchen, the desk was an oasis of order. Two ancient crocheted blankets were neatly folded over the back of the chair, presumably to ensure that she didn't freeze to death. Tidy stacks of books and files were placed side by side according to subject-matter. *The Perusine War: Causes and Consequences. Inventaire des mosaïques de la Gaule. Römische Staatsverwaltung. Anaemia: The Way Back. The Mind of the Horse. What Pony? Choosing a Mount for your Child.*

He picked up one of the pony books, and was leafing through a chapter called 'Equine Psychology' when Antonia came in. She stood in the doorway, her face a mask of astonishment. She was bundled up in a padded jacket, with the dark-blue scarf wound around her neck, and what looked like several sweaters underneath. Her face was thinner than when he had last seen her, and her eyelids were slightly reddened, as if she had been crying – although maybe that was the anaemia.

'I knocked,' he said, still with the book in his hands. 'I saw the lights and thought you must be somewhere around. So I waited.'

She closed the door and leaned against it.

He asked her how long the heating had been off.

'Um. Some time on Tuesday night. There's something wrong with the boiler.'

Two days? She had been without heat for two days?

She must have seen something in his face, for she added a little defensively, 'I had a hot-water bottle.'

He ignored that. 'You want me to take a look at the boiler?'

She shook her head. 'Thanks. I've got someone coming from Mazerans.'

He kept forgetting just how bad she was at asking for help. When Julian had sheepishly confessed to what he called Debra's 'little scheme' to buy the mill, Patrick had stayed near a phone all of Saturday, hoping Antonia would take him up on his offer and call for help. She had not, and he had cursed himself for a fool. He should have foreseen that. She had always been independent. And no matter how desperate she might become, she was unlikely to look to him.

'I thought you were in London for that trial,' she said.

'It's not for a few days yet. I came out this morning. Flying back tomorrow.'

She nodded, unwinding her scarf and emptying her pockets of a notebook, a pencil, and two baked potatoes. She caught him looking at them. 'I read about it once in *Cider with Rosie*. They keep your hands warm. Plus, you can eat them afterwards. Works pretty well. D'you want coffee?'

'Sure.' He pulled up a chair.

'I can't remember, do you take it black? I don't think there's any milk.'

'Black's fine.' He indicated the spattered walls. 'What's with the Jackson Pollock?'

'Oh, that. That was three days ago. I – lost my temper.'

He waited, but she did not elaborate. There was no need. After the stunt Debra had pulled, she had plenty to lose her temper about.

There was an awkward silence while they waited for the kettle to boil. Antonia stood with her back against the range, studying the floor.

How can she live like this? he thought. She's been here for what, three weeks? Four? How can she stick it for so long?

He asked her about the pony books, and she explained that she'd borrowed them from the daughter of a friend. He guessed it had something to do with Hippolyte. 'What are you trying to do, know your enemy?'

'Something like that. It annoys me that I get scared every time I see him. I thought maybe if I understood him a bit more . . .' She shrugged.

How like Antonia to tackle a problem by reading about it! She probably knew all about the development of the man/horse relationship down the centuries, but hadn't yet mustered the nerve to try patting a horse on the nose.

She bit her lip. 'I know how it looks. Same old Antonia. Still living inside her head and shying away from the practicalities.'

'Same old Antonia,' he said quietly.

She threw him a glance.

The kettle boiled, and she spooned instant coffee into two plastic mugs which still had the prices on them. She passed his over, then pulled up a chair.

He said, 'Julian told me about Debra buying the mill.'

She cradled her mug in her hands. 'You know,' she said quietly, 'I'd never have guessed that she had such a sense of humour.'

'What do you mean?'

'Completion – if that's the right term – takes place at midnight on the 23rd of March.'

'I don't get it.'

'The twenty-*fourth* of March is the Roman Day of Blood. One of the chief festivals of the Mother Goddess. It was also the day on which Cassius killed himself.'

She threw him a glance, and he saw with a shock that her eyes glittered with tears. She gave him a watery smile. 'How bizarre all this must seem to you! Quite a change from doing battle for multinationals. But in a place like this it sort of – gets to you. Well. It gets to me.'

It would get to anyone, he was tempted to point out, if they locked themselves up in a ruin and forgot to eat. But she didn't look as though she could take that right now.

'The Day of Blood,' he repeated. 'I don't think Debra knows about things like that.'

'Oh I'm sure she doesn't, it's just a coincidence. But still a bit odd, don't you think? Almost enough to make you believe in Fate.'

He could bear it no longer. 'Antonia, what are you doing out here?'

She blinked.

'The Perusine War?' he went on. 'How's that going to help you find the *kántharos*?'

'It isn't. Oh, I forgot. Since I last saw you, I've sort of – changed tack.'

He waited.

'I'm trying to solve the riddle.'

'What riddle?'

She spread her hands. 'The Cassius riddle.'

'The *Cassius* riddle?'

'Of course.' She said it as if no other existed.

'Wait, let me get this straight. You're trying to solve a two-thousand-year-old riddle that's baffled the best scholars for centuries—'

'Yes but I don't think they appreciated—'

'– all by yourself, in this appalling old ruin, with no proper resources, and no heat. That's what you're trying to do.'

Two spots of colour appeared on her cheeks. She

flashed him a grin. 'Well, someone's got to do it.'

He sat back in his chair.

Suddenly he caught a glimpse of the girl he had fallen in love with twelve years before. The straight-backed Minoan priestess with the warm brown eyes and the bird of paradise clothes, and that curious mixture of fearlessness and vulnerability.

How could he ever have thought she had changed? She had not changed at all. She was the same girl.

He remembered what she had told him about trashing her notes after the inquest. For twelve years she had turned her back on what she had once cared about so passionately – and now here she was in this freezing subterranean hole, clawing her way back to the sunlight: confronting the wrong turnings in her life in a way he never had, and fighting to regain what she had lost. She took his breath away.

'I suppose I must seem pretty crazy to you,' she said.

Not crazy, he thought. Magnificent.

'Listen,' he said abruptly, 'I think I can help.'

It was the last thing she expected him to say.

'I mean it,' he said. He was leaning forward with his elbows on his knees, and his hands loosely clasped. His eyes were troubled, as if he feared she might turn him down.

Her own eyes began to sting again. Since her crying jag on Monday night, she seemed forever on the verge of tears. It was probably just that wretched anaemia – but to have him sitting opposite her being kind didn't help at all.

'First,' he said, 'I need to see the paperwork on the sale.' He caught her puzzled glance. 'So I can figure out if there's some loophole to get you back the mill.'

When she did not move, he said gently, 'Antonia? May I see the papers?'

She swallowed. 'Yes of course. They're upstairs. I'll get them.'

On the landing she caught sight of herself in the mirror. Her eyes were dark hollows, her cheeks gaunt. She looked like a witch. Hardly surprising if he thought her mad.

'Antonia,' he said when she got back to the kitchen. 'First I have to ask you something.' He met her eyes. 'You don't believe I knew anything about this, do you?'

She stared at him. 'You didn't, did you?'

'Of course not.' He took the papers from her hand. 'I just needed you to know that.'

He took off his jacket and pushed back his sleeves, and began to read. He sat very still and read slowly, with complete concentration. As she watched him, it hit her that he really was, in truth, a lawyer. Patrick McMullan, the scruffy, too-thin boy from Dubois, Wyoming, with the dusty jeans and the black hair hanging in his eyes, was a barrister-at-law.

Perhaps, after all, Debra had been right in what she had said about him.

She had called Antonia the night before – to check that the message had got through about the completion date. 'I don't want there to be any misunderstanding,' she had said, sounding as calm and friendly as she had on the answerphone.

'Thank you, Debra,' Antonia had said, equally calmly, 'I believe everything's quite clear.' Her heart was pounding. It was horrible to be exchanging politenesses when they both knew that the moment Debra owned the mill she would have it bulldozed, concreted over, and probably patrolled by armed guards with Rottweilers.

Anything to crush Antonia's last hopes of finding the *kántharos*.

Rationally, Antonia knew that selling the mill need not be the end of the road. Armed with the completion moneys, she could stay in the area for as long as she liked, and continue her research. But she knew in her heart that it would never work. She had a nagging, irrational conviction that the *kántharos* was hidden somewhere in or around the mill itself. Once Debra became the owner, all chance of finding it would be lost. And when that chance was lost, she knew she would lose heart in solving the riddle.

'Good,' said Debra, 'I'm glad we're clear. Now I want to talk about Patrick.'

'Patrick?' Antonia echoed. The receiver became slippery in her hands.

'I'm very fond of that boy, you know. I admire his drive, and his good looks, but most of all I admire his talent.'

Antonia wished she had the courage to put down the phone.

'You have no idea,' Debra went on, 'just how good he is. You've never seen him in court. He's phenomenal.'

'What's your point, Debra?'

'Think of what that boy's achieved. He hauled himself out of that ghastly blue-collar town in the middle of nowhere—'

He is not a boy, thought Antonia. Stop calling him that.

'– he took a First, if you please. And in a couple of years he'll take silk. That's a certainty. And you know, he loves the law. He really does. No-one was more surprised by that than he.' She paused. 'Julian and I can do great things for him. Don't ruin that. Don't knock him off track just when he's getting somewhere.'

Antonia was so angry that she had to struggle to keep her voice steady. 'I don't think anyone can "knock Patrick off track" – as you put it – once he's made up his mind. But it's a nice try, Debra. Though I wonder why you bothered. I mean, what more do you want? The mill's in the bag, and soon I'll be gone for good. Just another unpleasant memory for you to sweep under the carpet, along with all the others. So congratulations. It wasn't the most honest way to go about it, but I don't suppose that's ever bothered you before—'

'Honest?' said Debra sweetly. 'Now what would you know about that?'

Antonia cut the connection.

She hadn't told Patrick any of this. What was the point? He would only feel torn. Soon Debra would be his mother-in-law. Stepmother-in-law. Whatever.

He was still reading, his eyelids moving back and forth. Watching him trying to help her made her want to cry.

He startled her by sitting back and meeting her eyes. She hoped hers weren't too red.

'I'm sorry,' he said, 'it's not good. Get your French lawyer to check it, but I can't find any holes. Everything's in place. It's a straightforward sale. No mortgage, no fancy *conditions suspensives*. And your guy did all the searches in advance, so there's nothing to stop it going through on time.' He paused. 'I guess you could renege on the deal, but you'd be in for a hefty penalty. I don't suppose you'd be able to afford—'

'I don't suppose I would.'

'Which means you're out of here in . . .' he glanced at his watch, 'a week.'

She pressed her lips together and nodded.

424

'I guess the good thing, if there is a good thing, is that you'll come into quite a lot of money. You'll be able to stay pretty much wherever you like.'

'Except where I want to stay, which is right here.' She shook her head. 'No, the reality is, if I haven't made progress by then, I'll pack up and go home.'

'What?' He looked horrified. 'You can't do that! This is too important.'

She was surprised that he should understand that.

'Surely you could put up with someone in the village?'

She gave a hollow laugh. 'I've already asked about that. No room at the inn. I think the truth is, they're all a little afraid of the wicked witch of Les Limoniers. And who can blame them? She must be by far the biggest spender in the village.'

He closed the file with a snap. 'Well, one thing's for sure. You can't stay here another night.'

She opened her mouth to protest but he wouldn't let her.

'Face it, Antonia, this place is a ruin.'

'I'll be fine.'

'No. You won't. There's no heat, the plumbing's shot, and before you know it the electricity will be too.'

'I told you, I've got someone coming—'

'– from Mazerans, yeah, I know. Like, when, exactly? When he feels like making the trek out here?'

She did not reply.

'Listen. The answer's staring us in the face. Take my house.'

She sprang to her feet. 'That's a ridiculous idea.'

'It's perfect! I'll stay with Julian and Modge for tonight – I can say my fax has broken down or something – and you can move in right now.'

'What about Debra?' she said angrily. 'Imagine

what she'll say! Not to mention Nerissa!'

'I'll handle that. Now listen. I'm not going back to London knowing you're down here in this sub-zero rabbit-hole while there's a warm, dry house standing empty about five hundred yards from your front door.' He paused. 'Come on, Antonia. Get real. Say yes.'

Suddenly she felt exhausted. 'Is this how you handle witnesses?' she muttered. 'Hammer away until they cave in?'

He gave her his lopsided smile. 'It's not subtle, but surprisingly effective.'

She stared at the floor. This was all wrong for about a dozen reasons. For one thing, he had underplayed the consequences of lending her his house. If Debra found out, she would probably excommunicate him on the spot, and as she was his Head of Chambers, the effect on his career would be significant.

And as if that wasn't enough, what about Nerissa?

No, Debra had been right about one thing: everything was going his way, and he didn't deserve to have it scuppered now. He had made an enormous success of a hugely demanding career. What right had she to blunder into his life, irreparably damage his prospects, and cause trouble between him and the woman he wanted to marry?

And what about the effect on herself? How could living in his house – the house he shared with Nerissa – do anything other than make things ten times worse?

She said yes.

CHAPTER TWENTY-NINE

'*First butterfly the fish*,' said the recipe cryptically.

Modge glanced doubtfully at the slab of turbot defrosting on the counter.

'*Lightly steam, then set aside, and while fish is cooling, scald cream and make a roux flavoured with scallions . . .*'

She bit her lip. She wanted lunch to be perfect, but she had a feeling that fish *quenelles* weren't going to happen.

Upstairs, the sitting-room door opened and she heard Patrick and her father coming downstairs. Patrick was telling a joke. She didn't catch the punchline, as it was drowned in her father's appreciative guffaw.

She thought: here come the two people I love most in the whole world.

Patrick had arrived unexpectedly the previous afternoon, and to their great delight had been forced to stay at Les Limoniers, as his fax had gone on the blink. 'Stay the whole weekend,' her father had urged over breakfast. 'Come on, old chap. It's Friday. No point going back to the metropolis. You can work from here.' So Patrick had stayed.

It should always be like this, thought Modge.

And why *can't* it? We could stay here for ever, just the three of us. Patrick and Daddy could use Mummy's office for work, and fly to London for hearings, and you could look after them both. You wouldn't ever have to leave. And Mummy would be pleased too, because she could stay in London and work. Maybe she'll come for visits if she can spare the time, and you'll pick her up at the airport in your new car.

She pictured herself at the head of a candlelit table. This Modge is thin and pretty, and her jeans are so loose that they gape at the waist. Patrick is filling her glass with champagne and laughing at something she's said, and Mummy's murmuring, *Darling, these* quenelles *are* delicious, *you must give me the recipe before I go back to London.* And Nerissa's gone away somewhere, because she's finally realized that she can never compete with the special understanding which exists between Patrick and Modge.

Her father entered the kitchen, startling her out of her daydream. Smiling at her, he went to the fridge for the lunchtime bottle of wine. Patrick wandered over to the counter and studied the recipe book, his black hair flopping onto his forehead in the way she loved.

'*Scarlet gills,*' he read aloud, '*shiny scales, and bulging eyes all indicate that a fish is fresh.*' He glanced at the white slab on the plate, and shook his head. 'Looks like you've got a problem.'

She giggled. 'I was thinking of doing sandwiches instead. Is that OK?'

'Fine by me,' said her father, pouring three brimming glasses of Côtes de Roussillon. 'Patrick, what are you doing in the fridge?'

'Getting a Perrier. D'you want one?'

'I certainly don't! For heaven's sake, have a proper drink!'

'Thanks, but this afternoon I have to—'

'*Work!*' chorused Modge and her father.

Patrick smiled. 'Am I that predictable?'

'Hopeless,' said her father, passing him a glass.

Modge hoisted herself onto the counter and beamed.

The night before, knowing that Patrick was only two doors down the corridor, she had slept right through till morning without having the nightmare once. For the first time since Antonia came, there had been no Highgate Cemetery, no horrible fluttering doves, and no lurking terror in the underground chamber.

Everything's going to be all right, she told herself. In a few days, Mummy will own the mill and Antonia will *have* to leave.

Thinking about Antonia set up a panicky fluttering in her stomach. She liked Antonia, and wanting her gone made her feel bad. But it couldn't be helped. She had to go. It would be better for everyone. Already Patrick was happier than he'd been in years.

She took a big swallow of wine. Everything was going to be all right.

Patrick took a bottle of Perrier from the fridge and held it up with a questioning glance: *Do you want some of this?* She nodded, and passed him two tumblers from the shelf, feeling cool and sophisticated at being able to read his thoughts.

You see? We know each other so well that we don't need words.

Her heart swelled with such happiness that it hurt.

At ten o'clock on Friday morning Antonia drifted awake after a dreamless sleep of fifteen hours.

She rolled onto her side and lay enjoying the warmth of the big, soft duvet and the play of slatted sunlight across the Mondrian prints on the wall. Then she padded into the bathroom and took the most wonderful bath of her life. She lay back and popped almond-scented bubbles beneath her fingers. Or rather, Nerissa's Hokusaido Bain Moussant Nutritif 'cleansed, conditioned and toned' her skin.

She knew it was Nerissa's, for Patrick and Nerissa had separate bathroom cabinets. Nerissa's held a comprehensive range of clinical frosted-glass bottles with Japanese labels. Patrick's was Spartan by comparison. He didn't even use aftershave. But he did go in for a lot of headache pills.

Wondering why he needed them, she sank beneath the surface. God, it was good to be warm again.

Wrapped in a fluffy blue towel the size of a bedspread, she padded downstairs to the kitchen. The marble tiles beneath her feet were smooth and level, and faintly warm. Everything *about* this house was smooth and level, and faintly warm. Recessed downlighters cast pools of silver onto gleaming granite work surfaces. None of the drawers stuck, and everything in the cupboards looked recently flown in from Heal's. She couldn't even hear the boiler. Maybe they had underfloor heating, like the Romans.

'Use everything,' Patrick had said when he showed her round the afternoon before. To give her the idea, he'd opened a couple of bottles of Crozes Hermitage, then re-corked them and left them on the kitchen table.

You are playing with fire, she had told herself as she watched him shoving sweaters in a holdall. Don't go down this road again. You'll only get hurt.

What would Kate say if she knew you were here?

But Kate didn't know. Nobody did. And in a strange way, that absolved her of responsibility. Or perhaps it was simply the hedonism of being warm and in beautiful surroundings. Clearly it didn't take much to lead her astray.

She got dressed, fixed herself brunch on a tray, and carried it out to the terrace.

It was the first warm day of spring, and in one of those sudden turnarounds which happens in the Fenouillèdes, the sun was strong enough for her to sit at the big teak table in jeans and a sweatshirt.

On the hill behind the house, La Bastide was coming to life. She could hear chickens complaining in a yard, the velvety thrum of sparrows in the trees, and the creak of shutters flung wide. From the bell-tower of St Pastou's, the public address system announced that the travelling fish shop would arrive at three.

She left the table, and went to the edge of the terrace. The view was breathtaking: a dizzying downward sweep through cypress, juniper and rosemary to the glittering river below – then up past a lattice of burnt-umber vines, to the jagged green and silver of the *garrigue*. Beneath a sky of high, tender blue the hills marched away to the horizon, splashed with anarchic patches of yellow broom. And in the distance, the Pyrenees dazzled like magic mountains in a fairytale.

Below her on the slope, bees fumbled the cobalt flowers of rosemary. A mimosa's powdery yellow pompoms shivered in the breeze. An almond tree nodded pale-pink blossom. Larches pushed new cones among the old: lime-green and succulent, like some new kind of vegetable.

Perhaps it was the half-glass of wine she had allowed herself, but when she returned to the table and began to eat, the food tasted miraculous. Coarse brown *pain de campagne* and Monsieur Vassals' *pâté de sanglier*, seamed with garlic and big, politically incorrect chunks of lard. Then more bread, smothered in dark mountain honey so thick and crystalline she had to cut it with a knife. Then another half-glass of fragrant Crozes Hermitage, a wedge of creamy local *chèvre*, and a handful of juicy green olives. Lazily she lobbed the stones over the wall into the waste ground for the lizards to nibble.

At the side of the house, a patch of level ground was shaded by a clump of wild pear trees. According to Patrick, this was one of Hippolyte's favourite spots for a snooze. She went to the edge and leaned over, and saw small crescent-shaped hoofmarks in the damp earth.

It was the same patch of waste ground which her father had chosen for his ill-fated dig, and which had brought him up against the unpalatable truth that his longed-for Roman villa was buried beneath this very terrace. Twelve years on, Nature had taken back the site: dwarf oak, rosemary and juniper smothered it in aromatic profusion.

She was reminded of a poem by Cassius which she hadn't thought about in years.

My place in the hills is small and simple,
but it has a fine view over the river
to the golden broom beyond,
And a terrace where you can smell the rosemary
* in spring.*

Idly, she wondered if she was standing on it.

She went back inside and wandered into Patrick's study, ostensibly to look for a pencil-sharpener before starting work. It was lined with bookshelves, and intimidatingly orderly. The books were mostly law reports, although to her surprise the single row of fiction contained a hardback translation of the *Poems*.

The desk was a broad expanse of polished beech, with a flatscreen monitor, a laser printer, and very little else. An aluminium mesh in-tray, an answering-machine, a ballpoint pen. No photograph of Nerissa. But you could make anything of that.

By the keyboard there was a silver coin which she recognized at once. Surely it had once belonged to Myles? She picked it up and turned it in her fingers. Yes, it was the same one. A present from his mother, of which he had been secretly proud. She read the inscription round the edge. *Fel. Temp. Reparatio.* The Roman version of: 'You *can* go home again.'

She wondered if Patrick believed that. She wondered if she did.

A sweater was slung over the back of the chair: sea-green wool flecked with amber. She recalled him wearing it at Julian's Sunday drinks.

Tentatively she picked it up. The wool was rough and warm, and had a clean, dry smell which she remembered.

The phone rang. Still holding the sweater, she froze. The answerphone clicked in, and Patrick told the caller to leave a message.

'It's me,' said Nerissa. 'Where are you?'

Antonia flinched.

'Your clerk said something about the fax being on the blink, but that can't be right, I thought you'd just got a new one. Anyway, I just wanted to remind you that we've got Suki Hemingway's lunch on Sunday, and *don't* tell me you've got to work because I've already said we can, and she won't take no for an answer. There'll be people there you should meet. Call me back.' She hung up.

Antonia breathed out.

Suddenly she felt ashamed. Nerissa's voice had been easy and familiar. They were getting *married*, for Christ's sake. And here she was, the lonely spinster, pathetically snooping through his things.

She replaced the sweater on the chair, fetched her coat, and went quickly down to the mill to check her post.

Ten minutes later, breathless and shaking, she was ripping open the envelope from the British Library.

Kriegführung der Romer turned out to be an unremittingly turgid 1928 text on late republican siege tactics. But its authors claimed the distinction of having trawled through more Roman papyri and military diplomas than virtually anyone else, and Antonia's A-level German – and the dictionary at the mill – allowed her swiftly to pinpoint what she had been hoping to find: a section on the Perusine War.

From a number of military diplomas and personal letters, the authors had established that in the spring of 40 BC someone had smuggled four magistrates and their wives and children out of the besieged city.

Her heart jerked. She knew as soon as she read it that the someone had been Cassius.

But what did that mean for Lycaris? For the riddle? Thoughtfully, she walked back up the track to Patrick's house. She paced the terrace. Then the pieces clicked into place.

Lycaris – whoever she was – had been trapped in the city, and Cassius had betrayed his own side to rescue her. Then, to avoid the inevitable trial – and perhaps to protect her as well – he had killed himself.

It all made sense.

So the question now became: who were the women among the escapees, and which one was Lycaris?

The text listed the four magistrates by name, so it *might* be possible to trace their family histories – particularly if they'd been patricians – and from that, to produce a shortlist of the women in the little group who might have been Lycaris. That would mean a trip to Toulouse for a couple of days. She would have to stay with Professor Meriot, her father's old friend.

An unwelcome thought brought her up short.

Even if all went well and she came up with a shortlist, how would she ever discover which of them was Lycaris?

She sank into a chair.

It would be appalling to get so close, only to fail at the final hurdle.

Then something dragged at her memory. Something that might help. She closed her eyes, willing it to return, but it had already slipped away.

Dismayed, she opened her eyes, and met those of a small, self-possessed green snake, which had been observing her from inside a drainage pipe in the far corner of the terrace. He had just caught an early cricket in his jaws, and the insect's wings fanned outward like a ruff, transforming him into a miniature dragon.

Again something tugged at her memory. Again it slid from her grasp.

The phone rang. She braced herself for Nerissa's voice on the answerphone. But it wasn't Nerissa. It was Patrick.

'Antonia it's me, pick up.'

She snatched up the cordless. '– Hello.'

'Hi.' A pause. 'How're you doing?'

'Fine. Actually, very fine.'

'You sound – excited.'

'I'm on to something. I really think I am.'

'That's terrific.' She could hear the smile in his voice.

'Um, before I forget,' she began, wishing she didn't have to spoil things, 'Nerissa rang. I didn't pick it up. She left a message—'

'I got it, she called here a while ago.'

There was an awkward silence. Antonia wondered why he had called.

'Antonia . . .' he began.

'Yes?'

'I – listen. I'm meeting old Panabière in the Bar-Tabac tonight. Every Friday he visits his wife in the cemetery, and he's always a bit low afterwards, so when I'm around we have a drink. I wondered – do you want to come?'

'Me?' she said stupidly.

'Yeah.'

'Um. Would he want me along?'

'Sure. Why not?'

'I don't think he likes me.'

'Sure he does. But maybe you – I mean, maybe it wasn't such a good idea—'

'No, no. I'd like to.'

'Good. I'll come by around seven and pick you up. I think I forgot to show you how to jack up the heating.'

He had not forgotten, but she didn't feel like pointing that out.

'. . . I forgot to show you how to jack up the heating,' said Patrick as he stood in the study with his back to Modge.

The day before, when his fax had broken down, he had cleared a space for his laptop at her mother's desk. She realized now that his fax had not broken down. He had only said that because he knew she got upset when he mentioned Antonia.

436

She stood in the doorway watching him. He was leaning against the window frame looking down over the jumbled rooftops of La Bastide towards his house.

'Sure,' he said into his mobile. 'I'll see you around seven.'

Modge backed away from the doorway and stood in the corridor holding her breath. She heard him ring off and return to the desk. She heard the creak of a chair as he sat down. But there was no scratch of his pen, no click of a keyboard. He must be staring into space. Thinking about Antonia.

Suddenly she understood. He was in love with Antonia. He always had been. They had fallen in love twelve years ago, and Myles had found out.

The thought of Patrick being in love with Antonia hurt terribly, far more than Nerissa.

She remembered her pathetic little daydream, and had to jam her fist in her mouth to keep from crying out. How could she ever have imagined that she had a chance?

Silently she made her way to the kitchen, took three tubs of Ben & Jerry's from the freezer, and went upstairs to her room. She locked the door, and propped a pillow against the wall. She moved carefully, for she felt as if she were made of glass, and might shatter into a million pieces.

On the floor by the mattress lay the paperback Prue Leith she had bought in Mazerans the day before yesterday. It was feathered with little yellow flags where she'd marked recipes to try. That struck her as agonizingly humiliating. Thank God no-one knew. If anyone found out, she would kill herself.

She curled up on the mattress and opened the first tub, mechanically spooning in Cherry Garcia without tasting it. She felt as if she were standing on a lava crust which was slowly cracking open. She and her mother were on one side, Patrick and Antonia on the other.

Her mother would never forgive him. It would be the end. She, Modge, would be left on the wrong side of the fault-line with a mother who resented her, and she would never see Patrick again. The pain was so bad that she caught her breath. Grimly she worked her way through the second and third tubs.

It was the first warm night of spring, and as if to celebrate, half the village had crammed into the Bar-Tabac. The air was thick with the smell of freshly ground coffee and roll-your-owns and the rich, wet-leaf odour of muddy boots. Every table was packed.

Patrick, taking a call from chambers on his mobile, could hardly hear his clerk above the din. Something about the Anderson trial being brought forward, and an impossible deadline for skeleton arguments. So what's new?

Only half listening to his clerk, he asked himself why he had invited Antonia along, when it could not help either of them to see each other again. Too much water had flowed under the bridge. It was way too late to change anything now. And it wouldn't be fair on her to try.

Across the table, she had just asked Monsieur Panabière why his wife had named their cart-horse Hippolyte. Surprisingly, the old man was telling her – his green wig rakishly askew, his turquoise cardigan spectacularly mis-buttoned.

She was watching his lips, for the old man's Catalan accent became impenetrable as he worked his way deeper into a bottle, and her face was flushed, her lower lip caught between her teeth. Patrick thought she looked wonderful. Like a priestess in a Minoan fresco. Excitement always did that to her.

He desperately hoped that her research would turn up what she wanted, but it sounded like such a long shot that he couldn't imagine how. She had told him about it as they waited for Monsieur Panabière. He couldn't follow all of it, but he gathered she had unearthed some reference which proved that in 40 BC, the same year as Cassius' death, someone had smuggled a clutch of republicans out of a besieged city. 'And I'll stake my career,' she said, pushing back her springy black hair in a gesture he remembered, 'that the man behind it was Cassius.'

He cleared his throat. 'How do you know it was him?'

She spread her hands, as if the answer was written on the air. 'It makes sense for about a dozen reasons. He was there, in command of one of the units camped around the city. And it was exactly the kind of plan he'd go for. Frontinus calls it "bold and cunning": turning one of the chief strengths of the besieging army – its network of spies – against itself. And he knew the city like the back of his hand, he'd been stationed there before the Civil War, so he could have planned it in his sleep. And if she *was* inside the city, he'd have moved heaven and earth to save her. He wouldn't have let her die. Not Cassius. And last of all, it's the only thing which accounts for that amazingly upbeat final poem of his.'

'So you think Lycaris was definitely among them?'

'She had to be. The only problem is, how do I ever find out *which* one she was.'

He turned his glass in his hands. 'If you had the cup, you'd know, wouldn't you? Something about it would tell you.'

She threw him a glance. 'It was nobody's fault, Patrick. It just happened.'

'– Yeah.'

Vassals *fils* brought the wine: a heady, blackcurrant-layered Merlot. After he had gone, Antonia said, 'It's just a shame that poor old Myles took the wretched line drawing too.'

Patrick nearly dropped his glass. 'The – line drawing?' he said hoarsely.

'The one I made of the *kántharos*. I don't suppose you remember.'

'But – why – why would that help?'

She shrugged. 'Maybe it wouldn't. But it might. It would at least be some record of those reliefs.'

He felt dizzy. He should have seen this coming. He thought about what she would say if he told her he had the line drawing safely locked away in his desk. *You mean to tell me that you've had it all along? All this time?*

That was when Monsieur Panabière had arrived.

His mobile rang again and this time it was Julian, calling from a golfing crony's near Antibes. He sounded well into his umpteenth brandy, and had decided to stay the night, rather than risk the long drive home. Fine, said Patrick dazedly. No problem.

When he rang off, Antonia was helping Monsieur Panabière into his jacket, and the old man was going through his customary search for his keys. He was seventy-six and increasingly frail, with a spine so bent that he could only just see over the steering wheel of his *camionette*. Whenever they met for a drink, Patrick argued about being allowed to drive him back to Le Figarol. He always lost.

Patrick finished his drink. Myles would have loved an

evening like this. Cigarettes, alcohol, and a comfortable crowd of villagers. Surprisingly, he had always got on well with them, particularly Monsieur Panabière. Perhaps he had felt that with the old man he didn't have to pretend.

Poor Myles. Poor, vain, selfish, insecure, lonely little bastard. Suddenly, Patrick wished savagely that his friend was still alive. *Achilles my friend*, he would say to Myles, *I've got myself into a hole. Can't seem to find a way out that won't hurt someone. Any ideas?*

He gave himself a mental shake, and called for the bill. Too much wine. And it had been a spectacularly bad idea to ask Antonia along. Way too much water under the bridge. No going back now.

Five minutes later they had waved off Monsieur Panabière's sputtering *camionette*, and Patrick told Antonia he would walk her home. What the hell. He had made so many mistakes, one more couldn't make much difference.

It was a clear, cool night without any wind, and in the moonlight the village looked its best. In honour of next week's Fête de St Pastou, the plane trees in the place de la Mairie had been hung with coloured lights, and the green bronze lion on the Mairie steps wore a dignified collar of bunting.

When they reached the house they stood awkwardly by the gate. Patrick felt reluctant to leave, but inviting himself in for a nightcap was out of the question, as she would probably feel obliged to say yes. He noticed that she did not suggest it herself.

So instead, they sat on the low stone wall in front of the house and watched the little bats wheeling like scraps of black velvet across the stars. He smelt pine resin, and the drifting sweetness of almond blossom. For the first time in months, his temples were free of pain.

He put his hand on the cold smooth stone between them, and wished things could always be this simple.

What would have happened, he thought, if it hadn't all gone wrong? Would we be married? Would we have children?

He would want a little girl like Antonia, with crinkly black hair and brown eyes and a straight Grecian nose.

That goddamned line drawing. He must give it to her, and soon. He wondered what he would say. *Listen, Antonia. After the inquest I meant to give it to you, but things got out of hand and I missed my chance. I miss a lot of chances. It's kind of my thing.*

How would she react? What would she say? Can you repair the past simply by saying you're sorry? *Can* you go home again?

To hell with it, it probably wasn't important, anyway. A horse with wings, trotting to meet a boy. What could that tell her about anything?

Which of course was a typical lawyer's argument to let himself off the hook.

'Antonia,' he said quietly.

'Mm?'

'If you had to choose between solving the riddle and finding the cup, which would it be?'

She threw him a curious look. 'Solving the riddle.'

That surprised him. 'Why?'

She paused. 'D'you remember in Plautius, when Cassius says he wants a libation for him and Lycaris?'

'Sure. That's the point of the riddle, right?'

She looked up at the stars, and nodded. 'The Romans believed that when someone dies, the person closest to them must give them the last kiss – to take in the soul which passes with the final breath.' Again she paused.

'Cassius knew that Lycaris wouldn't be around to do that for him. So he needed someone to ask the Goddess directly, after they were both dead, to bring their spirits together.'

'A libation.'

'Yes.'

Suddenly it dawned on him. Her audacity took his breath away. 'Jesus. You want to be the one to make the libation.'

She picked at the moss on the wall. 'Sounds ridiculous, I know. But you see, when I was little, Cassius was sort of – my friend. When I was unhappy he helped me. So I always wanted to do something for him in return.'

She made it sound as straightforward as doing a favour for a friend, instead of fulfilling the dying wish of a poet who had lived two thousand years before. But that was one of the things he loved about her, the way she could immerse herself in the past, fearlessly plunging in and bringing up great glittering handfuls of it. It was beautiful and unsettling and wildly unscientific. It was Antonia.

He thought back to when they had found the *kántharos* together. A hot, breathless night, spellbound with moonlight and wild sage, and the ancient murmuring voice of the Source. A night outside Time. He thought about that first incredible moment when he took her in his arms – his amazement and elation when she kissed him back. The softness of her lips, the minty fragrance of her hair. The unbelievably tender curve between shoulder and throat.

In the darkness of the waste ground, something large moved beneath the trees.

'Look,' she said, 'isn't that Hippolyte?'

*   *   *

As she said it she winced. 'Look, isn't that Hippolyte . . .' sounded like a transparent ploy to keep him there. That was the last thing she wanted. Having a drink with him had been a horrible mistake. She wanted him gone.

It should have been easy. Mending bridges over a friendly glass of wine sounded so civilized, but it had felt all wrong. As if she had been given the wrong part in a play. The truth was, she was not Patrick's friend, and she never would be. He hadn't realized that yet. Maybe he never would.

And now *this*. Bloody Hippolyte. So much closer than he'd ever got before. Too close. She could feel the sweat breaking out on her palms, her heart beginning to pound, as it always did when she got near a horse.

Go away, she told the pony silently. *Let me get out of this with some dignity, at least. Isn't it enough that I feel like crying when I'm with him? Do you want him to think me a coward as well?*

She had read that horses could sense people's feelings. Surely Hippolyte would get the message and bolt?

Unfortunately, if he got the message he chose to ignore it. As she peered into the shadows beneath the trees, the pony-shaped darkness resolved itself into his small solid form, and he trotted smartly past her and nudged Patrick in the ribs.

Patrick staggered and grabbed a handful of shaggy mane. 'Steady, boy!' Still hanging on, he felt in his pockets with his other hand and brought out a small bar of Suchard which he unwrapped and fed to Hippolyte.

Once that had been dispatched, he took another bar from his pocket and held it out to her. 'You want to give him the next one?'

She shook her head.

He was stroking the pony's neck. He had good hands,

and he seemed to know what he was doing. Apparently Hippolyte thought so too, for he was practically purring. From his good eye he gave her a reproachful look. *You see? This is how it's done.*

Bugger off, she told him silently.

But Hippolyte only nuzzled Patrick's chest for more chocolate, leaving a smear of froth across his sweater. Again Patrick held out the chocolate bar. 'How about it, Antonia?'

'No thanks. I don't feel like therapy tonight.'

'I just thought that as you're already closer to a horse than you have been since you were a kid . . .' He shrugged, letting her finish the rest for herself.

She licked her lips.

Hippolyte looked at her hopefully.

She said, 'They can smell fear, can't they? Any minute now and he'll bolt.'

He smiled. 'All this animal can smell right now is chocolate. Why don't you take it?'

'Why should I?'

'Because if you do, I'll go away and leave you in peace.'

That brought her up short. She wondered how much he had guessed. 'Oh well, in *that* case,' she muttered. Setting her jaw to stop her teeth chattering, she stepped forward and took the bar from his hand.

'Come up on my side,' Patrick said quietly. 'Then if he does decide to run off he'll bump into me, not you . . . That's right. Now unwrap the chocolate . . .'

'I thought of that,' she muttered, trying to keep her hand steady.

'Sorry.'

Her teeth began to chatter. 'How ridiculous! To be frightened of a pony!'

'It's not ridiculous,' he said quietly, 'it's you.'

'Stop being so reasonable.'

'Put the chocolate on the flat of your palm. That's right . . . Try to hold it a little steadier.'

'I *am* trying.' But she was shaking so much that it was all she could do to keep the wretched chocolate bar from dropping onto the ground.

Gently, Patrick took hold of her wrist and held it steady. 'That's good,' he said, from somewhere near her temple. 'You see? It's working. He wants to investigate.'

The blood roared in her ears.

The pony dipped his head, and her hand disappeared beneath a wiry mass of mane. She felt hot moist animal breath on her palm, smelt the sweet musky smell of horse. A tickling of horse-lips on her skin, as smooth and soft as dusty velvet. Then the chocolate was gone.

Hippolyte tossed his ugly little head, and trotted off into the rosemary bushes. Patrick released her wrist.

Absurdly, she wanted to cry.

Beside her Patrick said, 'I'm sorry. I pushed you too hard.'

'You didn't push me,' she muttered, 'I did it because I wanted to.'

He made no reply.

She wished she could stop shaking. 'It's just a nervous thing,' she said. 'I'm really perfectly fine.'

Briefly, he touched her arm. 'Spoken like a true Englishwoman,' he said.

She wished he hadn't touched her. It made her want to turn and bury her head in his chest.

'Antonia?' he said after a while.

She crossed her arms about her. 'Mm?'

'– I'm sorry.'

'For what?'

446

'For everything.'

She shook her head. 'It doesn't matter now.'

'It does. I screwed up. All the way down the line.'

She drew a shaky breath. 'So did I. All the way down the line.'

They stood side by side, in silence. He was so close that she could feel the rise and fall of his breathing.

'Do you think,' he began, 'do you think one can ever go back?'

She bit her lip. 'I don't know,' she said at last. She looked up at him. 'Do you?'

His phone rang.

Deep in the rosemary bushes, Hippolyte squealed, and cantered off into the night.

Patrick cursed aloud. 'Sorry,' he muttered. 'Guess I forgot to turn it off.'

Shakily, she went and sat on the wall while he took the call.

After he rang off he was silent, rubbing his temple as if it hurt. 'It's Modge,' he said at last. 'The fuses have blown. She's in darkness up there.'

She pressed her lips together. 'Then you'd better go.'

He stood looking down at her.

She got to her feet. 'Thanks for the drink. And the – um, equine therapy. Thanks.' She forced a smile.

He did not return it.

He left her standing by the gate, with the scent of almond blossom heavy on the night air.

CHAPTER THIRTY

Modge watched Patrick gazing unseeingly at his faxes, and thought, it's no good putting it off. You have to ask him *now*.

She was so nervous she could hardly breathe. She wondered if it showed. But what did it matter? In the mood he was in he probably wouldn't even notice. He hadn't even heard her anxiously concocted lie about fixing the fusebox herself. His face was distant and strangely raw-looking, as if he had just woken up after a long sleep.

Where are you? she asked him silently. *Are you still down there with her?*

She felt sick. Everything was unravelling before her eyes. That's why you've got to ask him, she told herself. A test. Then at least you'll know.

She went to the desk, and sat in her mother's big leather chair. That made her feel calmer and more in control, as if she were absorbing some of her mother's power. 'Patrick,' she said. 'Do you still have that drawing of the *kántharos* I gave you?'

The blue eyes fixed on her.

'I thought so,' she said. Amazing how calm she sounded. 'I want it back.'

Quietly, he asked her why.

She hadn't thought of a reason. The test was simply

to see if he would give it to her. If he did not, she would know that she had lost him for ever. 'Does it matter?' she said at last. 'It's mine. Myles gave it to me.'

'It wasn't his to give,' he said evenly. 'You know that. It's Antonia's.'

She gripped the arms of the chair. 'Is that why you kept it all these years? Because it's hers?'

He touched the desk with his long fingers. 'You see, I have to give it back to her.'

'No. Give it to me.'

Their eyes met. He was looking at her as one adult to another, not as Patrick to Modge-Podge, the little sister. She wondered how much he understood. Then he said gently, 'I'm sorry, honey.'

Desolation opened up before her. She said, 'You're still in love with her.'

'Modge—'

'My name is *Imogen*! Imogen Imogen *Imogen*! You used to get that right! When did you stop? When did you start talking like *them*?'

'I—'

'You can't give it back to her! What'll she say? What'll she think? She'll never forgive you. You know that!'

She ran from the room.

An hour later, she had worked her way through two packets of chocolate biscuits, four choc-ices, and a family-sized tin of rice pudding. Her mattress was littered with wrappers and crumbs.

She felt completely alone. As alone as the Little Prince in the story, standing on a desolate black planet spinning in space.

She tried to call her father at his friend's in Antibes, but they were out, and she only got an answerphone.

'Daddy, it's Modge. Can we go home tomorrow? Please. I really want to go home.'

Talking to a machine was worse than talking to no-one. In desperation she called her mother. It would be past midnight in London, but with the trial starting on Monday, her mother wouldn't go to bed until well into the small hours, if at all.

'Debra Swynburne,' said her mother curtly. Modge did a double-take. She was always forgetting that her mother practised under her maiden name.

In the background Modge heard phones ringing, people arguing, the staccato rattle of keyboards. She shut her eyes and pictured the war room on the top floor of Wilton Row. Computers and paper-strewn work-tops, and black halogen desk lamps like sinister cowled monks. An entire floor of teamwork and belonging, where everyone knew exactly what to do.

'Hello, Mummy,' she said shyly, 'it's me.'

'I gathered that,' said her mother. 'Is anything wrong?'

'No,' Modge said hastily. 'I just, I mean . . .' She groped for an excuse: 'I called to tell you we're coming back early. Tomorrow, actually. So I wondered. Is there anything special you'd like me to make for supper?'

'Supper? Oh darling, *supper* isn't going to happen! Not till this case is over.'

'Of course. Sorry.'

'Is Patrick there?'

'What? I – I think he's in the study.'

'Be a sweetie and put me through.'

'Could we possibly, um, talk a bit first? I'm kind of—'

Her mother sighed. 'Timing, darling? Now put me through, there's a good girl.'

Modge felt a rising panic at the thought of being cut off from that bright frenetic world. 'Could the trial wait a bit?' she mumbled.

'Sorry, darling?' Her mother's voice was muffled, as if she had turned away to talk to someone else. 'Oh darling, surely I don't have to tell you that at a time like this every second counts?'

Modge's fingers tightened on the phone. 'If it was Myles,' she said, 'the trial would wait.'

In the silence which followed, she pictured her words coursing down the telephone lines towards her mother: little crackling sparks of electricity which could never be recalled.

At last her mother said levelly, 'I'll pretend you didn't say that. That would be kindest. Don't you think?'

Modge shut her eyes. 'I'm sorry, Mummy. I didn't mean it. It's just that I'm so miserable, I—'

There was a click as her mother hung up.

On Saturday morning, after Patrick had waved goodbye to a hungover Julian and a stone-faced Modge, he went down to his house intending to retrieve the line drawing from his desk and give it to Antonia.

She wasn't there. Nor were her belongings. She had moved out. He pocketed the drawing and went down to the mill, but she wasn't there either, and her car was gone.

He dismissed the possibility that she had given up and gone back to London. Not Antonia. She had six days left to solve the riddle. She would do her utmost right up until midnight on Thursday night, when the mill became Debra's.

Besides, her answerphone was still hooked up, as he

discovered when he called from Les Limoniers. He left a brief message asking her to call him, then spent a long fraught day thrashing out a stack of last-ditch witness statements and cross-examination notes, and calling the mill without success.

Antonia still hadn't returned on Sunday morning, by which time Debra was apoplectic about having him back *forthwith*, and Nerissa wasn't speaking to him because of Suki Hemingway's lunch. Around noon, with just under two hours before the last plane out from Perpignan, he loaded the Discovery, closed up both houses, and drove down to the mill. This time her car was in the courtyard.

'I need to see you,' he said, when she opened the door.

She blinked. 'I thought you had a trial.'

'It starts tomorrow.'

She let him in, and asked if he wanted coffee. He said he did, and took a seat at the desk.

'I'm sorry I didn't return your call,' she said over her shoulder, 'but I only got back a few minutes ago. I've been in Toulouse since yesterday morning. At the library, ordering up references from stacks.'

'Any good?'

'I don't know, they're not up yet. I'll go back tomorrow.'

They waited in awkward silence for the kettle to boil. She spooned coffee into the mugs. 'The thing is,' she said, frowning at the coffee jar, 'I didn't feel right about being in your house. Creeping around avoiding the phone.'

He nodded.

Watching her go to the fridge for milk, he thought how extraordinary it was that a month ago he had believed he was doing just fine. Good job, surrogate family, beautiful fiancée. Not exactly happy, but then, who is? He thought he was doing all right. If anyone had asked about Antonia Hunt he'd have said, *Oh yeah, I remember her. But she's nothing to me now, hasn't been for years.* And yet here he was, ready to give it all up – *wanting* to give it all up – and he didn't even know what she felt about him.

He wanted to tell her that he loved her, that he'd been a fool for not realizing it sooner. That he would break up with Nerissa as soon as he got back to London, and could they try again? Could they?

But there was so little time, and his advocate's instinct warned him not to botch this by rushing her. *I'm sorry, Patrick, but it's too late to try again. Too much water under the bridge.* His stomach clenched at the thought.

He put his hands on the desk. 'I don't have much time,' he began. 'But I need to tell you something – I need to give you something.'

She put down the milk carton and looked at him.

'What I said at the inquest. That – lie. You know I did it because of Modge.'

'I know,' she said gently. 'It doesn't matter. Not any more. You must stop blaming yourself.'

'It matters. Because there's more.'

She waited, her face puzzled.

'What you don't know,' he went on, 'is that the night before the hearing, Modge gave me this.' He took the line drawing from his pocket and unrolled it on the desk.

She glanced down at it, then back to him. Her lips formed a perfect O of shock.

'Myles gave it to her,' he said, 'and she gave it to me.'

She stood staring down at it. Not moving. Not

touching it. '*Before* the hearing,' she murmured at last. 'She gave it to you *before* the hearing?'

He nodded, watching her take that in. 'You should have had it years ago. I'm sorry.'

He wanted her to look at him, but she did not. 'Why now?' she said.

'I needed to set things straight.'

She did not reply.

He stood up. 'Call me,' he said, and left.

This time the fluttering in Highgate Cemetery is very very bad. It's so bad that Modge does what she's never done before, and runs down into the underground chamber.

She finds that it's a cellar, carpeted with soft, evil-smelling mould which gives underfoot, and lined with hundreds of wine bottles with blank black labels. On a table in the middle stands the *kántharos*, bloody and glowing in a shaft of dusty light.

Her chest heaves with panic.

Suddenly the cellar is gone and she's out on the mountainside. The glare on the rocks is so bright that it hurts her eyes, and she's *furious* with Myles for sending her away. He made her steal, he made her scrape her tummy on the window-ledge, and then he laughed at her and told her to bugger off. *Pig*.

Still raging at him, she reaches the jeep. Just beyond it, she sees Monsieur Panabière's beautiful new aluminium gate.

'That'll serve him right,' she says aloud, tugging at the stone which wedges the gate open. Serve him right if he has to walk all the way home. And if he trips as he's climbing over and bumps his knee, so much the better.

She expects the gate to be heavy, but it swings easily into place, and she even manages to fasten the padlock, which is new and shiny, and locks shut with a satisfying click.

Serve him jolly well *right*.

Now she's with Patrick further down the slope, and they hear shouting behind them, and turn to see Myles in the jeep, bumpily reversing across the track. Suddenly the back wheels are spinning over nothingness, and the edge is crumbling, and the jeep is tipping backwards into the gorge. It's falling slowly, horribly slowly, and paper is fluttering all around it. Fluttering like pigeons' wings.

She screams. She goes on screaming.

She wakes curled in a ball with her knees under her chin and her hands over her ears to shut out her screams.

Oh god oh god oh god it was me. I *did it*. I *did it*.

Oh god oh god oh god.

I killed Myles.

It was six by the time Nerissa got back to the house which she shared with Patrick in Cornwall Gardens, after a ridiculously long lunch with an old flame.

To her relief, Patrick had not yet arrived from the airport. That was good. She wanted to appear as if she had spent the weekend in. A long, dull weekend, being neglected by him. And of course, now she had the trump card in reserve.

The lunch had been a spur-of-the moment idea. The minute Debra put down the phone, she had cancelled Suki Hemingway and called Stephen Mackenzie instead. It had worked out beautifully. The champagne had soothed her nerves, and so had poor old Stephen.

Debra's call had been brief to the point of rudeness,

although perhaps that was understandable under the circumstances. Did Nerissa know that Antonia Hunt had been staying at the house in La Bastide? Did she know that she had a rival?

No, she did not know about the house, and no thank you, Debra, Nerissa does not have a rival.

She had sat opposite poor Stephen in the restaurant, toying with her food in the way he adored, working out the best way to handle Patrick.

She *deserved* this marriage. She was so tired of going to friends' weddings and looking wonderful, and wondering why it wasn't her turn. Since the age of fourteen she had always had a boyfriend, even when she didn't want one – but curiously, none of them had ever proposed.

She deserved to be married. And it was only right that her husband should be brilliant and good-looking and successful.

Patrick's background was a huge plus, too. It gave her the edge. And the fact that his mother had been English and reasonably educated was irrelevant, for Nerissa knew that in such matters, it's only the father who counts. Patrick was blue-collar, because his father had been blue-collar.

Nerissa rarely daydreamed, but she had one fantasy which she often played out when she was shopping during 'audition' times. They are on their honeymoon, visiting his home town in Wyoming. The wooden pavements are lined with exhausted-looking women, with wispy hair and children on their hips, staring at her in awe.

So no thank you, Debra. Nerissa does not have a rival. She has never taken Antonia seriously, and she doesn't see why she should start now. On the other hand, this is not something that can be ignored.

Everything worked out beautifully. By the time she heard the taxi pull up outside the door she had showered, applied fresh makeup, and changed into a long, simple dress of cream cashmere which she knew Patrick liked.

She found him in the kitchen, adding water to a large whisky.

'You look awful,' she said, refusing his offer of a drink with a tiny shake of the head.

In fact he looked rather good. Bluish shadows around the eyes and an intriguing gauntness, as if he hadn't eaten or slept for days. But she saw no reason to flatter him.

'If you want food,' she said, 'I'm afraid you'll have to order something in. I haven't had time to shop.'

'I'm not hungry.'

'Neither am I. My agent rang yesterday, and I've been up to my ears in conference calls.'

That had occurred to her between courses at the restaurant, and she thought it rather good. Of course, once he knew about the trump card, he might think her a little callous to have been taking calls at a time like this, but she brushed that aside to explain away later. 'The audition's on Wednesday,' she said, knowing that he'd be in the middle of the trial. 'You will come with me, won't you? For moral support?'

'Nerissa,' he said abruptly. 'I have to talk to you.'

She licked her lips. She knew that tone. This might not be as straightforward as she'd thought. 'Can't it wait?' she said. 'I'm awfully tired.'

'I'm afraid it can't.'

She crossed her legs and waited.

'I guess you know what's coming,' he said. He paused. She could see he felt bad about this. Good. That would make him easier to handle. 'We haven't seen much of each other over the past few months, have we?' he began.

'Whose fault is that?' she said calmly.

'I know.' He looked her in the eyes and said, 'I'm sorry, Nerissa, but I can't marry you.'

The important thing at times like this was to admit nothing. Admit nothing, accept nothing. It would soon blow over.

She crossed and re-crossed her legs. 'I thought you might try something like this,' she said at last. 'Though I can't help feeling your timing is rather off.' At his puzzled glance she added, 'The audition?'

'Ah,' he said softly, 'the audition.'

She caught his tone and flushed. Not for the first time, she wondered if he knew. 'I wasn't only thinking of that,' she said quickly, 'I was thinking of you. Your career.'

She didn't need to say any more than that. He understood. But to her surprise, he simply shrugged and poured himself another drink.

'I suppose,' she said, 'this has something to do with Antonia.'

He took a sip of his drink and gave her a long, steady look.

'I had a call from Simon Toynbee yesterday,' she said. 'We had quite a chat. *Lots* of catching up to do. Of course, you do know that they're seeing each other again? He spent the night with her last week. But presumably she'll have told you herself.'

God, he was good. Not even a flicker. But she knew it had hit home.

Time to leave him on his own for a while, to let it sink in. And of course, she still had the trump card left to play. When he knew about that, he was going to feel terrible.

It was all working out beautifully.

When Nerissa had gone upstairs to lie down, Patrick called Antonia. At least, he tried to call her, but either she was screening or she was out, for she didn't pick up.

He told himself that Nerissa's little crack about Simon Toynbee was irrelevant, just the normal Nerissa stuff: a bit obvious, a bit lacking in subtlety. Usually that made him feel sorry for her.

But now he recalled Antonia's reddened eyes on the Friday afternoon. The broken glass in the kitchen, the wine-spattered walls. 'I lost my temper,' she had told him. At the time he had thought that must be over Debra. Now he wondered.

But not for long. If she preferred the Grand Inquisitor to him, she was going to have to tell him to his face. He would not let that affect things now.

He got up and paced his study. Then he called her again. This time he left a longer message. He told her that he'd split up with Nerissa, and could she call him right away. Please.

Twenty minutes later, she still hadn't called.

Nerissa put her head round the door. 'With all this business,' she said, 'I forgot to tell you. I did try to reach you earlier today, but you weren't around. I imagine Debra and Julian tried too.'

'Julian?' he said sharply. 'Why Julian? What's wrong?

'Of course,' she said, 'Debra's beside herself. And as for Julian, well, you can imagine.'

Suddenly he was sick of her little games. '*What*,' he said in a tone which made her nose turn pink.

'Modge tried to kill herself last night.'

CHAPTER THIRTY-ONE

'Je suis désolée, mademoiselle,' said the librarian cheerfully, 'mais vous devez patienter encore quelques jours.'

'*Quelques jours*,' said Antonia between clenched teeth. 'Which takes us to, what? Wednesday? Thursday? Perhaps you could tell me why I have to wait *quelques jours* when you're the one who misread my request form and called up completely the wrong references?'

The librarian gave a shrug which had obviously been perfected by hundreds of similar confrontations. *Take it or leave it*, said the shrug, *but hurry up. It's nearly closing time, and there are many more dissatisfied customers whose hopes I have to blight before I can go home.*

Biting down on her frustration, Antonia filled in another form, this time in insultingly large capital letters with little smiley faces instead of dots over the i's. She and the librarian parted with polite nods of mutual ill-will.

She went to the canteen, bought coffee, and took it to a table in the corner. God, she was in a terrible mood.

Call me, he had said before he left.

What did that mean? 'Call me and we'll get together'? Or 'Call me and grant me absolution for past sins before I go off and marry Nerissa'? What did he think he was doing, dropping the drawing on her desk, then calmly flying back to London without another word?

Turning the plastic cup in her fingers, she plummeted from exasperation to dejection. He would never break free of the Passmores. He would never break free, because he believed he must take Myles' place. He had to be the perfect son, the perfect brother, the perfect fiancé.

There was no point in calling him back.

But why, she wondered, had he kept the line drawing all this time?

For the twentieth time since he had given it to her, she took it from her bag.

Pegasus trotted joyfully towards Bellerophon, his head tilted, his nostrils dilated in a whinny of delight. About his hooves curled a naturalistic confusion of acanthus. And beneath one overarching frond lay a small, coiled snake.

She had recognized it at once. The coiled snake had been Cassius' personal seal. Like most educated Romans, he would have worn it on a ring and used it for sealing letters, and perhaps in his case, military orders. It *identified* him.

Which explained that odd little *frisson* she had experienced the other day on the terrace, when she had met the contemplative gaze of the small green snake. '*I recognized my young friend's seal on the note*', Plautius had written in one of his early letters, '*and I smiled to myself. A viper has never appeared so welcoming!*'

The wider implications had only struck her that morning as she lay in Professor Meriot's spare room gazing at the damp patches on the ceiling.

Cassius' seal – his identifying mark – had been carved at the feet of the winged horse. Surely that must mean that *Lycaris'* identifying mark would be found at the feet of Bellerophon, on the *other* side of the cup – which, a frantic re-examination of the line drawing revealed, Antonia had not, twelve years before, got around to sketching in.

In the bleak neon light of the canteen she stared at the blank patch of paper where Bellerophon's toga petered out. The blank patch which held the key to Lycaris.

Cassius and Lycaris.

The truth is in the cup.

She struggled to remember. What was on the other side of the cup?

But nothing came.

And yet she knew she was right. Only this would explain why Cassius had told his friend that the riddle would be solved when Lycaris was dead. Because when Romans died, they were cremated, and their ashes placed in an urn, which, if they were wealthy, would be decorated with their seal.

So the task became to identify the seals of the women whom Cassius had rescued, and then to recall, somehow, if the cup had borne anything similar.

It sounded simple. But it was complicated by the fact that some Roman women kept their seals on marriage, and some did not. And some didn't bother with seals at all.

Of course, there was no guarantee that she would be able to locate even one of the seals.

The problems multiplied. But at least, after a day's trawl in the library, she had narrowed down the candidates to three.

There had been twelve people in the little group which escaped Perusia, of whom five had been female. At first, Antonia had wondered why the group had been so large. Why rescue twelve people if you only wanted to save one? Then it dawned on her. Camouflage. If Lycaris was still married, Cassius would not have wanted to draw attention to their past liaison by singling her out.

Of the five females in the little group, *Kriegführung* mentioned that one had been in her sixties, and one a girl of ten. Which left three who might have been Lycaris.

Of these, the first, Aemilia Saturnina, had been a patrician who had married at fifteen, and would have been twenty-two in 53 BC, when the affair took place. At that time she could have been either a widow or a divorcée – and therefore quite possibly Cassius' lover.

Then there was Valeria Atilia, the daughter of a wealthy wine merchant from southern Spain, who had married well, and was about eighteen in 53 BC.

Finally there was Tacita Cornelia, another patrician, who at sixteen in 53 BC had been the youngest of the three – although since Roman girls married from the age of twelve, that by no means ruled her out.

Eenie, meenie, mynie, mo.

So far, the clear favourite was Aemilia. The affair had been a stormy one – the *Poems* mentioned fights in which Cassius beat a rueful retreat with bites on his neck and scratches on his cheeks – and it seemed more likely that a woman of twenty-two would have had the assurance to attack her lover than a girl still in her teens.

The other point in Aemilia's favour was that Antonia had a good chance of identifying her seal. By a stroke of luck, she had learned that Aemilia's own cinerary urn lay somewhere in storage beneath the Glypototek in Copenhagen. She knew one of the assistant curators there, and although he was busy preparing for a dig, he had promised to see what he could do.

But as she sat in the canteen nursing her coffee, it

occurred to her that even if a miracle happened – even if she uncovered all three seals, and one of them jogged her memory, so that she clapped her hand to her forehead and cried, *Eureka*, I remember, there was a four-leafed clover at Bellerophon's feet, *this* woman is the one! – she still wouldn't know for sure. Because memory plays tricks. Sometimes it serves up what you *want* to remember, rather than the truth. She would not know for sure that she had found Lycaris unless she held the *kántharos* in her hands and saw for herself the symbol at Bellerophon's feet.

Her spirits sank. What was she doing here, chasing after impossible dreams? All around her students were flirting, holding hands, getting on with their lives. What was she doing?

The rational thing would be to go back to the mill, pack her bags, and return to London. Get on with her life.

And forget all about Patrick McMullan.

'How do you feel?' said Patrick, pulling up one of the hospital chairs.

He must have come straight from court, for instead of a tie he was still wearing his stock, and his hair was ruffled from his wig. Modge thought he looked exhausted.

She pulled the blanket under her chin and said, 'I feel like a fraud.'

He waited for her to go on.

'Pretty pathetic suicide bid,' she said. 'According to the nurses it was hardly enough aspirin to merit a stomach-pump. The only reason they're keeping me in is because Mummy insisted, and that's just because she doesn't want me at home. How's the trial going?'

'It's going,' said Patrick, refusing to be sidetracked. 'How do you *feel*?'

She had been longing for him to come, but now that he was here, she wished he would go. How could she ever have fooled herself into thinking he could be more than a brother to her? Now all she wanted was for him to leave. It hurt too much to see him, when she knew she must begin facing life without him. 'I told you,' she mumbled. 'I feel like a fucking fraud. I can't even kill myself properly.'

'You didn't try.'

'Yes I did.'

'No you didn't,' he said gently. 'If you'd wanted to kill yourself you'd have succeeded. You're an effective person.'

She thought about that. 'I should have had more guts.'

'What you did took more guts. That note of yours got a whole lot of stuff out in the open for the first time in years. It was a brave thing to do.'

She looked at him. 'I wanted Mummy to know everything. Everything. Do you understand?'

'I understand.'

She blinked. 'I told her that Myles took the *kántharos*.'

'I know.'

'And now she'll hate me for ever.'

'No.'

Her eyes began to sting. 'She will,' she whispered at last. '*I* shut the gate. *I* killed Myles.'

'No, honey.'

'*Yes*.'

He leaned forward with his elbows on his knees and looked her steadily in the eyes. 'No-one killed Myles. It was an accident. A whole lot of mistakes and missed chances and plain old bad luck had to come together for that jeep to go into the gorge. Each one of us played a part in it. But only a part. It was an accident.' He paused. 'It's taken me years to accept that. I think that in time, you're going to be able to accept it too.'

She wiped her eyes with her fingers and sniffed. 'Try telling that to Mummy.'

He glanced down at his hands. 'I don't think anyone can do that. It's something she'll have to come to on her own.'

'She never will.'

'You don't know that.'

But she did. Her father had stayed with her virtually all the time – he'd slept at the hospital and was in the waiting room now – but her mother had waited till visiting hours on Sunday afternoon, and stayed for precisely ten minutes.

She had taken a chair at the foot of the bed and given Modge a brisk meaningless smile, and asked if there was anything she wanted from the house.

'Did you get my note?' Modge had asked.

Her mother placed her hands on her knees and pressed down. 'Don't worry about that. We won't talk of it.'

'But I want to.'

'Best not to, darling.'

'Mummy—'

'You mustn't worry about anything, darling. You're going to be fine.'

'I'm not fine. I haven't been fine since Myles was killed. I'm twenty years old and I weigh twelve and a half stone, and I hate everything about me. I'm sick of it.'

Her mother put both hands to her temples. Her face

was pained. Modge had grown up with that expression. It meant, *Darling*, please. *I'm up to my ears in work, don't make it worse, there's a good girl!*

It always worked.

Modge turned to find Patrick watching her. She said, 'Why did you bother to stick around all these years?'

He thought for a moment. 'Myles asked me to look after you. Plus, and I know you'll find this hard to believe, I've always kind of liked you.'

Again her eyes filled. 'You've come to say goodbye, haven't you?'

He studied her face. 'For a little while. I think it's better.'

She rolled onto her side with her back to him. If he would leave now, this minute, she wouldn't break down. 'Go on then,' she muttered.

There was a pause. Then she heard him stand up. He placed something on the pillow in front of her.

'What's that?' she mumbled. But she knew what it was. It was Myles' Roman coin, which Mummy had given him years ago.

She remembered Myles teasing her one afternoon, holding it just out of reach and making her jump for it like a puppy. When finally she caught it, he let her keep it for a while. But she accidentally dropped it in the cattle trough in the rue de la Clouette, and howled, because she thought it was lost for ever. He had been surprisingly nice about it. 'Modge-Podge,' he said with a long-suffering, big-brother sigh, 'you *are* a silly little cow, aren't you?' And after he'd fished it out, he'd let her keep it for the rest of the day.

She hadn't remembered that until now.

She fingered the coin; then pushed it way. 'I don't

want it,' she declared, still with her back to Patrick. 'Take it away.'

'No. It's yours now. It should have come to you a long time ago.'

'I don't *want* it. Take it away or I'll chuck it in the bin.'

'You can do what you like with it. It's yours.'

'Right,' she muttered. Tears were sliding down her cheeks. She picked up the coin and threw it in the bin. 'Satisfied? Now go away.' She drew the blanket over her face and shut her eyes tight. Go away, Patrick. Go away now. I can't bear this.

'Maybe some time when you're better,' he said quietly, 'you'll give me a call?'

'What's the fucking point?'

'We'll go out for lunch. You'll drive up from Newmarket for the day, if the stables can spare you—'

She covered her ears with both hands.

'It'll happen, Imogen. You're going to make it happen. I know you. And you'll tell me all about Newmarket when we meet for lunch.'

'Get out. Get *out*!'

She heard him move to the door. 'I'll see you for that lunch, Imogen,' he said.

A long time later, when she had reached the hiccuping stage, she opened her eyes. Beneath her cheek there was a big damp patch, and her head was pounding.

I wonder if they'll give me an aspirin, she thought. Not bloody likely, with my track record.

She got up and went to the basin and splashed cold water on her face. Then she sat on the edge of the bed.

The coin had landed on a pile of crumpled tissues and some half-eaten grapes which her father had brought from the hospital canteen. She sat contemplating it for a long time. Then she snatched it up, wrenched open the bottom drawer of the bedside cabinet, and shoved it in, on top of Antonia's green hair-clip which she'd made her father bring from home. Right at the back, where she could pretend it wasn't there.

On Monday night when Antonia didn't call, Patrick told himself not to worry. Hadn't she said she would be in Toulouse? She would call on Tuesday, when she got back.

He immersed himself in the trial. Which was easy, for in the bizarre high-pressure world of High Court litigation, a thermonuclear war could break out, and no-one would notice.

Debra was in her element, for victory was close at hand. Since the trial began, she and Patrick had rarely been out of each other's sight, yet not once had she mentioned his broken engagement, or Modge's pitiful bid for attention. He knew she must be aware of his feelings for Antonia, for Modge's 'suicide' note had been comprehensive – but she gave no sign of it.

'Isn't she incredible?' murmured the clients. 'You'd never believe she's got a daughter in hospital. Now *that's* professionalism.' It struck Patrick as grotesque.

Antonia did not call on Tuesday morning, so he did. She wasn't there. Just before he left for court, he left a message on her answerphone. 'Antonia, it's Patrick. Can we meet up? Call me, would you – please?'

She didn't call. He spent Tuesday night in Debra's war-room with the litigation team. He watched himself reassuring clients, joking with solicitors, and debating with Debra and the others over the best way to tackle each witness. The ease with which he could dissemble astonished him.

It was three in the morning by the time he got home, to find a note from Nerissa on his pillow – *audition now in Paris, back Thurs. (?)* – and no messages on the answerphone. Perhaps, though, that was not surprising, as he realized he had forgotten to give Antonia his number.

Early on Wednesday morning he called the mill again. Again there was no answer, so he left all his telephone numbers, and asked her to call.

In court that morning he was cross-examining the other side's expert witness, a self-important little man who thought he could second-guess Patrick's questions. That only made Patrick's task easier, and irritated the judge. It also left part of his mind free to wonder what was happening out at La Bastide, and to face the slowly dawning possibility that maybe Antonia did not intend to call him back. Maybe she wanted nothing more to do with him.

'*Antonia,*' he remembered Myles remarking, '*is not the forgiving kind. Nope. Nyet. No way, José.*'

During the lunchtime break, when the team returned to chambers for sandwiches and strategy, he slipped out to his own room and called the mill again. He felt as tongue-tied as a seventeen-year-old. Jesus, why is it so hard to say what you feel? Answerphones are the worst invention on the planet. 'Antonia, uh – could you call me? Please? This thing – this trial – it'll be over soon, I think they're going to settle, maybe today. Anyway, I'll catch the first plane out.'

At five to two, just before he left for court, he called his travel service and bought a ticket on the first flight out in the morning. The hell with this. If she didn't want anything to do with him, she would have to tell him in person. What's the use of being a barrister if you can't plead your own case?

At a quarter to four the other side asked for a short adjournment, during which they accepted the settlement proposal they had been given on Saturday night. The judge was delighted: now he could go off and play golf. The clients were ecstatic. It was eight by the time Patrick and Debra managed to tear themselves away, and then only with promises to meet up later at Langan's, for more champagne.

'I need to talk to you,' Patrick told Debra as they reached the clerks' room.

'Finally,' she said, walking into her room and shutting the door behind him. 'Would you care for a drink?'

He shook his head. He chose a chair which faced away from the portrait of her father over the mantelpiece. No reason to give himself a handicap. Lord Justice Swynburne's basilisk stare had faced down better men than he.

'I take it,' said Debra, pouring a generous measure of Scotch into a tumbler, 'that this is about Antonia Hunt?' Her face was as serene and unreadable as when she was running an impossible argument in court.

'It is,' he said smoothly. If she hoped to wrong-foot him, she would be disappointed. He had known she would try to seize the upper hand. She was a litigator, after all.

He added, 'I take it Julian also told you that I've split up with Nerissa?'

She gave him her small, tight smile.

He had told Julian that morning at breakfast, just before the older man left for the hospital. He had felt bad about burdening Julian at such a time, but he had no choice.

Julian had listened in silence. Then he slowly folded his *Times* and placed it on the table beside his plate. 'I was afraid this might happen. I suppose I always knew that Nerissa wasn't right for you.'

'It's not her fault.' He paused. 'I'm still in love with Antonia.'

How simple it sounded when you said it out loud. How simple. And suddenly everything fell into place. No more headaches. No more papering over the cracks and wondering why nothing felt right.

But plainly, Julian had not expected this. He looked shocked. 'Oh my dear boy, you can't! You must know how Debra will take this!'

'I can't help that, Julian. No-one can.'

The older man did not reply.

Patrick attempted a smile. 'It's not as bad as all that. I'll still see you, you know. It's not as if I'm going to Australia.'

Julian took off his glasses and polished them with his handkerchief, blinking furiously. 'You're right, of course. It's not as though you're going to Australia.'

Debra was studying her father's portrait with a narrow gaze. She looked as if she were devising a litigation strategy.

Patrick felt worn out. He thought, why can't we take off the gloves and get on with it?

'I must say,' said Debra, still with her eyes on the portrait, 'I'm disappointed that you felt you had to mislead me all these years.'

'About?'

'You knew my son had taken that artefact, yet you covered it up. You knew my daughter had shut that gate, yet you never said. You—'

'I didn't know about the gate.'

'And now to resume your relations with that woman behind my back.' She reached for the decanter and

473

poured herself another drink. 'It seems I've misjudged you from the start. Perhaps what they say about silk purses and sows' ears is true.'

Patrick let that pass.

'So,' said Debra, 'it turns out I've been wrong all along – as my daughter was at pains to point out in her little note. My son was a thief, and that woman is in fact an angel of light, whom I'm expected to welcome into the fold with open arms.'

'No-one expects you to do that,' said Patrick quietly. Then he said, 'May I speak now?'

She inclined her head with exaggerated courtesy.

'What I have to say won't take long. And before I forget, I've already spoken to the Anderson lot, and they're not expecting me tonight.'

'Why not?' she said sharply. 'The CEO particularly wants you to be there.'

Steadily he met her eyes. 'Because I'm leaving.'

'Leaving?' she echoed.

'Resigning my tenancy.'

She blinked. 'That's impossible.'

'No it isn't. Not very usual, perhaps, but not impossible. I've made all the arrangements. My clerk will box up my things and send them round to Cornwall Gardens. He hasn't taken on any new cases for me recently, and as regards my current ones, they're all up to date. I'll prepare leaving notes tonight so that whoever takes over will be able to—'

'You can't just *leave*. You can't just throw everything away. Everything you've worked for.'

He was surprised. Clearly she had never envisaged this. 'Not everything,' he said. 'I'll still practise law.' His lip curled. 'Perversely, I get a kick out of it. But I'm thinking of changing allegiances.'

She laughed. 'You, a plaintiff's lawyer? Helping the underdog take on the multinationals? Oh, I don't think so!'

'Why not? I know enough about large companies to give them a run for their money.'

'Come off it, Patrick! We all get these sorts of doubts from time to time. But we get through them.'

'Maybe. But I'd still like to give it a try.'

She studied him. 'After all I've done for you.'

Calmly he met her eyes. 'I've learned a great deal from you, Debra. For that I'll always be grateful. But we both know that what I've achieved, I've achieved myself.'

She looked down at her drink, and frowned. 'Don't leave, Patrick. I don't know if I could carry on without you.'

The personal appeal. He had been expecting that. Maybe she even meant it, too.

He stood up. 'Goodbye, Debra,' he said.

Julian passed Patrick on the stairs, and thought he looked exhausted, even for the end of a trial.

'Julian,' Patrick called from the foot of the stairs.

Julian leaned over the banister.

Patrick looked up at him and tried to smile, but didn't quite make it. 'Goodbye, Julian,' he said. 'I'll – see you around.'

Something twisted in Julian's chest. 'Patrick—'

But he had already gone.

Oh God, thought Julian. God, don't let this happen.

Debra was alone in the clerks' room, standing by the fax machines leafing through the new arrivals.

'I thought I'd find you here,' he said. 'Congratulations on Anderson.' He tried to kiss her cheek but she twitched away. 'I saw Patrick,' he said. 'He looked terrible.'

She shuffled the faxes into a stack and gave him a brief smile. 'He's gone.'

Again that painful twist in his chest. Feeling very old and tired, he sank into a chair. 'What do you mean, gone?'

'What do you think I mean? Resigned. Departed. Left. Out of our lives.'

My boy, he thought numbly. My son in law. The son I never had. The clichés were endless. And they all had teeth.

At last he said quietly, 'And you didn't expect him to leave?'

'I thought he was more focused than that. Obviously I was wrong.'

He rubbed a hand over his face. 'Perhaps you left him no choice.'

Abruptly, she asked if he wanted a drink. He shook his head, and watched in silence as she retrieved her favourite Waterford tumbler from her room.

'I've come from the hospital,' he told her when she returned. 'Modge seems a little better. The doctors say she can come home tomorrow.'

She sat on the head clerk's desk and took a large swallow of her drink.

'Debra,' he said carefully, 'it wasn't Modge's fault.'

She put down her tumbler. 'She chose the worst possible time. The day before a major trial, when I—'

'Not everyone runs their lives by the court lists. She did it because she couldn't cope any more. If that's anyone's fault, it's ours.'

'I don't see how you reach that conclusion.'

Glancing down, he realized that he had placed his palms together, as if in prayer. Please don't be angry with our daughter any more, it's tearing us apart. Please don't force me to choose, as you did with Patrick. Please don't reject what I'm about to say. Quietly he said, 'We need to seek help for Modge. Professional help.'

She became very still. 'We talked about that years ago.'

'No,' he replied patiently. 'I suggested it, and you turned it down.'

'Because there's no point.'

'I think there is.'

'I disagree.'

He sighed.

She took another swallow of her drink. 'I don't need some "therapist" telling me I can't handle my own daughter. Telling me it's all my fault. No. Absolutely not. It's out of the question.'

'It's not a question of "handling" her. It's a question of helping her come to terms with what happened to Myles. And the point is, Debra, for the first time in twelve years, she wants to. She wants to get better. But she needs help.'

She did not reply.

He looked at her sitting on the desk in the empty office, surrounded by faxes and law reports and tottering stacks of briefs. She was all alone. She had rejected Modge. She had sent Patrick away. If he backed down now, he would be left alone with her in this sterile wilderness of paper. In this dead zone, where nothing could survive.

'I'm going to seek help for Modge,' he said again.

'I told you—'

'And I told you.' He paused. 'I cannot stand by and watch our daughter go the same way as Myles.'

Her jaw tightened. 'Are you saying that was my fault?'

'Of course not.'

'You think it was my fault. You think Modge was my fault too.'

'For heaven's *sake*!' he cried, 'this is not about *you*, it's about our daughter! Can't you see that?'

She was shocked by his outburst. He was shocked too. He could not remember the last time he had raised his voice.

'Julian,' she said at last. 'If you go through with this, I shan't forgive you. You need to be clear about that.'

'I can't help that, my darling. Modge needs me.'

'And I don't?'

He sighed. 'She needs me more.'

In silence they faced one another. Then he got to his feet and made for the door.

As he was leaving, he heard a phone ring behind him.

After four rings, Debra picked it up. 'Debra Swynburne,' she said.

By the time Nerissa reached La Bastide on Wednesday afternoon, she had begun to feel more than merely irritated with Antonia.

It was too much. The woman had to be made to face reality. And if that meant a trip out to this dreadful place, then so be it. Better to deal with it face to face. Point out how much Patrick needed a well-connected wife, how far he could go.

She rang the number Debra had given her, but either Antonia wasn't answering, or she wasn't at the mill. Nerissa never cursed, but on this occasion she was tempted. It hadn't occurred to her that Antonia might not be there.

She brought her bag in from the Discovery, locked the house again, and set off on foot for the mill. The old building was in darkness when she reached it, and Antonia's ghastly little Citroën was gone. Nerissa tried the door. To her surprise, it opened. Antonia must have forgotten to lock it.

She went in. The kitchen was positively medieval, but on a counter by the sink was a phone and an answering machine. Antonia had four messages. Nerissa pressed PLAY.

When she heard Patrick's voice, she gasped.

She listened to all four messages. They were all from him. '. . . I'm going to catch the first plane out,' ran the final one. 'I think we can work this out, Antonia. I really do. That is, if you want to. I know I do. I – I love you. I don't think I ever stopped loving you.'

She was incredulous. She had never heard him talk like that.

Dear God. He had really meant it about splitting up. The thought appalled her. The *idea* of having to start all over again with someone else. It wasn't fair. She *deserved* this marriage.

She erased all four messages, and left the mill.

CHAPTER THIRTY-TWO

The Discovery was not in its usual place at the airport when Patrick reached Perpignan on Thursday morning.

He stood blinking at the oily spot on the concrete. It took him several minutes to work out that Nerissa must have got there before him. He wondered why that was so hard to figure out. Maybe it was lack of sleep. He had spent most of the night drafting leaving notes on his cases, then another couple of hours clearing his desk before catching a cab to the airport. Forty minutes' sleep on the plane had left him with a head like cotton-wool.

He tried counting up how many hours' sleep he'd had over the past week, and gave up at around ten. Something about astronauts and sleep deprivation buzzed around the edges of his memory, but he couldn't catch hold of it, so he let it go.

Rain on his face pitched him back into the present. He returned to the terminal and rented a car, and reached La Bastide around eleven-thirty. The Discovery was parked outside the house. Oh, bloody hell. He didn't have the energy for another showdown with Nerissa.

The answerphone in the hall was blank, and there were no letters on the table. He swore under his breath. He had been counting on finding a message from Antonia.

He found Nerissa in the kitchen with her coat on,

writing him a note. 'I was just leaving,' she said, pocketing the note. 'I came to collect my things.'

Her face was serene. She seemed to have accepted that it was over between them.

He sat down and put his elbows on the table. The room floated gently round and round, reminding him of those astronauts again. Nerissa put a mug of black coffee in front of him and told him he looked absolutely terrible.

'I'm fine,' he muttered. 'Just a bit tired.'

It was good coffee, and after a while the room stopped going round. He told her briefly about resigning from chambers and saying goodbye to Modge.

She raised an eyebrow. 'What's this, clean slate time?'

He tried to smile, but it wouldn't come. His face felt like cardboard.

She picked up her keys. 'I'll leave the car at the airport in the usual place.'

'Sure.'

He carried her bags out and loaded them in the back. As she opened the door, she turned and said over her shoulder, 'Oh, I almost forgot. I bumped into Antonia yesterday evening in the village. She said to say hi.'

Somehow he managed to take that without a flicker. 'Did – she say anything else?'

Nerissa was tying her scarf. She shook her head. 'She was in a hurry, she'd only come back from somewhere or other to collect her messages, then she was off again.'

He went cold. Yesterday evening. She had been here yesterday evening, she had collected his messages – and the only reply she had for him was 'hi'.

Well, you can't get much clearer than that, can you? Nice work, Patroclus. You've gone and lost her all over again.

He became aware that Nerissa was studying him curiously. 'Sorry,' he said. 'You want to be going.'

She gave him a wry smile which had something else behind it that he couldn't read. Then she put her hands on his shoulders, stood on tiptoe and kissed him lightly on the mouth. 'Goodbye, Patrick. And good luck.' Another odd little smile. 'Something tells me you're going to need it.'

At half-past eleven on Thursday morning Antonia switched off her laptop, shouldered her bag, and left the university library in search of a proper cup of coffee.

Once inside the smoky little café which had become her haunt over the past four days, she resisted the urge to order a glass of wine, and sat down soberly with a *café Americain* to contemplate defeat.

Over the past two days, she had learned a surprising amount about her three candidates, but it still wasn't enough to get her home.

Valeria Atilia, the wine merchant's daughter, seemed the least likely of them all. According to *Roman Inscriptions in Britain*, she had ended her life in Colchester, where a funeral plaque described her marriage by the conventional acronym *SVQ*. That was short for *Sine Una Querella*, or 'Without A Quarrel'. It didn't sound like a woman who had once bitten her lover's neck, and drawn blood from his cheeks with her nails.

Aemilia Saturnina remained the most likely candidate, for although Antonia knew little about her, the colleague in Copenhagen had at last called back and told her that the cinerary urn was decorated with a relief of pomegranates. To the Romans, the pomegranate had been a potent symbol of eternal life. Of course, it was a bit of a stretch to assume that the fruit had been Aemilia's personal seal rather than just a general motif for the afterlife. But pomegranates pointed the right way, and Antonia had a hunch that Aemilia was the one.

Finally, there was Tacita Cornelia, whom Antonia liked the best, even if she was probably not Lycaris. Her name turned up in a letter by Pliny the Elder written more than a century later, in which she was cited as an example of the influence which a strong, intelligent woman could have on her children. '*By all accounts this was a woman of courage and depth of feeling,*' Pliny wrote, somewhat sententiously, '*who passed on those qualities to her young.*' The young Cornelii had grown up in Athens. From an 1893 catalogue of Greek papyri, Antonia had learned that in later years they had adopted as their seal the crescent moon of their mother's family.

A pomegranate or a crescent moon.

Neither jogged her memory. She could not picture anything in the blank spot on the cup. It looked as if her stab at solving the riddle was doomed to remain just that. A stab in the dark.

Toying with her coffee, she watched the people strolling along the pavement in the spring sunshine. A young man put his arm around his girlfriend's shoulders and hugged her, and laughed aloud. Maybe he was laughing because his girl had said something funny, or maybe it was simply for the sheer joy of being young and in love under the sun.

My heart went up and sang in the sky.

Suddenly Antonia thought, how petty I am. To treat this riddle like some kind of intellectual puzzle. To be upset because *I'm* not the one who's going to solve it. It isn't a game. It never was. It means something.

Two thousand years ago, a man loved a woman.

When he lost her, it blighted his life. Then, years later, she fell into danger, and he found a way to save her life – at the cost of his own. But before he died, he did everything he could to ensure that one day their spirits would be together.

To him it was not a word-game. It mattered. He believed in it.

She wondered if Lycaris – whoever she was – had ever learned what Cassius had done for her. Did they meet again, one final time? Did they find some way to overcome whatever had separated them thirteen years before? Or were they swept apart by the war, their last chance at reconciliation gone for ever?

She watched the dancing shadows of the young leaves on the pavement, and thought about last chances, and mending the mistakes of the past. Then she got up and went inside, and dialled Patrick's chambers.

His clerk answered, sounding harried. No, Mr McMullan wasn't in chambers. And no, he wasn't at home either, they'd been trying to reach him there too. She could always try the hospital, although—

Antonia's heart lurched. 'The *hospital*?'

The clerk became evasive. Clearly if she did not know about that, he did not consider it his place to enlighten her. Perhaps she should speak to Mr Passmore or Ms Swynburne, although as Ms Swynburne was in conference, Mr Passmore was probably her best bet, he would be home around now, would she like the number?

Julian answered on the second ring, and did a valiant job of concealing his disappointment when he heard her voice. They had a brief, awkward conversation in which he did most of the talking, and when she put down the phone she needed a drink, a real one this time. When the waiter brought the *coup de rouge* it was an effort not to down it in one.

To try to *kill* herself? Poor little Modge. And poor Julian. And Debra. And Patrick.

Julian had sounded shattered, as well he might, and he had been vague about Patrick's whereabouts. He wished he knew, he said. He was worried about Patrick.

She had a sudden picture of a young man walking down the rue de la Clouette, while an eight-year-old skipped in circles round him and pestered him for *pain au chocolat*. Patrick in the pot-shed, sitting patiently on a bench while Modge instructed him in the art of numbering shards. She wondered how he was taking this.

She finished her drink and called for another.

'It's no-one's *fault*,' Julian had said. 'In fact, it's time we got things out in the open. Rightly or wrongly, what Modge has done is a catalyst. We need to *deal* with things. For her sake. And perhaps also for ours.'

To hear him struggling for optimism had been heartbreaking.

The waiter brought the second glass. She contemplated it. Another drink was hardly a good idea, given that she had to drive back to the village that afternoon, pack up her things, and be out – God knew where – by midnight, when the mill changed hands. The thought filled her with a great weariness. She just wanted to talk to Patrick and make sure he was all right.

She held up the wine-glass, and watched the sunlight turn it to ruby. 'This is for you, Modge,' she murmured. 'And for you too, Patrick. Wherever you are. "A cup of wine for the afternoon . . ."'

A cup of wine . . .

She frowned. Where had she heard those words before?

Slowly she put down the wine-glass. A cup of wine . . . Then it came to her.

Myles crouching like a leprechaun on a sun-baked hillside, waving an empty champagne bottle as he shouted down an irreverent toast: '*A cup of wine for the afternoon, and* don't *let the water-jug near it. The Bacchus from* these *cellars flows* neat!'

Suddenly everything fell into place. Of course. *How* could she have been so stupid? Myles had hidden the *kántharos* in the cellar – the one place where neither she nor her father had thought to look. No-one ever went down there. The cellars were too big, too dark, too unexplored. Besides, they were always kept locked. Although that would have presented no obstacle to Myles. On the contrary, he would have enjoyed the challenge.

She glanced at her watch. It was shortly after noon. She had just under twelve hours in which to hurry back to Professor Meriot's and retrieve her things, drive down to La Bastide, search the cellars – *and*, on top of all that, make contact with Patrick and find out how he was doing.

Just before she left the café, she tried his chambers again. This time she was put straight through to the head clerk, who told her starchily that no, Mr McMullan still wasn't in, and no, he was not expected back. Mr McMullan had resigned.

Resigned?

They wouldn't tell her any more than that. She dialled the number which – after considerable prevarication – they gave her for his house in London, but all she got was an answerphone, and she didn't leave a message in

486

case Nerissa was there. The same thing happened when she called the house in La Bastide. Where *was* he? She thought about calling Julian again, but decided against it. He had enough to deal with as it was.

She would call again when she reached the mill.

It was noon, and as Patrick had missed breakfast on the plane, he was hungry, but he couldn't decide what to eat. Eventually he gave up the idea altogether. Food was irrelevant. The important thing was to find Antonia.

He stood in the middle of the kitchen, trying to think. But his thoughts kept skittering off at a tangent, and it was becoming harder and harder to bring them together.

Come on, think. You're not just going to let this happen. You're a lawyer, for Christ's sake! Surely you can bring her round?

Maybe you can. But you've got to find her first.

One thing was certain: at midnight tonight, the mill would become Debra's. Which meant that at some stage today, Antonia would have to return to collect her belongings, or Debra's bailiffs would chuck them out onto the road.

So what are you waiting for? he thought. Get down to the mill! Hell, maybe she's already there!

He threw on his jacket and left the house.

But there was no sign of anyone at the mill, although puzzlingly, the door was unlocked. He went inside. No messages on the answerphone. His last hope – that Nerissa had been lying, and Antonia had not in fact been back and collected them – drained away.

On the floor he found a scattering of mail and a couriered envelope from Paris, marked urgent. He wished he had thought of sending her a couriered letter from London. Maybe she would have taken that more seriously than a clutch of incoherent telephone messages.

He went over to the desk, tore a leaf from Antonia's memo pad, and scribbled a note: *Antonia. I meant what I said. Every word. Patrick.* He stuck it on the fridge beside the postcard of Cassius, where she was sure to see it.

As he did so, his eye was caught by a fluorescent green Post-It underneath. KATE! it said in big red capitals, with a London number scrawled underneath. He pocketed it and left.

Back at his house he called the number, and somewhat to his relief, found himself speaking not to the mad friend herself, but to a reedy-voiced male who described himself as the mad friend's husband. No, said the reedy voice, Antonia hadn't been in touch in the last couple of days, wasn't she overseas? Yes, he would tell his wife that Patrick needed to get in touch with Antonia *urgently*, and if she rang, they would be sure and pass on the message.

The husband sounded more amenable than the wife, but worryingly vague. It didn't help that he called Patrick 'Mr Toynbee' when he rang off.

Again Patrick found himself standing in the middle of the kitchen wondering what to do. It wasn't even two o'clock yet. It might be hours before she arrived at the mill. He could not face waiting in the house. He had to do something. He pulled on his jacket and left.

Despite the mildness of the afternoon, the track up to the Source had the stillness of midwinter. It was too early for cicadas, and too cold for lizards. The roar of the Sarac was a muted thunder far below.

As he walked, inhaling the sweet resin-scented air, his

mind cleared, as it always did when he approached the Source. You can't give up now, he told himself. If you do, you'll only be repeating the same mistake you made twelve years ago.

It was three o'clock by the time he reached the end of the track, and although fitful sunlight pierced the clouds, the Source was already a well of darkness.

A door in the mountain, he thought. A gateway between the worlds of the living and the dead. He wondered if Myles was inside.

He ducked his head and entered, and underfoot the ground was as dry as on the night they had found the *kántharos*. He knelt, and let a handful of dust trickle through his fingers. In the darkness at the back of the cave, the spring sang softly to itself: an ancient, bubbling mystery that hadn't changed in ten thousand years.

He remembered how Antonia had looked as they knelt in the dust before the *kántharos*. Her face transfigured, her dark eyes glittering with tears.

She was still the same girl. Why had it taken him so long to see that? She hadn't changed, and neither had he. You could try to convince yourself that people grew apart, that times moved on, that events got in the way – and maybe sometimes they did. But not this time. Not unless he let it happen.

On his way out, he cracked his head dizzyingly against a stalactite, which brought him smartly back to the present. *Watch your step, son*, the Goddess seemed to be warning him. *You're not out of the woods yet.*

His easy optimism drained away. No wonder Antonia hadn't called him. He should not have left her like that, with no indication of how he felt.

He emerged unsteadily into the sunshine. Black spots darted before his eyes, and when he put his fingers to his temple they came away covered in blood. Chastened, he started back down the track. But when he reached the little bridge where it branched off up the Ravin de Verdura, he came to a halt.

It was still only half-past three. If he kept going, he would be back at the mill in half an hour. What if she still wasn't there? He didn't think he could face that. So to kill another hour he decided to take the side-track up to the ridge. Maybe he would meet her on the way down. Knowing Antonia, she would not leave La Bastide without saying goodbye to the Source.

The track wound up through a beech wood carpeted in crisp, bronze-coloured leaves which made the sound of his passage loud in the still air. When he halted for breath, the wood fell eerily silent. No wind stirred the bare grey branches. No cry of a hawk, no solitary piping wren. He was alone.

The track narrowed and became steeper. The leaf carpet deepened to knee-high drifts.

This must be years of leaves, he thought as he ploughed through them. Years and years, maybe right back to that last summer. Right back to Myles.

Thinking about that, he stepped on a tree root that turned out to be a fallen branch, which upended and nearly pitched him off the track. He landed heavily on his right foot, and a bolt of pure white lightning shot through his knee.

The pain was worse than anything he had known. He fell, and for several heartbeats all he could do was roll in the leaves and fight it.

Panting and shivering, he lay staring at the tracery of naked branches against the sky.

Of *all* the times for his knee to go.

One botched attempt at standing told him that he was

in trouble. As soon as his foot touched the ground, the pain flared to a white, engulfing agony which felled him at once. Ah, fuck. *Fuck*. He broke into a sweat. He locked his jaws to keep from crying out.

The cut on his head began to throb in unison with his knee. He forced himself to lie still and figure his options.

Obviously he couldn't stay here. Hikers did not come this way in March, and he doubted that hunters did either. Of course, he could always use his mobile, which – by sheer luck – he still had in his jacket pocket. But hell, this was hardly an emergency, he'd only buggered up the ligament in his knee. So forget about that.

How far was he from the mill? It must be about two miles back to the main track, then another mile and a half, maybe two, down to the mill. So say four miles in all. Which on two legs would be an easy one-hour hike. On one good leg and a couple of crutches, it would take maybe three hours, maybe four. OK, so say four hours at most, and you're back by seven-thirty at the latest.

And maybe by then, said a snide little voice in his head, Antonia will already have been and gone. He told the voice to shut the hell up, and began looking around for crutches.

An hour later, he was not even halfway back to the main track, and already it was beginning to get dark. The branches he had found for crutches were helping, but they weren't really long enough, so it was slow going. And it hurt like hell. The pounding in his temple was now marking time with admirable precision.

He stopped to rest, noticing vaguely that the temperature had fallen sharply. Glancing up at the darkening sky, he wondered if there would be a moon tonight. If not, things might get tricky.

He hated the idea of calling for help. Who was he

supposed to call? Antonia? Hers was the only local number he had, given that both his house and Les Limoniers were empty, and although Monsieur Panabière had a phone, it was a village joke that he never answered it. So it looked like it was either Antonia, or the emergency services in Mazerans. But come off it, this wasn't an emergency.

He took out his mobile and punched in Antonia's name. Nothing happened. He tried again, with the same result. No reception. He bit back a laugh. Should have thought of that one, shouldn't you? That'll teach you to rely on technology.

Once again he struggled to his feet – foot – and began shuffling through the leaves like an elderly drunk.

After a while it occurred to him that no-one knew where he was. Hell, no-one even knew that he was in France. He hadn't been up to the shops, hadn't bumped into anyone, and since Nerissa had taken the Discovery, it was unlikely that anyone would associate the anonymous rental car in the road with him. And of course, he had left nothing in the house to indicate where he was headed.

Oh, terrific. This time he had really screwed up. What was it he used to tell the townies on the dude ranch before they set off on a hike? *Always tell someone where you're going, always take plenty of water, and never hike alone.*

He had a sudden image of a collie dog a week from now, scrabbling through a pile of leaves, and tugging at his decomposing body.

Why a collie dog? he wondered, and started to laugh.

CHAPTER THIRTY-THREE

Antonia reached the mill around four o'clock, and found it unlocked.

A rapid scan of her mail told her that none of it was from Patrick. To make matters worse, there were no messages on the answerphone.

She suppressed a flicker of exasperation. 'Call me,' he had said. Surely it wasn't beyond *him* to call her?

Then she thought of Modge, and was contrite. He had other things to think about right now.

The official-looking envelope from Paris turned out to be from Debra's French lawyers, formally notifying her that if she stayed in the mill a minute past midnight, she would be evicted. She chucked it in the bin. If Debra wanted to waste money paying lawyers to tell her what she already knew, that was her problem.

But in the same envelope was a note from Debra herself which brought her up short. It had been written in longhand with great care, and was dated the previous day. *'I thought you would be interested to learn that my daughter has tried to commit suicide. I hope you are satisfied with what you have done. Debra Swynburne.'*

To have been included in the courier delivery, the note must have been faxed to the lawyers' Paris office from Debra's chambers. Antonia found such meticulous ill-will strangely chilling.

'No, Debra,' she murmured. 'I'm not "satisfied". But don't worry. You'll get what you want. In eight hours you'll have won, and I'll be out.'

Eight hours. What could she achieve in eight hours? The cellars would need five times as long for a proper search.

Wearily she went to the fridge for a Coke, and found a new Post-It stuck crookedly next to Cassius. *Patrick?* Patrick had been here and left a note?

The handwriting was terrible. She could barely decipher his name. *Antonia. I meant what I said. Every word. Patrick.* What did he mean, 'I meant what I said'? What he'd said about what? And when had he been here? Where had he gone? Had he flown back to London, or was he still in La Bastide?

She felt a prickle of unease. Was he all right? The writing was all over the place. Then she remembered Modge telling her about his scrawl, and how he'd had to learn how to write from scratch, because of the burns to his hand. So was this normal for him, or what?

She rang his house, but got no answer. Then she rang his house in London – again no answer. Finally she rang chambers, who were beginning to expect her, and told her wearily that no, they didn't know where he was either, but if she caught up with him before they did – which they had a feeling she might – would she be kind enough to ask him to get in touch?

It's probably nothing, she told herself as she put down the receiver. He's probably just avoiding the phone – what with Modge, and resigning, and everything. He's probably in London right now, having a long, late, expensive lunch with Nerissa.

Telling herself severely not to over-dramatize, she put together the Calor Gas lamp she'd bought in Toulouse, and started down to the cellars to begin the search. She had seven and a half hours in which to find the *kántharos*. And no-one – not even Patrick – was going to get in the way.

Five minutes later she ran back upstairs, threw on her jacket, and set off at a run for his house. She had to know whether or not he was still in the valley.

The stars were out when Patrick came to.

He was lying on his back under the oak tree at the mouth of the Source. He had no recollection of how he had got there, although a quick inspection showed him that at some point he must have fallen and smashed his watch, for it had stopped at nine-fifteen.

Nine-fifteen? What had happened in between? Maybe that crack on the head had been worse than he thought. Or maybe he'd simply decided to catch up on some sleep.

Funny place to do it, though. And cold. Really cold. Hadn't there been piles of leaves somewhere? He remembered great drifts of dry, rustling leaves. Would've been better if he'd stopped for a nap in one of those.

Ah, the hell with it. He was too tired to worry about it now. And his head hurt like crazy.

Some time later, Hippolyte came by to visit, and nudged him with a warm, wet nose. Patrick told him to go fetch Antonia, and obediently the pony trotted off. But somehow Patrick didn't think he'd got the idea.

Maybe Pegasus would do better. After all, he could fly, which would make him a whole lot quicker than Hippolyte, with his stumpy little legs.

He tried to locate Pegasus among the stars. Years ago, he had looked him up in a book on astronomy, and been surprised to learn that in the northern hemisphere, Pegasus was upside-down. He scanned the heavens for an upside-down horse falling out of the sky, but couldn't find one.

Snatches from the astronomy book drifted through his mind. '. . . *the chief star of the constellation is suspected of variability . . . when observing, take care not to forget extinction . . .*'

Looks like I forgot about extinction, he thought hazily.

Then he recalled that the constellation didn't have any wings. Just a neck and a nose, and two prancing front legs. *I guess we're supposed to infer the wings, huh?* he heard himself say, twelve years before. He couldn't remember what Antonia had said in reply, but he knew that shortly afterwards he had kissed her for the first time. And she had kissed him back.

Gradually, the darkness above him filled with little winged horses toppling out of the sky. He closed his eyes and flew up to meet them.

'I haven't got *time* for this,' Antonia muttered as she ran up the road to Patrick's house.

To her relief it was lit up like a Christmas tree. Someone must be home. But instead of the Discovery she found a blue car with Hertz number plates parked in front.

That can't be Nerissa, she thought, puzzled. A Nissan Primera is hardly her style.

She rang the bell, but no-one answered. Then she saw that the door wasn't properly shut. 'Patrick?' she called. 'Nerissa?' Cautiously, she pushed it open and went inside.

On the kitchen table she found a scattering of loose

change, some keys, an Air France ticket, and a crumpled wad of car rental papers. The rental was in Patrick's name. So at least she knew he was still in the valley.

But where?

Then she noticed that the fridge door was standing open. It had obviously been like that for hours, for it was well into the defrost programme. On the counter beside it stood a carton of milk torn raggedly open, an unopened packet of crackers, and a jar of peanut butter with a knife sticking out. It looked as if he'd wandered over to the fridge for something to eat, then lost interest halfway through, and forgotten all about it. What was *wrong* with the man? Was he sleepwalking? Or drunk?

Or maybe, she thought, he simply got a better offer, and left the house in a hurry. Maybe Monsieur Panabière called, and he went up for a drink at the Bar-Tabac. Maybe he's up there now.

She scrawled a quick note asking him to call her, propped it up against the milk carton, and left the house, running all the way to the Bar-Tabac.

Wherever he was, he was not at the Bar-Tabac or anywhere else in La Bastide, according to the assembled drinkers. No-one had seen him for days, and they all confidently assured her that he was in London.

He's probably fine, she told herself as she arrived back at the mill. He's probably just gone for a walk and forgotten the time.

It was half-past six.

If she was going to make a start on the cellar, she must do it now. As far as Patrick was concerned, she had done all she could. From now on it was up to him.

Three and a half hours later, as she was struggling to shift a crate of ancient and extremely heavy empties, the phone rang. She fell upstairs and snatched the receiver just as her answerphone started telling whoever it was that Antonia couldn't take the call, so please leave a message.

'Where the hell have you *been*!' she cried. 'I've been calling your house every ten minutes for hours!'

'Ah,' said Kate. 'So he hasn't been in touch.'

'What? *What?*'

There was silence on the other end of the line. Then Kate said, 'Antonia, I'm really sorry. But my useless dork of a husband only just remembered that he took a message from your barrister hours ago. Apparently he said it was urgent, so I thought I'd better call.'

Antonia gripped the receiver. 'What did he say?'

'Phil can't remember exactly.'

'Oh, *Kate*!'

'I know, I know, he's getting sixty lashes in the morning. But he really can't remember, except that it was urgent, and could you call back as soon as possible.'

'When? When did he call?'

A whispered discussion on the other end of the line. 'Around lunchtime. Phil remembers, because he was eating a sandwich.'

Lunchtime. That was hours ago.

'Where was he calling from?'

More mutterings. 'Sorry. He didn't say.'

Antonia shut her eyes.

Kate sighed. 'Antonia, love, you can't go on like this. Why don't you just tell the man how you feel?'

She drew a ragged breath. 'Because I can't *find* him! I know it sounds bizarre, and there's probably a perfectly reasonable explanation, but I've been all over the place and I can't find him! He's here, I know he is, because his car's here. But his front door was open and the fridge was defrosting and I can't shake off this horrible feeling that something's happened.'

There was another silence. Then Kate said in her most pragmatic and managing voice, 'Listen. I won't tell you not to worry, because it won't help. But when I spoke to your chap on the phone the other week he sounded pretty robust to me. For Christ's sake, Antonia, he's a lawyer! He can look after himself. And he can't have got very far without his car.'

'That's true,' said Antonia hopefully.

Kate paused. 'Having said all of which, if you haven't heard from him by midnight, call the police.'

When she rang off, the mill seemed very dark and quiet. Antonia stood by the fridge wondering what to do. It was half-past ten, and she had barely scratched the surface of the cellar – which, as she had feared, was turning out to be an obstacle course of wine-boxes and unwieldy pieces of what looked like ancient farming equipment. The place must have been a paradise for Myles, he could have hidden the *kántharos* anywhere. And she had one and a half hours in which to find it.

Or looked at another way, she had one and a half hours in which to go stumbling around in the pitch darkness on a freezing mountainside making a complete idiot of herself, while the man she was trying to find was probably dining happily with his fiancée at the three-star Michelin in Sainte Eulalie.

She sat down wearily on her desk, and met Cassius' contemplative gaze on the fridge.

But that isn't the point, is it? she told him silently. *The point is, Cassius, I've got to go and find Patrick. And if that means giving up my last chance of helping you, I've still got to do it.*

She wiped her eyes with a grimy knuckle. 'I'm sorry, Cassius,' she said aloud. 'We were nearly there, weren't we? We were so close. So close.' She drew a ragged breath. 'But I have to do this. You understand, don't you? Wherever you are, you of all people understand. I have to make sure he's all right.'

Patrick was drifting in the sky somewhere around Betelgeuse, and it was becoming terrifically difficult to avoid the moon. It kept zooming straight at him: an enormous, erratic silver disc whose glaring brightness drilled savagely into his aching head.

Then someone was shaking him by the shoulders, and the moon resolved itself into a gas lamp with Antonia kneeling beside it, calling his name.

'Antonia,' he murmured, struggling into a sitting position which sent lightning shooting through his skull.

'What the *hell* are you doing up here?' she cried, gripping his shoulders with both hands.

'I was—'

'*Look* at you! Blood all over you! Face like fucking paper! What d'you thinking you're *doing*, not telling anyone where you were going? Not even a note!'

She fished in her pocket for a handkerchief and ran inside to the spring, then ran back and started roughly wiping the blood from his face. The water felt wonderful, but she was shaking so much that most of it went down his neck. He tried to take the handkerchief from her to do it himself, but she smacked his hand away.

'What happened to you?' she demanded.

'Hit my head,' he mumbled. 'And my knee's kind of shot. Christ, but it's good to see you, I—'

'Your *knee*?' she exploded. 'Great God in Heaven, I can't *believe* you never got that fixed, you were supposed to do it years ago!'

That made him laugh. 'You're not going to give me a hard time about that now, are you?'

'It's not funny, you moron, I thought you were dead! I thought you'd gone over the fucking cliff! What the fuck were you doing up here, wandering around in the dark? D'you know what time it is? It's a quarter-past fucking *midnight*!'

She was swearing like a trooper, which she never did, and clutching his shoulders with both hands as if she never meant to let go. In the silvery gaslight her face was smooth and pale and glistening with tears, her lips as white as chiselled marble. She looked marvellous.

He told her so.

She sniffed, and wiped her nose on the back of her hand.

He touched her cheek with his fingers. 'Don't cry.' He struggled upright, ignoring the iron rings constricting his skull. 'Antonia—'

'Don't you move,' she said, pushing him down again. 'I'm going for help. Now you stay put. I won't be long.'

He grabbed her wrist. 'Wait. First I have to tell you something. It's important.'

'What?'

He searched for words. Shit, he was beginning to drift again. He knew that he had to tell her something and he knew it was incredibly important, but he couldn't remember what it was. So instead he asked her if she'd got his messages.

'The one on the fridge? What the hell was that supposed to mean?'

'No no, the other ones. On the phone.'

She looked at him blankly. 'You left messages?'

'Oh Christ. You didn't get them. That's why I came up here.'

Again she looked puzzled, and he realized that that didn't make any sense. 'I was waiting for you,' he explained. 'You hadn't answered my messages, but I knew you'd come up here to say goodbye. I mean, not to me, but—' He took a deep breath, then started again. The iron rings around his skull were tightening, and the stars were beginning to zoom at him again. 'I let everything get in the way,' he muttered. 'Shouldn't have let everything get in the way . . .'

He had a nagging feeling that there was a much, much simpler way of saying this, but his brain refused to tell him what it was.

Then he felt her put her arm around his shoulders and bring his head against her breast, and her warm hand was smoothing the hair back from his forehead, and her breath was heating his cheek. She bent close to him, and he caught the peppermint scent of her hair. 'Patrick,' she said softly. 'It's all right now. I understand.'

He was immensely tired. 'We let everything get in the way,' he mumbled. 'That has to end here, Antonia.'

'I know,' she whispered, and he felt her lips brush his, and tasted her salty tears. 'That ends here. You're going to be all right, Patrick. We're both going to be all right.'

He opened his eyes and met hers, and knew that for the first time in twelve years, it was true.

CHAPTER THIRTY-FOUR

Near Lake Trasimene, Umbria, 1 March 40 BC

Tacita didn't know what she would do if he refused to see her.

She paced the barn, straining for the sound of footsteps in the courtyard. But all she heard was the drip, drip of melting snow, and the occasional thump as an icicle dropped from the eaves.

Even if he came right now, they wouldn't have much time. In the farmhouse across the courtyard her husband and the others were still sleeping, exhausted by the terrors of their nocturnal flight through the hills. But she could not count on that for long.

If only he would come. Now more than ever, it was imperative that she should see him. He had to know the truth before – before he died.

She still could not believe it. Faenio had told her just after midnight, when their little group finally reached the deserted farm. The old slave couldn't help himself, it had come out in a rush. He had wept as he told her.

She had been too stunned to cry. What a fool she had been not to see at once what this rescue must cost him! What a fool! Although perhaps in her desperation, she had not *wanted* to see. Thinking about it, she had lain awake all night, while around her the others slept in the straw where they had dropped.

An hour before dawn she had risen silently and left the farmhouse, crossing the muddy courtyard to the barn, where Faenio had a fire blazing. Yes, he told her, he had got word to his master that she must see him. No, he didn't know what the response would be. She must wait and be patient.

She was not patient.

In the glow of the brazier she had washed as best she could, put up her hair, and tried to smooth the worst of the wrinkles from her dress. It was a cruel parody of those heady spring nights when, sick with excitement, she had crept from her father's house and run breathlessly through the streets to the Porta Capena, and into his arms.

A footstep in the courtyard.

And there he was, standing in the doorway looking at her, his face expressionless. 'You wanted to see me,' he said. 'I can't stay long. It's too dangerous.'

She put a hand to her throat. Words deserted her.

He looked magnificent. Beneath a general's cloak of heavy scarlet wool he wore a doublet and kilt of gilded leather with buckles of burnished bronze. His half-boots were tooled in silver. She pictured him riding his horse at the head of a column of men. Tall, upright, intimidatingly in control.

After that first long look, he did not glance at her again, but brusquely asked if she wanted wine. She did. She needed it.

He walked to the table beside the brazier, and she saw that his limp had worsened since the poetry reading seven years before. She watched him pour wine into two bronze beakers, add hot water from the jug, and leave hers on the table for her to take. He doesn't want to touch me, she thought. Her heart contracted.

He held his cup in both hands and frowned at it. 'Your children,' he said at last, 'they are – coping with this?'

She picked up her cup and took a long swallow. It was good wine, and after months of sour *posca* it tasted ambrosial. She felt its warmth stealing down into her belly. 'The twins are with my brother on his estate,' she said. 'I only have my eldest with me.'

He nodded. 'That's good. It'll be a hard journey.'

'Gaius—'

'You need to make your way to Puteoli by the back roads,' he said, still without looking at her. 'Don't go anywhere near Spoletum. That's where our forces are massing for the final assault. When you get to Puteoli, take ship for Corinth. Then cross the isthmus overland—'

Carefully she set down her cup, wondering how to begin.

'– then take another ship for Athens. But remember: overland at the isthmus. Don't try it by sea. This time of year the storms around the Peloponnese are at their worst. And go to Athens, not Alexandria or Ephesus. It's more out of the way.'

He drained his cup and set it down, wiping his mouth on the back of his hand. 'I'm giving you my slave, Faenio. He'll see that you get there safely. He'll look after you.' He paused. 'My father gave him to me when I was a boy. You can trust him completely. He won't let you down.'

Thirteen years ago, as she lay in his arms, he had told her about the tricks he used to play on Faenio when he was ten. Did he think she had forgotten all that?

'You can't give me Faenio,' she said. 'He's been with you for so long—'

'Precisely. Besides, I won't be—' He cut himself short.

She knew what he had been going to say. *I won't be needing a slave for much longer. Not where I'm going.* She couldn't stand it any longer. 'Gaius, I can't let you do this!'

He shot her a glance. 'What do you mean?'

'I know what's going to happen to you. I know what you mean to do.'

His face hardened. 'Who told you? Who?'

'It doesn't matter—'

'That bloody Cretan! I expressly forbade him to say anything!'

She twisted her hands together. 'I've been such a fool. I never thought. You must believe that. I assumed that with your rank, you'd get away with it. I was such a fool!'

He waited awkwardly, while she brought herself under control.

'I'm sorry,' she muttered, 'it's the wine. I'm not used to it.' She went to the table and took another swallow, and put the cup down again. Then she said, 'I need you to know something.'

'I don't want—'

'I need you to *know*,' she repeated fiercely, 'that I've never loved any man but you. I never stopped loving you, Gaius. That's the truth.'

He looked stunned. He opened his mouth to speak, then closed it again. At last he said, 'I didn't know.'

She went to him and took his hands. They were rough and brown, and notched with scars: a soldier's hands. Beautiful, she thought. 'Well,' she said, 'now you do.'

His hands tightened on hers. 'Tacita. You haven't changed.'

'Neither have you.'

They stood like that for a long time. Then at last he drew her into his arms and held her tight. She put her head on his shoulder and shut her eyes, and felt his warmth about her, and caught the faint scent of wine from the lees he used in his ink. In one breath she was back in the tomb in the Porta Capena. She couldn't bear it. 'It's not fair,' she said brokenly. 'We could have been happy.'

His arms tightened. 'No,' he murmured into her hair, 'not in this life.'

'Do you think there's another?'

'Oh, yes.'

'You sound so certain.'

'You used to tease me about my peasant faith. Remember?'

'But you weren't always so certain.'

'No.' He took her face in his hands and looked down into her eyes. Close up, his own were as light and vivid as she remembered, and hard to look into for long. He said, 'It took me years to realize that what I felt for you – what I *feel* – is all the proof I'll ever need.'

Outside, an icicle hit the ground. They both started.

'We don't have much time,' he said. 'The others will be waking up soon.'

She felt a rising tide of panic at the thought of leaving him. There was so much still to tell him, and she had scarcely begun. If they were interrupted now, how would she bear it?

She put her hands on his shoulders. 'Gaius, there's something else I must tell you. You need to understand why I left.'

To her dismay he shook his head. 'I don't want to know. That doesn't matter any more, it—'

'It matters,' she insisted. 'I tried to tell you once before, but—'

'I know, I sent back your letter. I'm sorry. That was wrong of me.'

She brushed that aside. 'I have to tell you, Gaius. We won't get another chance, and this is something you must know. Not for me, but for you.'

He watched in puzzlement as she ran to the door and called softly to Faenio. After a few moments the slave entered, gently pushing his charge before him. Then the old Cretan withdrew, to resume his watch outside the door.

Tacita turned back to Gaius, who had gone very still. She put her hands on the boy's shoulders and said simply, 'This is my son, Titus.'

Fearlessly, Titus stepped forward and extended his hand, and thanked the general for saving their lives.

Gaius did not move. He stood with his hands at his sides, gazing down into the twelve-year-old's face, into the startling grey eyes – his own eyes – gazing solemnly back at him.

Then he raised his head and looked at her over the dark, tousled curls of his son. His lips parted, but no words came. He cleared his throat. Started again. 'Why . . .' he began, 'why didn't you tell me?'

She licked her lips. 'How could I? You would have tried to stop me. You would have got yourself killed.'

She watched him take in the truth of that – and also the truth of what she had not said. If her father had discovered that his only daughter was carrying a provincial officer's child, he would have had her killed as well.

'And you never guessed?' she said.

Dazedly he shook his head. 'It – occurred to me, of course. But I thought – I thought I would have known.

I thought one sensed these things. Somehow.'

It moved her painfully to encounter such ignorance in so intelligent a man.

Titus was glancing from one to the other, trying to follow what was going on, and scowling, because he couldn't. He looked exactly like Gaius when he was angry. The same lower lip thrust out, the same strong brows drawn together.

'What you did,' Gaius told her slowly, 'by leaving – you saved my life. And yours. And – his. All three of us.' He listened to the sound of that. 'And I thought you were *weak*! I thought you left because you were frightened!'

Slowly he went back to the table and sat down, and put his hand across his mouth.

He sat with his bad leg stretched before him. Intrigued, Titus edged closer. 'Are you wounded, sir?'

Still with his hand over his mouth, Gaius studied him. 'A long time ago.'

'Does it hurt?'

'Only sometimes . . . Come closer, will you? – Titus?'

Titus moved forwards.

Gaius took the boy's small hand in his. Frowning, he turned it in his fingers, examining it as if it were some exotic and fragile object which he must commit to memory. At last he said, 'Titus, you have ink-stains on your fingers.'

Titus gave a small smile. 'So have you, sir.'

'So I have. I was up late, writing.'

'You're lucky, sir! My mother won't let me stay up late.'

Still frowning, Gaius studied the boy's hand in his own.

Titus sucked in his lips. 'You're left-handed, sir,' he said.

509

'And you're observant, Titus.'

'I noticed, because I'm left-handed too.'

At last, Gaius released the boy's hand, took him gently by the shoulders, and looked into his face. 'And what do you write? Hm? Do you write poems?'

'Oh, no, sir. I write *plays*.'

'Ah, *plays*.' He nodded. 'That's good.'

'Father doesn't think so. He says writing isn't proper work, and I've got to be a magistrate when I grow up, but I won't. I'm going to be a playwright.'

'You stick to that.'

'That's what Mother says when Father isn't there.' He cast Tacita a doubtful glance to check that he hadn't overstepped the mark.

She nodded encouragement, and tried to smile.

'Your mother's right,' said Gaius. Over the boy's head, he met her eyes.

She said, 'I know I should have sent him to safety. He should be with the twins at my brother's—'

Titus rolled his eyes. 'Oh, *Mother*!'

'– but I couldn't. I couldn't bear to be parted from him.'

Gaius said to her, 'Will you tell him?'

'Of course. When he's sixteen.'

He nodded.

'Tell me what?' asked Titus.

'A secret,' Gaius replied.

'Why can't you tell me now?'

'Because it's too dangerous. Not just for you, but for your mother.'

Titus thrust out his lower lip rebelliously.

Tacita knew that look. It meant trouble. Gaius noticed it too, and said smoothly, 'But instead I can give you something, another kind of secret.'

Titus looked at him hopefully.

Gaius untied the pouch at his belt and brought out a small, figured bronze inkwell.

'Oh look, it's an owl!' cried Titus in delight.

'It's for travelling,' said Gaius. 'You'll be on the road for a while, so you'll need something to write with.' Again he fished in the pouch; he brought out a little bronze canister about the length of his middle finger, and snapped open the lid. 'And something to write *on*, of course. There's some paper already in there, to get you started. Have you a pen?'

Eagerly, Titus nodded.

'Well, then. You're ready to begin.' He put the canister and the inkwell into the boy's hands, and closed them with his own. For a moment he held the boy's hands in his. It was painful to see the expression on his face. 'Keep these with you always,' he said with a catch in his voice. 'They're for jotting down ideas as they come to you. Otherwise you'll forget them. Trust me on that. I know.'

Titus looked up at him. 'Is that what you do, sir? Keep them with you always?'

'Always.'

'*Always*,' repeated Titus with satisfaction.

'There's a trick to opening the inkwell. Here, I'll show you . . .'

Tacita watched the two heads bent close together one dark, one fair, both unruly. Titus was frowning and breathing heavily through his mouth. His small hand rested on his father's forearm.

Suddenly Gaius raised his head and met her gaze. His eyes glittered. *Thank you*, he mouthed.

She gave him a shaky smile.

Titus said earnestly, 'I've read every one of your

511

poems, sir. Mother keeps a book of them with her always. Personally, I like the one about Pegasus best.'

'Personally,' said Gaius with a smile, 'so do I.'

'When I'm grown up I'm going to write a play about Pegasus and Bellerophon, but I'm going to change the ending. Everyone says Bellerophon lost Pegasus for ever, but I bet that's not true, I bet they made up and were best friends in the end.'

'You write it the way you think it happened,' said Gaius. 'That's always the best.'

Titus nodded sagely. 'I think so too.'

Outside the door, Faenio coughed.

Tacita caught her breath. It was time to go.

Gaius touched the boy's shoulder one last time. Then he passed his hand over the tousled black curls. 'Titus,' he said, getting stiffly to his feet.

'Yes, sir?'

'Promise me you'll write that play.'

Titus looked up at him and smiled. 'I promise, sir.' He caught his lip between his teeth. Then he said, 'And when I do, will you read it, and tell me *honestly* what you think?'

Tacita pressed her hand to her mouth.

Gaius stood looking down at his son with a longing which would never be satisfied. Once again he touched the boy's curls. Then he made himself smile, and said, 'I'd like to, Titus. Very much.'

I can't bear it, she thought. She went to Gaius and said quickly, 'Come with us. Come with us tonight.'

'Oh *yes*!' cried Titus.

'I can't,' said Gaius.

'*Why* not—' she began.

'It's impossible. You know that.'

'No I don't!'

'Tacita. It would put you all in danger.'

She shook her head. She could no longer speak for the tears.

Titus went to her and took her hand. 'Why are you crying, Mother?'

'Because I'm sad.'

Gaius put his hands on her shoulders and gave her a little shake. 'You mustn't be sad. This is how it was meant to be.'

'No. I don't believe that.'

'Yes.'

'So I'm supposed to leave you here?' she cried. 'Is that it?'

'That's it.' Then he added, 'But when you get to Athens, you might drink a toast to me, hm? That'll be my reward. The best wine you can afford. Let Titus have some too.'

'Oh, yes!' said Titus, clutching his treasures to his chest.

The tears were running down her cheeks, and she made no attempt to keep them back.

Faenio put his head round the door, and then withdrew.

Gaius' hands tightened on her shoulders. 'This is how it was meant to be, Tacita. We weren't meant to be together in this life. But we've had this time, which I never expected. And now, after all these years, I can do something for you at last. For you both. You've given me that.' He paused. 'Some day we will be together.'

'How can you say that!' she burst out passionately.

'Because I know it's true.'

'*How?* How do you know?'

'If the Goddess wills it,' he said simply, 'it will be so.'

CHAPTER THIRTY-FIVE

Mazerans Hospital, 2 p.m., 24 March, the Present

Patrick was standing at the window in a hospital dressing-gown when Antonia entered the room. He was talking on the phone. His face was grave. 'Yes. Yes. – No. It'll be all right.'

When he heard her come in, he turned awkwardly on his crutches.

She gave him a brief smile, which he did not return. Obviously it was not an easy call.

He had not yet shaved. With the dark stubble on his chin and the long strip of white sticking-plaster on his temple, he looked like a pirate. A pale, thoughtful kind of pirate, after a rough night out.

The doctor said he had been extraordinarily lucky. Apart from the crutches and the sticking-plaster, there was nothing to show that he had walked into a rock, hobbled two miles with a torn ligament, and spent half the night on a freezing mountainside.

He put down the phone. Then he shook his head and murmured, 'Son of a bitch.'

She waited, but he did not enlighten her.

Feeling unaccountably shy, she picked up the bag she had brought from his house, and put it on the bed. 'Clothes and shaving things. The doctor says you're free to go, and you're lucky it wasn't worse.'

He gave her a strange look she couldn't read, then picked up the bag and hobbled into the bathroom. She sat on the bed and listened to the clatter of things falling off shelves, some swearing, then the splash of water as he started to shave.

The events of the previous night felt increasingly unreal. After several hours at the hospital, she had got a lift back to Patrick's house and spent a bizarre few hours trying to sleep. He had called at six to check that she was all right, and she had been awkward and tongue-tied.

'How did it go at the mill?' he called from the bathroom.

'Fine,' she replied. It was not fine, but she didn't feel like going into that. During the night, Debra's minions had emptied the place and dumped everything in the courtyard, where a thin rain had given it a thorough soaking. Her sister's 'good' pieces were ruined, but luckily one of the minions had taken pity on Antonia's laptop and notes, and shoved them in a plastic bin-liner under the eaves.

'I almost forgot,' she said. 'There was a message from Modge on your answerphone. She wants you to call.'

'Uh-huh. That was her just now.'

She was on the point of asking how Modge knew where to reach him, when she remembered Julian. She had called him that morning, to tell him that she had found Patrick and that he was OK. Julian had sounded so worried when she spoke to him the night before that she hadn't the heart to leave him in the dark.

She went to stand in the doorway.

Patrick had jettisoned the dressing-gown, and wore the jeans she had brought from the house, and nothing else. He still looked like a pirate, but a clean-shaven one. She wished he would put on his shirt.

She asked hoarsely how Modge was doing.

'I think she's going to be all right. Given time.'

'What did she want?'

He tapped his razor on the edge of the basin. Then he met her eyes in the mirror and said, 'We need to go to Le Figarol.'

'What?'

He repeated it.

She wondered if the doctors had got it wrong, and he did have concussion after all. 'What are you talking about?'

'We need to go and see old Panabière. Right now.'

'Now? But – why? Surely it can wait till tomorrow?'

He shook his head. 'Today's the 24th. The Day of Blood, right?'

She had been trying not to think about that. The anniversary of Cassius' death had very nearly claimed Patrick, too.

In bemusement she helped him on with his shirt. Visiting Clovis Panabière was not how she had imagined they would spend their first day together. Patrick ought to be home in bed. They both ought to be home in bed. Preferably the same bed.

He leaned down and kissed her gently on the mouth. 'I can't tell you any more in case it doesn't come off. Just trust me. OK?'

She met his eyes. Then she reached up and brushed the black hair from his forehead. 'OK,' she said.

Monsieur Panabière had been foraging in his wine cellar for what seemed like hours, hunting out a special vintage of Pic-St-Loup which he insisted they should try.

He had been delighted to see them, for he took a proprietorial interest in Patrick's recovery. Antonia had run to *his* farm in the middle of the night, and *his camionette* had brought them back to the farm, where they had called for help on *his* phone.

Antonia wished the old man would hurry up. They only had a couple of hours before dusk, and she couldn't face driving back to the village in darkness. She was still shaken from the drive up, which had been horrible, with the Citroën lurching from pot-hole to pot-hole, while Patrick waxed paler and paler and tried not to show how much every jolt hurt his knee.

The worst point was when she overshot the turn-off and had to reverse downhill past the accident site.

'This,' she had muttered between clenched teeth, 'is why I didn't bring the bloody car *up* here last night.' She crunched into first, and tried not to think of Myles. 'I take it old Panabière knows we're coming?'

Patrick shook his head. 'I called, but he didn't answer. You know what he's like.'

'Terrific. So we don't even know if he's in.'

'He's in. Trust me.'

'You said that before.'

As they turned into the courtyard, scattering chickens in all directions, Patrick said, 'Promise not to be angry with him. He's an old man who had a bad time in the war and misses his wife. Remember that.'

'What are you talking about?'

He looked at her steadily in a way that made her stomach turn over. 'Just remember not to be angry.'

At last Monsieur Panabière emerged triumphantly from the cellar, his olive-green wig lightly filigreed with cobwebs. In his arms he carried two dusty and extremely serious-looking bottles of Pic-St-Loup – 'Le *meilleur* que vous avez jamais gouté' – and a large, apparently pre-war tin of patent hair restorative: TONIQUE AMIEUX: LE PLUS EFFECTIF DU MONDE POUR RESTITUER LES CHEVEUX.

With a flourish he placed the tin on the kitchen table in front of Antonia, then took three tumblers from the draining-board, and poured them all a drink.

'Santé,' he said.

'Santé,' they replied.

The wine was wonderful: strong and punchy, with a peppery undercurrent.

Antonia indicated the tin. 'What's that?'

Patrick and Monsieur Panabière exchanged glances.

'That,' said Patrick, 'is why Modge called.' He turned his glass in his fingers. 'It's taken her a while to get up the courage to tell me. Or anybody.' He frowned. 'In fact, it's taken her quite a while.'

Antonia looked at him. Then she understood. 'God. *God*. I got the wrong cellar.'

'What?' said Patrick.

'I got the *wrong* cellar! I was on the right track, but in the wrong place.'

'You? Wrong?' Patrick smiled. 'Not possible.'

When she made no move to touch the tin, he pushed it towards her. 'Go on. Open it.'

Looking back on it afterwards, it seemed to Antonia that at the moment when she opened the tin, a stillness descended on the kitchen. The little black cat by the stove stopped licking its paws. The chickens outside fell silent. The sun went in.

'It's even more beautiful than I remembered,' she said as she lifted the *kántharos* from its nest of wadding.

She held it in both hands and turned it slowly, and the light caught the reliefs and brought them alive.

Pegasus trotted joyfully over a field of waving acanthus, where a small coiled snake sheltered beneath an overarching frond. Bellerophon walked like a young prince, his face serene and joyful, his palm outstretched to greet his long-lost companion. And behind his shoulder, a crescent moon rose into the evening sky.

With her finger, Antonia traced the outline of the moon. 'Her name was Tacita,' she said softly. 'Tacita Cornelia.' She swallowed. 'After the escape from Perusia she went to Athens. She stayed there until she died. That's where her children grew up. "*A woman of courage and depth of feeling, who passed on those qualities to her young.*" Oh, I'm *glad* it was her! I liked her the best.'

Carefully, she set the *kántharos* on the table. Then she glanced from Patrick to Monsieur Panabière, and back to the old man. Steadily he returned her gaze.

'Remember what you promised,' warned Patrick.

'I didn't promise,' she replied. She turned to the old man. 'Monsieur. Pourquoi ne m'avez vous jamais parlé de ceci?'

Monsieur Panabière regarded her with the eyes of a man who has seen seven decades of human wickedness and folly, and learned not to take anything too seriously. He lifted his thin shoulders in a shrug. 'Parceque, mademoiselle, vous ne m'avez jamais demandé.'

It was half-past four by the time the Citroën emerged from the turn-off to Le Figarol.

Antonia had no choice but to park where they always used to park, in the widest part of the track, just uphill from Monsieur Panabière's aluminium gate.

Neither of them spoke as they sat in the car fifteen feet from the site of the accident.

You've done it, she thought. You've found the cup

and you've solved the riddle. Now all that's left is to make the libation.

Ever since she could remember, she had wanted this day to come. But now that it had, she felt bereft. It was too much.

Patrick sat beside her in silence. She wondered if he guessed what she was feeling. Or perhaps he was thinking about Myles.

They got out of the car, Patrick moving awkwardly on his crutches. She opened the back and took out the elderly hunting-satchel which Monsieur Panabière had donated, and the tin with the *kántharos* inside, and the second bottle of Pic-St-Loup, which the old man had opened for them, and then re-corked.

She placed the tin on the bonnet of the car, and settled the bottle in the hunting-satchel for the walk up to the Source. 'It's not Calenian,' she said, 'but I think it'll do.'

She glanced at Patrick. He was leaning against the bonnet, looking pale. Her heart sank. She needed him with her for this. She didn't want to face it on her own. But plainly he was in no state to come. 'I think you'd better wait here,' she said.

He shook his head. 'I'll come. I don't want you to do this alone.'

'I'll be fine.'

'That's what you always say.'

She made herself smile. 'I will. Really.' She tried to make light of it. 'And the Goddess prefers women. Remember?'

He inclined his head. 'She looked after me pretty well last night.'

Their eyes met. She didn't want to think about what would have happened if she had not found him.

He took hold of her wrist and glanced at her watch. 'I figure you have just under an hour to get up there, make that libation, and get back here before I start worrying and come after you.'

'Fine,' she said.

Unfortunately, Monsieur Panabière's hunting-satchel was not big enough to take the tin of hair restorative. Patrick held the satchel open while she lifted the *kántharos* from its nest of wadding.

It was a clear, warm day, and although the Catalan sun was already low in the sky, it still shone brightly. For a moment Antonia held up the *kántharos*, and they watched it fill with light.

'You be careful up there,' Patrick said.

She did not reply.

Something inside the rim had caught the light. She brought it closer. Her mouth went dry.

'What is it?' said Patrick. 'What?'

She cleared her throat. 'He didn't leave as much to chance as we thought.'

'What do you mean?'

'The truth is *in* the cup,' she said quietly. She placed the *kántharos* on the bonnet of the car, and with her forefinger traced the short, stark inscription hidden just under the lip. She spelled it aloud: '"C. et T. et f."'

Patrick said, 'What does the last bit mean?' Then he turned to her. 'Jesus. *Jesus.*'

'Cassius and Tacita. And son.'

Again she touched the letters.

She knew who had made it. In contrast to the professionally executed inscription on the base, this had been roughly cut. It was the sort of carving which might be done by a man with no special expertise in stone-cutting, using his own knife. He would have needed a good knife, and a lot of determination, for this was sardonyx, and as hard as nails.

Cassius had drunk Calenian wine on the Day of Blood, and eaten a meal of bread and salt and pomegranates with his old friend Plautius, before he opened his veins. Antonia thought of him carving the initials on the miraculous cup which he had commissioned, so that someone – he didn't know who – would, at some future time, make the libation he needed. She thought of him carving the initials with his knife. Like a boy scratching his sweetheart's name on a tree-trunk.

'*We drank wine,*' ran the famous passage in Plautius' letter,

> *and I followed my young friend out onto the terrace. I struggled to keep back the tears, but he seemed almost serene. 'Why, Plautius,' he said, 'I hadn't realized until now, but today is the Day of Blood.' Then he astonished me by breaking into a smile. 'But how fitting that is! It's a good sign, don't you think?'*
>
> *I fear that I did not understand what he meant, nor did I have the spirit to ask him, or to return his smile. From this day on, I thought in desolation, I shall be less careful how I live.*

The setting sun filled the *kántharos* with ruby light.

Sunset on the Day of Blood, thought Antonia. A good time for a libation.

Again that sense of disbelief. It was too much. Her eyes began to sting.

Patrick leaned against the bonnet of the car and put his hands on her shoulders, and drew her into his arms. 'I'm coming with you,' he said.

She shook her head. 'You can't. Your knee—'

'I'll manage.'

'But—'

'What you've got to get used to,' he said gently, 'is that you're not alone any more.'

He looked down into her face, as she took in the truth of that.

She wiped her eyes with her knuckles, and blinked at him. Finally, she nodded. 'Come on, then,' she said.

THE END

AUTHOR'S NOTE

I thought I should deal with a few points which may have occurred to some readers concerning the Roman sections of the story.

First, on dates. The Day of Blood on 24 March was made an official holiday by the emperor Claudius, some years after Cassius' time. However, there is plenty of evidence that ceremonies and processions honouring Cybele were held long before then, so I don't think it's too much of a stretch to have brought forward the Day of Blood by a few decades. (Another point, of course, is that since Cassius' time the Western calendar has changed, so that 24 March in our present-day calendar almost certainly doesn't correspond with that in Cassius' world. But I don't believe either Cassius or Antonia would have worried about that.)

Readers may also have noticed that I've been a bit inconsistent about using Latin and English place names. For example, I've translated some names into English (such as Victory Hill), while leaving others (such as the Porta Capena) in the original Latin. The reason for this is simple: I've used whichever seemed most natural in the context.

Concerning Cassius himself, some readers may wonder at his being 'six foot something' tall: weren't people much shorter in those days? Yes, they generally were, but so was the Roman 'foot': about half an inch shorter, in fact. This makes Cassius about five feet ten or so in modern terms – which would have made him tall for those days, but by no means a giant.

Another question: would Cassius have worn a beard, when in his day it was usual for Roman men to shave off their beards when they reached manhood? Despite the prevailing fashion of the time, there is evidence that some men chose to keep their beards: for example, those who were particularly keen on Greek culture, and certain Roman generals who fought in the eastern Mediterranean during the first century BC. As Cassius was both a philhellene and a career soldier, I felt it was appropriate for him to keep his beard.

Finally on Cassius, what about his penchant for neat wine, when we're told that Romans drank their wine diluted with water? On this, I would simply point to the Roman poets, several of whom talk in their poems of drinking their wine neat. With Propertius and Catullus as fellow-drinkers, Cassius is in good company.

This brings me to the poetry itself, and here I must acknowledge the debt I owe to three luminous sets of translations which helped to inspire much of Cassius' poetry: *Propertius – The Poems*, by W. G. Shepherd (Penguin, 1985); *The Poems of Catullus*, by Peter Whigham (Penguin, 1966), and *Ovid – The Erotic Poems*, by Peter Green (Penguin, 1982).

Michelle Paver

WITHOUT CHARITY
by Michelle Paver

Now was the time for him to leave. If he did not leave now, if he allowed her to catch sight of him, there would be no going back. She stood before the great stone horse, absorbed and unaware. She looked small and upright and brave. And easily hurt. He took in the slow sweep of her lashes as she traced the line of the horse's neck. The clarity of her profile. The warmth and tenderness of her mouth. All his careful reasoning collapsed about him.

When Sarah first saw Harlaston Hall, its grandeur unnerved her. How could this great mansion have anything to do with her family, and in particular with her grandmother Charity? Reluctantly, Sarah had taken on the job of writing up the history of the hall, mainly so that she could get away from London and the misery of her broken love affair. But as she became immersed in the poignant story of the house, and in particular of Robert, the last Lord Harlaston, it became vital that she uncovered the truth.

From present-day London to the windswept Lincolnshire fens, from the battles of the Boer War to the rigid hierarchies of a small village in Edwardian times, this sweeping novel tells a breathtaking story of a family and its long-buried mysteries.

0 552 14752 4

APPLE BLOSSOM TIME
by Kathryn Haig

'There are ghosts. The air is buzzing with them and I have to sit and listen while they whisper to me . . .'

Edwin Anstey died a hero's death in France in 1918. Of that his daughter, Laura, had been assured – by her grandmother, the formidable Lady Anstey, by her mother, by her stepfather Tom, her father's old comrade-in-arms, and by the old people in the village of Anstey Parva. But they were all strangely reluctant to talk about this hero; his name did not appear on the village war memorial, and in the picture gallery at Anstey House his portrait had not joined those other men of the family who had served King and Country with distinction over the centuries. Was there some terrible secret? Why was Laura not allowed to know about her father, whom she had never seen?

A child of the Great War, Laura was twenty when the Second World War broke out, and as an Anstey she had to do her bit. In the ATS she was posted to Egypt and learned at first hand about war and what it means. She found love – or thought she had – but realised, almost too late, that her heart belonged much nearer home. And always, haunting her, was her father – handsome (she believed), brave (she hoped) but always, mysteriously, absent.

'A beautifully sustained and ultimately romantic read'
Good Housekeeping

0 552 14537 8

If this engrossing love story doesn't find a place in your heart...

... you'll find a cheque in the post

If you don't find *A Place In The Hills* one of
the most unputdownable love stories of the year,
we'll put our money where our hearts are
and refund you the purchase price.

Just return your copy of this book
with your till receipt, stating where and when
you bought it and the reasons for your
dissatisfaction, and we will give you
your money back.

A Place In The Hills Guarantee
Marketing Department (KA)
Transworld Publishers
61-63 Uxbridge Road
London W5 5SA

Offer applies UK and Ireland only.
Offer ends Friday 31st August 2001